C000145505

Anne Marsh writes sexy [contemporary?] romances, because the wo[rld can always use another] alpha male. She started wr[iting when she was] laid off from her job as a t[echnical writer and] decided happily-ever-after[s be]a[t] software manuals. She lives in North Carolina with her two kids and five cats.

New York Times and *USA TODAY* bestselling author **Cathryn Fox** is a wife, mother, sister, daughter, aunt and friend. She loves dogs, sunny weather, anything chocolate—she never says no to a brownie—pizza and red wine. Cathryn lives in beautiful Nova Scotia with her husband, who is convinced he can turn her into a mixed martial arts fan. When not writing, Cathryn can be found Skyping with her son, who lives in Seattle— could he have moved *any* farther away?—shopping with her daughter in the city, watching a big action flick with her husband, or hanging out and laughing with friends.

If you liked
Have Me and *Devoured*
why not try

In the Dark by Jackie Ashenden
Bound to You by JC Harroway

Also by Anne Marsh

Ruled
Inked
Her Intern
Hot Boss
Hookup

Also by Cathryn Fox

On His Knees
On Her Terms
Under His Touch
Under His Obsession

Dirty Rich Boys

Corrupted

Discover more at millsandboon.co.uk

HAVE ME

ANNE MARSH

DEVOURED

CATHRYN FOX

MILLS & BOON

First Published in Great Britain 2021
by Mills & Boon, an imprint of HarperCollins*Publishers*
1 London Bridge Street, London, SE1 9GF

Have Me © 2021 Anne Marsh

Devoured © 2021 Cathryn Fox

ISBN: 978-0-263-29790-4

MIX
Paper from
responsible sources
FSC® C007454

This book is produced from independently certified FSC™ paper
to ensure responsible forest management.
For more information visit www.harpercollins.co.uk/green.

Printed and bound in Spain
by CPI, Barcelona

HAVE ME

ANNE MARSH

MILLS & BOON

PROLOGUE

IGNITION

Liam

A NAKED COUPLE bangs enthusiastically behind the rhododendrons by the pool, ignoring the pile of people conducting an orgy on my front lawn. God bless California's outstanding nighttime weather. I tend to skirt the group sex thing. Not because I'm prudish but because if I get too close, I'll join in and I shouldn't have sex tonight. Mostly because when I drink this much, I black out and then I do the filthiest, half-remembered things that I completely hate myself for. My Napa sex parties may be popular with the Silicon Valley elite who make the two-hour drive north from San Francisco, and my guest list may boast more start-up founders and CEOs than a venture capital fund, but certain people on a certain board don't like them. I've been spanked and told to stop and apologize for past bad behavior—or else.

I haven't taken orders since earning my first billion dollars, and I'm definitely not apologizing for anything. Turning over a new, reformed leaf is also not part of my plans for tonight. Instead, I head for the music and lights of the nearby big top. The enormous tent wasn't included with my purchase of the ten-thousand-square-foot château, although there's more than enough room for it between the French-style formal gardens and the acres of grapevines. Tonight's party theme is Fun Under the Big Top and I've imported an entire circus and midway, complete with a Ferris wheel, naughty arcade games and a three-ring show of sex acts. Waiters pass champagne and carnival food, but the snacks aren't the focus of attention. That would be the acrobats building a complicated pyramid of naked bodies in a showy display of minuscule loincloths, sequins, muscles, tits and asses. I work up some applause and devote myself to draining the remainder of my bourbon.

This is where the night starts to blur and jump thanks to what I've knocked back from the bottle of ridiculously expensive bourbon in my hand. Drunk me time-travels in tiny hops, skipping from one moment to the next so that I can gloss over the boring parts, like how I've got from a tent of naked people to the base of the Ferris wheel. I'm not blackout drunk, not yet, but I'm close. The ride spins in a dizzying circle, spokes flashing past me as the riders shriek.

I'm thinking I do want sex. Dirty, filthy, anonymous sex. The kind that makes you hate yourself in the morning for what you were willing to do or let be done. The kind of sex that hurts and leaves a mark.

So of course that's when I spot the girl. Woman. She stands out, a quality about her, a hot, magnetic pull between us that gets my dick hard. Mostly, I want to fuck her, to drag her down to my level, but she has to say she wants this, too. That's the one rule of my nasty game. You have to admit your secret wants out loud.

She's one of my few guests who hasn't raided the adult aisle of the Halloween store for her costume. I mentally mark her up for that because she's stunning anyhow, even all covered up. A black-and-white-striped dress bells out from the curve of her waist to mid-thigh, the hem decorated with a row of pom-poms. It's more cute than sexy until I get to the red-and-white stockings in a naughty pair of red fuck-me heels. And as if she hasn't hit all my hot buttons already, she wears fingerless gloves and carries a tiny black umbrella that she twirls as she tips her head back to watch first the Ferris wheel and then me.

"Are you taken?" She grins at me, face still upside-down, her voice soft and irrepressibly mischievous. A black velvet mask conceals most of her features but strawberry-blond hair spills down her back in an unruly ponytail.

"By you." It's cheesy, but entirely true. Right now, right here, I'm all hers and she's welcome to do whatever she wants with me.

She's so completely covered up, I want to strip her bare, brush my mouth over the column of her throat and then move lower. I could fist her hair as I drive into her and make her scream with pleasure. Her eyes laugh at me, happy, pleased to be here.

I really shouldn't go near her.

So of course I do.

I stride right over until my shoulder is brushing hers when she straightens.

As soon as I touch her, as soon as I pull on the ties of the mask until they sag in my hand, I realize that there's an obstacle to my hookup plan. My little strawberry blonde isn't a beautiful stranger. She's a gate-crasher.

Hana Valentine.

My best friend's sweetheart of a little sister. It's too late to put her mask back on, so I shove it into my pocket.

Twenty-three now, but still way too nice and far too innocent for my kind of game.

"I didn't invite you." Drunk truth at its finest.

She grins at me. "I borrowed Jax's invitation."

"Felonies are frowned upon, Ms. Valentine." I wait for her to look guilty, but she just stands there staring at me and my brain cells have clearly been replaced with bourbon because I stare right back. Sixteen-year-old A.H. Hirsch doesn't lend itself to logical decision-making. So I give in and do what I want—I'll feel bad about it in the morning, which was the plan all along, right?—rather than calling for security like I should. Her hair feels so soft beneath my fingers, and she doesn't protest at all when I wrap its length around my fist and gently draw her backward. Instead, her eyes flare with excitement, making me think she has a hidden submissive side.

Her hair…her hair is something else, fresh-smelling, like cucumbers and herbs, summer and the outdoors. Or maybe those are just the memories of our Berkeley summers. She grew up in the house next door and I used to see her all the time. I shove those thoughts in a box and toss the box into my mental dumpster. It's not as if I care about her hair. Or her. In my world, my ladies wear whichever scent I like best. The last thing I want to admit is that she could be special.

I pull her tighter against me and she comes willingly, still sweetly submissive, her body melting into mine. Her back cradles my front and I've missed a few important memos about Hana Valentine. Firstly, she's grown up since we met as kids in Berkeley. I wait a beat, absorbing the sexy, soft give of her body. I don't want to feel this, not with her, but the longer I hold her, the less I can fight the feeling. Because secondly, something has shifted between us from when I spotted her and when drunk me decided it was okay to touch her because it would feel good now and I'd thoroughly regret it later.

Time skips again.

Now she rides my thigh as I press it between hers, and I can barely register the searing heat of her because I'm back to trying to figure out when she grew up on me. She's more pocket-sized than tall, although I'm a big bastard, so she shouldn't have the upper hand. Bourbon. I blame the bourbon. I feel her gaze move over my face as she tilts her head against my shoulder, the better to watch me.

I'm totally letting her do this.

This is my choice to allow her to take control, to lead.

I am such a liar.

"You shouldn't be here, Hana."

She shrugs, her dimples peeping up at me. I can't help but notice she doesn't move away. Instead, she bears down gently on my thigh, as if she's making her pussy goddamned comfortable on me and it's no big deal.

"Does that make me a bad girl?" It's cute, the way she tries to talk dirty. She blushes and then she laughs because she knows she sounds funny, too. It's like one of those bad pun games that get funnier the drunker you get.

"No." I tuck her more tightly against me and push my thigh slowly up. She's wet and I need to find out if it's for me.

"You're looking at me." She sounds breathless. It matches how I feel inside, which is really unacceptable.

"Yes." I run my finger down that smooth curve of skin, from her ear to her collarbone. "I am. You don't belong here. I didn't ask you."

"Sometimes I like to break the rules, Liam."

My dick throbs from its contact with her and my bastard side wants to shove her dress up and show her what happens to bad girls when they trespass in my kingdom. I'm just drunk enough that it seems like a good plan.

Instead, I offer her the bourbon bottle. "Drink?"

Her fingers close over mine, guiding the bottle to her mouth.

"Are you corrupting me?" she asks when she comes up for air.

"Don't tell your brother."

Jax would kill me if I debauched his sister. Warm brown eyes assess me, as if she sees someone entirely different than I do when I look in the mirror. She'll be disappointed when she learns the truth.

"Are you okay?"

Not really, but I don't talk about it. Not ever.

I press my lips against her throat instead. She's mouthwatering, too sweet for a man like me. If I'd ever thought about this darling off-limits girl, I'd have imagined her doing it missionary style in a bed, on her back, her arms wrapped around her lover with candles or mood music to set the scene. Boring stuff.

I let her go. Or try. My free hand slides down her arm, my fingers tangling with hers. The shock of pleasure is unexpected but addictive, as are the words that fly out of my mouth. "Ride with me."

Fuck, I'll hate myself in the morning.

She lets me pull her toward the Ferris wheel, but apprehension flashes across her pretty face for the first time. "Am I safe with you, Liam?"

"Always." Right then, I mean it. I won't do anything to hurt her, not permanently, or so I think. I lie when I'm under the influence, too.

Hana is just so very Hana. I haven't spent all that much time with her because she's Jax's little sister, five years younger than me. I double-check mentally once more just to make sure. She's old enough, although it's probably alcohol math doing those sums. But I've always liked her, the way you like dogs and cats, distant family members, and the Starbucks barista who pretends to be interested in your life. She's one of those super nice people who smiles a lot and never says shit about anyone. Frankly, she's too nice for her own good and Jax worries about her.

I would, too, if she were mine.

Her gaze bounces from couple to couple, amusement and arousal crossing her expressive face as she realizes what they've been doing on the Ferris wheel. She's smart. She immediately flashes ahead to thinking about what we could do to each other. I look at her big eyes and I know I'm going to show her more. I'm a bastard, but she either doesn't know or doesn't care. Maybe she'll blame the bourbon, too.

When we board, she curls up on my lap, wrapping her arms around my neck as if I'm safety net enough. The carny running the ride shrugs and adjusts the safety bar, putting the belt around the two of us. I'm sure he's seen it all tonight and I don't feel like letting go anyhow.

The wheel shoots into motion and Hana shrieks. She's a curvy girl, sweet and hot on my lap, and I'll fucking hold on to her to the moon and back so she doesn't need to worry about falling off or getting hurt that way. I don't deserve this chance, but consequences are for tomorrow and time skips faster and faster.

Skip.

Hana squeals as the wheel reaches its zenith and then plummets downward. Her arms tighten around my neck, her thighs gripping my waist. This was the best worst idea ever.

Skip.

Skip.

We skim over the ground, my circus, the carnies, the whole party a drunken blur of lights and watchers. Hana's fingers dig into my hair, pulling my face toward hers, and I kiss her. I've never been so aroused, so turned on for another person's touch before. My thumbs trace her cheeks and those damned dimples, holding her in place for my kiss.

She trembles in my arms, all heat and need, and of course I'm lost. This is bad, even for me. This is the ultimate line and I'm throwing myself across it. I open my mouth and cover hers, erasing the distance between us. Her lips are softly submissive, parting when my tongue presses for entry. I make a rough sound and she sighs, her tongue stroking gently against mine. Too soft, too easy. I kiss her harder, deeper, angling her head so I can take all of her. She lets me, her hands pulling at my hair as she meets each slide of my tongue with hers, answering my groans with needy sounds of her own.

Skip.

Skip skip…

I've pushed her skirt up around her waist and lean

back to see panties. They're pink and lacy and I can't look away as I touch between her legs for the first time. Her surprised gasps and greedy moans drive me crazy. She's all I can think about as I shove her panties to the side and push a finger into her. She's hot and tight, then hot and yielding as she makes room for me inside her.

"Is this what you want, Hana?"

"Yes." Her hands pull at my shoulders as she licks and bites at my throat for punctuation.

"Good girl." I add a second finger, testing her reaction, and she moans louder. This is what I love, the feeling of being in control, of pushing her body higher, faster, tighter. I circle her clit slowly, teasing her, and am rewarded with another moan.

How drunk is she? Probably too drunk. It feels like we're flying, so I hold her extra tight as we swoop down from the top and the ground soars up to meet us. It's not free fall, but it's close.

Hana murmurs something, startled. I nip her bottom lip, tasting the alcohol on her mouth. I'm drunk-slow or maybe that's just the Ferris wheel gliding to a halt.

"Get me down now." She buries her face in my throat, which means I can't kiss her anymore. "God, I'd marry you if you just got me down."

"Deal," I growl, my voice bourbon-rough.

I shouldn't, but I'm going to. I'll add Hana to the list of things I've touched and made dirty.

Skip.

We're back in the big top, but this time I'm in the

ring rather than the stands and the tent has mostly emptied out. Outside the sky has that not-dark, not-quite-light quality it gets when dawn and regrets are coming fast. The bourbon is long gone. The ring-master looks at me, and my beautiful girl giggles. I don't remember how we got here, but it was my idea. I'm pretty sure I remember that.

"It's your turn."

So I say it. "I do."

Skip.

Skip.

…

CHAPTER ONE

WE'RE A NO GO

Liam

MY EYES ARE CLOSED, but the morning sun turns my vision red. My bones—along with my head and my morning wood—decide this is the perfect moment to start aching like a motherfucker. It's my first clue that I did it again. I bite the inside of my cheek while I take stock.

I end up in places I shouldn't when I drink.

I also do things I shouldn't. Admittedly on purpose, to make myself feel bad, but still.

Mentally, I review what I know, which turns out to be absolutely nothing.

Breathe in.

Breathe out.

Breathe in.

See? I recognize the panic. It's what I deserve. I don't know what I did last night because I was out of control. Blackout drunk like my asshole dad when he'd finally come home after weeks or months away and then get into it with my mother.

Mission thoroughly accomplished.

Picking my way along the road of last night's memories yields nothing helpful. The memories' disappearance correlates with the decreasing level in my bourbon bottle. I'd been drunk. I'd partied. I'd…

Done something.

No.

Some*one*.

This last guess is cheating because I'm not alone in the bed. My arms clutch a curvy, naked body close. The last thing I want is company. And particularly not the female kind. Mornings after come with more expectations than Christmas does presents.

I disappoint when it comes to relationships. My sexual repertoire doesn't include explanations, apologies, commitments or anything other than straight-up dirty sex. It works better for all parties involved if I put out and then get out before expectations are engendered. I turn my face into the hair of my sleepover companion. She smells clean and sweet, like fruit and something herbal.

I like it.

I need to figure out who I screwed. Then I'll reach out to my lawyer and he'll draft an NDA with the appropriate legal names and financial incentives. I spend a moment trying to blind guess who my companion is but last night is fuzzy, the details blurred other than some truly spectacular sex, and even that is more highlights reel than full-length documentary.

I'll have to ask. Or at least open my eyes. I've seen too many acquaintances burned badly to let a random hookup escape without signing. If I intend to start sleeping with random unknown girls on a regular basis, I should institute a name tag policy. *Hello, My Name Is...* stickers to make everything easier. The benefits of being the party host.

"Liam?" My naked sleepover buddy shifts in my arms—why am I *spooning* her?—and murmurs my name. The sound is feminine, husky and not entirely awake, although she sounds like she's getting there. She has the voice of a phone sex operator and both my dick and my brain decide that maybe we're not dying after all. This may have something to do with the way her backside cushions my front as she stretches. I press my mouth against her throat and discover she tastes as good as she sounds.

As my brain isn't entirely online yet, however, all that comes out of my mouth is an uninspired, "Right here, sweetheart."

I'll make it up to her with my tongue.

I swear.

My mystery guest responds with more garbled phone-sex syllables, clearly not averse to maintaining her side of the conversation, but the angry buzz of my phone drowns out her follow-up remark. I slap an arm in the approximate direction of the noise but come up empty. The buzz rapidly escalates to the volume of a horde of murder hornets. When I give up and crack an eye for a visual, I see strawberry-blond hair and the morning sun bouncing off a sea of crisp white cotton Frette that's devoured my phone.

We're in my bed.

I brought her upstairs, whoever she is.

I'm twenty-eight. I'm rich and single, and my external packaging is generally acknowledged to be A-plus. I like dirty sex and I refuse to pretend I'm doing anything but fucking. Romance is not something I offer, so getting out of this will cost me.

My companion fishes my phone out from underneath a pillow and helpfully dangles it behind her. "Here. Answer before whoever it is has an aneurysm."

Slim, sun-kissed, with three freckles perfectly aligned like the stars in Orion's belt, her arm is toned yet feminine. Do I know this arm and its owner? Eh. I could just roll her over and check. Sit up and know. But since that feels like reading the last chapter of a mystery novel first, I settle for taking the phone. She's got great hands. Her nails are short and shapely, but completely without polish.

Which all seems unimportant compared to the enormous rock of a diamond nestled against a platinum band. My heartbeat picks up. Is she married? That's a new low, even for me. I'd tell drunk me that he needs to acquire some standards, but he's shameless.

Trying not to think about what I can't remember—it's counterproductive—I scroll through Leda's messages, the ones that shouldn't be blowing up my phone because I should have blocked my ex-girlfriend the moment I confirmed her duplicity three months ago:

I hate u.
U shouldn't have ended things.
We were good together.
Fuck u.
Don't be stupid.
U don't get to replace me.
I'll tell.
U know u miss me.

Fucking hell.

I roll over, away from Mystery Girl, my thumb hovering over the button that will block Leda. I deserve this for being stupid, for thinking words would work instead of numbers. Still, Leda's growing impatience means she'll eventually do something that even I can't fix with a really big check.

There's good news mixed in with the bad, though. My lab manager has shared more pictures of my baby Mars rover. The first mission won't carry people or I'd sign up today, if only to get away from Leda and the shitstorm she's generated. A planetary landing is still too risky as Mars lacks the ozone layer that keeps us comparatively safe here on Earth. Until we figure out how to deal with that, lethal doses of solar ultraviolet radiation would hit any astronaut who landed on Mars.

It's a complicated problem and one some of the best minds in the world have been working on for years, so I'm not going to suddenly come up with the answer while I'm naked in bed. Not yet. But sue me, I still like to dream about it. Unfortunately, the board of Galaxtix knows that this passion project is my personal weakness, and they've threatened to shut the entire project down if I don't reform or resign because my repeated educational forays into the birds and the bees are apparently costing them in terms of foundation donors.

When I asked if they were *serious*—it's an educational foundation and I'm just conducting sex research of the Kinseyian variety—they informed me that I'd better meet their demands fast. And then they gave me a timeline and actual goddamned deliverables that included donating money to charities for puppies and kittens and never, ever making my sex life public again. They'll collectively shit themselves when they find out about last night.

Which they will.

Because…internet.

Bare skin brushes mine as my companion shoves herself upright and swings her legs over the side of the bed with indecent energy. A soft sigh escapes the mouth I can't see and don't remember kissing, two issues that I also need to fix. In fact, my brain screams that compensating for that neglect is far more critical than making my Leda problem go away or even solving the intriguing challenges of a Mars landing. *Stupid brain.* Bleary-eyed, I roll back.

The room smells like sex.

Also? Mystery guest is stunning, with a tiny waist

and a generous, pear-shaped ass that begs for licking and biting. I squint. Based on the physical evidence, that already occurred.

"Don't go." I mute my phone and shove it under my own pillow before curving a hand around her waist. She's softly rounded where my fingertips stroke.

"No worries. You're stuck with me forever." Laughter fills her voice as she stands up. She's short, but those legs of hers go on for days. Weeks. Multiple interplanetary cycles. All I can think about is that bare skin, so it takes a moment to process that she's turned toward me, wiggling the enormous diamond on her ring finger in my direction as if it's some kind of bizarre fishing lure. Diamonds aren't my thing, but breasts…

Even better than a Mars rover.

Hers are fantastic. Round and lush, perfect martini-glass-shaped handfuls with pale pink nipples. I don't remember these breasts, but her voice—

No.

I'm a filthy bastard but even I wouldn't have—

There's no chance—

I shoot upright, alarm sirens wailing in my brain. "Hana?"

"Liam." Hana beams at me. My brain whimpers.

The one woman in the world who should never be able to pick my dick out of a naked lineup is in my bed. I might have gone above and beyond on my plan to incite maximum self-loathing come morning.

Hana is *naked*.

And also—*married.*

I'm strangely hurt she didn't invite me to the wedding, although I guess that would have been weird since she had the biggest teenage crush on me. I've known for years, of course—in a strictly hypothetical and entirely abstract way—that Hana Valentine had grown up to be a stunning woman. When we first met, however, she was twelve to my seventeen and she blew raspberries on my arm.

There was zero attraction between us.

Zero.

I'd carried that attitude over to her teenage years when she'd developed boobs and then a crush on me. Eventually, she'd learned about the wonders of the bra and now she's clearly outgrown her puppy love if she's got a husband tucked away somewhere.

I glance around just in case I've developed a brand-new interest in ménage, but it appears it's just the two of us in my bedroom.

I don't have many rules, a character flaw that helped make me a billionaire before the age of thirty. Still, I've always respected the golden rule of friendship: thou shalt not bang thy friend's little sister.

Said off-limits little sister shifts.

Onto her knees, my dirty brain supplies. There are *possibilities.*

She ups the smile wattage as if today is just the best day ever.

I end up watching her because it's hard not to stare at Hana. She's always happy—it seems to be her perpetual condition—and when she smiles, she lights up the room. I give her a head tip while my brain scrambles for the right thing to say.

Her breasts jiggle.

And I panic. Because I look down and then over. Up. *Anywhere* but at the amazing, new-to-me rack that's right *there* at mouth level. Her eyes still crinkle at the corner when she's happy. That hasn't changed in the six months since I last saw her. We'd been wining and dining her brother in some weird vegetarian Berkeley restaurant she'd chosen for his birthday party. I'd dutifully tried to look like a meatless family dinner was my idea of fun while Jax laughed at me. I don't have the slightest idea what the fuck Hana's doing here, but I need her to go away until Jax's next birthday. And find some clothes.

And stop.

Being.

Naked.

She's rocking a serious case of sex hair—Christ, what did we *do*?—but her brown eyes twinkle happily at me. She still has the freckle she loathes on her cheekbone and a spray of less loathed, smaller freckles on her throat.

She complains about those freckles all the time, but they're like a kissing road map, a deliciously sexy detour that I've never noticed and I'm absolutely, 1,000 percent not taking. Ever.

But because I'm bourbon-weakened, my eyes make an involuntary dip south that I blame on the tiny black-and-yellow tattoo of a bee pollinating a daisy inked above the soft curve of her right breast. How long has she had *that*?

Bees are Hana's jam and her avowed first love. She earned a degree in entomology from the Santa Cruz campus of the University of California and now she harvests socially responsible honey that she sells at farmers' markets and online. She has both a bee farm and a mortgage, which makes her a grown-up in the eyes of the world and the IRS, although I have my doubts, doubts Jax has echoed more than once. Frankly, neither of us understands the whole working-hard-for-a-pittance approach to life. It seems counterintuitive, so I've suggested strategies to better monetize her product whenever our paths cross. The last time, she'd sent me a paperback copy of *Men Are from Mars* bristling with sticky notes. Message received. I'd stopped offering unsolicited business advice that other people pay me for, although I had set up an anonymous weekly order for two cases of honey.

Jax's Hana is a cheerful dork, a granola-to-the-bone, outdoorsy, justice- and fairness-oriented person. She truly believes that as long as her bills get paid on time, she's good, and that it's bad karma or something equally woo-woo to want more than you technically need. Plus, she's an introvert and Jax swears each Christmas that he's going to buy Walden Pond for her so that she can officially become a hermit. She *barters*—and she doesn't always come out ahead financially because she believes feelings should get factored into a deal. Do I understand her? Not at all.

Something else I don't understand? Why she leans in and brushes a kiss over my forehead. An off-limits, naked body part skims my arm and I glance down.

No.

Erase.

Hana isn't hookup or spank bank material. She's younger than me, she's my best friend's little sister, and honestly she drives me nuts with her organic, do-gooding, naive approach to life. I'm a negotiator.

"How do you feel?" Concern slowly replaces happiness on Hana's face. Just imagine the sun ducking behind a cloud.

Heavy drinking always hurts, which is the whole point of doing it. "My head is pounding, my mouth is drier than the Sahara, and I have a bizarre urge to find the nearest twenty-four-hour diner and order obscene quantities of waffles and fried eggs."

Her brows draw together. She has a new eyebrow piercing, a delicate gold hoop that winks in the morning sunlight. It's cheerful, which is typical Hana. "I meant about last night. *Us.*"

Right. Somehow we've ended up in bed together, naked and spooning. Tread carefully. If I'm lucky—and unfortunately I believe in opportunities, not luck—then we've just had a harmless sleepover because there was nowhere else in my fifteen-bedroom mansion for her to crash. Or clothes to wear.

"What exactly happened last night?"

The furrow between her brows achieves Grand Canyon-like depths. "You don't remember?"

Do I?

I flop back on my pillow. I'm sure my party planner picked some suitably exotic theme for last night's sex party, but I can't remember what I approved. I do recall a circus tent (what the fuck?), a clown (again—WTF?), someone's hands holding mine and mine holding hers, and then some disconnected flashes of lips, boobs, a great ass, and coming like there was no tomorrow. I spend an extra six seconds with that last memory because as sex memories go, it's a good one and today is shaping up to suck.

She huffs out a breath. "Do you remember riding the Ferris wheel with me?"

"No."

More loud exhalations. I'm pretty sure that not only is her memory working perfectly but she's about to hold each and every one of those memories against me.

"So you don't remember getting stuck at the top? Or what I promised if we got down?"

"No."

Christ, I hope we didn't have public sex under the big top. If we did that, the pictures will surface shortly on the gossip sites because that's how my life has gone lately. It won't matter that there's a strict no-pictures-and-no-phones rule at all my parties or that I hire security to enforce that policy—someone will have bent the rules. That beeping sound is the Karma Bus backing up over me.

"Or how you swept me off my feet when we were back on solid ground?"

From the slightly dreamy look on Hana's face, *sweeping* is 100 percent euphemism and the actual activity involved orgasms. Jax is going to kill me. This is his sister. His sweet, innocent little sister.

I need to kill me.

"Can you please put on some clothes?" I grab the sheet and tuck it around myself like a six-hundred-thread-count toga. We haven't even touched on the wedding ring she's sporting because I'm not ready for that conversation. I would have said I don't sleep with married ladies, but clearly last night was a series of truly abominable firsts for me. I may have just hit the bottomest bottom of the moral abyss otherwise known as my soul.

Her gaze catches on my waist and dips downward. Is she checking me out? And what the hell? This Hana seems remarkably different from the one I've known for years. More self-possessed, less tongue-tied and blushing—although just as wholesome.

She chews on her bottom lip. "No."

That's also different. I don't recall Hana being utterly unreasonable, despite her adamant dislike of all things corporate and that bizarre love of organic farming. This makes her refusal to do as I've asked unexpected. Frankly, she's hero-worshipped me from her tween years onward and my few suggestions have been solid gold commands in the Hana-verse. Since it was cute and useful, I'd taken shameless advantage to keep her safe. What the hell happened to her?

She rolls her eyes. "When did you turn into a prude?"

"I'm not a prude." Normally when someone accuses me of holding back sexually, I do something particularly, publicly dirty like fuck on a San Francisco cable car or visit one of the city's many sex clubs. Since this is neither a childhood game of one-upsmanship nor the moment to explain just how dirty I am, I practice self-restraint.

Okay. I try to.

I can practically hear the board of Galaxtix laughing their collective asses off.

Hana looks right at me. "We had sex."

What's left of my conscience goes supernova.

She can't be serious.

Fucking *hell*.

I mean, I'm naked, I'm in bed, and I was looking to hook up in the most inappropriate way possible, but I guess I'd been holding out hope that I still had some secret, well-hidden shred of decency and I'd had amazing, mind-blowing sex with someone else before my drunk ass passed out next to a naked Hana. Her expression tenses, her cheeks flushing. Unless she's really changed, that pretty pink color is a dead giveaway that she's about to lose it. She doesn't get mad often, but when she does, it's best to not be in the way.

"I shouldn't have done—that." I wave the hand that isn't clutching the sheet to my abs like I'm a vestal virgin. A nice person would apologize and provide aftercare for any dirty things I'd done to her last night. What are the chances that we had sweet, innocent sex and I haven't scarred her for life?

Low.

"You're unbelievable." She hops off the bed, bare knees bumping against the edge of the mattress. Jesus Christ, why is she still naked in my bedroom?

"I get that a lot." I wink at her reflexively, the words shooting out of my mouth before I remember that this is *Hana* and not some casual hookup. I can't flirt with her. She's off-limits.

"*Un*believable," she repeats and saunters across the room. Slowly. Still naked. Still clearly ready to rip my balls off and feed them to me for breakfast.

"So about last night—"

She turns and shoots a look at me. Usually, Hana is all smiles and laughter. She's a California girl through and through, sunny and warm and level-headed. I'd have said she's my honorary little sister except that would put last night's bedroom activities squarely in the realm of Victorian pornography and that's an even harder no for me.

"Show and tell," she announces. "Show."

She yanks at the rings on her hand and sends them flying through the air toward my face. I catch them automatically with my left hand. A hand, now that I'm paying attention, that sports a matching band. A big, shiny, new gold ring.

"Tell. We got married," she says. "Also? You're a dick."

CHAPTER TWO

GRATEFUL IT'S NOT MY CIRCUS

Hana

LIKE ANY TODDLER or alpha male, Liam Masterson is *not* used to not getting his way. Fortunately for him, he has me in his life—a life I'm newly determined to shake up like a soda can. He prides himself on his calm, take-charge demeanor, but I've always been able to rile him up if I put my mind to it. It's a gift, although currently it's also a gift he clearly would like to return to the store because apparently our spur-of-the-moment marriage was not in his letter to Santa or his five-year master plan. Too bad, so sad. Making this easy for him would be a colossal mistake. He's spent years dismissing me as a sweet, slightly annoying and totally asexual being. That changed last night and there's no way I let him tuck me back into the baby sister box.

We had sex.

I saw his penis.

Truly, *saw* doesn't begin to cover what I did; I touched, licked, fisted and rode said penis and it was every bit as amazing as I'd ever fantasized. Better, in fact. My first reaction when I woke up was to pull his big, cranky, standoffish self to me and kiss the ever-living daylights out of him. I wasn't ready to let go of my fantasy Liam.

Fantasy Liam would have taken charge—like Real Liam—but he'd have rolled me underneath him and demonstrated a perfect understanding of *to have and to hold.* Hands-on demonstrations are the best, so yes, the current state of things isn't ideal. He doesn't seem to want to hear *have me*—at least not from my lips.

In fact, for the first time in forever, I'm mad at Liam. Usually he makes a brief but compelling appearance in my sexual fantasies, I get off, and then the next time I see him IRL, I blush and hope he hasn't acquired mind-reading powers. If anyone could, it would be Liam.

The man's never met a skill he couldn't master. It's like he just wakes up on a random weekend, and then when most of us would think *oh good, it's Saturday, so maybe I'll zip over to Walmart and buy a nice geranium for that empty plant pot and satisfy my new gardening aspirations*, he teaches himself hydroponics and constructs a greenhouse by noon for the one-of-a-kind flowers he's germinated from seed. And then he'd sell those seeds for a million bucks, invest the proceeds and have a country named after him by dinnertime.

If you asked me to pick two adjectives to describe Liam, *smart* and *ruthless* would top my list. He's unbelievably good at making money because he doesn't hesitate to use both of those qualities. The thing is, I've never really questioned his morals. Does he love money? Absolutely. I don't think too many people would argue that being broke is an ideal condition, and he was dirt-poor growing up. I'm a fan of keeping my bills paid, too. And it's not as if he's a Scrooge McDuck, gleefully swimming in pools of gold coins. He gives back generously to his community and I know for a fact he's super hands-on with a big science education foundation.

Because behind the expensive suits and private jets lurks a secret Boy Scout. He's the person you call when the ride-sharing service declines your credit card and you're facing an eight-mile walk, the guy who will come over at 4:00 a.m. to fix your backed-up toilet, the one who never yells even when you reverse your first car into his truck and there's all sorts of bumper damage. He just buys an aftermarket rearview camera and installs it while you're crying in the bathroom and then moves on as if it never happened. He has this pathological need to fix a problem and tie it up with a badge-worthy knot.

The last thing I want is for him to fix and dismiss me, however, so I force myself to saunter out his bedroom door. This requires ignoring the authoritative way he says my name, as if I'm a pet he can order to stay. It also requires ignoring certain inconvenient facts, like my being naked. Nudity is a common side effect of alcohol for me. Not only does drinking make my clothes melt off, but it leads to those articles showing up in the strangest places. You'd think my panties at least would be on Liam's bedroom floor, but the wide-plank, artisanal, bloody expensive wood is as immaculate as an iceberg. Wherever we started our wedding night, it wasn't here.

One of the few things Liam and I have in common, other than my brother, is our fuzziness on the precise sequence of events.

In addition to my naked state, the second inescapable fact seems like a multipart disaster. A veritable list of sad truths.

1. It's 10:12 on a Saturday morning.
2. I've just spent the night making my dirtiest dreams about Liam come true.
3. I proposed to him because why *not* make my dreams come true?
4. Answer: because he doesn't remember our getting married.
5. He hates himself for not remembering.

If I'd known amnesia was a possibility, I'd have whipped out my phone and recorded the consummation the way he did the ceremony itself, but it's too late now. Whatever changed his mind last night about my little sister status and had him agreeing to my drunken marriage proposal, it was an aberration and he's now reset to his default factory mode of older brother. Next will come the patronizing, well-intentioned overprotectiveness that makes me want to scream—and not in the mind-blown-orgasm-achieved way.

I do my best to come to terms with this sad reality as I stand in the hallway outside Liam's bedroom. I haven't spent much time at Château Sin since Liam bought the palatial Napa Valley property a few years ago. Napa's gorgeous on the outside, all vineyards and rolling hills, but once you see inside some of the gated enclaves (or sneak inside like I did), you realize a few things fast. It's an expensive playground for San Francisco's wealthy socialites, philanthropists and tech billionaires, the kind of place where an acre of grape land sells for ridiculous amounts of money and then the owner has outdoor sex parties with a hundred of his acquaintances.

I'm not allowed here because he appointed himself the protector of my virtue when I started high school. Still, I'm not stupid and I know how to use the internet. The man has fan pages. By the time I was thirteen, I knew he was a sex god and that he believed he was protecting my innocence. In theory, I appreciated this evidence of a moral character, although his scruples inevitably got in the way of my teenage lust. At sixteen I'd fantasized about gifting him with said innocence, and by eighteen I'd taken care of business thanks to a coed freshman dorm.

My few Liam-sanctioned visits to Château Sin prior to last night had been brief and largely confined to the massive swimming pool surrounded by grapevines and ridiculous faux Grecian statuary.

We've spent as much time discussing the reasons for the estate's unofficial but horribly tacky nickname as I've spent up here—none. Liam's house is as rigidly compartmentalized as his personal life: he lets anybody and everybody wander all over the ground floor, touching his shit and enjoying themselves, but the second floor is strictly off-limits. I've always assumed his forbidden spaces held his secret man cave/dragon lair. Batmobile storage. Dead bodies. Discovering it's just a clothes-eating, orgasm-granting black hole is weird.

And a little disappointing.

I feel like I just shoved the Liam statue off its special pedestal in my heart, which is stupid. Just because he's the first guy I fell in love with doesn't mean he deserves me even if on paper, he's total husband material—employed, has health insurance, doesn't live in his mom's basement, remembers major milestones.

Château Sin is definitely not a basement. Absolutely everything is expensive and oversize, from the ceiling height to the wall of windows that line the western side of the house. You could fit an entire forest of redwoods in there and still have room leftover for a bonus mountain. Sunlight pours in through the glass. It's California, so the light isn't unexpected, but I take a second to appreciate it anyway. Sunshine is definitely going into my gratitude journal later today. Parading in front of glass when I'm buck-ass naked is probably more exhibitionist than is socially acceptable, but this *is* Château Sin—home of legendary kinky sex parties—and my give-a-fuck is broken. I'm tired of being written off as a good girl. I want my shot at being dirty.

I stick to the sunny spots while I consider my good-girl conundrum and an urgent need to seek warmth. Liam's house is severely air-conditioned. He must be a top 100 individual contributor to global warming.

Although I like my naked statement, the goose bumps are unpleasant. Stumbling across a well-stocked linen closet with a stack of fluffy bath sheets or maybe a guest robe would be optimal, but I've clearly used up my karmic deposits for the week as no towels magically appear. Liam's massive windows are also sans curtains, so I can't even fashion an impromptu toga, a handy skill acquired at college. Equally lacking is a convenient trail of panties, dress and shoes leading to Liam's bedroom door. Sucks to be naked me.

When said bedroom door opens behind me, I glue myself to the closest window, under the guise of admiring the sun-browned hills and perfect rows of grapevines. *Play it cool.* You do *not* show fear to Liam—he'll walk all over you, issuing well-intentioned orders.

So I watch him in the reflection and wait for him to make a move.

God, he's gorgeous.

Bossy, arrogant, far too domineering—and so, so drop-dead gorgeous.

I give up on playing it cool and turn around to appreciate the view. Liam's a big bear of a man, wearing a pair of misbuttoned faded Levis and nothing else. The jeans hug an impressive bulge and a pair of wickedly muscled thighs. His sun-bronzed chest is all chiseled abs and a faint trail of golden hair leading down to a very, very happy place. I stare shamelessly. He props one broad, muscled shoulder against the door frame, jamming a hand into his pocket. Warm, amused eyes watch me. He's barefoot, and despite his huge size, he looks downright cuddly. He also looks like he's once again very much in control. That first part is an illusion. Liam didn't claw his way to the high throne of Silicon Valley by being nice. Or sweet. Or anything other than whip-smart, ruthless and willing to do whatever it takes.

Part of me finds said ruthless intelligence sexy.

The same part that likes to tease him.

It's also the part that sends me sinking into a warrior pose, straightening my arms over my head. *Yes, let me salute these delicious, warm rays of light with my boobs.* I must have been a cat in a former life because I freaking love the heat.

Deliberately, I arch my back, meeting Liam's gaze. "Morning, sunshine."

Would it be over the top to roll the tips of my nipples between my fingers like he'd done last night?

"Don't be a bitch, Hana."

He sounds slightly desperate, which is new. Bet he'd panic if I dropped into a downward dog.

"No naked yoga. Got it. Are there other house rules at Château Sin I should know about? A menu of dirty sex acts to pick from? Do you offer room service?"

He keeps his eyes on my face. *So* disappointing. I've followed this man around like a puppy for years, so the less mature part of me (along with certain southern regions) badly wants him to notice me. Because I'm not ten anymore, I remind myself not to wish bad things on his inattentive, cranky, unappreciative self. Ill thinking will just boomerang back on me. It's basic cause and effect.

He pads toward me and holy wow, I have another item for today's gratitude list. The man is poetry in motion—dirty, hot, 100 percent confident, epic poetry. If I'm a happy, sunbathing housecat, Liam is a predator feline and I hope I'm lunch.

He holds out a shirt. Of course. "Get dressed."

"You're surprisingly prudish for a man who hosts sex parties."

When I take the shirt from him, our fingers brush. He might have earned a billion dollars with his big, beautiful brain but he doesn't sit on his ass 24/7. The man has a serious rock-climbing addiction, witnessed by the calluses and collection of small scars decorating his fingers. I've fantasized about his strong hands, sure, but my new firsthand knowledge sends little shivers through my lower belly.

"Maybe I don't share." There's not so much as a hint of a smile on his face now. I can't tell if he's pulling my leg or making a delicious caveman statement.

"So group sex is off the menu?" I tip my head to the side, trying to read the truth on his face. It's not that I think he would lie to me—Liam is scrupulously honest and will avoid answering questions rather than outright prevaricating—but he hates sharing details about himself.

"This isn't the time." The look he gives me says I should know what the etiquette is for this situation.

I'm neither Miss Manners nor Emily Post, so I indulge myself in some shameless staring to give him time to remember who I am. His eyes are hazel (a Liam fact I knew already), but the sunlight reveals they're flecked with gold because Mother Nature marked him as a rich boy from the day of his birth and he could have been an underwear model if he hadn't decided to be an evil business genius instead.

His gorgeous eyes move over my face, analyzing, as I slip into his shirt. I consider leaving it unbuttoned, but he's right.

Bitchiness will only come back to bite me.

Plus, I'm cold.

I compromise and do up everything but the top three buttons. Since Liam's built like a lumberjack, this leaves enough cleavage on display to remind him I'm no child.

"What you said back there—" He tips his head toward his bedroom. Stops. Frowns, clearly marshaling his thoughts. I wonder just how bad his hangover is because this is the first time I can recall Liam being at a loss for words. "That we got married last night—"

God, he's cute.

"You did buy me a ring." I give him a smile, half teasing, half pissed he's forgotten.

He pulls his hand out of his pocket and unfolds his clenched fingers to reveal a stunning bridal ring set. He's holding half a diamond mine in his palm. The stones dazzle in the morning sunlight and I wonder just how much money Liam spent. Probably more than my poor mortgaged bee farm is worth to the bank. I definitely had far less to drink than he did, but my memories are still less clear than I'd like. I do remember that after we got married beneath the big top, he made a phone call and someone in a dark suit showed up with a case of rings. I'd argued for something less costly than the GDP of a small nation, but I'd lost that battle.

"So these are yours." He holds the rings out to me. Liam has always been generous when it comes to money. He shares cash easily—it's himself that he keeps locked up tighter than a bank vault. He also tends to think that everything—and everyone—has a price tag.

I reach out and close Liam's fingers over the rings. "You keep them."

"Is that all I did, buy you jewelry? Did I fuck anything up?"

I step into him, looping my arms around his neck. I can't help but notice that he freezes—and that his arms most definitely do not close around me. "I proposed. You said yes. Then you said *now* and we may have traded small sexual favors until I agreed. Turns out the ringmaster of the sexual circus you hired is an ordained minister in the state of California."

Disgust flickers across his face. "I'm an ass. Jesus."

"Pretty sure he was nondenominational."

His eyes roam over my face. "We're really married?"

"One hundred percent." I wink at him. *Play it cool.* "However, I'm sure you have about a million security tapes you can pull if you'd like independent verification. Also, you recorded the ceremony itself on your phone. I was unclear at the time if you wanted spank bank material or a souvenir for our future grandkids."

"I never planned on getting married," he says. I can't help but notice he's not holding me back. "Not because you're not great but, you know—"

Right. Everyone who lived on our block in Berkeley would have voted his parents most likely to kill each other. The lots were small, the houses close, and his parents were never quiet about their disagreements. Whenever they fought, Liam would climb over our fence and hang out with us.

"I know," I say.

I step away from him, stupidly hoping he'll pull me back into his arms. I suppose the ringmaster-slash-minister could have been a lying liar, but whatever team of lawyers Liam has on speed dial will undoubtedly sort it all out. In addition to melting my clothes off my body, alcohol gives me a big-time case of fuzzy logic. Last night, marrying Liam seemed like an excellent idea, the perfect way to transform myself from *innocent and off-limits little sister* to *hot, sexy woman* while making my teenage fantasies come true. Today, however, I have doubts.

He reaches out and snags me with his free hand, his warm fingers braceleting my wrist as he tugs me gently to a stop. Liam is always careful with me, even when I wish he wouldn't be. "I'll fix this. I swear."

CHAPTER THREE

PANTS ARE OVERRATED

Hana

WITHOUT WAITING FOR my response, Liam starts towing me back into the bedroom. I feel like a little Hana barge bobbing in the wake of Destroyer Liam. It's not a good feeling, but apparently I used up my quota of those last night. I let him lead for the moment, though, because he's great at fixing things and I'm stupidly tempted to let him.

Except that we both still want different things. Why did I think we actually had a shot at us? Too much bourbon? Too many daydreams? I'm not naive, but I'm not exactly jaded, either.

I'm the kind of hopeful where secret heart wishes made at the top of a Ferris wheel seem like an actual plan, something that can come true even when my feet are firmly back on the ground. I grabbed my chance at Liam when he said *yes*.

Liam stops abruptly, fixing his considerable at-

tention on his massive, mussed-up bed. Just a handful of buttons stand between us and being naked.
Heat rushes through my body and my palm hovers
over the small of his back and the hard, bare curve
of his skin.

That's the bed where we had *sex*.

I came about a million times thanks to Liam's
generosity in all matters oral alone. It deserves ac-
knowledgment, a massive statue, maybe even a
dildo-shaped one like the Washington Monument.

"I love your big, beautiful bed." I step up next to
Liam and pat the mattress, mostly just to get a rise
out of Liam. I hate it when he ignores me.

He lets go of my wrist as if burned, and reverses
course to hurtle toward the wall. I fight the urge
to make chicken noises and settle for sitting cross-
legged on his bed. His shirt rides up my thighs and
he swallows audibly. *Yes, this was yours last night.*

I feel marginally better, enough so that I fish his
phone out from underneath the pillow and hold it
out to him. The screen is filled with text alerts that
I studiously don't read. "Check it."

"It's not that I don't trust you," he says. "It's not
personal."

Truth. Liam trusts no one, and I'm no one. He also
does best with facts. He likes life to be cut-and-dried,
but he's either too polite or too hungover to tell me
to my face that he won't be convinced we're married
until he's seen photographic proof. I don't toss him
the phone, though. He's going to have to come to me.

Eventually, he gives up and strides across the room

to take the phone. Even better, he drops down onto the bed beside me, impatiently thumbing the billion text alerts away. The video didn't turn out half bed. Bad. Oops. That's a Freudian slip right there. We watch together as the on-screen Hana and Liam promise to have and to hold, for better and for worse, and for richer and poorer.

Since he's the billionaire and I'm not, he definitely got the worse end of the deal.

"We got married on purpose." Liam's got that stoic glare thing going on, the I'm-a-hard-ass stare that's probably really effective in the boardroom but that has zero effect on the hardware in his hand. It does make me feel hot and dirty, which is likely not what he intends.

"I'm pretty certain marriage isn't like a pothole or a bumper. It's not something you hit by accident."

The corner of his mouth quirks up. "Do you leave a note when you bang some poor guy's car in the Whole Foods parking lot? Or do you just sneak away?"

"First of all, I do *not* shop at Whole Foods. They've got great stuff, but I'd have to sell a kidney to buy my groceries there, and since I've only got two, that's a two-week death wish and not a viable long-term plan. Second, it sounds like you're asking me what my plans were for today. I wasn't planning on leaving you a note with a fake phone number and ghosting."

He exhales and nods. His gaze flickers over my face but I can't tell what he's thinking. Typical. He says, "First, you can buy whatever you want. Billion-aire." He points to himself just in case there's any doubt about who is rich and who is financially chal-lenged in this not-relationship. "Second, yes, I would like to hear how you envisioned today unfolding."

"I had planned on today being a whole lot more naked."

Honesty makes everything so much simpler. Liam being the boardroom type, however, he's more devi-ous and less accustomed to blunt statements of truth.

He practically bolts upright. "Christ."

"You're such a baby." I tweak his nipple. "I can't believe you have this reputation as a sex master and Don Juan."

He slides me a look. "Let us have wine and women… Sermons and soda water the day after."

We've clearly moved on to the day after, which is just my luck.

"Impressively well-read. I'm glad you're more than just a pretty face. It bodes well for our children."

He sets the phone onto the bedside table and rolls, pulling me underneath him. Muscled forearms brace my head and he glares down at me, all grumpy and mussed. "Be serious."

"You asked if we were really, truly married. I an-swered. I'm not a Magic 8 Ball you can shake until you get a better answer."

This is why we'd never work as a couple. I mar-ried my fantasy Liam. Real-life Liam, however, is proving deeply disappointing.

I poke his chest. "Off."

After he removes his person from mine, he deposits the rings on the bedside table, next to his phone and a stack of condoms that is much smaller than it was last night when we started.

"Ambitious," I observe.

Liam counts, gives the floor a quick survey (again, ewww), and turns back to me, visibly anxious. He's either imagining unpleasant dick diseases or suspects me of trying for a honeymoon baby.

"I'm on the Pill." I pat him one more time—the man is built—and then slide off the bed.

Last night I was focused on bringing my not-so-secret Liam fantasies to life when I proposed. This morning, okay...nothing's changed since yesterday morning. We'd still never work as a couple in real life. He's not Mr. Monogamy, nor does it appear he's willing to try. I don't have any diseases, I'm a decent person, I'm super loyal, and he could have said no. Plus, we'd had amazing chemistry. Alcohol-fueled, sure, but I'd also been willing to try sober sex. Clearly, however, it can't work out between us because I refuse to be the *punishment* half of a *Crime and Punishment* love story. Liam somehow manages to be both uptight and a player, while I deserve someone who will embrace my sexy goddess goodness.

Or badness.

Honestly, I'm not sure how that works, but I'm determined to learn.

The first step in my Must Resist Liam Masterson plan is to find clothes. It's always harder to think about non-sex things when naked, so I laid a course for Liam's closet. He can spot me a shirt and some pants. Nude at home is one thing, but I draw the line at naked driving. My pickup truck has vinyl seats and no AC. You just know that's when Officer Too Friendly pulls you over. It might even be illegal to drive naked. I make a mental note to google that in the near future when I find my phone.

Liam's closet is—color me not-shocked—a masterpiece of organization he probably paid someone else a small fortune to arrange. The rods, the drawers and the shelves are done in tasteful shades of beech with loads of gold hardware. It's all terribly shiny and expensive. I run my fingers over a rack of suits. Kiton, Brioni, Zegna. Liam has come a long way since we were kids. He needs to wear more Levi's. Live life a little unbuttoned. If we'd worked out, I would have helped him with that.

Nope.

Don't go there.

I grin maniacally at myself in the enormous floor-to-ceiling mirror—Liam either *really* likes looking at himself or he has sex shenanigans in his closet—and ransack his drawers. He has far too many but I hit the mother lode early and uncover his stash of boxer briefs. Fortunately, they're big on me (my ego isn't ready to handle having a bigger butt than my man), so I fold the waistband over until I'm firmly in wedgie territory and things seem likely to stay put.

When I turn around, Liam is standing in the doorway. He does that a lot, but it makes sense. He's neither in nor out. Also, it's just an all-around good look for him. One broad, muscled shoulder is propped against the frame and his jeans ride low on his hips. The man has a happy trail pointing south that I really hope I explored.

The corner of his mouth tugs up in a lopsided grin that I first encountered last night. It's his sex god smile, the one that says he's feeling it. I sort of want to shuck the shirt and drop my stolen panties, but I know I need to stick to the plan.

"Are you taking my stuff?" His voice is light—he's either gotten over his anger or he's tamped it down. Probably B. The man is the king of repressing feelings.

I point a finger at him. It might be my middle finger because I'm not quite to Zen yet. "Find my clothes and you can have yours back. Consider this a hostage situation."

"I'm happy to buy you a closet full of shirts, Hana." He smiles, and it's the familiar grin now, not the new I-want-to-sex-you-up one. The crinkles at the corners of his eyes have always done something to me. When I was sixteen, he'd look at me and I'd turn into a hormonal puddle of goo even though he was really looking through me. Or over me or around me. Never *at* me. Today, right now, his eyes are completely, determinedly friendly.

This isn't happening. I can't be just his best friend's baby sister. Not anymore. He'd flicked my nose. Made monthly drugstore runs for tampons and barbecue potato chips. Vetted my dates, threatened to break bones, offered emergency cash and picked drunk me up from a bar one memorable, never-to-be-repeated college night. He listened on the rare occasion I cornered him. I talked. So much listening, with a side of well-intentioned, older-brother judging. He'd always wanted what was best for me, but I was the only one who'd ever thought that might mean *him*.

"Hey." Big fingers tip my chin up until I meet his eyes. "I'll get this fixed."

"Of course you will." I somehow manage to smile as if it's no big deal. As if that isn't exactly what he said before we stepped into his bedroom.

I'm once again Liam Masterson's little problem.

"Tell me something."

He nods.

"Why did you say yes last night?"

His jaw tightens. "I drank too much."

"So when you said yes, it was an accident?"

He hesitates, then says quietly, "No. It was a plan."

"So you wanted to marry me?" I'm an idiot for asking, but the part of me that's Team Cinderella, that believes in magic and fairy godmothers and morning-after second chances? That part of me wants to happy-yell the question.

He braces one big, bare arm on the wall beside my head, his muscles bunching. I'm surrounded by a delicious Liam cage.

"No," he says, and my heart does a free fall to my feet. "I do things when I'm drunk, things I shouldn't. I let other people make choices for me. And I drink knowing that's going to happen and that I'll feel terrible the next morning because I wasn't in control."

The hand that's not flattened against the wall comes up and squeezes my shoulder gently. "I shouldn't have had sex with you, so I did. Saying yes was the wrong thing to do, so I didn't say no."

I stare at him because—

I'm his punishment?

My mouth falls open just a little. "You married me because you'd feel terrible about it when you sobered up? You used me to make yourself feel bad? Do you do this in all of your relationships or am I just special?"

"Yes?" He flinches. I'll give him that. Or maybe that's just a reaction to his phone buzzing wildly from where he's buried it in the bed.

"You haven't asked me why I proposed."

"I know why," he says. "It's why you've stared at me since you were thirteen."

"Because I had a crush on you?" At least he didn't claim it was his money. "That was teenage me. I've grown up some since then, Liam. Mostly in the last half hour, because I'm not sure how to react when you tell me that the words we said last night to each other, words that meant something to me, were just some kind of freaking self-flagellation for you. I took a chance on us, and you took some kind of messed-up self-revenge. What you said last night, you said for you."

He stares down at me, and for the life of me, I

can't figure out what he's thinking. His phone goes nuts in the other room again.

"You should get that."

He shakes his head. "I really shouldn't."

"Because of—" I wave my hand between us.

"That's my—" He grimaces. I can tell he's not sure which noun to use next. "Ex. Leda. We dated. We broke up. She's made it clear she won't let me go."

"Wow." I can't find the words to respond that will make it clear just how cocky that sounds. I also add inappropriate and provoking to my mental list because now I'm dying to know more. I just hope he's not drawing some kind of stupid, man-brained parallel between his ex's behavior and mine. "I agree it's not a good idea to be chatting up your ex when you're married."

He nods. "I wouldn't. Do that. Not to you."

That's the Liam I've known for years, protective, casually affectionate, determined to make sure I go through life happy and safe. It's hard to turn my back on all that, particularly when it comes wrapped in such a sexy package. I know I should let him go.

I should walk out the door, out of his life.

The problem is that he's taken something that was my dream come true and turned it into a nightmare. Standing here in front of him, I feel naked and it's a thousand times worse than the pants-less dreams or the dreams where my teeth fall out or I have to pee but can't find a clean bathroom. I want to scream at him, to make him hurt the way I do, except this isn't entirely his fault. I loved the man my sixteen-year-old heart had invented, so of course real-life, morning-after Liam disappoints.

So I push past him and start walking because I won't be like this Leda, whoever she is. I won't stay where I'm clearly not appreciated, although I still pause in the door because I'm still a little weak for this man. "Isn't this where you apologize for being such a colossal dick?"

"I'll take care of this," he repeats instead. "The lawyers, the paperwork, everything."

I have no idea what that means or how you un-pick a marriage that's barely had a chance to begin, but I'm sure he'll handle it. "Money fixes every-thing, right?"

He doesn't have to think about it. "Not quite ev-erything, but almost."

"Let me know when you've fixed us, then," I tell him.

I feel him move behind me and I can't stay here. I valet-parked my truck last night, so my keys will be in my vehicle and I'll figure everything else out later. I walk away from Liam and by the time I reach the front door, he's no longer behind me.

CHAPTER FOUR

A COMM CHECK

Liam

I PRACTICE WHAT I'm going to say to Hana while I sit in my Market Street office in San Francisco. *I would find it very convenient if we could stay married for the next four to six months. I'll make it worth your while.*

Too blunt?

Maybe.

Wrong approach? Definitely. Hana's never been interested in money.

Plus, just because I'm an asshole doesn't mean I want to make Hana feel bad. I just don't want to apologize. It's not like saying *I'm sorry* magically fixes shit anyhow. Those are just two little words that people throw around. Because they're covering their asses. Because they want you to stop complaining or crying or making demands. Because words are cheaper than money.

Am I sorry?

No, I'm not. When you get to the apology stage in a relationship, it's game over. Apologies don't cut it in the business world any more than they do outside the boardroom. Or in bars, parking lots and bedrooms. My father apologized over and over to my mother before leaving to do the same stupid shit again.

My parents weren't picture-perfect. They had a difficult relationship with more blasts and rocky orbits than a space shuttle. Our Berkeley house was colorful and chaotic even by the hippie college town's standards, with one wildly unpredictable, dramatic scene after another. My parents would fight, then Dad would storm out for a few weeks or months, and come back right about when the money ran out and the electric company started taping shutoff notices to our door. Harmony would be briefly restored and then the cycle of fights and apologies would repeat. If I hadn't been there, the third wheel in their drama, maybe they could have worked it out.

If Berkeley hadn't been so staunchly anti-establishment, anti-big corporation, anti-money, maybe I wouldn't have gone over to the dark side. I love making money. Money's easy. It's about patterns and algorithms. Not only does two plus two make four, but it makes four every single time. There are no surprises in math, unlike relationships, which is great. I'm maxed out on exploding shit, so I prefer to limit my personal interactions to my dick or my bank account when possible. This definitely worked for Leda, but Hana has always insisted she won't touch my money or Jax's, but those are just her emotions talking.

Leda, my ex, has also been doing some serious talking.

For years I've been the business golden child, the moneymaker, the acknowledged king of Silicon Valley. I build tech companies that eventually sell for mind-blowing numbers of dollars and everyone involved goes home happy and rich. And then I do it all over again. And again. You can't have too much money or success, and I've never failed when I've made the effort, so my current situation is difficult to process. The first blow to my throne was the day I realized that the portfolio of patents held by Leda's company, Swan Bio, was worthless because none of the tech she'd patented had ever worked. She'd lied to me, to her investors, and to the United States Patent and Trademark Office. There were a few casualties of the lawyerly type as well. I'm the king strutting around in a really expensive set of invisible clothes with my dick hanging out for the whole word to see.

It's a problem.

A half-billion-dollar problem.

When I'd done some private investigating, the problem had grown exponentially worse. Not only was there no product, but there was no seed money left. All the dollars that had been poured into her company had vanished.

Which brings me to my current problem. I haven't revealed my suspicions of financial malfeasance to the world, as I fix my shit in private. The rumors swirling around the city are that I'm a dick who shut her company down because she broke up with me. The senior members of the Galaxtix board have explained, in progressively stuffier speeches, that being labeled unrepentantly dickish makes me look unprofessional. These are people who follow the big rules in life, the biggest of which is: thou shalt not get caught. Therefore, I'm also accused of being immature, shortsighted and a liability. Ruling Silicon Valley doesn't require the moral character of the Pope, but apparently I'm not allowed to look like one of hell's lesser demons, either. They were getting ready to invite me to resign.

I'd pointed out that I broke no laws—federal or state—and that I gave them money. They should have been grateful. Nope. They'd insisted that I "clean up my image" and "show the world that I'm a good guy." I'm not a good guy. I'm a businessman and a billionaire.

In fact, they'd suggested I eschew additional sex scandals, and instead give monogamy and personal reformation a serious second look. Also, they thought I should give apologizing a shot, starting with Leda and then moving on to the board, the shareholders and Joe Public. I'd refused repeatedly and had instead thrown that sex party last weekend. The one where I'd accidentally ended up married. They'd have had a collective aneurysm if they'd found out about that.

I'd been about to tell them where to shove their ultimatums when I'd realized that last weekend's challenge was the perfect solution to the board's collective aneurysm about my personal life.

I'm married.

To a bona fide good girl.

Settled down, completely reformed, upstanding citizen.

Totally true story if I can convince Hana to play along. Since she told me to let her know when we were divorced and stormed off, however, my desire to play temporary house with her will come as a surprise.

By ten o'clock, I've successfully started the process of purchasing Hana's mortgage and verified she has no other financial liabilities. Some guys send roses when they fuck up—and some of us just smooth the road of life a little with a judicious application of cash. She's not in this marriage for money, but it can't hurt to show her what I bring to the table. By noon I've cleared out my inbox and taken care of what can't wait. So I'm genuinely 100 percent free when Jax texts at 12:10 that he's outside my building and I should get my ass down there now.

The *or I'll beat the shit out of you* part is just understood. Clearly, Hana's told him about our marriage. She's probably also told him that I'm a first-class dick (true), but that's just one more thing I won't apologize for. I'll give her a bee farm instead.

When I get outside, Jax is slouched against a low retaining wall full of perky summer annuals, glaring at the flow of people headed to lunch. Most of them are wearing suits or business casual and when they catch sight of him, they adjust their course on the crowded sidewalk so they don't have to get too close. It's like watching a trail of ants detour around an unpleasant obstacle.

Jax wears blue jeans, a black leather jacket and motorcycle boots, so he must have ridden his bike into the city today. He looks tough, his arms crossed over a muscled chest. We've been friends since he moved in next door all those years ago in Berkeley, but that doesn't mean he isn't thinking about punching me. I deserve it, so the real question is: Will I let him? We're evenly matched in size, but he's always joked that I look like the angel Gabriel while he more closely resembles the dark side.

Those devil looks mean there's little resemblance between him and Hana, on the outside at least. He's a dark-haired, dark-eyed menace, his shoulder-length hair pulled back in a short ponytail. I was with him when he started the sleeves that decorate his arms, colorful swirls of ink that record each step he's taken to get where he is today. Hana doesn't know half of what he's done to make sure she's safe, and we've always just known we'd do whatever it takes to keep her that way. This is why he's here, of course, because marrying her doesn't seem as if it's in her best interest.

He holds out a paper bag to me with a muttered curse and I take it.

"Is it poisoned?"

"Too quick," he growls. "Eat. I have a start-up to go hammer into shape after I kick your ass."

One of Jax's particular talents is taking underperforming companies and cutting away the dross until they shine financially. It doesn't make him the most popular guy in the room—people lose jobs when he takes over—but the ones who stay never regret it. Not financially, at any rate. I suspect he's a bit of a bastard boss, but then again, hell will freeze over before I work for him.

I open the bag to find a hot dog with onions and sauerkraut. The combination all but guarantees kissing Hana will not be on my afternoon agenda. I hesitate, but I'm hungry. He nods when I start eating, and for a few minutes we both focus on eating with maximum efficiency.

"What are the chances you're *not* married to my sister?" Jax crumples his now-empty bag and lobs it into a nearby trash can. It's an impressive three-point shot and I hand him mine so he can do it again.

I appreciate that he starts with facts and not feelings.

"My lawyers double-checked everything."

He hits the trash can again. "And?"

"And we're married."

"Hana deserves to be happy." The look on Jax's face warns that he doesn't see any further association between me and Hana leading to that state.

"I won't hurt her. We're going to work out a deal."

My phone goes nuts in the pocket of my suit jacket as Leda deluges me with a new flurry of texts. She hasn't let up, her endless messaging making it clear she has plenty more to say about the end of our relationship. I, on the other hand, ran out of fucks to give weeks ago. My fuck-less state coinciding with her decision to share the alleged details of our relationship with a gossip website has caused me a world of unresolved problems. I'm finding it increasingly hard to resist the urge when Leda comes up to run around shouting *liar, liar, pants on fire*. Mostly this is because I cringe when I think about Hana reading these things and deciding they're one more piece of evidence in the mountain of my dickishness.

While Jax considers what to say, I unlock my phone and inventory my messages. Nineteen angry texts from Leda demand, in increasingly hostile progression, that I repent of my sins, explain myself, text her back, don't bother texting her back and drop dead. *Shit. Delete.* I also have new emails from multiple business and entertainment reporters requesting I comment on my starring role in Silicon Valley's biggest start-up scandal. They don't mention my marriage. *Delete.* My PR team has reached out with a plan to handle the fallout from said scandal. I scan it. Like their last two proposals, they strongly urge me to go down on bended knee and apologize. I fire off a one-word response—no—and delete their email as well.

Jax plucks the phone out of my hand. Since not having to sum up saves me time, I let him. He glances down at the screen, his eyes skimming over the messages.

He pins me with his hard-ass glare when he looks up. "Why haven't you fixed this? Block Leda. Make her go away. You can't be texting her and be married to my sister. It looks like you still have a thing for her."

He's probably not soliciting murder, so I go with the next logical assumption. "Are you asking me to pay her off?"

Jax curses but doesn't deny the thought of money has crossed his mind. Instead, he hands me back my phone.

"Isn't there another way to get her out of your life?"

This is dangerous ground. "Eventually there will be legal charges, but I don't own that timeline and I can't guarantee they'll stick."

"But you think they will."

I hesitate for just a moment. Jax is one of the few people I trust with the truth. He's also just about the only person I'd explain myself to. "This is about her business relationships, not something personal." Not a revenge fuck in the literal sense. "She lied to a lot of people. She took their money knowing she didn't actually have a product—and then she spent that money, but not on R&D. Or she moved it. Whatever happened to it, it's gone, and since she was the CEO, she's responsible."

Jax's frown deepens and a slim guy in a well-tailored summer suit veers hard left and almost stumbles off the curb. "Why don't you just say that? Everyone thinks you're an ass who is wrong and won't apologize."

"The ass part is true."

When I stop there, he does some more cursing.

He's known me for years, so you'd think he'd appreciate the whole no-apologies approach. My parents used to terrorize the neighborhood with their fights. They'd yell—or discuss at full volume—everything that had gone wrong since the last time my dad had come home, and then he'd "apologize," my mom would call him on it and there would be more words. Nothing ever got fixed, he never stopped doing the stuff she hated, and it just made our family look like candidates for Dr. Phil's show. I used to head over to Jax and Hana's place whenever I heard my dad's Dodge Charger pull into the driveway.

"So if it's true, tell people it's true." Jax looks like he might want to throw his hands up in the air like a 1950s housewife and have a fit of the vapors. Whatever those are. "What does Hana think about all this?"

This one's easy. "She knows Leda and I broke up."

Usually I'd point out that Hana hadn't asked for details, but she was pretty focused on our impulsive marriage. Any questions probably occurred to her later and were answered with Google.

"Are you crazy? Your ex is texting you constantly and the rest of the world believes, with some grounds, that you fucked up her business to teach her some kind of lesson. What if Hana thinks you'd do the same to her?"

"You'd kill me," I point out. I think I sound quite reasonable.

"Yes, but she shouldn't even have to think it." He definitely looks like punching me has risen back to the top of his to-do list. I'd rather not be sporting a black eye when I go see Hana, so I just nod in agreement. I consider telling him I'm in the process of acquiring the mortgage on her bee farm, but it's completely different, right? I'm not buying her note to shut her down or take the place away from her (okay, so the thought crossed my mind that it would be leverage, but Hana is *nice*—I won't need to bribe her into compliance). I mostly did it to smooth things over, but it also makes a better thank-you present than flowers for helping me out. She'll never have to worry about things like recessions or billing departments again.

"What happens next? Eventually Hana's going to outgrow her crush on you, and then what?"

"Is this the twenty questions game? Am I supposed to drink if I don't have an answer?"

Jax grunts something I don't catch. "Are you staying married?"

Danger. "It would help with a work thing if we were a couple for the next few months."

"And then?" Jax doesn't look particularly happy, although I know he understands. Sometimes you have to do shitty things to get where you need to go—and I understand that he'll stop me if he decides that's what Hana needs. He's my safety valve.

"And then I guess it's up to Hana. I'm not calling all the shots here."

"She doesn't tell you that you work too much?" From his tone, I assume Hana's been on his case, either about putting in too much time at the office or accumulating too much money. She's idealistic, which can translate into her announcing that enough money is enough money and Jax should let someone else have a chance at the next billion dollars.

I throw him a bone. "Leda thought I put my work first. It made her mad."

Jax just nods. "You did. We both do. Hana's my one exception."

He stops and then gets this weird look on his face. Possibly, his hot dog is talking back to him, but I'm not sure. Leda was right that she came second after my career. But Hana is different. A sense of rightness settles over me.

"So you have to think about what you're going to do." Jax stares at the sea of lunch-seeking business-people, but he clearly doesn't see them. If I were a better person, I'd ask him who he does see. I'm not sure it's my Hana. "Plan for the future and stuff."

Generally, I see my future in terms of earning quarters. I'm only twenty-eight, which means I have some serious money-earning years left. And while I'm a risk-taker when it comes to work, I've already made sure that there's plenty set aside and sewn up tight in case something unexpected happens. While I can't envision myself failing, I'm also completely certain I never want to be broke again. This is prob-ably the point at which Hana would tell me I'm an ass and suggest living off the land or some other granola-type approach to a wholesome life. I can feel my lips curving up in a smile.

"You need to tell her the truth. She's going to hear stuff."

"And she'll believe what she believes."

Jax heaves a pained sigh. "She had the biggest crush on you when she was a kid. She thought you were Jesus Christ walking on water, that there was nothing you couldn't do. You have to ease her in to the actual you. Why did you really marry her? Not the crap business reasons story that makes your life sound like a movie plot, but the real reason."

"She asked me."

He doesn't look surprised—Hana's crush on me drives him nuts—but it doesn't shut him up, either. "She couldn't have forced you to say yes."

"No guns were involved," I say lightly.

I decide not to tell him that there's every chance we could annul our marriage because both of us were drunk off our asses and that's grounds enough in California.

"Just do your thing and fix it," Jax orders. "Find out what she wants. Give it to her. Fucking apologize for once in your life."

I look at him. "Right. Or else."

"Or else," Jax agrees.

He sounds as if he's talking to himself.

CHAPTER FIVE

MAN ON A MISSION

Liam

A WEEK AGO, I was a bachelor billionaire and the host of a now-legendary sex party. Saturday morning: I woke up with a ring on my finger and a wife by my side. Sure, the point of getting drunk off my ass was to do things I'd regret the next morning, but marrying Hana is a whole different category of messed up. Worse, I can't stop thinking about her, and my lunchtime conversation with Jax just feeds my inner beast.

Hana naked.

Wrapped in a sheet wearing just my rings.

Bending her hot body into a yoga pose.

Her hot *naked* body.

We had sex, but seven days later I still can't remember all of the details, although not for lack of trying. I wanted to punish myself, but instead I think I ended up hurting Hana. She's not forgettable and although my blacking out is entirely my fault, not hers, she may not see it that way.

An hour after Jax roars off on his bike to kick ass at an underperforming start-up, I give up pretending to be productive. Instead, I stare out the window of my office. I can see both the Bay and the Transamerica Pyramid from where I sit. Despite the sunshine, smog dims the colors of the sky. It's probably hot and bright in Marin where Hana has that farm of hers. I haven't been out there, although I know Jax is a frequent visitor. I've teased him more than once about his newfound hippie tendencies and asked if he had urges to swap out girl hugging for tree hugging. A quick inbox check tells me that the investment bank in which I own a significant if private stake has done as I asked and acquired Hana's mortgage. I know she won't let me pay it off if I ask—Jax tried to gift her the money for the original purchase and she refused—but this way no one will ever foreclose on her or sell her loan. I just won't tell her until it's a done deal.

Leaning back in my chair, I stare out at the soaring buildings of the San Francisco Financial District. I'm only here in our city office today because I had a meeting. I jiggle my knee, trying to force myself to think like I normally do, but I don't want to make more money or start another company.

Hana occupies the prime real estate in my brain as she has all week.

Since she's not here, I fall back on my phone, firing up the video of our wedding. I've watched it so many times that I know exactly what will happen and when. Hana and I join hands and repeat our vows after the ringmaster. He's included the standard stuff about love and honor, sickness and health, riches and poverty. While I'm not sentimental, the way Hana beams at me feels special. And then the cheesy circus music starts up, almost but not quite drowning out the ringmaster's invitation to kiss my bride.

There's a pause and then Hana throws her arms around my neck, hauling my face down to hers because she's a tiny bit of a thing and I'm a big brute. She kisses me enthusiastically and I pull her up for a decidedly X-rated kiss. My hands thread through her hair, angling her mouth as I devour her onscreen. I sort of want a do-over because she'd been smiling up at me with wide brown eyes, looking happy and dazed, and then I'd fucked her mouth with my tongue like a barbarian, bending her backward over one arm because we had an audience that I was clearly playing to.

Usually she wears faded blue jeans or Bohemian dresses that are big on fabric, tassels and flowered prints. The dress she wore to our wedding looked vintage. One of my groundskeepers had found the black-and-white dress and I'd had it dry-cleaned and returned to her, along with the red fuck-me shoes that had turned up in my kitchen.

The video stops and I promptly restart it.

At some point, I have to delete it because I'm turning into a fucking creeper.

What started out as an impulsive bad idea is now an opportunity. I need to get her attention and fast. She drove away from my Napa Valley place as if her gorgeous ass was on fire. Normally I don't give a shit what my hookups say or do after we've had sex, but Hana is different and not just because she didn't sign an NDA. I promised her that I'd take care of her. Twice. First in our vows and then the morning after.

Mortgage security aside, an unexpected way to achieve this goal has come up and I need her to consider it. I'm thinking of her. Not me.

Mostly.

I cringe. Okay, so a quick annulment is still the easiest option for Hana and at first I thought it was what I wanted, too. Except I've already spent an hour today being berated by the board of Galaxtix about the circus sex party and how bad it looked. Apparently, we'd lost another potential private investor and it was all my fault. I'd looked from one suit to the next, calmly meeting their judgmental gazes, and had come perilously close to telling them to stay out of my personal life. I could fund a dozen science education foundations. I could buy another space project.

But it wouldn't be this one.

This is the first time I've been invited to join a board for something other than my money, and I really love the direction our research has been headed. It's weirdly addictive, putting my MIT degree to work, and while I honestly don't expect to be driving a Bugatti on the surface of Mars in the next decade, it's a great dream. I don't want to lose it because a bunch of smart people, consisting mostly of engineers and nerds, have decided my dick is in charge of my brain. I've poured my money and my heart into this space rover thing, and it means something to me, so I won't let them kick me out without a fight. Which was when I'd opened my mouth and overshared accidentally on purpose.

When I'd casually mentioned that I might, possibly, have been there that night with my new *wife* and that there would be no more public orgies because naturally she frowned on that kind of thing, being a nice girl and a huge fan of monogamy, they'd stopped yelling and started asking questions. Unfortunately, those questions included *What's her name?* and *Why was she at a sex party—are you swingers?* I'd put them off, but eventually I'd have to provide answers.

As it stands now, I've been strongly requested to bring my new wife to a charity gala next month hosted by one of the board members. I don't particularly want to be married, but it will smooth over ruffled feathers and it has been made clear that as long as I'm married to someone who can serve as my public face, all will be forgiven.

So I'll just convince Hana to stay fake-married to me for a few months. I'll trot her out in front of the board, bring her to a few charity gigs, and then we can quietly split up just as soon as people have forgotten about the whole Leda thing. I'll make it easy—she won't have to do much besides move into my place and go to the charity gala. Smile, take a few photos, let me buy her dinner and a bee farm. Maybe some really nice earrings. I've already determined through some judicious texting with her brother that she isn't currently seeing anyone, and a quick hack into her checking account revealed that bee farming is even less lucrative than I would've guessed.

So her cash flow issue plus my image issue adds up to us staying married for now. She used to have a huge crush on me, so maybe she won't even mind.

I like the thought of that.

Giving up on work for the day, I head out of the office, making a quick stop at the reception desk to let them know that I'll be unavailable unless it's an emergency.

I try texting Hana again from the elevator. Her voice mail is full and she doesn't pick up. It's possible she's genuinely busy. She sells her honey at three different farmers' markets, so she should be in Marin right now. I'll pay her a visit and lay our options on the table.

So far, no specific public revelations about our marriage have come to light. There's just been the usual content on the celebrity gossip sites with pictures of guests arriving and leaving. The costumes definitely got coverage, plus half the world seems to be wondering if circus is the new kink. The big top and the Ferris wheel were visible from outside my compound and the paparazzi shot what they could. Sooner or later, however, they'll find out about Hana, especially if I start introducing her as my wife. After the Leda debacle, they'll dig into her background, expecting to find something salacious.

And they'll find bees.

Hana is fucking perfect.

CHAPTER SIX

AND WE'RE GO FOR LAUNCH

Liam

BUILT FOR SPEED, my limited edition Bugatti Veyron eats up the highway. Driving anything less than sixty would be criminal, and I'm in the mood to go fast. I shoot out of the city and then floor it as soon as I've cleared the Golden Gate Bridge with its obstacles of slow cars and gawking tourists.

The Veyron rides smooth, its wheels hugging the road, the seductive purr of the motor filling the white leather interior. Jax calls it the international playboy accessory, but he's just jealous because it's way harder to have sex on the back of his stupid motorcycle. I feel like a European prince in this car, life is good, and I have a plan with a limited window to execute so I let the ocean and palm trees whip past my window until I hit Marin County's infamously bad traffic.

At least there's plenty to look at as I slow to a forced crawl. Marin is gorgeous, all ocean and wetlands, stunning views and stupidly expensive scraps of houses tucked into epic-sized redwood trees and palm tree groves where people making stupid amounts of money in San Francisco live alongside longtime families. Owning real estate here is a golden ticket. Houses sell the day they come on the market. Less advantageously, all those new homeowners bring their cars—and all of them seem to have decided that today would be a great day to buy a truckload of organic tomatoes and eggplants at the farmers' market.

I follow a sea of cars, bikes and walkers to a parking lot that's really a dusty field of ruts and weeds. Leaving my Veyron surrounded by destructive particles of nature sucks, but I need to find Hana and request her buy-in on our temporary but public future. As soon as I get out, however, I realize I've underestimated the chaos factor.

The Friday farmers' market is a disorderly sea of pop-up awnings. I scan the aisles, but come up empty. There are endless piles of local produce, fresh-grown strawberries, jams, soaps and more leafy stuff than I can possibly identify. A service delivers my produce in a box so all this choice is an unwelcome novelty. Maybe the crunchy granola goodness will rub off and I'll start a garden? Plant some seeds and do good-for-me shit? Or maybe not, because the dress code seems to be organic cotton, beads and reusable hemp shopping bags. My three-thousand-dollar business suit and tie stick out and not in a good way.

I wave off a half dozen vendors eager to load me up with produce. I don't need organic zucchini or purple carrots—just a wife. Eventually, through a combination of blind luck and strategic direction-asking, I discover Hana's stand on the far edge of the market. Her love of all things bee is obvious even from a distance. A black-and-yellow awning protects her tables covered in red-and-white-checked tablecloths and dozens of wooden crates of honey, mason jars filled with waxy combs, dark honey, light honey and flavored honey sticks. The world of honey products is far larger than I knew. I still don't understand how she makes enough money to live, but her workplace smells sweeter than mine. There's even a display case housing a live slab of bees that must be a serious liability. What if the glass broke? Or someone knocked it over and then the two thousand bees trapped inside rampaged through the farmers' market?

Thanks to the bee analogies or possibly the constant thinking about sex, I feel unexpectedly light-headed. Hana's seated behind one of the tables, waving her hands as she explains something to a middle-aged lady purchasing a half dozen jars of honey. No one needs that much honey but it's hard to say no to Hana, as I've learned.

She's hot in a cute, wholesome way that I attribute to the straw fedora half sliding off her head as she agrees vigorously with something the other lady says. Two strawberry-blond braids poke out beneath the brim and a cheerful smile tilts her pretty mouth.

It might be funny or a really good story—or it could also be boring as fuck and something she's heard twice already today. Hana has a way of focusing on you, though, as if she really can't wait to hear what you say next.

Hana used to look at me like that.

I stride toward the stand, trusting that the milling, ambling, aimless crowd of shoppers will get out of my way.

She rockets to her feet as soon as she spots me, green dress belling out around her in a floral explosion. The hem stops above her knees, so I get an eyeful of toned, suntanned thighs. The rest of her is regrettably covered up by the long sleeves of her dress, which gather at her wrists in a big puff. The front dips low in a vee to reveal some kind of lacy thing that's probably intended to hide her boobs. The lace just draws attention, however, to the freckles that dot her cleavage. I do my best not to stare because I really am here to talk with her, not play connect-the-dots with my tongue.

I want to at least kiss her hello, but that seems likely to lead to a repeat of the sex scandals the board has been riding my ass about as I don't seem to be able to keep my hands off her once I get started. Instead I stop on the public side of the honey-loaded table and consider my options for getting past the barrier. Crawling underneath would lack dignity and vaulting over feels like showing off and could end poorly for the glass jars.

I settle for bracing a hand on the edge and leaning toward her. "Hana."

"Liam." Laughter fills her gorgeous eyes.

Christ, she's beautiful.

"Hi." I've fantasized about our reunion a half dozen times, usually while in the shower. At this point, I've swung back and forth between reminding myself that she's my best friend's little sister and my hot weekend hookup so many times that I might have permanent whiplash.

Her gaze skims down my body, taking in my suit. "Did you make another billion dollars today? Commit any acts of big business?"

"Enough to buy you lunch. Can you take a break?"

I hold up the paper bag I'm carrying. After considering the best way to approach her, I decided on food-based bribery. Hana's favorite place to eat in San Francisco is a raw food restaurant that serves only vegetables and plant-based products. They don't cook anything on the menu and it's so farm-to-table fresh that you can pick the dirt out of your teeth.

"Is that—" She reaches for the bag and I only hold it out of her reach for a second. I'm playing nice today.

"Rabbit food," I agree. She already knows how I feel about meat substitutes. Our fingers brush as she takes the bag. She's wearing an inexpensive mood ring where her wedding band should be, the stone a rich golden amber.

She ducks over to the next table and asks its occupants if one of them can temporarily babysit her honey. The sinewy, built guy who follows her is way too good-looking.

"Thirty minutes," she tells me once she's got him situated with a gunmetal cash box.

"Not long enough."

"Take it or leave it."

"Hana. Since when do I negotiate?" I lean down into her. She could back up, but she doesn't and she looks so fucking beautiful that I kiss her for a sweet, quick beat. Her lips part beneath mine and suddenly I'm devouring her mouth, eating her up in a wet, obscene tangle of tongues and lips.

When I pull back, she looks dazed.

"Tell me where we're eating lunch or I'll choose."

She mutters something, but points to a rusting truck that's an antique without any of the investment value. Its paint job was left behind at some point in the 1950s and I'm amazed the California DMV ever approved it for road use.

I follow her, picking my way around the maze of tables and produce. I feel like the tail end of a parade, so I catch up, cupping her elbow with my hand. Not because she can get lost when her truck is sitting there in plain, ugly sight, but just because I like touching her. Her skin is soft and she smells mostly like coconut and vanilla, although there are notes of honey and tomatoes in there.

The truck is less private than I like—we're definitely not having makeup sex without attracting an audience. She sets the bag in the truck bed and lets down the gate, revealing a disorganized jumble of stuff: wooden crates stamped with the farm's name, a plaid blanket, random tools, driftwood and a flat of succulents.

She points to the lunch I brought her. "Are you bribing me?"

"Is it working?"

She hops up onto the gate—which puts her at eye level—and looks expectantly at me. "Not yet."

Grinning, I lever myself into the truck bed beside her. Thanks to her weird collection of stuff, there's not much room. Our knees touch, the fabric of her dress brushing my suit pants. The metal is sun-warmed but also streaked with yellow pollen. Hana never parks in the garage at her farm. She just leaves her truck outside wherever she stops driving. It makes Jax nuts because he's a clean freak, and in this case, he has a point. There's every chance our asses will be pollen-colored when we stand up.

She does a stretchy thing with her arms, bending them behind her head one at a time. "What do you want?"

I nudge the bag toward her. "To have lunch with you."

And sex and a temporary marriage but…details. She'll be more amenable after she's eaten. I know how she gets when she has a hangry going and she can't have had much time to eat today.

"God, you never change." She digs into the bag with a sigh, pulling out a biodegradable paper-wrapped object, and eyes the words Sharpied onto the side. "Bean sprout taco?"

"Christ, no."

"Your loss." Her eyes twinkle at me as she relaxes, popping open a cooler hiding behind one of the crates and pulling out two cans of Coke. I love that she hasn't changed. She's always had a weakness for it. No diet, no other brand. Just Coke. I've added it to my weekly grocery order for both my San Francisco place and my Napa château.

I take a can from her, wrapping my fingers around her hand. I feel like an asshole—more so than usual—because instead of focusing on today's plan or thinking about what Hana needs, I'm mostly aware of how easy it would be to ease her legs apart and slide under that tent of a dress. I'd lick a line from her knee to her clit and then I'd eat her out. Maybe later she'll let me do it.

"Liam?"

Hana's sweet voice cuts through my fantasy. It brings my attention back to the here and now, but does nothing to deflate my inconvenient hard-on. I try reminding myself that she's off-limits, but my dick points out that we're married, which introduces certain possibilities, the biggest of which is turning out to be hard to hide in dress pants.

"Are you ready to tell me why you're here?"

Not a chance. "How was your week?"

It's been six days, 144 hours, or roughly 8,640 minutes since she hightailed it away from me and our impromptu marriage. Not that I've been counting.

The look she gives me starts somewhere around my knees and lingers far too long on the front of my pants. Color stains her cheeks, but she launches into a lively description of how she's spent our time apart. It involves wildflowers, bees, and a pressing need to determine whether or not her particular colony will accept lavender snacks or if they're holding out for echinacea.

Beekeeping is not something I've given a lot of thought to, but Hana loves it and I like listening to her. Eventually, she falls silent, working through her second taco.

"Penny for your thoughts?" I stroke my finger down her nose. The gesture is an old habit but it somehow feels different. I pop open her Coke and set it down beside her. I can feel the warmth of her skin and I have an urge to push two fingers into her to see if she's that warm and soft everywhere. I resist because I'm not a total pig. I know what's wrong.

"What do you want? Right now? And don't tell me you're not here for something, Liam."

She pulls her legs up, making a barrier between us of her body. *Fuuuck. Me.*

"Maybe I'm just having lunch with my wife." She's not thinking about the same things I am, I remind myself. I'm just her older brother's friend and a drunken hookup that she proposed to for some reason that made perfect sense to her but that the rest of the world would see as crazy.

"As if. Are we still married?" She eyes me calmly over her "taco."

"Yeah." I lean back against my side of the truck, soaking in the sun-warmed metal. I can't remember the last time I slowed down and just took a nap in the sun. I'm always busy launching a new company or shepherding a critical project to success, so the urge to close my eyes feels strange. I'm in the middle of a freaking farmers' market with a thousand people walking past us.

"You didn't end it?" Her cheeks have a new flush of color that wasn't there before. I tug her cute little hat lower, angling the brim for better coverage.

Just because sunburn's a serious risk and she's mine.

Temporarily.

"Not yet." My eyes drift down her body, trying to see through the surprisingly opaque yards of floral material.

"Why not?" She scrunches up taco wrapper number two in her hand.

"That's exactly what I wanted to talk to you about."

CHAPTER SEVEN

NOT SO SMOOTH NOW

Liam

"WE SHOULD GET MARRIED. Stay married." *Real smooth, Masterson.* I cringe at the way I just blurt the words out. I hadn't rehearsed in the car because I'd wanted to sound natural, but this is too much of a good thing.

"They have family law courts for this kind of thing," she says. There's an impish look in her eyes that doesn't bode well for my dignity—or my self-control. If I don't take charge, our discussion will derail or take a detour. Detours with Hana are turning out to be super fucking fun, but I also don't want to sit through another board meeting like the one earlier today.

Ergo, I suck in a deep, calming breath and try not to think about kissing her.

Or touching her.

I remind myself that I don't believe in problems—

only challenges. The situation with my board is *Titanic*-sized, but this is also the moment when I storm the wheelhouse and turn that ship the fuck around.

In the pro column, Hana is sweet, lovely and obviously exactly the kind of nice person who can be invited to charity galas and cocktail hours. We're also already married, which makes her convenient. And since she's broke or close enough, she can use my money.

In the con column, Hana is Jax's sister and I'm never, ever supposed to think about her as someone I'd like to have sex with. After our wild Friday night, however, I don't think I can go back to seeing her as almost a relative. It's disorienting having seen her naked, compounded by the fact that we really are married. I went from being a single guy to her husband, and skipped all the dating stuff that usually fills in the middle. You'd think I could just chalk it up to drunken shenanigans, write her a check and move on with my life, but somehow I can't.

"Earth to Liam." Hana leans over and pokes my stomach, aiming for my belly button. She did this for a while as a kid until I learned to watch for it and preemptively grab her hand. It feels different now. I can't help thinking what that finger is connected to. The hand, the wrist, the arm, the deliciously curvy torso, ass and legs. I might not *remember* particular details, but I definitely have the big picture cemented in my head as I thread my fingers through hers.

"We can annul on grounds of unsound mind. We were extremely intoxicated and not capable of making decisions," I say carefully. "But I'd like to do this as quietly as possible. I'm not sure if you're aware of my current situation, but I'm in negotiations with the board at Galaxtix. They're concerned about how my personal life may be perceived by donors. So I'd propose that we stay married for now and then we'll split up later when it's convenient."

She drops the remnants of her taco into the bag with her free hand. "You're kidding."

"I'm not." This is the tricky part. "Four months would probably do it, although a year would be better."

For a second, I think it's my lucky day and she's going to agree without arguing. Her lips part and she gets this soft look on her face, but then she presses her lips together and stiffens up. It's time to sweeten my offer.

"I'll compensate you, of course. Generously." I reach into my suit jacket and pull out the post-nup my lawyer drafted. "I would need you to sign this, but it's to protect both our interests. That way I don't get half a bee farm when we split up, and you're not saddled with my business."

Hana makes a choking sound. I shift so I can reach behind her and pat her on the back. Since she can breathe—based on the number of audible *freakity-fudge-freaks* I hear—she isn't dying and doesn't need my help. I run my fingers down the delicate knobs of her spine. She feels fragile, but we both know she's made of steel—except when it comes to me. I've always been Hana's soft spot and I've never been so grateful for that.

"No." She shakes her head, making her braids dance over her shoulders. "I don't want your money."

I've heard her have this exact same argument with Jax on multiple occasions, but this time she'll lose. No one is more stubborn than me when I want something.

"Tell me what you do want then." I flatten my palm against her back. Any lower and I'll be cupping her butt.

"Did you really think you could stride in here and pay me to be your wife for whatever nefarious reason you need one?"

"Yes?"

"No." She shifts away from me, clearly done with lunch, with me and with this conversation. That doesn't work for me, so I use the hand I'm holding to pull her onto my lap. Without hesitation, she wriggles around, making herself comfortable. I'm less so, but that's only to be expected. "Do you really think you're qualified to be someone's husband?"

I pretend to think about that for a second. The honest answer is no, but that's not going to get me what—who—I want. "I'll be an intern husband."

"Are you sorry that you got me into this mess?"

I debate reminding her that the "mess" is half her responsibility, but decide against it. "No."

"Are you serious?"

"I'm also not not-sorry." I shrug. "We got married. It isn't the end of the world. I told you I would fix it and I will. I'm just here to lay out options for you. If you're looking for apologies, you should have married someone else. I don't apologize. You should know that by now."

She hesitates, clearly not sure what to say next. Hana is nice. In her sweet, honey-centric world, people apologize when they screw up and they probably mean it most of the time. She's trying to understand my point of view because that's what nice people do, and I need to close the sale. All I really want to do, though, is kiss her and possibly crush her between my body and the truck while we have sex.

"Apologies are just words." I might possibly press my forehead against hers because I'm a greedy, *desperate* bastard. "But I give awesome make-up sex and now would be a great time to tell me what color you want your Porsche to be."

She sighs. "You're really unbelievable."

She could be referring to my offer to buy her a car or sex her up, or my refusal to apologize. The likeliest answer is a *D, all of the above* scenario. I drop her hand and pull out my phone, making a note in my to-do app to have a car delivered to her. It'd be funny if nothing else.

Then I return to our negotiations. "We have three options. Option A is divorce. We're looking at 180 days from whatever date we decide our marriage ended on. I'd suggest that's the second day, but you can let me know if you feel differently. Option B is an annulment. We'll need to convince a judge that one or both of us was of unsound mind that night because of intoxication, which won't be hard to do. Option C I already mentioned. We stay married for now and then we go for Option A later."

"Did someone tell you to do this?" She looks around.

"Who are you looking for?"

"Jax. I may have to kill him."

"Jax has nothing to do with us. This proposal is all on me."

"So you're genuinely here on your own?"

"Yes." She still doesn't look as if she believes me, so I continue building my case. "Does it matter? You pretend to be my wife, I pay you. Imagine how many bee farms you could buy."

"I only need one."

This is another difference between us. If I owned a bee farm, I'd franchise it or grow it into a national conglomerate that controls the honey market.

"Tell me why." Her finger drills into my chest again. "Make it good."

"I'm getting pushback from my board about my 'lifestyle choices.'" I make air quotes and she shakes her head. "We're a publicly traded company and the situation with Leda doesn't look good."

"They think you screwed her company over because you were mad at her."

Somebody's been googling.

"I bankrolled her company. I poured venture capital dollars into it. Anyway, it turns out that there were a few issues with the product she was developing—" *like it didn't exist* "—and so I shut down the funding. I guess she took that the wrong way and she's been accusing me of shit ever since. I look like a first-class asshole, though, and my board is pressuring me to do some damage control and shine up my image."

"So I'm damage control and an image buffer."

"It would definitely help if we looked like a normal married couple. We could live together, do couple stuff."

She eats another taco while she thinks my statement over. "This has to do with my being *nice*, doesn't it? I'm the good cop in this scenario and you're the bad one."

It does. I nod.

"So you want my help."

"Yes. Fine. I do."

"Except you don't want to call it *help*—you want to call it something else and pay me."

"It sounds bad when you put it that way."

"So how would you envision this temporary marriage working? You said we'd live together? Act like a real couple?"

I've given this extensive thought. While last weekend's quickie marriage is by and large a secret, the truth will inevitably come out. There are just too many holes for me to plug. While the ringmaster signed a general NDA before I allowed him onto my property, money talks and sooner or later he'll be tempted to share his side of our story with the press. The other guests are also a liability.

"Yes, we'll live together. Be seen together." I spread my hands. "But I'm not asking you to have sex with me. If you want it to be, sex is off the table."

She slides me a sidelong glance, mischief dancing in her eyes. "I haven't had sex on a table. It seems awkward and uncomfortable, but maybe you've had different table experiences than me."

"Don't be a brat." I recapture her hand.

"What are you going to do? Spank me?" She blushes. It's adorable, but it also emphasizes the differences between us and makes me want to teach her a lesson.

"If that's what you want."

Her mouth falls open a little, but no words come out.

I smile, leaning forward, my free hand stroking her thigh just high enough that we both know it's not a friendly accident.

"Is that what you want, to spank me?" The tip of her tongue traces her lower lip.

Her curiosity is going to kill me.

I shake my head. "You're a nice girl, Hana. We both know you're not running around the San Francisco sex clubs, asking strangers to spank you."

Because I'm not the nice person here, however, I raise her hand to my mouth and nip the tip of her finger. Her breath catches when my tongue swirls over the sensitive pad.

I let go of her hand and sit back. "I don't want to hurt you. You're safe with me, Hana. I only want to make you feel good."

"But not in bed."

"Hana—"

"Yes, yes, I'm aware that we little sisters aren't supposed to think about sex, let alone talk about it. I'm entirely certain that Jax would like to believe I'm planning a life of celibacy until I'm ninety. He'd volunteer me for a convent if he could, but neither of us is Catholic. I don't want money, Liam. We'd kill each other if we lived together, for so many reasons."

"How many?"

She thinks for a minute. "Three."

Three is manageable. "Hit me."

CHAPTER EIGHT

THIS COULD NEVER WORK

Hana

FRIDAY NIGHT WE got married.

By Saturday morning, I'd walked out on him after he made it offensively clear that, per his supersmart man brain, our marriage could never work as I was practically family. Oh, and that I was his own, personal hair shirt and self-flagellation tool. Tired of always coming up short, I'd left.

In retrospect, giving Liam space was a mistake. He's clearly used his alone time to come up with a new plan, and equally clearly, he thinks I'll require convincing to go along with it and he's here ready to play hardball. The delicious vegan tacos I just finished are proof of that.

I cup his cheek with my hand. Stubble shadows his jaw, inviting me to rub my face against his until his bristles mark my skin. The sexual jolt I feel is stupid, so instead I answer his question.

"One. You're filthy rich and I'm not. Two. I like having sex and you've made it clear you're not putting out. And three: you don't fit into my life—it would be like adding a chef's kitchen to a double-wide. The kitchen would be expensive and the appliances top-end, but the infrastructure work would be a bitch and no one would ever be able to figure out the resale value."

He gives a slow blink.

"I'm trying to do the right thing here," he says. And just like that Liam is back to being the suit. You know how medieval knights wore all that armor when they rode into battle and you pretty much had to pry them out of it with a can opener? Just substitute designer suits for chain mail and you have Liam. He's happy if he gets to be the one discussing spanking and other sex acts, but he shuts down if I mention those three little letters: S, E and their best friend X.

"I could ignore the first and third issues if we established a few ground rules like I pay my own way, but the no-sex thing is a deal breaker, so perhaps you'd care to discuss the sexual elephant in the room?"

"Not particularly." The growly look he aims my way might scare the pants off someone who hasn't known him for years, but he's said it himself. He'd never hurt me. It undermines his ability to negotiate a killer deal.

"We did it. We had sex. Based on your reaction the other night, I either really did it for you, or you'd just come off a sexual drought. Since the Instagram posts seem to suggest you're a man-whore and generally make yourself available to San Francisco's population—mind you, I'm not judging—I think you just really liked getting your rocks off with me. I'm not going to force you to tell me if you've been entertaining secret fantasies about me for years, but I'm not averse, either."

The look on his face turns contemplative. "How is *man-whore* not judgmental?"

"True." I make a show of tapping my lower lip with my finger. "Okay. We'll call you the Father Christmas of sex, passing out orgasm gifts to all the good little girls. I want a turn while you want a vestal virgin for some nefarious business purpose. It puts us at an impasse, if you see what I mean."

I'm hoping he won't figure out for himself that I can't actually stop him from keeping me on a sexless pedestal. His penis really has to cooperate with the idea, and I won't cheat on him. He kind of already has what he wants.

Would I have agreed if he'd asked me before the sex party? I honestly don't know.

I'm still holding on to his hand, so I force myself to let go. It's harder than I expect—my fingers want to cling to his, to stroke his hand, to tickle the palm with my nails until he gives me his slow, lopsided sex-god grin. I'm not ready to let go of him yet.

Because holy shit, the man gets hotter every time I see him, which may have something to do with the fact that I've seen him naked. There's no unseeing naked Liam.

He looks at me with his poker face. "What are you proposing?"

Play it cool. "This would have to be a partnership, Liam. Not an employee-boss relationship."

Hot boss would be a super fun fantasy to role-play, but I'm not going to make it a real-life thing. Liam would run roughshod over me.

He narrows his eyes. "Okay."

I grin at him. "Give a man a fish, and you'll feed him for a day. Teach a man to fish, and you've fed him for a lifetime."

Does it sound like a tangent? Sure, but Liam rolls with it. "Confucius?"

"Probably." I wave a hand dismissively. "But getting back to the bigger picture, you have an image problem. People don't think you're nice. I'll teach you how to be nice and then you won't need me as a prop."

His forehead puckers in a frown, but I barrel ahead. "And in exchange, you'll give me bad-girl lessons. Based on today's conversation, I clearly need more practice in that department. I'd never even considered spanking, so obviously you have a ton to teach me."

And…

There is one more sexual elephant we need to address.

"Unless you're not attracted to me," I continue, so quietly that it takes him a moment to make out what I've just said. I know when he has because he tenses beneath me. "In which case, I get that certain things are off the table. I'd like to have really memorable sex with you, but only if that's what you want, too."

His eyes darken, his fingers tightening on my bare shoulders. "Attraction's never been the problem."

He runs a finger down my shoulder and along my side and my breath catches.

"I want you," he says roughly. "And if dirty sex is something you're curious about, I can help you out with that, too. But are you sure it's what you really want?"

"Is it a binary kind of proposition?"

"Maybe you'd like a taste," he said, his finger moving lower. "Before you make up your mind about us. Say yes and I'll show you what I could give you."

I straighten. "We're in public."

The problem is that Liam thrives on a challenge. His fingers skimming lower, his big body beneath mine, the obvious ridge of his arousal between us— these things make it clear that he's more than willing to get busy in the back of my truck. When he touches me, when he's close, I can't think. All I can do is feel, and it scares me as much as it pulls me in and makes me want to hold on to him. "People will see."

He drops his other hand between us, shifting me until I'm straddling his outstretched legs, my knees hugging his thighs. I feel his palm slip beneath the fabric of my skirt. "Yes? Or no?"

"I can't think. I should say no."

"But you want to say yes. Think of me as the treat you're allowing yourself. I'm going to make you feel good and then later I'm going to fuck you."

He pauses, clearly wrestling with his Boy Scout. "If that's what you want."

"I can't imagine not wanting this."

You.

What happens if I always want you?

What happens if you don't feel these things for me?

I lean back, trying to force my sex-focused brain to think objectively. This is what I wanted, right? This is Liam finally seeing me as a sexual partner. It's exactly what I asked for, but it's also a little more immediate than I'd anticipated. If pressed, I'd have said that I'd imagined a bed with luxury sheets, possibly after a nice Chianti. Better underwear and mood lighting would also have factored into my fantasy.

He trails his fingers over the bare skin of my thigh, tracing small circles as he moves higher. "Tell me yes."

Liam Masterson is touching me.

"Tell me you're not drunk."

He shakes his head. "Never again."

"And you'll remember this—" *me* "—later."

"Absolutely."

Heat flushes my face, sweeping down between my legs, part arousal, part nerves. My heart pounds, unsure and excited. Liam is in charge and I both love and hate it.

"What if someone sees?"

"You'll enjoy it." His fingertips curl over the edge of my panties, stroking through the cotton.

My breath catches. "Liam."

"You'll have to be quiet," he says. "If you don't want anyone to hear you."

God.

Oh.

Maybe?

I glance around, as if somehow cataloging our potential audience will help. It's noisy enough that I *could* probably scream his name and no one would notice. The usual cheerful cacophony of the farmers' market is like a noisy, comforting cocoon that suddenly seems fraught with dirty possibilities. My truck is a fairly safe distance from the main aisle, parked on what's pretty much the edge of the market. And if I'm really doing sexual math, the truck bed is deep enough that no one will see more than our heads and upper chests. It will just seem like I'm sitting on Liam's lap and possibly grinding on him. Totally normal dating behavior, right?

And yet I feel my cheeks grow warm. This is why I need to practice my bad-girl vibe.

"Can I do whatever I want?" Big fingers tug on the cotton of my panties and heat sears through me.

I nod because if I actually try to speak words, all that's going to come out will be babble or maybe a plea for him to *fuck me now goddammit*.

He eases my panties down, tucking them beneath the curve of my butt. I can't believe he's doing this, that powerful, smart, take-charge Liam Masterson is playing a game with me.

And he's *totally* rocking it.

"Should I make you come?" He whispers the question against my ear.

It's not as if I want to say no, not now, but I could. He'd stop right away and put me back together and somehow we'd finish our conversation. But I want him to touch me more than I want dignity or privacy or anything else.

"Do it."

He grins, as if we're just two people in the back of the truck having a picnic and not a dirty conversation. Not—

He moves his fingers, stroking lightly up and over me as if he has all the time in the world. As if we haven't both been waiting a week to do this again. His hands are amazing, his fingers roughened by all the rock-climbing and manly extracurriculars but also strangely gentle.

I can't believe we're doing this. We've been a possibility in my head for so many years and then after last weekend, I'd thought that maybe that was it. I lean into him, pressing my face against his shoulder. There's the faint scent of starch and cotton, and beneath it, the woodsy, outdoor scent of his cologne and the warmth of his skin. God, I could breathe just him forever.

His fingers brush over me. Up and then down, as if he's testing his control or maybe just spinning the moment out because it feels good to him, too. My eyes drift shut, my world this man, his shoulder, those *fingers*. I squirm with each little shock of pleasure as he slides back and forth, carefully screwing himself deeper into me.

A dog barks and I jump. His other hand—the one not between my legs—presses against my shoulders, tugging me tighter against his chest. I remember this feeling from his ridiculous circus party, the secret thrill of almost, maybe getting caught, of giving in to the pleasure and doing exactly what I wanted because Liam would make everything okay.

"Is that all?" I whisper, surprising myself. "You've left me waiting for a long time."

"Rude," he agrees quietly. "I should make it up to you."

"Right now," I demand.

He sinks one finger knuckle-deep into me, his thumb moving around my clit in small, controlled circles. His other hand is wrapped around my shoulders, a warm, delicious weight. I don't understand this beautiful, dirty man who is somehow my husband, but my body recognizes his touch.

I turn my face harder into his shoulder, pressing my cheek against his dress shirt. I know *he's* watching *me*, watching me get lost in his touch. He can hear each catch in my breathing, the rough sound I make when he slides a finger down me and presses inside. He makes opening up for him easy, petting my slick skin. I breathe into his shirt, tasting the warmth of him, my fingers curling against his chest, slipping beneath the buttons of his dress shirt only to find more cotton, another barrier. I want him naked but I can't have that here.

I've fantasized about him for so long, and now suddenly, he's here with me. I ease my head to the

side so I can watch his face. He looks gorgeous, his
forehead furrowed as he concentrates, watching me.
He said he'd make me come and I don't think Liam
has ever lied to me. This was just sex—not even sex,
just a game—but it was the most intimate thing I'd
ever done. I needed to come, but he made me wait for
it, his wicked, dirty fingers teasing me. My muscles
tightened, my breath catching, all of me freezing and
lifting and it was right—

there—

yes.

I'm afraid to blink, afraid if I look away, I'll wake
up and this will be just an amazing sex dream and
I'll be alone. I have to close my eyes, just for a heartbeat, just while the delicious, hard pulse between my
legs goes supernova and Liam makes a quiet grunt,
a rough sound that says maybe he's imagining making space for himself there and sliding inside me. I
want to pull him in deeper, take him all the way, melt
beneath him as I whisper to him that I'm coming.

And he tells me that he knows I am.

That he needs me to come right now.

Here.

So hard.

I know this is a game, and I know we're playing
by Liam's rules—Mr. In-Charge, who has sex parties
and wild sex in positions I've never dreamed of—but
he's here with me, his beautiful mouth whispering
words into my hair. Words like *yes* and *please* and
you're so fucking gorgeous, and so I let go.

Liam's got me.

CHAPTER NINE

DANCING BILLIONAIRES ARE THE BEST

Hana

IF I ACT like a tween spotting a pop star, Liam will run.

I know this from firsthand experience—of the Liam variety rather than the rock-star variety.

When I was thirteen, Liam was the kind of hot that made me blurt out random thoughts and hang around my front yard for hours, hoping he'd drive up in his beat-to-pieces Jeep, big hands on the wheel with easy confidence. He'd been built along football player lines, rawer and less polished, and because he'd just started his conquest of the business world, sometimes he'd skip the suit. That his blond hair had been surfer-long, perpetually tousled from driving too fast with the doors off had factored in mightily in my adolescent fantasies. Sometimes he'd spot me and raise a hand in greeting, and I'd wave back furiously, alternating between smiling like a loon and blushing. My adoration had not been subtle.

Liam either figured out the cause behind the effect or Jax had clued him in because around my fifteenth birthday, he stopped casually dropping in at our house, and that absence lasted three years. Whenever he had stepped foot inside, he'd glued himself to Jax's side. Flirting in front of your older brother is almost impossible, so I'd gotten over big, Boy Scout–worthy, take-charge Liam, or so I'd thought. Last Friday I'd learned an important lesson.

Liam is still my sexual kryptonite.

I also thought I'd learned that I was his, but Saturday morning he'd been right back to treating me like little-sister material. Or trying to. He won't admit that I have boobs and a perfectly lovely vagina. The handful of hours I spent riding him like a sexy cowgirl and then tucked up against him as we slept were an aberration as far as he was concerned, something to beat himself up over and fix. Sure, he'd been amazing in bed. Not only was Liam generous in the giving department, but his Boy Scout tendencies made him insist on doing things "right." I came first, I came often, and he was all about my pleasure. That part got an A-plus.

In the long-term aftercare department, however, he sucked. He'd booted me out of his bed with mortifying speed.

He hadn't apologized.

And yet the man has definitely made his case today.

On the Richter scale of orgasms, I'd rate his most recent effort an earthshaking 8.9. He'd destroyed my defenses and left me sprawled on his lap trying to find some vestige of the good sense I used to possess. It's hard to kick a man to the curb when you're still feeling the aftershocks between your legs. Despite our very public situation, I'm seconds away from unzipping his dress pants and refreshing my memory about his awesome penis.

This is mortifying because there are obvious reasons the two of us would never work, starting with his plan for our marriage to be a temporary, sexless sham where I play the good girl to prop up his business image. I add to the list in my head because I need a distraction. Liam is also too rich, too domineering and too big. He sucks the air out of a room when he saunters in and most people rush to give him what he wants without waiting for him to actually take charge and start issuing commands. I'm sure part of it is the money. Jax hates the way people look at him and see an opportunity to cash in.

I believe in gratitude, though, and being happy for the good things the universe sends my way. Happy, but realistic. Mentally, I add today's orgasm and my memories of Liam's full frontal nudity to my gratitude list, and then I promise myself I'll hide that list away because some things are a onetime thing and shouldn't happen again. I'll just have to jill off to my Masterson memories and never see him again.

Shifting off his lap is trickier than I expected, thanks both to the monster erection that wants to come out to play and to the twisted rope my underwear has become. The man got my panties down effortlessly, but getting them back up myself proves to be a challenge. When I tug, my skirt gets caught in the cotton twisted around my thighs. I get up on my knees, trying to measure the distance between the top of the truck bed and my waist so I can hike things up and get on with my day, but then I spot ancient Mrs. Abernathy peering at me from behind a mountain of crab-apple jelly jars. I can't traumatize an old person with my panties, so I sink back down onto Liam's legs, trying to pretend I was just doing some kind of really athletic yoga pose.

The third time I try to wiggle everything discreetly back into place, Liam makes a rough sound and takes over with his usual efficiency. "On or off?"

I consider protesting but I can't go back to work panty-less and if I try to hop out of the truck in my current state, there will be an accident. "On. Tell me you can fix this."

He nods. "Hold still."

His fingers stroke over my thighs, straightening out the twisted fabric with a minimum of tugging. Liam Masterson, panty whisperer. At least they're on and not off. I'll add that to my gratitude journal.

As soon as he's put me back together, I get out of the truck bed. Clearly I can't be trusted on horizontal surfaces around Liam, plus I need to get back to work. There's still a few minutes before the farmers' market officially closes, and I have a million things to do, some of which involve honey sales and other responsible, nonorgasmic adult tasks.

Now that I'm standing on solid ground again, embarrassment sets in. Okay, not really. But I feel like I should at least pretend that I'm semi-mortified he fingered me while we were in the back of my truck. And since the man's wearing my bite mark on his shoulder and has a baseball bat in his pants, I'm probably supposed to apologize or offer him a BJ. I try to figure out where that fits in our good guy/bad girl lesson plans and give up. I'll have to stick to the social niceties.

"Thanks for lunch."

"You're welcome." Liam does some discreet adjusting of his own that makes a mockery of my gymnastics. He's clearly going to be the coordinated half of our couple.

And…I guess that means I'm doing this?

"Sorry it wasn't reciprocal." I may stare at the giant trouser anaconda he's packing.

I also announce this far too loud.

Mrs. Abernathy starts fanning herself with extreme vigor. I think she may be craning her neck for a better view. I don't blame her.

Liam does that thing where he smiles with his eyes while the rest of his face impersonates a sexy, frozen glacier. "Hana. It's okay."

It's only been seconds since I came, I've apparently already made a life decision, and he's acting all normal. I grin at him and wrap my arms around him. "Ten out of ten, Mr. Masterson. That was most definitely memorable."

The corner of his mouth quirks up. "So then we have a deal."

There's a moment of silence while I try to decide if negotiating post-orgasm is even possible. Probably not. The man literally has me in the palm of his hand.

"Right now what I really want is a margarita and a nap."

He leans in, resting his forehead against mine. "Say yes and I'll throw those in."

"Tempting." Both the man and the booze. "But I have a business to run here, so we have to say goodbye."

He pauses, perhaps running through what's probably an amazing, well-thought argument. "Say yes instead."

I lean back in his arms until I can see the blue sky overhead. It's a picture-perfect afternoon and this is the best position to watch it from. "That's all you've got? At least describe a day in our new, couple-y life for me. Help me see how it would go."

His arm dips me lower as if we're tangoing. "We're having sex?"

"That's it? Is that a question or a statement? Do you see sex as a daily thing?"

He pulls me back up effortlessly, spinning me around in a lazy circle. "Let's explore that. How often do you like to have sex?"

Honestly, I tend to prefer a side of commitment with my sex and it's been a while since I've been in a relationship. Liam may not take that the right way, so I fudge. "A couple times a week?"

He stops the almost-dance-number and looks at me. "That's it?"

Is there some kind of standard deviation normal number thingy here? "I can do less. Or more. When I asked for lessons, Professor Masterson, I wasn't imagining a seven-period school day."

"Pity." His slow grin just about melts my panties right back off.

"Pervert. I have sex when I feel like it. It's not like cardio where I'm trying to hit so many miles per week. How often do you like to do it?"

His grin grows. "As often as you'll let me."

"But when we're not having crazy monkey sex, how do you see this happening between us?"

He thinks for a moment. "I'd like for us to live in the same house. Go places together. I have work events, and I'd appreciate it if you came with me."

"I could do that, but we'll have to stay at my place. Bees, you know. It's hard to telecommute."

He nods. "Counterproposal. We hire someone to take care of the farm—it'll be like a vacation, okay?"

"Seriously?" I'm tempted to introduce him to my hive personally. "You think you can swap someone in for me, but you'll keep going to the office because there's only one Liam Masterson?"

He has the grace to flinch. "Right. That came out wrong. I would like to make this as easy as possible for you. For the record, I know you're good at what you do. I'm sure your bees would miss you. Why don't we spend weeknights at my place and weekends at yours?"

"That's hardly even," I protest. "But okay."

He opens his mouth, but I don't want to think any more about how he's made all this money and practically runs the world. His being good at his job doesn't mean I suck at mine or that I'm worth any less. I mean, financially, of course I'm worth less, but that's just bank accounts and stock options.

I flash him a half-assed thumbs-up and turn toward my stand. While farmers' markets are loads of fun and have the best free snack options ever, it's also sadly true that they're not raging business opportunities. I mentally count up the unsold jars, balancing them against their departed companions. It's not a sophisticated form of accounting, but it works for me. I pretend I can't feel Liam cringing behind me. I'm sure he runs his business with some kind of super sophisticated, double-column-whatever, Mensa-rated accounting system. He can adjust.

Jars first, I decide. My neighbor, the one who volunteered to fill in for me on my "lunch break," shoots me a grin as I approach and I pretend that I'm sweaty and flustered from the California sunshine and not because of any truck-bed shenanigans or bad-girl lesson previews. I almost think he believes it, too, when I send him off with three jars of honey and my thanks.

I risk a backward glance and am just in time to see Liam vault lightly over the side of my truck like he's some kind of world-class athlete. It never occurred to me that all the rock climbing he and my brother do on the weekends might come in handy in real life. Wow. I'm considering whether I should give the sport a shot when Liam strides up beside me.

He gives my poor stand a very Judgy-McJudgment-pants look. He's probably thinking that by now he'd have moved all of his product and probably franchised sales to Europe, Africa and the outermost reaches of Siberia. I'm just thinking that I have to get all this stuff back into my truck—and *out* of it again when I get back to the farm.

I think I might groan—and not the good sex kind of sound—because Liam nods at the mountain of glass jars and honeycomb.

"Tell me how I can help." He pulls his suit jacket off, hanging it on the back of my folding chair.

"You don't have to ride off into the sunset and do whatever it is billionaires do with their Friday afternoons?"

"You're my business." He levels one of those indecipherable Liam looks at me, calm and steady. He feels like a really complicated sudoku puzzle, all empty squares waiting for me to figure out what goes where. Unfortunately, math and I are not on speaking terms. His hand tucks an errant strand of hair behind my ear.

"Just so we're clear, you're volunteering to be the orgasm fairy, my sexual guru and my farm boy?"

His face pokers up as he works through my list. "Farm boy?"

He can't be serious. "*Princess Bride*? The helpful,

do-anything guy Buttercup keeps around her farm for fetching and carrying?"

Liam blinks at me. "Do I need to know more or should I just assume that everything I see goes back in your truck?"

"Farm boy grows up and becomes a really successful pirate." I pat his arm, taking a moment to appreciate the muscles beneath his sleeve. "You have lots in common. Jars, hive, tables, chair, tent all go back in the truck."

I point to each item as I rattle them off. Boxing things up seems like a big step down for a man who runs a billion-dollar company, but he offered.

"How much for the shirts?" He motions toward the small stack of Hey Honey Farm T-shirts on the far end of the table. They're bright yellow with a frisky cartoon bee getting it on with a flower on the front. As usual, they've been my bestseller today.

"On the house." Frankly, I'd pay to see Liam in one of those. He's always so put together and dignified.

He groans and pulls out his wallet. "You can't give things away, Hana. That shirt cost you money to produce, plus you have intellectual capital sunk in it."

We both eye the copulating bee on the front, clearly coming to the same conclusion. That's not *intellectual* capital sunk in my design. He hands me a twenty and I dutifully make change from my cashbox while he sorts through the pile for something that will fit.

When he finds one—of course it's the XL—he

sets it on top of the table and then his fingers go to his tie. Loosen the knot slowly while he watches me with his bedroom eyes. Undo his shirt buttons, one neat, orderly flick of his fingers after another. *It's just a shirt, Hana. You've seen him naked before.* Even before our drunken lovefest at Château Sin, Liam had occasionally gone shirtless around me. Not as often as I'd have liked, but his chest wasn't terra incognita. I could be totally cool, right?

Naked Liam.

I stare while he strips off the tie, and the dress shirt follows with a loose shake of his shoulder. Rats. He's wearing a perfectly respectable white T-shirt underneath. While I mourn his not-nudity, he sets the tie on top of his suit jacket and then folds his shirt with retail-store-precision into a neat rectangle.

His fingers curl around the edge of the T-shirt and slowly tug upward. My breath catches and Mrs. Abernathy lets out a wolf whistle.

I clap enthusiastically because oh my *God*, playful Liam is the sexiest thing ever. He hums something as he teases the shirt up over his perfect abs and then pulls it over his head. For a moment our eyes meet and then he winks at me, giving the shirt a saucy twirl in the air, before he treats it to the same meticulous folding job.

The sight makes parts of me melt, and not just the sex parts, although those are definitely paying attention, too. He just looks happy and a little goofy and nowhere near as remote as he usually does.

"You're hired." I slip my fingers underneath his

belt and his pants to tuck the handful of dollar bills from his change into the waistband of his boxer briefs.

I'm not surprised that he spends the next hour methodically working through my usual closing tasks. He charms the last few customers into buying honey. He loads the unsold jars back into their crates and then shifts those crates to the back of my truck. He breaks down my tables and awning, fitting the equipment neatly into the bed around all the crates, although my lack of tie-down cables concerns him.

His Hey Honey Farm T-shirt hugs his perfect chest and I spend more time admiring the way his biceps bulge as he effortlessly moves my stuff around than I care to admit. He may have a big, bastardy brain that's disgustingly good at making money, but it's not all he does. Finally, though, we have everything in my truck and the beehive strapped in the spot of honor in the passenger-side seat. I fidget, not sure what to do next.

"Thanks. I appreciate the help."

He tips his head, acknowledging my thanks, and snags a honey-and-cracker taster from the tray on the table.

"Help yourself," I say.

He winks. "Your honey tastes amazing." I'm pretty sure there's a dirty joke in there, but before I can respond, he snaps into what I've decided is Pirate Liam mode, all take-charge and corsair-y. "Friday is a weekday. Come to my place."

"Normal people consider Friday *night* part of the

weekend," I point out. "That's when the fun starts. Your raunchy sex party could be considered an example."

He gives me a dubious look. "Arguably, that was a business event."

"Seriously?" God, billionaires are weird.

"Seriously." Humor twinkles in his eyes. "You can make all sorts of connections there. People are relaxed, their guards down."

"Naked," I interject. "It's naked business. Yuck."

He rocks back on his heels. "It's a business I'm out of, seeing as how I'm married."

Should I go there? Absolutely not. Instead, I wave a hand at my truck. "I have to take that home. There's honey to harvest, combs to straighten. Plus, the bees don't just look after themselves. I have to check their water, and since these guys can be bullies, I have to make sure the stronger hives aren't trying to rob the weaker ones or it'll be outright bee war. And I have to look in on the queens and make sure they're laying well."

"You're a bee Peeping Tom." The laughter is back in his eyes.

Also? The man has a tiny dimple. How did I not know that?

He follows me over to my truck and opens the door for me, motioning for me to get in. I do, feeling a whole new fondness for my vehicle as I remember what we did in the bed of my truck. I'd like to drag him into the cab and ride him like a cowgirl.

While I contemplate mauling him, he pulls a sleek

silver pen out of the suit jacket he's draped over his arm. Then he picks up my hand and scrawls a scary-looking series of digits on the back.

"Are you giving me the nuclear missile launch code?"

"Gate code. I'll text you my address." He cups the back of my head and pulls me into him for a quick, hard kiss. "Go put the bees to bed for the night and then come to my house. Or I can follow you to yours."

I look down at my hand. Somehow, while he's been kissing me, he's gotten my rings back on my hand. I hold them up so they catch the sunlight like the world's most expensive prism. They cost way too much and I should be making plans to sell them and donate the money to a food bank. But I can't even pretend to think about it. My weakness for all things Liam is shameful. I conned him into marrying me in a moment of drunken weakness and now I'm essentially taking his money, which makes me at best like all his other girlfriends and at worst some kind of weird gold digger. I don't like this version of me. And I still don't want to take off his rings.

CHAPTER TEN

FLIGHT, GO!

Liam

WHEN HANA DRIVES off in her beat-up truck, waving out the window, it's all I can do not to follow her. Objectively, chasing is a poor dating strategy, so it stands to reason it would make a poor marital building block. Also, I make her nervous—at least when I don't have my hand in her panties—and she clearly needs some space to process the terms of our new agreement. She came on my fingers, so I'm counting that as both a win and an enthusiastic yes. I'll debauch her a little— she'll polish me up socially a little. Everyone wins.

I head back to my car and make it into the city in record time. Traffic laws may possibly have been broken, but since there's no evidence, I can deny it. When I pull up in front of my house on Lombard Street and punch in the ten-digit gate code, it's still light out. My real estate agent had tried to sell me on a sleek penthouse in one of the exclu-

sive residential towers in the Financial District, but
I'd wanted my own space and the ability to come
and go without saying a word to anyone. Condos
are just upscale dorms—you pass a hundred people
in the hallway and everybody knows who's throwing a party. Housekeeping comes three times a week
and a service stocks my kitchen, but otherwise my
place is a ten-thousand-square-foot fortress of soli-
tude with killer city views.

Hana will give me shit for having enough space
to house a small European village, but I plan to convince her to move in anyhow. I'm not bee farm material *and* I have a pool. She can swim and look at
the Bay at the same time. Hana's crazy for water, so
I'm hoping that'll convince her.

I take a quick shower and then throw on jeans
and an ancient MIT T-shirt. My new Hey Honey
Farm shirt isn't smelling too fresh after loading her
truck, so I toss it in my hamper and then I stare at
my phone, willing her to text that she's on her way.

It's possible she's not home yet. Marin traffic is
slow, and too many dumbasses try to make up for lost
time once they break free from the gridlock. There
have been accidents and Hana lives pretty far out on
some super-windy roads.

I fire off a quick text, checking to make sure she's
made it home safely. Then I map her route here on
my phone, realizing it's going to take her at least an
hour to drive down. I should have gone with her or
asked about how she was feeling, but all I could think
of was getting her here and in my bed.

I make arrangements for a pitcher of margaritas to be delivered.

I order dinner.

I may stew.

I'm allowed one more text, I decide. Just to make sure she's not upside-down in a ditch with two thousand angry bees.

You don't need to hand-feed each bee. You know that, right?!

Her silence is suspicious. I'm considering driving up there just to check on things when my phone finally buzzes with an incoming text.

Busy being a busy bee!

After half an eternity more, she texts to let me know she's about to leave and that I should be ready to start my "good guy transformation." It sounds as if I should have ordered a cape and maybe some tights instead of Chinese, but I'm willing to play along.

Need list of good guys plz

There's only a brief pause before she responds, so I suspect she's put the bee maintenance on hold. For someone who's supposed to be tearing down to my place, she's certainly taking her time.

Why?

As answers go, it's highly unsatisfying.

For my vision board. Need inspiration for my transformation

She texts back a list:

Han Solo
Professor Snape
Sir Patrick Stewart
Diego the saber-toothed tiger
Gandalf

I do a quick internet search that just confirms my
suspicions that most of the guys on Hana's list are
fictional and that the tiger dude is actually a baby-
eating-wannabe from an animated film who has a
change of heart and becomes a foster dad instead.

Hana sets a high bar. It's not as if I have a ton
of real-life examples to choose from. My earliest
memories of my dad are of him leaving, a departure
typically accompanied by a percussion of slamming
doors, yelling and car tires. Both he and my mother
liked to make their points with auditory aids. He
never stuck around for long, although until I was
eight or nine, he did come back every few months.
He'd drink, they'd fight, and he'd wake up and remember nothing. I'm already more like him than I
should be.

Because personal safety is important, I refrain
from blowing up her phone with messages while

she's driving. Instead I send a quick *Bee safe* and unpack the dim sum that arrives on my doorstep. Then I wait.

And wait.

I've seen Hana drive, so I know it's not the speed limit holding her up. I'm considering sending out a search party when she finally texts an SOS. My city house *is* screened from the rest of Lombard Street by some very clever landscaping, although I'm certain she can't miss the enormous fence—or the multi-level contemporary mansion behind it. I go out and spot her half a block in the wrong direction. When she pulls up, I show her how to punch in the code so the gate slides open, revealing the decadence of off-street private parking.

As soon as she's maneuvered her boat of a truck into a spot next to my Veyron and killed the engine, I pop the passenger-side door and grab her bag.

She pats my arm. "You just passed the first test."

"In learning how to be a good guy?" When she nods, I grin at her. "Bring it. I'll be a cartoon character next."

She makes mock saber-tooth fangs, which is cute, and we manage to fill the time it takes to get from the truck to the house with her reprise of the key plot point in the *Ice Age* movie. There are apparently multiples of this thing and everyone but the baby hooks up and gets married. I'm sure his time will come, too.

Things get less cute, however, once we're inside. I'm not trying to dangle my money in her face—that's not a negotiating tactic that will work with

Hana—but it is part of who I am. I've worked for it, and my available square footage is commensurate with my bank account balance. Tastefully. The house has won more than one architectural award and for a while it had the distinction of being the most expensive property for sale on the San Francisco market. My real estate agent still sends me Christmas presents three years later.

"Wow." Hana stares around her. I try to see my place through her eyes, but then I give up, mostly because up until now she's been wrapped up like a fluffy pink burrito in some kind of shawl or poncho. She shrugs it off and I'm speechless. Like someone slapped duct tape over my mouth or hit the mute button on a conference call, because there are a million words beating inside my head and trying to come out, but nothing makes it.

So far I've mostly seen Hana in her flowy dresses or giant hoodies and faded Levi's. Date-night Hana is even more spectacular. She's wearing a lacy white tank top that dips low over her chest and hugs her curves. Her farm-ready jeans have been traded for a pair of white leggings that showcase her legs and ass. A soft gray cardigan slides down one shoulder toward a pair of cute, slouchy knit boots because even though it's summer, San Francisco is notorious for its cool weather. Her outfit's soft and sexy in a way that makes me want to pull her into my arms and hang on.

"So," she says. "Here we are."

She peers at me and then she starts giggling.

Within seconds, she's full on snort-laughing, smacking her hand across her mouth as if that will somehow help. I lean a shoulder against the door frame and decide to wait her out.

"Oh my God." She sucks in air as if she's dying. "We're like a bad porno, right? Or one of those books where two people decide they just *have* to get married for Reasons and now they're trying to figure out how you politely ask for sex."

"You can ask however you want." I change my mind about waiting and shove off the door frame. "We can practice that as part of your bad-girl lessons."

It may be wishful thinking, but her eyes soften. "You're doing the prowly thing."

And then she giggles again.

I hook an arm around her waist and toss her over my shoulder. Her chest brushes my back and she shoves her hands into my back pockets. I'm not sure if she actually thinks I might drop her or what, but she feels amazing. I promptly remember the way she felt underneath me in bed, and I'd very much like to repeat the sensation.

I decide margaritas are called for and head in the direction of my outdoor bar.

"Are we getting naked?" She gives up groping me and wraps her arms around my waist.

I pat her butt with the hand that's not positioned perilously high on her thigh. "I thought I'd feed you first, if that's okay."

"Why?"

"Because it seems like a nice-guy thing and we're taking turns?"

I stride outside and set her down carefully. Her hair is a casualty of our play, exploding out of the fantastical twist thing she's had it confined in on top of her head. The whole pile shifts left and she automatically grabs it and undoes it the rest of the way. I fight the urge to bury my fingers in it.

Hana opts for dinner outside because "city views are awesome." There are terraces and a pool on three different levels and the landscape architect has divided them into outdoor "rooms." Running a bee farm is impressive, but people give her shit that it's a losing business proposition. She shrugs it off as "just money" and after helping her tear down her stand this afternoon, I can attest that she knows how to work hard. Still, I'm glad that for tonight at least, she's willing to enjoy what I can give her.

Tonight that's going to be mango margaritas and Chinese takeout from my favorite dim sum place in Chinatown. I may have helped fix a small financial difficulty the owners found themselves in, so I get stuff that's not on the menu. Tonight's haul includes pork buns, four different kinds of dumplings, shrimp balls and fried pastry stuffed with barbecued pork. Hana's ridiculously excited about how I "have an entire lawn on my roof" and "could put a beehive right *there*." I try to keep up with her as she checks out the different spaces, calling out plants by name and pointing to various building landmarks.

Eventually she winds down and collapses onto

the grass. I make her a plate of food and hand her a margarita before sitting down next to her. I have perfectly good patio furniture, but she wants to sit on "actual grass in the city." Hana devours her plate in record time, then flops on her back, squinting up at the stars. She frames a passing jet between her fingers, then turns her head to contemplate the pool.

"Do you lose guests here on a regular basis? Your house is huge."

I grin. I love her enthusiasm, although I'm not looking forward to hosting her future bees. "You're my first guest."

"No way." I'm not sure she knows how to sit still because she pops up and toes off her boots. She's wearing white ankle socks dotted with little cherries. Naturally, the cherries are smiling. I can feel myself smiling back.

"Jax has been here. A few other friends."

"But no lady friends?" Her eyes laugh at me over the rim of her margarita glass.

"You're the first one of those, too," I say immediately.

"Really?"

"Yes. New topic." Talking about where I bang my hookups seems like a bad idea. There's no way to make it sound good, plus she's already had the grand tour of my Napa place.

She wanders over to the edge of the pool and dips the toes of one foot. "You could have told me to bring a swimsuit."

I decide I'm tired of behaving myself. It's been

an entire evening. "We're moving on to the bad-girl lessons. Skinny-dipping."

"Oh, really? Does anyone under the age of fifty still use those words?" The corners of her mouth twitch, as if she's trying really hard not to laugh. Given her response to a simple phrase like *here we are*, I'm impressed.

"I'll demonstrate. If that's what you'd like."

I had no concrete plans to jump her tonight. Hopes, yes. Aspirations, absolutely. But the only thing I was *planning* on was dinner and drinks. That seemed pretty non-offensive to me because everyone has to eat, right? I definitely don't want her to think that she has to have sex with me, even if she let me finger her earlier today and now she's at my place. *No* is an important word, although I prefer *yes*.

She grins at me, twisting her hair back up into that ice cream cone thing she had earlier. "Go right ahead. Make my night."

I strip down efficiently, setting my clothes on the back of a lounger. By the time I've pulled my T-shirt over my head, Hana's sitting on the foot of the lounger watching me like I'm her favorite television show. She shifts to keep me fully in view as I unbuckle and unzip, shoving my jeans and boxer briefs down my legs. My dick is full of hope as she can see for herself by the time I've finished.

She applauds enthusiastically. "We need music!"

"Your turn." I tug her sweater over her head.

She grins and lets it slide down her arms. Followed by the rest of her clothes.

"You're gorgeous." I shamelessly look her up and down.

I last saw her naked days ago and I haven't been able to stop thinking about her. It doesn't make any sense—it's not like she's the first naked girl I've ever seen. She's got a great body, but it was a sex party full of naked people. It's hard not to be jaded.

There's just something about her that really does it for me. She's like the best pocket-sized present, short enough that her head barely reaches my shoulder. Now that I've finally got her naked, I'm reminded that she's all curves and surprisingly long legs. She's definitely worth waiting for. My eyes dance over her body like balls in a pinball machine, admiring the soft tease of her belly, the way her waist dips in and her hips curve out, the amazing boobs. Since I'm naked, there's no hiding my enthusiasm or the way I'm losing focus because stripped-down Hana is gorgeous.

Though my pool is heated, I turn it up some more because I don't want Hana to freeze. The control panel's tucked into the wall, so my back's to Hana when I hear the first splash.

When I turn around, she's easing into the water, careful to keep her hair above sea level.

I follow her without really intending to. She's on the far side, arms folded on the edge of the pool as she stares at the city lights. I don't see anything but her.

She lets out a little murmur when I come up behind her, bracing my arms on either side of her. Her back brushes my front as I step into her, and I like that. I like the way her fingers try to cover mine, the way she leans back into me. I like everything about her, but that's a problem for another day.

She makes a small sound, her fingertips stroking the backs of my hands.

I lean into her, breathing in the herbal scent of her shampoo. "Can I touch you?"

She pushes off the bottom of the pool, floating against me. "Always. Hold me."

I turn her in my arms. She reaches for me because this is Hana and she'll never let it just happen. She's going to jump in, all the way. We come together in a tangle of mouths and hands, kissing and sucking. She runs her hands along my shoulders, traces the line of my back and squeezes my ass. There's more kissing, her hands dragging my head down to hers as pool water splashes and we twist into each other. Her legs scissor around my waist, so I pull her against me, cupping her butt with my hands so I can hold her up.

When I finally carry her across the pool and set her down on one of the lounge chairs, she's got her arms locked around my neck, letting out these little whimpers that are the best sound ever. I pry myself free long enough to retrieve a condom from my pants and roll it on, and then I press her down into the cushions.

"Is this okay?" I ask.

She whimpers something and pinches my ass.

"Can I have you here?" I kiss a path down her shoulder and over her chest.

"Have me," she groans. Her hands fist my hair, pulling. "Don't be so slow."

She's working herself against my dick, rolling her hips against mine. Any faster and it'll be a quickie. I drop down between her thighs, pushing them apart with my shoulders.

"What are you—"

I slide my hands between her legs, opening her up. My tongue strokes up the space I've made for myself and she squeals. Despite our time in the pool, she's slick. I circle my tongue around her clit.

"Liam—" Her heels dig into my shoulders, her hands twisting in my hair. I cup her ass with my hands. I don't think there's anyone who can hear us, but I don't care. She just lets go and lets me make her feel good. It's the sexiest thing ever.

She wriggles against the cushions, shoving her hips up. I don't care if an entire fleet of sightseeing helicopters does a flyover because holy fuck, this woman is everything. She tenses and squirms, her hands using my hair to steer me to her favorite spots. I push a finger inside her, searching, and then I feel the first pulse.

When she's desperate to come, I move up her body with one last lick of her clit. I need her as desperate for me as I am for her as I push forward into her. She wraps her arms around me and buries her face in my shoulder. I hold her back, moving slowly until she's gripping me tight. Her nails bite into my skin and her teeth sink into my shoulder as she squeezes down on me hard. I go off like a rocket at the way she comes.

I've got just enough game to roll off her and pull her to my side. I need to buy bigger patio furniture if we're going to make this a habit.

"You okay?" I whisper the words into her hair, my hand caressing her back. She rubs her cheek against my chest and mumbles something, but the only words I can make out are *sex god*, *freaking machine* and *later*. The possibility that I've boned her senseless makes me grin.

When I shift her so I can see her face, she's asleep. I watch her face for a while before I pick her up and move our party inside. I debate taking her to one of the guest rooms—I have seven—but don't. We're married, we just had pool sex, and I totally want to wake up naked next to her again.

CHAPTER ELEVEN

SNEAK ATTACK

Hana

I WAKE UP in Liam Masterson's bed.

Once again, I don't remember getting here. I do remember the pool, the world's best orgasm and Liam's big hands pulling me close. I think I also told him there was a fine line between sex maniac and sex god, and I'd get back to him on which he was later. I may also have been very, very bad.

Déjà vu.

Since my French is limited to food words like *croissant, vin rouge, s'il vous plaît*, I might not have the phrase right, but I decide I like the way it sounds. Liam is asleep next to me. He's facedown, his head pillowed on one muscled arm. I haven't seen him like this before, not really. Last weekend I'd only been awake for seconds before his phone went nuts. I don't want to creep on him, but I also don't want to lose the opportunity. It's still early enough that

the sky is an inky, dark gray like that poem about
cat's feet. I try to remember how it goes but I'm not
that awake yet.

I don't think Liam picked out the stuff in his bedroom. It's gorgeous, all tasteful grays and creams.
A big armchair in the corner is piled with faux fur
throw pillows and a stack of books about space exploration. I imagine Liam sitting there and reading,
maybe checking his phone or trying to find Mars or
whatever planet has wandered into view this month.
I like this room, much more than his sex shrine in
Napa Valley, probably because I've decided to believe him that I'm the first girl he's invited to have
a naked sleepover here.

Floor-to-ceiling windows open onto a balcony
with more incredible views of the city. I take a moment to wonder if the lack of curtains means people
with binoculars will be able to look in and see us
having sex. It's a question I probably should have
asked last night before we had pool sexy times.

Unlike last time, Liam's not gone. He's perfectly
lined up on his half of the bed while I'm sprawled
everywhere.

It sort of feels like we're starting over. Last night it
was dark and I was in a hurry, so I take the opportunity to totally perv on him. The man's a freaking Go-
liath, although I guess I'm trying to make him over
into the hero David. I might need to rethink that. His
hair is loose and tousled in a way that screams lion's
mane or pirate. Even asleep, there's a rock-hard line

to his jaw that says he's got this. I'm not surprised he's king of the business world.

I stare some more, mentally tugging down the sheet that's tucked around his waist. I bet he has manly butt dimples. He just keeps sleeping, though, like a big, predatory cat catching some rays. Except, you know, the room is mostly dark and I've got half the bed so he can't even stretch out. Will that be his side from now on? Do I have to stick to the right side? What if we both get tired of that?

Too much reality bites before coffee, so I slip out of bed and borrow Liam's bathroom before I can talk myself into a panic attack. Like everything else, it's completely over-the-top fancy, all sleek marble counters and floor-to-ceiling windows with sweeping views of San Francisco. Clearly, Liam's not a fan of curtains. I brush my teeth with a new toothbrush he's laid out for me—my bag is somewhere in his McMansion—and then perform a little basic housekeeping to my person, pee, wash my hands and tiptoe back into the bedroom.

I'm strangely nervous when I get back in bed. This feels like a big deal or at least as if I should have a workable plan. The problem is, I'm still not sure what he wants from me. The good guy/bad girl lessons are a joke. On the one hand, we had awesome sex, so that bodes well for us. On the other hand, he clearly needs some kind of picture-perfect accessory wife for his business functions, so I'm not sure he's thought this through with his usual logic. I'm loud and colorful and I happily raise bees and wear clothes with pom-poms. He, on the other hand, has a closet full of three-thousand-dollar suits, a car service and a building full of people who willingly call him Mr. Masterson. What if he wakes up and decides I'm too much, too quirky, too unlikely to fit into his business lifestyle?

He rolls over, still asleep, and that has me wondering what exactly it would take to wake him up. It seems mean to strip the covers off him, so I burrow underneath. I hadn't factored in the whole no-light thing, but I just start at the bottom and go up. Fortunately, he's already naked, so I don't have to deal with the logistics of undressing him.

I run my hands up his legs, trying to go slow so I won't startle him. My mouth is right behind my fingers, my tongue gliding over his skin until I'm inches from my goal. I blow lightly, cupping his balls with my fingers. Even semihard, he's impressive.

"Hana?" His big hand tangles in my hair, tugging gently. He folds back the covers so he can see my face.

"One advantage of dating a farmer is that we get up super early. I mean, apparently you do, too. Which is great. I wouldn't want..." *Shut up shut up shutupshutup.* Why did I think I could be sexy before coffee? "I mean, I know you're a businessman, not a farmer, and you like it that way, but if you *wanted* to come to the dark side with me, now you're kind of all primed and—"

There is no good way to finish that sentence, but mercifully I find myself stopping. I do this by sliding my hands up his thighs and wrapping my lips around his penis. He says something, but I miss whatever it is because I'm deafened by all the blood rushing to my head and pounding in my ears and other parts.

God, there's just so much of him to enjoy. I claim him with my mouth, dragging my hands up until they meet my mouth coming down. He's hard and hot, and there's no way I can take all of him without tons of practice. I lick and suck what I can, teasing him with my lips and my hands. I don't want any part of him to feel left out, so I fist what's not in my mouth. He makes a rough sound, like a jaguar or some other very large, very predatory animal. It's very motivational, as is the shudder he makes when I drag my tongue about him and swirl it around the thick crown. My heart's pounding like a one-man band, which may have something to do with the way he keeps growing. And growing. He may be in the running for world's biggest dick.

"Jesus, Hana." My name is a hoarse mumble that I take to mean *do it more* and *don't stop*. His hands thread through my hair, further confirming my impression. I pull him deeper, relaxing the muscles of my throat because I need him inside me.

The way he pumps in and out of my mouth expresses his total agreement with that need. I mentally fast-forward through all the *Cosmo* articles I've read and my firsthand experiences (nowhere near as diverse as Liam's), but I can't remember any special techniques or secret sauce to make him feel extra good. It's slightly panic-inducing, but there's nothing I can do about it now so I give up trying to be extra dirty and just enjoy myself.

It's not hard.

I find a rhythm that has him making rough, needy sounds while I'm porn-star humming around my mouthful of dick. I need him to be crazy for me, for him to lose it the way I do when he touches me. So I just keep kissing him, sucking on the fat crown, then licking my way down so I can do it again. It's like dirty sledding or something. He gets harder, his thrusts a little less controlled until he's hitting the back of my throat.

"I'm going to come." His hand strokes the top of my head, urging me to let go.

I pop off long enough to ask, "Mouth or boobs?"

"Let's negotiate." He bites my ear. "Inside you, yes."

"That works for me." The words come out as a garbled sigh.

"Good."

He flips me over onto my stomach and reaches into the bedside drawer. Thank God one of us is a Boy Scout. There's a tearing sound as he opens a condom, a muttered curse, and then he's on top of me, his thighs pushing mine wide as he eases inside me. I moan his name and reach for the hand he's braced on one side of my head.

"Is this okay?" he asks.

"Better than," I gasp. "A-plus, in fact."

My body's tight from all the sex we had yesterday, but he pets me with his fingers until I relax and he gets all the way in.

"You're—" He makes another one of his sex sounds as he pulls back.

"You, too." I wrap my fingers around his wrists, this part of him he lets me have.

CHAPTER TWELVE

IT'S ALL FUN AND GAMES UNTIL SOMEONE GETS HURT

Hana

LIAM REFUSES TO tell me where he's taking me. He says it has nothing to do with shoring up his business image or our temporary marriage of convenience—rather, it's a chance to "make things up to me." I decide to let him. We've hammered out a compromise: we each are giving up one day. This means that the bees are going to be on their own on Sunday and Liam's minions and the moneymaking world will have to fly solo on Monday.

We head out on Sunday in another fancy car. He has a thing for vehicles with fast engines. They're total pinup material for him. It may also explain his fascination with space travel. When he finally finishes working out the design for his Mars rocket, I'm betting he flies it.

The first hour speeds by. Liam's packed us some

road trip snacks because he's a genius and doesn't even cringe when a few loose pieces of gravel ping off the side of his car. There's a fancy Bluetooth speaker set up that just begs for a driving playlist, so I thumb through the music on his phone. He has terrible taste and I tell him so. Then we argue amicably over which songs are best for a drive up the California coast.

The thing about long car rides is that they make me sleepy. The snacks and the music debate help, but eventually my eyes start to drift shut and I do the embarrassing head jerk thing. Even worse, I think my mouth might be open.

"You could take a nap," he suggests, patting his leg in invitation. Amusement colors his voice, so clearly I'm not fooling him.

It takes a few moments of tense maneuvering to get my head onto his leg without sending us careering over the side of the highway and down into the Pacific Ocean, but Liam's as good at this as he is everything else. My leg-pillow is also outstanding. Liam makes a deliciously muscled and warm bed; whenever he shifts his leg to push a pedal, I get an endorphin hit.

My thumb is way too high to be socially acceptable but I'm practically using his dick as a pillow, so I figure he's aware that it's up to him to tell me to stick to my side of the car. Since he's now stroking my hair away from my face, his talented fingers rubbing away the tension and massaging my scalp, I decide that's tacit approval.

I blame my state of extreme relaxation for the

words that I blurt out next. "God, you're amazing. Don't make promises you don't want to keep."

"Never."

I peek up at his face. My view is kind of cut off by the steering wheel, but he looks hot from this angle. Which sounds odd, but this is pretty close to my blow job view, so I decide to go with it. Plus, he looks charmingly intense as he promises to fulfill my strange, scalp-related sexual fantasies, so I'm not going to question a good thing. The yawn that escapes from my mouth is completely involuntary. My vagina protests even as my eyes feel like someone's rubbed them with sandpaper.

"Sleepy?" His fingers make another delicious pass over my scalp.

"Someone has an insatiable sex drive," I nap-slur. Staying awake now might require superhuman strength.

Liam's amused "sorry" comes from very far away. I'm pretty sure the distance between his mouth and my ears is doing that magical distance-stretching taffy melt I've seen in cartoons. I'm definitely not knocking the ball out of the park in the sexy wife-slash-girlfriend department, but he's at least partially to blame because his fingers keep working their magic.

My brain short-circuits at this point and I fall asleep. When I wake up hours later, Liam's easing me out of the car. I try to quick-check for drool spots and bedhead, as car trips don't bring out the best in me. Oh well. He's seen me post-sleep before anyhow, and at least this time we haven't spent the night at his kinky circus.

"You should put me down."

He grins. "But I like this position."

Uh-huh. "We'd get inside faster if you weren't forced to carry my deadweight."

Liam lifts me higher, so he can brush a kiss over my mouth. The advantage of this position is obvious. I can kiss him and feel his biceps bulging beneath his shirt. The only thing better would be naked, bulging Liam. "I'm bigger than you."

"And?"

"That means I get my way." He moves toward a cute little cottage that's surrounded by an entire field of lavender. I should probably protest, but I'm still sleepy and Liam's taxi service is a turn-on. I settle for curling my arms around his neck and doing some kissing of my own.

He takes the steps two at a time—show-off—and I get a good look at where we are over his shoulder. Fields of purple stretch in every direction. The sun is going down now, but it's summer and so there's still plenty of light despite our late start from San Francisco. Having sex surrounded by all that lavender would be like starring in a historical porn. Oooh. Maybe Liam could borrow a white charger from somewhere and gallop up, and then our clothes would magically fall off our bodies, and we'd have amazing, anatomically creative outdoor sex. It's an ambitious plan, but I think I'll mention it. My breathing sounds a bit like a freight train now and I'm sucking air and—

"This place smells amazing!"

"I thought you'd like it." He pushes open the front door—it's not locked—and steps inside. "Welcome to Chez Masterson-Valentine. It's all ours for the weekend."

Not only is the cottage surrounded by downright decadent quantities of lavender—I think I may have a contact high from the scent—but it's ridiculously luxurious. I won't lie. There are advantages to dating a billionaire. I catch a brief glimpse of what looks like an open floor plan full of squashy white furniture. A bottle of wine is breathing on the kitchen counter next to a crudités platter and a cheese board. I've stumbled into a love nest prepared by Martha Stewart.

"Can I interest you in a tour, Mrs. Masterson?" Liam's cocky grin leaves no doubt as to his intentions.

"Is this a sex tour? Is it interactive or is this more of a museum tour and I'm limited to looking but not touching?" I walk my fingers up his chest. Truly, the man has muscles on his muscles. It would be a shame to pass up an opportunity to properly appreciate them.

He leans in and nips my bottom lip. "You can touch the artwork, baby. You have the all-access pass."

"Tour it is." I reach around him to pat his mighty fine ass. "Do a good job and I promise to tip well."

Liam either has keen navigational instincts or he checked out the floor plan before he booked the place, because he heads straight for a spiral staircase that leads to the bedroom.

It probably has all the usual bedroom accoutrements, but I barely get a chance to admire the iron canopy bed before we're magically naked. My yoga pants hit the floor, my tank top and flannel go flying in the other direction, and somehow he's managed to lose his clothes, too. The man is a paragon of efficiency. He totally deserves a sex memorial or maybe a knighthood. Lord Liam, His Sexship. When I giggle, he takes that as a personal challenge, pulls my legs over his shoulders, and proceeds to suck on my pussy with diabolical cleverness.

Not until I'm whimpering his name after coming all over him does he slide back up my body and lower himself onto me.

"Are we paying attention now?" There's a possessive look in his hazel eyes that sends a corresponding thrill through me.

"You give good tour." I wrap my arms around his neck and my legs around his hips.

He rocks against me, rubbing his amazing dick against the part of me he's just been loving on. "Yeah?"

The rest of our conversation involves a lot of moaning and invocation of deities. He whispers that I'm fucking beautiful and I may moan-pant a few compliments of my own. It's intense and fast and once he's inside me, Liam doesn't hold back.

He thrusts deeper, harder, finding a fast, familiar rhythm that makes me groan his name. He's so good at making me lose myself. I wish—

I could make you feel the same way.

That you got lost in me, too.

That I was enough.

His fingers tighten on my hips as he moves in me. The sensations radiate through me, white-hot pleasure, the brighter pulse when he finds my G-spot—my body locks up, grabbing this moment to come harder than I've ever come before. I barely manage to hold in the words.

I love you.

I still love you, Liam.

Liam.

CHAPTER THIRTEEN

BROTHERLY INTERVENTIONS SUCK

Hana

"EXPLAIN TO ME again why my best friend felt the need to perform a public striptease for you."

My brother frowns at me from across the table, the corners of his mouth turned down in a man pout. I've already been through this once, and Jax has rejected my perfectly normal explanation that Liam didn't want to get his pretty suit dirty helping me load the truck so he opted to change his clothes in public. With half of a very busy farmers' market watching.

"Maybe it was my birthday." I wink at Jax. "Maybe Liam's got a side gig as a happy birthday stripper."

Jax's frown deepens. He's going to have wrinkles before he turns thirty next year. "Your birthday isn't for another three months."

We're currently squeezed into a booth masquerading as the world's smallest bure. A thatched "roof" covers our table and we're separated from the other guests by bamboo walls. The Tiki Bar is several enormous, uphill blocks from my last sales call of the day on San Francisco's tony Pier One, so I'm still red-faced and breathing more deeply than I care to admit. My inability to get words out gives me a good excuse to come to terms with the decor, which is all horrible, wonderful, super fun South Pacific kitsch. The booths are little bamboo bures with plastic palm thatching that I'd impaled my scalp on when I slid in; the bar itself serves up a full complement of waterfalls, talking parrots and flaming tiki torches. I probably should have worn a sundress or something fun and tropical, but it's San Francisco. Even midafternoon in July, it's not particularly warm.

Schlepping crates of organic honey around all day hasn't helped my energy levels, although I scored two new restaurant accounts, so that's something. I've also done tons of driving back and forth between San Francisco and Marin this week in the name of responsible beekeeping. As of yesterday, I officially have my first employee, who will start next week, but my butt is sore from too much driving and my vagina might actually be in need of a vacation. My sex muscles haven't been this sore since I had a marathon jill-off to a particularly sexy werewolf shifter book. I may have announced to Liam last night that one of us was going to have to either take it in the ass or sleep in one of his billion guest rooms, which led to him offering to kiss everything better, me arguing that he does not (contrary to whatever he might have read on the internet) possess a magic sexual cure in his tongue, and then awesome oral sex. Judging by my extra sore sit muscles, I did a lot of clenching.

I grin at Jax. "Liam rocked it."

Liam's striptease apparently brought out the phones, and of course those videos made it online. Nothing escapes the gravitational pull of the internet.

Naturally, I've downloaded the video to my phone and the only reason I haven't achieved ten thousand views is that I had to drive to Hey Honey Farm at the crack of dawn, load my truck and then get back into the city. I deliver honey once a month to a handful of restaurants and bakeries I sell direct to. Thanks to our sex marathon last night, I'm both sleepy and unable to concentrate, plucking my phone out of the pocket of my jeans every chance I get so that I can watch him over and over.

Just to torture Jax, I press the play button on the screen, making Liam dance for the dozenth time. Our late lunch has turned into drinks and a pupu platter. I'm done working and I have no further plans to drive today. My truck is currently parked in Liam's obscenely expensive off-street parking and I've declined a "car service" in favor of an Uber and my independence. Liam wasn't happy about that, but since he was stuck in a business meeting, he couldn't do anything about it. I'd also slipped out of his Lombard Street McMansion at the crack of dawn before he'd properly woken up—thank you, farm hours—so he's doubly unhappy with me right now.

In the video, sun blazes around Liam, lighting

him up like an angel. Not for the first time, I edit that thought. *Fallen angel*. There's no point in attributing angelic qualities to the man. I've always thought of him as a Boy Scout, but he's actually 100 percent devil once you get him naked. Although the video has no sound, I fill it in from memory. The chatter of people, dogs barking, cars on a street somewhere nearby. And the whisper as his clothes came off.

Video Liam loses his tie and unbuttons his shirt one button at a time, revealing the white cotton T-shirt. It was probably something perfectly normal like Hanes but on him it was godlike.

And then gone.

Thank *God* because his bare, suntanned chest was a masterpiece. He's a surprisingly good dancer for someone built like a lumberjack. I like that I'm the only one who knows he's humming just under his breath. His hips circle, lazy, certain. I need to get him in a club. Or my kitchen. I wonder if he'll turn out to be the kind of guy who swears he never dances but then busts a move to a phone playlist when he thinks no one is looking. Or is that too domesticated for a billionaire bad boy?

Jax groans. "Stop eye-fucking him. We need to talk about your marriage."

I drag the platter to my side of the table. "We absolutely do not."

"Do, too." He grabs a wing.

"Do we discuss your sex life?"

He gives me an evil smile. "We could."

The best defense is a good offense.

I steal the last egg roll from the platter. "He's really good in bed."

Jax groans. "I don't need to know that."

"Discussing my sex life was your suggestion. Liam's awesomeness should come as no surprise to you." I consider miming a little something-something with the egg roll, but Jax will probably stroke out. Plus, I'm hungry and it's a waste of a good egg roll. "You get invited to sex parties. Have you never seen Liam in action?"

"People go to those things to talk business."

"Uh-huh. Maybe the oldest profession in the world, but honest-to-God legitimate business? Really?"

"Yes. They do. Sometimes, although not always. People are relaxed at those things. They're open to meeting new people or talking about stuff informally."

"See, the problem I have," I tell him, "is that there's a whole lot of sex at these things."

"Okay, so no, it's not *all* business." Jax scrubs a hand over his face. "But you shouldn't assume everyone's there just to get off, okay? And sue me if I want to make sure that Liam doesn't hurt you."

Usually, this is where I'd point out that Liam's packaging is gorgeous and he's a better ride than my favorite dildo. I have no idea why everyone in my life seems to be under the mistaken impression that I'm Miss Sweet Thing. Just because I *haven't* tried out the kinkier pages of my *Cosmo* doesn't mean I *can't*. I just hadn't met anyone I wanted to have wild, adventuresome sex with before.

"We're spending weeknights at Liam's place," I blurt out. "The fancy one on Lombard Street, not Château Sin. He wants me to be his temporary wifey, go around with him to a few high-profile social functions or something."

Jax rolls his eyes and snags a wing from our pupu platter. "Because the man can't get a date on his own?"

"He's still in hot water over his ex." I'd never seen her in person, but my mad internet searching skills had turned up a ton of photos. She's extremely photogenic even if she seems to wear black exclusively. In more recent photos, she does a lot of hanging on Liam's arm and staring coolly at the cameras. She looks put together and confident, whereas I'm wearing duck sauce on my shirt.

"What does that have to do with you pretending to be his wife?" Jax points a chicken wing at me. "Which you are, no pretending necessary. I'm going to get you a lawyer."

"He won't hurt me."

Jax gives me a look that says he's quite certain that Liam totally *would*.

"You've had a crush on Liam since you were this high." Jax holds his hand a few feet off the ground.

"Yes, I wanted to marry him when I was fifteen. Yes, I got over that." Mostly. "I also kind of hoped my crush wasn't obvious, but clearly I embarrassed the shit out of both of you. And FYI? I know that version of Liam was all in my head, okay?"

Jax pounces. "So you married a stranger. Or did

you? How long has this been going on? Do I need to kick his ass?"

"Liam had nothing to do with my fifteen-year-old self—and *I* asked *him* to marry me. Since then, he's pointed out repeatedly that I'm his best friend's little sister, so he's done just fine kicking his own ass. I'm pretty sure having sex with me has scarred him for life. Plus, we're not about to fly off to Bora Bora for a romantic honeymoon."

Not that I'd be totally averse. The Tiki Bar is hardly authentic South Pacific, but the pictures on the wall look amazing. Sitting on the deck of my overwater bungalow with my special someone while dolphins and manta rays gambol in the water around us would not require hardship pay, although I imagine I'd have to save for at least fifty years to afford it. Liam's money is a problem because I will never be able to do for him the way he does for me.

"I really can't explain it."

"Why were you even at his party in the first place?" Jax's face darkens. "Did he invite you?"

"No, he didn't invite me. Are you nuts? Until he woke up next to me, married, he was convinced I was eternally sixteen years old. He's even worse than you. I stopped there because I'd been visiting wineries, trying to place my honey. I was hungry, I was hot, and I had to pee. I was just going to make a pit stop. And then one thing led to another and I stayed for his party. It had been a shitty day and I needed free alcohol."

This is a partial truth. I *had* been on a winery

tour, but I'd also snagged Jax's invitation to Liam's party and I'd packed a costume in the trunk of my car. Fortunately, either Jax hadn't shown up or our paths hadn't crossed, so he's unaware of this detail.

Jax frowns. "I can't believe you didn't tell me you need money."

"How did you get that from what I just said?" I may throw up my hands because, dammit, he's right.

"You just told me," he growls. "You were driving all over Napa Valley trying to sell your shit. If you *had* sold it, you'd have shared that. The last time you tried the cold-calling thing, you informed me you'd do it again only if hell froze over or the bank sent goons to collect. Let me help you this time."

"No."

"Let Liam help then. He owes you a favor."

"Are you crazy? Again—no."

While I appreciate Jax's desire to be supportive, I also want to do this on my own. *This* being my life. Hey Honey Farm is not just a paycheck. That I love what I do and I'd happily continue to do it without earning zillions of dollars is a plus, since my cash flow has been lower than my lender would like. I'm working on it, though, so I don't need Jax to come riding to the rescue.

CHAPTER FOURTEEN

FARM BOYS ARE THE BEST

Hana

"I'D LIKE TO RENEGOTIATE."

Since Liam says this while he's inside me, I'm both distracted and immediately suspicious. This also has something to do with the man's uncanny talent to hit my G-spot.

This ability really means that our conversation mostly consists of me moaning like a porn star in between electric-white bursts of pleasure.

"If you want sentences with actual subjects and verbs, you have to pull out. I'd rather you just—" I moan-squeal this because of course he doesn't stop. "Do that again."

His mouth nips mine. "As you wish."

I bribed him into watching *Princess Bride* last night—yes, blow jobs were involved—and he hasn't stopped stealing Westley's line ever since.

He does an awesome thrusting thing, his arms

braced on either side of me, so close that his fingertips stroke over my shoulders each time he enters
me. My sleep tank is shoved up to my collarbone,
my shorts have disappeared into the tangle of sheets
at the bottom of the bed, and dark o'clock sex has
never been so welcome.

He tips his head to look down at me in the dim
light, his mouth kissing distance from mine. "Let's
stay here all day."

My bastard husband stops thrusting and actually
waits for me to respond. The corner of his mouth
curls up in a knowing smirk.

I expect him to move but he doesn't, so I may
smack his ass. "Really?"

"I'll make it worth your while." He pushes into
me. Slowly. Because he's a freaking tease and he's
holding out on me. He kisses along my throat while
I try to remember why this is a bad idea.

"Say yes," he coaxes shamelessly.

It's two more strokes before I remember that since
last night was Friday, it's now technically Saturday—
which means it's *my* day to make him live at the
bee farm instead of this really horrible, super swank
mansion in San Francisco. Since he's debauched me
nightly for the past week in his quest to turn me into
a bona fide bad girl, I get a shot at teaching him to
behave in public. It's like dog school for sexy billionaires or something.

I grin up at him. Two can totally play this game.
"You're coming with me, farm boy."

I squeeze my inner muscles around him and he groans.

"You're not playing fair," he whispers.

"I learned from the best."

Liam

I rarely lose a business negotiation.

Trying to renegotiate while naked was clearly not my smartest move, however.

When I brought up the possibility of exchanging farm time for quality bedroom time, she proved that she'd been paying attention to all those feminist theory classes Jax complained about at UC Santa Cruz, flipping the script on me and kissing me senseless. Ordinarily, I'd applaud her for being clever and pulling a good gender-role-reversal, but the end result is that I'm now riding shotgun in her ancient truck and it's barely light out.

"Good guy lessons," she reminds me, sliding laughing brown eyes in my direction.

"Eyes on the road." I scoot over and tuck my arm around her shoulders. If she gets sleepy or distracted, I can take over. Plus, she smells great. Hana takes one hand off the wheel and slides it up my thigh. Her gentle grip has me considering the merits of a pit stop, but the road's narrow and her farm has to have a bed. Or a hay loft. I'm pretty sure that's required for farms. "And both hands on the wheel. You can maul me later."

She makes a pouty face. "You're so safety-conscious. It's weird."

When life drops something good into your lap, you look after it. Anything else would be stupid.

"If I'd stuck with being the unethical corporate monster you think I am, I'd still be in bed," I point out. "Instead I'm driving to Marin at the ass crack of dawn in a truck that's incapable of exceeding sixty miles an hour."

"You're lucky I didn't make you leave at 12:01," she points out.

I press a quick kiss against her neck. "That's because I produced an excellent counterargument."

"It was very impressive. Feel free to bring it up again later just in case I didn't fully get your point."

Her eyes are bright with laughter. While dawn is never going to be my favorite time of day, I'm a fan of this. I try not to read too much into it and instead concentrate on what's happening outside the truck. It's not as gorgeous as Hana, but I can see why she likes living up here. There are flashes of ocean, lots of steep hills and some obvious perilous drop-offs. It's like being in a video game except there are no free lives and the birds aren't angry.

The time passes quickly, no one falls asleep, and before I know it, Hana's hitting the brakes and making a ball-jarring left-hand turn off the main road and onto a gravel track. A jaunty white sign with a plethora of bright yellow bees putting the moves on a flower flashes past my window and then she sends us hurtling downward. Fortunately, I started the day out with amazing sex, so I'm still mellow enough that I don't yell.

Hey Honey Farm must be located on the lowest level of hell. We jolt down the middle of the road, propelled partly by gravity and partly by Hana's lead foot. I'm sure she'd know whether or not it's likely someone else would be coming *up* the road, right? Just in case the potential for a devastating head-on collision isn't enough, the road is lined on one side with enormous trees, redwood and otherwise. Drift left—hit trees. Drift right—plummet down a steep cliff that ends in the ocean.

Once things level out, the ocean view disappears behind a curtain of trees and we coast into a large clearing. There's a small white farmhouse with a wide porch, tons of flowers, a handful of outbuildings and poor cell phone reception. I don't see bees, but they must be here somewhere. I'll be lucky if they're not in the house. This place is as alien as the asteroid belt between Mars and Jupiter.

"Remember that this is my first time on a farm. You have to be gentle with me."

"You like rough." I do, but I hope that the way Hana's yanking on the parking brake isn't supposed to be a metaphor. "You've really never been on a farm before? No school field trips? Community gardens? Romantic weekend getaways to a dude ranch in Montana where you could commune with nature?"

I'd mostly skipped field trips because they'd cost money and I hadn't wanted to be someone's charity case. "Give me the grand tour, okay?"

The first thing that hits me when I get out is the smell. It's not so much bad as it is unexpected. There's a shitload of flowers, which I'd guessed there'd be, but there are also notes of decomposing greenery, salt water and a whole lot of compost. The sun filters through the trees, painting Hana with little gold flecks and bouncing off the red-and-white roof of the farm cottage. As we get closer to her house, there's a soft droning noise from the lavender massed around the big front porch. I've found the bees.

She barrels up the porch and pushes the door open. Of course it's not locked.

"You're not worried about the woodsman paying you a visit? Or the Three Bears?"

She grabs my hand, laughing. "Come on, city boy. I'll show you around."

I've never been in here before but I think I would have recognized it as hers. It's sunny and cheerful, with a steep staircase on the right. A bright floral pattern covers the treads and bookcases crammed with books fill the landing above. She leads me through the living room, which has a fireplace, glass-faced built-ins and a squashy sofa. I catch just a glimpse of a dining room on the left and then we're hotfooting it through a dollhouse-sized hallway, past a bathroom dominated by an enormous claw-foot tub and into the bedroom.

She turns and plants her hands on her hips. The laughter's back in her eyes. "What do you think of farm life so far?"

"Is it nap time? Do good farm employees get a

ten-minute break?" I pounce on her and toss her onto the bed. In no time at all, I've got her clothes off, and mine follow.

"There'll be a performance review later," she says with mock gravity.

The next day brings more of the same. Lots of sexing mixed with outdoor time while we work through her chore list. After we check to make sure the bees are well-watered and that no enemy mites have tried to move in since we checked yesterday, Hana whips up a stellar PB&J for lunch. It turns out we get the afternoon off since the bees are good.

"Come on." She reaches for my hand as if it's the most natural thing in the world for us to be joined together like that and then she starts down what looks like a rocky, wildflower-covered hillside.

I let her pull me along although this is crazy.

"Is there a path? A destination? For the record, I prefer to climb up mountains and not down."

For all I know, she's decided to resolve our marital status the old-fashioned way. She could just roll me down the hill—honestly, it's nearly a mountain—and no one would ever find my poor, dead body once my cell phone had died and the signal had vanished.

She turns—still moving down the path/track/whatever it is—and grins at me. "God, you're so old."

I think my mouth falls open, which is a mistake at a bee farm. Who knows what will fly into it?

"I'm only five years older than you. Turn around and watch where you're going."

She rolls her eyes but turns around. My heart settles back into my chest.

Once I'm convinced Hana isn't about to barrel-roll herself into an early death, I can appreciate the view. There's definitely a path, although it's mostly just a dirt thread that's almost entirely swallowed up by the clouds of meadow grass and flowers on either side of us. If this is what Hana's bees live on, it's no wonder her honey tastes so fantastic.

And then we step into a grove of tall pines, the sunlight muted for a handful of seconds, and out again onto a beach that's hidden at the bottom of the mountain-hill we've just climbed down. A pocket of cream-colored sand and dune grass separates us from the water and there's a darker strip of wet sand where the ocean breaks. A ring of rocks juts out from the cliff on the right, taking the brunt of the incoming waves.

Hana drops my hand as if it's on fire. "I'm going for a swim."

"Now?"

She beams at me. "Unless you want to come back at midnight. Moonlight on the water is amazing."

I consider asking her if I could take her somewhere safer—and warmer. Fiji maybe, or the Bahamas. The ocean waves pound against the sand rather too similar to a jackhammer for my taste. I don't even want to think about her swimming alone in the dark.

Wait.

"*Do* you swim here by yourself?"

"You're my first farm boy." Her answer is muffled

because she's busy whipping her tank top over her head, revealing a cute polka-dotted bra.

Something about her makes me worry, like I need to wrap her up and keep her safe. Not because she's not capable of taking care of herself—she is and she's proved it—but because I don't want to imagine a world without Hana in it. I need her to tell me everything she's done since she was that sixteen-year-old girl with the awkward crush because I want to know. I want to know *her*.

She's right.

She's not just Jax's baby sister.

She's not just the girl I've sort of watched grow up like a holidays-only uncle.

She's not even just my temporary wife, as much as I wish she would be.

She's an uninhibited, take-no-prisoners, curious, funny woman who's busy stripping off her clothes because apparently it's time for naked swimming.

CHAPTER FIFTEEN

SEX IN WEIRD PLACES

Hana

I'VE COME TO an obvious decision: if I'm going to make Liam really and truly mine, I'll have to make him see me. Not the teenage girl I was or even the woman who possesses a sometimes grudging but lifelong membership in the Jax Valentine's Baby Sister Club. I love my brother, but I have to be more than just some kind of weird extension of him. I should probably also borrow a leaf from Liam's meticulously organized planner and come up with a *plan*. No more winging it and then pouting when I don't magically get my happy ending. Relationships are exactly like sex: you have to say what you want, then demonstrate, and then you still end up responsible for your own happy ending.

Step one is to strip Liam naked. I'll pry him out of his expensive designer wardrobe, and then I'll open his soul with my metaphysical can opener and get a good look inside that. Bare Liam will be amazing. I'm certain of it.

Currently, though, he's eyeing me as if he thinks insanity might be grounds to annul our marriage. I'm not sure if it's the swimming conditions that have him so uptight or my willingness to strip down outside.

"Hana."

His voice is low and stern, the take-charge tone that gets me wet, although I'm not stupid enough to tell him that. Instead, I drop my tank top on the flannel I've already shucked. It may be July in California, but the bee farm is surrounded by trees and fields. Going bare-armed would be like walking into a bar of horny sailors naked. There are mosquitoes and ticks everywhere. This leaves me in my jean shorts, boots and bralette. I should come up with a plan for shimmying out of these, but instead I plop my butt down on the sand and unlace, unbutton, and generally beat all known land records for stripping down to a tiny pair of lacy yellow panties. From the way Liam stares, he likes yellow just as much as I do.

He opens his mouth to say something else that I bet is either super practical (about the water's undoubtedly frigid temperature or the lack of toweling and personal safety devices) or dirty. Dirty Liam is the best, but after last night's dream, I'm too sleepy to come up with a witty response. So instead I drop my panties and sprint toward the water, trying to ignore the goose bumps crawling over my skin.

"Last one in pays a forfeit!"

I hear Liam's bark of laughter behind me. It's

going to take him a minute to catch up because I've
got a head start in the naked department. I lose time,
though, twisting my head around to check out his
progress. Liam's competitive, so he'll strip down.
The biggest question is whether he'll decide to wear
those cute boxer briefs I spotted peeking over the
waistband of his jeans or if he'll meet my challenge.
I'm betting on the latter.

I crash into the water, slowing down only a little
when the waves slap at my knees. I'm hot and sticky
and this is heaven. The next wave hits my crotch and
I suck in a breath. Okay, so it's also a little like going
for a polar-bear swim in January, but it's still good.

I don't so much hear Liam as I sense him. He
comes up from beneath the water, pulling me down
with a quick, hard tug on my ankle. I go under, but he
anchors me, cradling me against his big, warm body
as we bob toward the surface. I should get even, but
instead I thread my arms around his neck. My legs
go around his waist like they've been doing all week.

"That was mean."

"You started it." He gives me his lopsided sexy
smile, the one that makes my heart pick up speed
as if we've just hit the final mile of a marathon
and maybe, just maybe, that's the finish line right
there and all I have to do is run a little faster, a little farther.

"Truer words," I say as lightly as I can. I don't
need him to point out that I started everything between us. For a handful of minutes, I float, loosely
anchored by his arm, my face tipped up toward the

sun and the bright patch of sky above us where a pelican is chugging by.

"Could you climb that?" I point to the cliff on our right, the one that sticks straight out of the water and then keeps on going and going for what feels like miles. The rock face is all craggy bits and old birds' nests, ledges and crumbling stone. Somewhere, even farther up, is the public road that leads toward Stinson Beach.

"Yes." Liam anchors himself against a larger wave, assessing the cliff face in a way that makes me think that next weekend we'll be rock climbing.

"Why do you do it?"

"I like the challenge. I like getting to the top." He shrugs as if it's no big deal. I give up pretending that I'm not curious if he's gift-wrapped in wet cotton briefs and shimmy lower until I discover that not only is Liam completely naked, but he's superhuman. Despite the chilly temperature of the water, he's semihard.

"You're naked." The words come out on a yawn.

His brows draw together. "Am I boring you?"

"I didn't sleep well last night."

"Bad dreams?" He starts walking us toward the beach, which is a good thing. It's cold enough that I can't feel my good parts anymore.

"No. The opposite. I had an amazing sex dream— the kind where you wake up because you're coming and you wish you could go back to sleep and do it again."

God. The look on Liam's face is priceless. I can

barely keep my own expression straight. Poor guy. He's just so convinced that I'm this sweet, innocent princess.

Liam

Jesus. I just about trip over my own feet and drown us. The ocean is cold, but it would take prolonged exposure at this point to shrink my dick. Any temperature-induced siesta has been abruptly aborted by Hana's dream announcement. I know she mostly says these things to get me going, but it works. I wade out of the surf with a raging hard-on.

"Are you superhuman?" She asks this question while patting beneath her with one hand, just in case I'm unclear why she's asking. When her hand closes around me, I grit my teeth to keep from groaning out loud. Her palm is barely warmer than an ice cube, but my dick doesn't care. It kicks happily in her grip.

She looks up at me through her lashes. "Should I tell you about it?"

I snort. We both know there's not a chance in hell I say no.

"Every last detail. Feel free to reenact."

Jax said I should share what I'm thinking and open up more. Seeing as how he's Hana's brother, I'm entirely certain he didn't mean I should tell her about the dirty dreams she routinely stars in since our wedding, but I'm just adapting his plan to fit my current needs. I can tell her later, when we're substantially warmer, about my childhood woes or my intense dislike of art films. If it goes really well, I might even share the feeling I get when I close a business deal and add another zero to my bank account. If nothing else, it'll offer her a chance to give me shit.

"Alrighty then." Her fingers walk up my chest and circle my right nipple.

Somehow I get us back to our pile of clothes, which suddenly seems woefully insignificant as there's a definite breeze to go with all of the California sunshine. I hold her against me while I straighten out my hoodie. As makeshift blankets go, it's not great, but I don't want to wait until we've put on clothes and made our way back to the house to have this conversation, so I drop down and tuck her onto my lap. At the same time, I thread her arms into her flannel. The way the wind makes her wet nipples pucker is amazing, but I don't want her to freeze.

"Start talking."

Hana

While Liam's satisfying himself that I'm not about to imitate a Popsicle, I lean back to better see his face. He has bedroom eyes and he looks like pure sex as he swipes a little errant salt water off his face. Licking him suddenly seems like an equally good alternative to mostly naked story time. But…

Promises.

I lace my arms around his neck.

"Okay. So my dream starts the way they usually do: I'm naked. I'm running through a meadow and it's sunshiny, full of flowers and bees, and it's all great. There's none of the crap that makes outdoors sex so uncomfortable like pollen or sticks that poke you in weird places. It doesn't matter that I'm barefoot or that I'm not wearing a sports bra."

"No need for sunscreen or bug spray." He grins at me, drawing his fingers up and down my sides in a delicious, scratchy-light tickle.

I can't tell if he's teasing me because so far this is probably the least sexy story ever. I eye him.

"Do you think I could get a side gig as a phone sex operator?" I blurt it out as soon as the thought occurs to me. "Although maybe that's a relic of the noble past now, kind of like my truck, and everyone just watches people on webcams. Have you ever done that? I'm talking about the purchasing end. Not the strip down and show off part."

His fingertips slide up my sides. There's laughter in his voice when he says, "You're running through a field for an awful long time."

I probably should have committed to memory a few pages from an erotic romance because I'd love to have that magic, where I'm casually, effortlessly sexy and he goes off like a rocket. Oh well. It's too late now. He either gets me or he doesn't.

"Someone's chasing me," I say. "Someone big and male. He's faster than me, and stronger."

"Does he catch you?"

"Yes." I can't bite back my smile. "Of course, I'm not trying too hard to get away."

"You don't want to be rescued?" His fingertips trace the undercurve of my boobs.

"Not even a little. White knights are pretty boring, although they get bonus points for armor and horses." I draw a curvy swirl against his shoulder. "When he catches me? He hooks an arm around my waist and there's this moment where I'm flying and my only connection to the world is where we touch. His dick is enormous and it's right there, pushing against my butt, sliding up and down."

Liam makes a rough sound and his hands cup my breasts.

I cover his fingers with mine. "Did we discuss audience participation?"

"I always want to participate with you." He circles a nipple, pulling gently. "Continue."

"And then he tumbles us both to the ground. First he's on the bottom, then I am, and then we're rolling around and he's tickling me. Not hard, just a gentle scrape of his fingers. It feels so good."

"Like this?" Liam's forehead creases as he moves his fingers up my side and then back down again. It tickles, but it also definitely does it for me.

When I whimper, he does it again. The sun on my back is warm, Liam is warm, even the sand is warm now. His big hands skate up and down my back, following the line of my spine lower until he's tracing the top of my butt. It's possible I might spontaneously burst into flame. Instead, I babble some more.

"I can't get away, but I don't want to. He's bigger and stronger, but he's making sure I get what I need."

The thing about Liam is that he always listens, so of course he nods. "He should."

"His nails scratch up my back, over my shoulders. I'll show you."

I draw my hands up my body, nails dancing over my bare skin. There may be moaning.

"Jesus. Hana."

Liam's breathing sounds tortured. The full-on sexy rasp is tempting to explore closer, but right now I just feel so good that I don't want to stop. Instead, I draw my nails up my neck and into my wet hair, my eyes drifting closed as my head tips back.

"Can I—"

Liam waits until I nod, and then his hands follow the path mine took, pressing small circles over my sides, moving higher until his big hands cradle my head and I relax into his hold. His nails scratch lightly over my scalp.

"Finish the story," he says roughly. "Please."

I shrug. "We wrestle. And then I feel his fingers tickling up my thighs, scratching lightly. He doesn't stop when he gets to my panties."

Liam groans. "I thought we were naked in a field."

"It's a dream." I nip his bottom lip. "I'm allowed to have magic panties."

I lean a little closer, bracing my hands on his big bare shoulders. The man's built like a lumberjack and I have plans to appreciate every inch of him. I spread my fingers so I can get started on that and also because I just love touching him. The way my legs are spread and I'm planted on his chest, he has to know how I feel about him. I'm wet despite skinny-dipping in the ocean, and I desperately want to reach for him and make him mine.

"Sometimes, if I haven't had sex in a long time or it's a really good dream, I come when I dream."

"Did you come last night?"

"I always come with you."

He blinks.

"You." I run my fingers over his shoulders. "I was dreaming about you, Liam. The end."

He presses a kiss against my lips. "Do you—"

"Want to have sex on the beach? Yes, please, right now, and thank you."

CHAPTER SIXTEEN

HOUSTON, WE HAVE A PROBLEM

Hana

WE POP MY high society cherry a few weeks after we strike our deal. Liam has some gala dinner for a science education foundation and he invites me to accompany him in the spirit of making progress in the "good guy" and social-image-polishing direction. I'm beginning to think I might prefer to focus on my bad-girl lessons because the orgasms are spectacular, but I can't deny him this. Plus, he makes the valid point that dinner out in nice clothes is really a date, which ought to thoroughly reform his bad-boy self.

I get in the spirit of things and make my own on-line donation, although Liam assures me he's got us covered. I'm sure his contribution would make my eyes water.

He also goes all out to help me look fancy. A stylist magically appears in the living room with a rack of designer dresses. There are shoes and bags,

wraps and underpinnings. All I have to do is point.
I sort of feel like I should refuse on principle and go
find something at Ross, but the dresses are pretty,
I'm weak, and so I let myself be zipped into a sparkly gold floor-length gown that leaves one arm and
shoulder bare and demands four-inch heels. A hair-
dresser transforms my hair into a mane of soft waves
and I resist the urge to ask if my new look comes
with a tiara.

Knowing Liam, he either has a spare one somewhere in his McMansion or he has a jeweler on speed
dial.

When I come downstairs, Liam is leaning against
the wall, staring out at the city lights. He turns before
I can say anything, and I stare shamelessly at him. He
looks exactly like the billionaire he is. The laughing,
sandy lover from my beach has been replaced by a
powerful man wearing a tuxedo that showcases the
raw beauty of his body.

I groan. "I'm going to have to fight them off with
a stick."

"Them?"

"The Liam Masterson fan club. I've heard it's
really popular." I faux-waltz toward him, twirling
in loopy circles like I'm Cinderella. The ridiculous
heels make it hard, but I manage. Barely. "Wait. Will
there be dancing?"

"Yes." He strides to meet me, catching my hands
in his. His gaze focuses on me, hot and intense. "Will
that be a problem?"

"I have basic ballet and sexy club moves." I shrug. "Will that be enough?"

"Follow my lead," he suggests.

"That should probably be our theme song for when we're getting grilled tonight. Maybe I should write it on my inner thigh with a Sharpie so I'm reminded every time I pee." When the corner of his mouth quirks up, I nudge him. "I know you like to put everything in spreadsheets, but this will work way better for me. I don't want to screw up your big night."

Liam has mentioned several times that tonight is a big deal for him and that he was specifically asked/told to bring his wife with him. Given his original pitch to me about us keeping up temporary appearances in the interest of image management and his strong dislike of being told what to do, I can only assume that we'll have a very important audience tonight and that it will be awkward.

Liam brushes a careful kiss over my mouth. "They'll love you."

I mock-glare at him. "That's like your mom saying you're smart and talented. It's highly suspicious."

Liam actually gives it serious thought for a moment. "What specifically do you think anyone at the event would dislike about you?"

I don't particularly want to point out my shortcomings in the social mingling department, but he waits me out and eventually I cave.

"I haven't done big, fancy social stuff before. The last party I went to where the guys wore tuxes was my high school prom. I don't do social chitchat, I blurt stuff out, and if someone asks about our wedding, I may overshare. Plus, they're all going to be super successful businesspeople, so while I'm proud of the farm and what I've accomplished there, I know how it looks to other people."

"You run a business and you're smart. If you ask them about themselves, they'll adore you. If they don't, fuck them." He reaches into the pocket of his tuxedo jacket and pulls out a long blue box. "This is for you."

"The dress and the shoes were more than enough, but thank you." I pop the box open. Thank God I already said something polite because Liam turns out to be a master present giver. There's a bracelet cuff made of tiny diamond bees and a pair of super sparkly diamond earrings. They're part me, part him. I love them.

He fixes the bracelet onto my wrist, but it turns out the earrings are made for pierced ears and I never bothered to do that.

"I can get my ears pierced?" I offer.

He frowns. "Only if you want to."

It takes twenty minutes for our car service to cover the last block to the hotel where the gala is being held. A long line of limousines and town cars wraps around the block. I fight the urge to roll the window down and stick my head out. Liam just laughs when I suggest we get out and walk the last hundred yards.

When we finally pull up in front of the hotel,

Liam gets out first. It's his job to make sure I don't flash anyone or step on my hem. He achieves this by reaching into the car and scooping me up off the seat as cameras go off like fireworks. When he sets me down on my feet, he brushes his mouth over my ear.

"Beautiful."

His hand presses against the small of my back, steering me toward the red carpet. He's coached me on what to expect, but I flinch when the cameras explode. As we step onto the carpet, the photographers yell for us to look left, right, our other right, over the shoulder. I stop when Liam stops, which seems to get me through the worst of it. People call for *Mr. Masterson, over here. Mrs. Masterson.*

The energy is high and although it's not my kind of scene, it's hard not to get excited as the photographers snap photos of me as if I'm some kind of A-list celebrity. Other couples stand and pose on the red carpet behind us, but the paparazzi are all over Liam. Flashes go off as reporters unleash a volley of questions at him.

"Did you elope…"

"Any comment on Leda Swan…"

"Is it true you bought a controlling interest in Leda's company…"

"Have you apologized…"

"Raunchy pictures leaked…"

My smile feels more and more forced and the gala's minder moves purposefully toward us. I turn instinctively toward her, needing to get out of the spotlight. Somehow, I expected people to be nicer at a charity gala.

"This beautiful woman is my wife." Liam pulls me into his side. His grip is gentle and protective but I still move stiffly, my heels catching in the fabric of my dress, and I bump into his side with an audible *oops*. Shutters click, immortalizing my awkwardness.

He feels tense. There's a brief pause as the reporters digest his bombshell and then there's a roar of sound as the reporters spring back into action, barking out follow-up questions.

Liam holds up a hand. "I have no comment on Leda."

One of the reporters launches a new question despite Liam's embargo. "Do you feel like you have something to apologize for?"

Liam pauses. For a moment, I think he'll ignore this question like he has the others. "I don't apologize."

The minder tugs urgently on my arm, motioning for me to move along. We can all tell this interview has headed south. The reporters continue to pepper Liam with questions.

One of them waves a tablet at us. "Have you seen the photos?"

There's a good ten feet between us, but that's not enough distance to blur all of the details. Naked Liam, for instance, is perfectly clear. As is his very flexible, extremely creative partner. She's wearing just a pair of thigh-high leather boots with dizzyingly high heels. I blink because I really don't want to know what they're doing in that picture. That's Liam's past, not his present. I think.

Because the next pictures that flash across the screen of the tablet *are* familiar. That's me and Liam kissing—and more—on the Ferris wheel. I stare at my bare ass and wonder if it's possible to spontaneously combust from embarrassment.

And then the reporters turn on me. It's clear they knew who I was before I stepped foot on the red carpet. It's even clearer that they've dug into my past and have drawn their own conclusions.

"...true that you met your husband at a sex party..."

"Financially troubled farm that Mr. Masterson bailed out..."

"Prenup..."

"Public sex kink...exhibitionist..."

Liam ignores the reporters, steering us single-mindedly toward the entrance. As soon as we're inside, I let my smile drop.

I don't know what to think. My ears still ring from the roar outside and light spots dance before my eyes. I want to go home. I want to yell at Liam. This isn't a fairy-tale evening out and he hasn't been honest with me. Has everyone here seen me riding Liam's fingers in public?

I don't have to do this. "I'm leaving."

Liam tugs me over to an alcove, waving off the guests drifting toward him. They look like sharks scenting chum. "Stay."

He stands in front of me, blocking me from sight. I want to tell him to move, but I need to catch my breath. I'm pissed, too. "They have pictures of my ass."

"Not for long." Liam whips out his phone, firing off a series of texts. Or maybe he's inputting missile launch codes. Nothing about his world makes any sense. How can normal people live this way?

"Why are they bringing up my farm?"

He rests his forehead against mine, his hands cupping the side of my face.

"I need you to stay." He hesitates. "Let's talk about the farm later."

"What did you do?" I'm so pissed.

"I have to give the keynote," he says, which is not the answer to my question. In fact, it's not an answer at all. "And if you leave now, people will believe that everything that was said out there is true."

"Of course they will! You didn't deny it!"

I turn, trying to slip under his arm, and he groans. His mouth finds mine in a brief, sweet kiss.

"Stay for my keynote. Then we can go. My PR firm will handle this. No one will bother you again."

He doesn't remind me that I agreed to do this. That attending tonight's gala was a promise I made to him. That he never actually said helping him with his image problem would be easy or pleasant. I hate that I've been so focused on what I want from our relationship that I haven't considered what he needs. And right now that's someone to stand by his side—and airbrush him with respectability.

"We do your keynote. Then we leave. I'm expecting an explanation, in case that's not clear." I may
not sound happy—I'm not a freaking saint.

He nods.

"Okay." I brush my mouth over his. "Then let's
do this."

People are still circulating as if there's nothing
wrong. There's a long line at the bar, a string quartet
plays something classical, and no one's screaming at
me. Although I guess the night is young.

I don't recognize anyone, which is hardly surprising. Farmers' market circles are very different. I do
meet several state politicians, two mayors, most of
the city council and a large number of executives.
A number of B-list celebrities mingle with the other
guests, taking more photos. I explain repeatedly that
I'm a small-business owner with a bee farm; other
than the guy who owns a restaurant, no one seems
to be able to grasp the concept of a business model
that doesn't involve either widgets or bytes and pref-
erably both.

We're seated at a table in the front. Liam will
be giving the keynote, so more men in tuxedos and
women in fancy ball gowns make a point of stopping
by to introduce themselves. Although the waiters
start bringing out the salad course, not many people
seem to eat. I try my salad and it's excellent.

When Liam gets up to speak, there's an electric
energy in the room. People watch him and hang on
his words. He's good. He talks about the power of
science education and how every child deserves the

chance to believe in spaceships and exploring new frontiers. New worlds, new journeys, new opportunities to learn. He shares how he was convinced that he'd move to Mars someday, and then he talks about Galaxtix's work on a Mars rover and its plans to launch a private space mission in the next five years. He's getting people to think about who might benefit from the foundation's work, and I wonder how many extra checks will be written tonight because of him.

It's surprising, then, when the older man seated on the other side of Liam's empty chair murmurs something to his dinner date. It takes me a moment to process what I've just heard.

It's a pity Masterson is such a wild card—unpredictable, and those parties, such a liability.

Liam strides back to our table to thunderous applause. I'm tempted to elbow the complainer and point out that Liam totally rocked his speech. It's also clear that he loves space exploration and Galaxtix's mission, even if he self-sabotages.

The old guy promptly gets into it with him, too. I try to pretend that the two of them are sitting in their own little bubble, but it's hard not to hear what's said.

"I gave you exactly what you asked for, Malcolm. No scandals, just nice, wholesome romance." Liam's voice is tight with impatience. I suspect Malcolm has brought up Liam's *unpredictability* again. "I've been a fucking saint."

Malcolm says something I don't quite catch, but it sounds bitchy, unhappy or both. He's not a cup-half-full kind of guy, that's for sure.

Liam sets his glass down with an audible click. "I won't go any further. That's nonnegotiable. She's my wife and she's exactly what you asked for, so show some appreciation. She's settled, she's the antithesis of Leda, and that's what matters. She loves me. The press will love her."

It makes me uncomfortable to hear my relationship with Liam being discussed like this, especially since it seems entirely impersonal. Liam was perfectly clear when he approached me at the farmers' market that he had a business agenda and that staying married would help, but I haven't really paid too much attention to that since. That was a mistake. I'm the pretty wallpaper in Liam's little redecorating project and not the love of his life.

I can't decide if I'm overreacting or not. Liam's amazing in bed and he can be super thoughtful. Sure, he was aware of the monster crush my younger self had on him, but he'd pretended to be unaware because that's what a nice guy does when his best friend's little sister cranks up the idolatry to level ten. We've never talked about love. He's never said that he loves me and I don't think I missed that part of his conversation. Why would he mention that now?

CHAPTER SEVENTEEN

CRASH LANDING

Liam

So THAT WENT to shit fast.

Malcolm confirms he's an ass by going off on Hana. She gives him a look that should eviscerate him and then excuses herself from the table. When he realizes that she's heard pretty much every asinine word he just shared, he freezes, but just for a second. I'm sure he'll claim next that it's her fault she can't take a joke. That he didn't really mean it. Watching him scramble to cover his ass would be funny if I weren't wrestling with regret. I've spent my adult life avoiding both regrets and apologies. But I have a feeling that if I want Hana to be in my life, I'm going to have to open the door to both.

My phone is going nuts, but none of the messages are from Hana, so I silence it. I can't believe I said what I did.

Hana's gorgeous. With her it's an inside-and-out

kind of beautiful. Leda had the supermodel looks but there was nothing attractive underneath the surface, and that matters. I'm fucking lucky Hana looked at me at all, even if she was doing it through bourbon goggles.

First I got the earrings wrong. I should have noticed she didn't have pierced ears.

Then we got here and dozens of people had asked what she did, instantly dismissing her because she doesn't pull down millions of dollars a year.

And then there were the photos of her, and Malcolm pushed me and I lost it. *She loves me. The press will love her.* I regret those words. Yes, Hana had a crush on me for years. For the most part, it was painfully awkward and I tried to avoid being alone with her. Sometimes, I took advantage of it. I don't think she still feels that way for me. Most of all, I hate that I took something personal of hers and made it very, very public.

I look at Malcolm. "Do you want me to quit the board?"

He pretends to be nursing his whiskey and water, but we both know he's running the odds in his head on *yes* being the right answer. He hates me.

"I want what's best for the foundation." He sounds as if he has a ruler permanently stuck up his ass.

"Funny, that," I tell him. I don't think the expression on my face is any too pleasant. "Because that's what I want, too. I meant what I said earlier tonight, about every kid deserving the chance to dream about exploring. For some kids, that's going to be science.

Other kids will pick a different direction. I've put a lot of time and money into this because I want to give those kids opportunities. And maybe I'm not a nice person or even a good person, but my personal relationships are no one's business but my own, and I'm not telling those kids we're supposed to be helping that they're not smart enough or good enough or whatever adjective you want to use as an excuse. If my trying to help is hurting them, I'll bow out."

Malcolm opens his mouth but I'm not through with him. "And you owe Hana an apology."

When he looks blank, I realize he's forgotten her name. Or maybe he never bothered learning it. As far he's concerned, her real name is Mrs. Masterson and her only value is as my wife.

You can't fix stupid, so I go after Hana.

Hana

Although the charity gala appears to have raised a significant amount of money in the name of elementary science education, no one looks happy. When I step out of the ladies' room, still not sure what to think about Liam's conversation with his asshole neighbor, Liam's mouth is drawn in a tight line and quite a few tuxedo-wearing, important-seeming people are either scowling at us or ignoring us.

"It's like we've contracted some kind of super-nasty STD and they're all afraid of catching it if they get too close," I say, running my hand down his arm. Mostly, I'm trying to make him less tense, although

I also like the way his muscles bunch beneath the jacket of his tuxedo.

He surveys the room and I can't help but notice that several of the other guests suddenly disappear toward the bar or the bathroom.

"Are you trying to scare them off?"

He looks down at me. "Keynote and then out. Shall we move on to step two?"

"In the interest of not completely burning all of your foundation bridges, please and yes, thank you."

It turns out there's a cable car stop not too far from the hotel where we are, so rather than wait for our town car, Liam suggests we hop on that. I'm game. Since it's San Francisco, my fancy dress doesn't even get too many sidelong looks. People are used to everything here, and one panhandler asks if we just got married, then beams at whatever Liam drops into his cup.

It's late, so the cable car isn't jammed like it would be during the daytime. I guess most of the tourists are back in their hotels by now. We stand at the back, hanging on to the poles that are supposed to keep you from pitching out onto the street. I have my doubts, but Liam wraps an arm around my waist and tucks me between him and the wall of the car. At first we just ride, but the farther we get from the hotel, the more certain things bother me.

Liam is smart, rich and generous. It makes no sense that the board of Galaxtix would try to force his resignation just because he throws sex parties for consenting adults.

"Why does Malcolm want you to resign so badly?"

His fingers tighten around the pole. "Galaxtix invested quite heavily in Swan Bio. The company was poised to become the biggest IPO in Silicon Valley's history. When it went bust, Galaxtix took a hit. Malcolm also had a significant position."

"Who founded that company?"

"Leda."

"And he still thinks that you somehow scuttled her company because of a bad breakup?" Liam is rich enough that I suppose he might even be able to do it, but I sense there's more to the story.

"That's exactly what he thinks." Liam's fingers tighten on the pole. "Leda and I split up, I discovered her patents were worthless despite her claims, and very shortly thereafter, she discovered that the funding for her company had evaporated. She couldn't bring a product to market with no cash. Companies go bust all the time, but one minute she was the golden child, and the next minute no one would lend her a dime. Malcolm thinks that's how I conduct all of my relationships."

I consider that while the cable car clangs its way through an intersection. "All of them?"

He rests his forehead against mine. "Including ours."

Okay, so maybe I'm being paranoid, but that's not a denial. It sounds more like a statement of fact and because that freaks me out just a little, I press harder than I might have.

"But I'm not the founder of a Silicon Valley start-up. I'm just a small business owner, if we're being objective. That's stupid. You don't have anything to do with my farm."

Liam's silent long enough that my chest goes way beyond tight and threatens to explode straight on the spot. This should be an obvious answer. *No, Hana, I did* not *do anything with my billions of dollars that would directly affect your business.* I know he's rich, I know that money translates into power, and I'm aware that he has far more influence than, say, an organic honey farmer, but I also thought I'd made my position plenty clear. I'm not for sale, no matter how good his intentions are.

"This is where you explain why Malcolm has this mistaken impression, Liam. I know he thinks you're a giant dick on principle, but this cone of silence you insist on living under isn't helping."

I feel Liam sigh against my hair. His arms tighten around me, and I want to lean into him and forget this whole conversation. But I can't. If he's done something, I need to know so I can figure out my next move. We may have a connection in bed, but I need to be able to trust him when we're not naked, too.

"I own your note, Hana. I bought it a few days after we got married, before you agreed to a temporary deal. In theory, he's entirely right. I could shut you down exactly like I shut down Leda."

I can't even process what he's telling me. No. I don't *want* to. While Jax has made strongly worded suggestions on several occasions about paying off my mortgage and start-up loans, I've made it very clear to him that I'm doing this by myself. It's great that he wants to be supportive—not everyone has family like that and it's a gift—but financial hand-outs are still a *no, thank you* from me and he's re-spected that. Liam, however, has completely ignored my boundaries.

"Why?" I want to say so much more, but that's all that comes out.

Why do you keep secrets?

Why did you think I couldn't do this on my own?

Why do you get to trample all over my boundaries but I'm not allowed to get close to you?

"You were struggling. That made you vulnerable." He glances away at the buildings trundling past the cable car. "It's the carrot and the stick. I could re-ward you by making your financial shit go away, or I could use it to make sure you did what I needed you to do. But since I'd screwed up, helping you out seemed like the right thing to do and so that's what I did. I know you don't want my money, but I want you safe."

"By buying my *farm*?"

"I bought the mortgage and I've already filed a satisfaction releasing the lien. It's a gift. Like flow-ers. There's nothing to be upset about."

"I'm not upset." *Lying liar.* The cable car stops and Liam jumps down, reaching up to swing me to the ground. "I'm sad because we don't get to be a nor-mal couple. You have all this money, so you just go ahead and do whatever you think is best. You don't have to check with me or anyone because it's not as if we're sharing a checking account and I'll notice when a half-million dollars vanishes. Instead, you just do stuff."

He sets his hand at the small of my back. Lombard Street is famous—or notorious—for its hairpin turns. It looks like a dancing snake and it's all uphill from here. Ugh.

Liam looks at me. "We can have a joint checking account if you want. You can yell at me when I spend too much at Whole Foods."

"I don't think that's the answer."

"I want to fix this."

I believe he does, too. I don't have any magic answers, though. We've kind of been living in a bubble these last few weeks. The sex is amazing and I'm not going to say I don't love his house on Lombard Street. I do—because hanging out there with Liam is fun. It's his space and it's where we do couple things. But it can't be all fun and games. It can't just be sex and him buying me expensive surprise gifts like an entire freaking farm. He's gorgeous and he's amazing in bed. We have off-the-charts good sex and the kind of chemistry I've never felt before. It's unicorn sex, something most people never find. It's just that I thought our connection existed outside of our naked times, too.

Liam's so much more than my brother's hot friend. He's funny and thoughtful, even if he pretends he's not. He's generous and scary smart and, up until now, he's made me feel safe. I've never thought he'd lie to me—but he has. I could have cut him some slack for buying my mortgage at the start of our relationship, but he should have told me so we could discuss how we were going to move forward.

He punches in the gate code. "We'll talk about it, okay?"

"It's too late for that."

He holds the gate open for me so I can go first. "I'll fix this."

My chest tightens as if someone's squeezing my ribs into my heart. "No."

"Hana?"

"I don't think there's any fixing this." I wave a hand between us. "This is something you shouldn't have done, but having done it, you should have figured out really fast that you'd trampled on a pretty big boundary and you should have laid it out for me. You should have apologized, except you *never* apologize, right? I don't see how we work because there's not a *we* here—there's you and then there's me, who apparently you don't think can handle her own business."

His jaw tightens. "I'm sorry if you find financial freedom offensive."

"It's not the money, Liam."

"Then what is the fucking problem, Hana?"

He really doesn't get it. I'm not sure I did, either, not until tonight. He has all that money, and I don't. Honestly, I'd probably have been okay with his helping me out eventually, but it would have had to be mutual. I have to be able to give back to him, too. He has to take my help. Otherwise, I'm still just his best friend's baby sister and he's just the guy I hero-worshipped. When we woke up married, I thought that was my chance to get to know him and to do all the things with him. Sex things, yes, but also date things, daily things, me-and-him things. I thought we were starting a relationship.

"I'm tired of being a problem you have to fix."

"You're not." He rests his hand at the small of my back, urging me forward. "I like spending time with you. I thought we were having fun and that this was what you wanted."

"Yes. That's true. But—" I fish in my clutch for my truck keys. "But I'd like to be more, Liam. No. Scratch that. I'd like to be enough. Just me, just as I am. I need to be an equal partner, not the lesser share of some seventy-thirty deal."

"Am I supposed to sell your mortgage to some shark of a lender so you can feel like a martyr? Is that what you want?"

"No." I start walking toward my truck. I don't know if I'll have the strength to leave if I go inside. Whatever stuff I've left in his house, it's just stuff. It doesn't matter.

"Are you *leaving* me?" He sounds incredulous and that's the problem, isn't it? Whether he's willing to admit it or not, he thinks he's the boss, that he holds the upper hand in this relationship. It may be a benevolent dictatorship, but I can't live like that.

I won't.

So I give him the only answer I can. "Yes. I can't do this anymore. You wanted a temporary marriage while you sorted out your business stuff, and now we're done."

I have no idea what comes after a fake marriage ends, but I'm sure Liam will take care of it like he always does. It's just good business.

CHAPTER EIGHTEEN

KNOCKED OUT OF ORBIT

Liam

LOMBARD STREET ISN'T the same without Hana. I manage to throw myself into work for the first week, which increases my bank account significantly but does nothing to make my oversize mansion seem less quiet. It's no more than I deserve.

She's left little pieces of herself in my house. She has a drawer full of random stuff in my bathroom, and one of her ancient but beloved Santa Cruz T-shirts on a shelf in my walk-in closet. Her weird coffee pods for the Keurig. Some kind of Norwegian yogurt in my fridge that curdles my teeth when I try it. I don't understand what went wrong, why I couldn't fix this. The charity gala was definitely not a win for me, but the real issue seems to be my buying her mortgage. I turn it over in my head, looking for new angles, trying to figure out where I went wrong. I thought I was being nice and looking out for her. Or maybe that's what I wanted to think. Maybe it was easier to give her stuff, to share money but not myself with her.

I was kind of a dick.

She hasn't filed for divorce, but I worry that she will. I guess then she'd have to talk to me, but I don't think a conversation in the presence of a court-ordered mediator will go particularly well.

I don't want to lose her.

I work all hours of the day, trying to forget that I've fucked things up so badly; however, that has already happened. She set the rules when she agreed to be my temporary wife and then I went ahead and ignored them. I made her feel small.

I remember my mother screaming at my dad when he wandered home. I didn't like the way he made her feel, as if she wasn't reason enough for him to stay. He'd send money home, but there was never enough of it. And besides, what we both really wanted was him.

I think Hana may have wanted me until she realized she deserved a whole person, someone who could love her and be there for her. Someone who wouldn't walk away and send a check.

Now that it's too late, I know I want her back.

I love her.

Jax won't answer my texts or calls either, but I'm a stubborn bastard and I'm willing to fight dirty. I finally resort to stalking him outside his current start-up. When he comes out the door, he can't miss me.

"I need to talk to you." Hana hasn't answered any of my calls or texts, and I'm going nuts.

"No." He turns right, headed for a park that's down the street from the converted brick warehouse that houses his current start-up.

I fall in beside him. Since it's the Mission District, we have to step over the occasional passed-out drunk. There are a shit ton of pigeons in the park, but there are also snack carts.

"Tell me how I fix this."

For a moment I think he's going to instruct me to fuck off, but then he sighs. "Hana is not happy with you at the moment."

I want to seize on those last three words and ask if that means she's happy with me some of the time or is planning on being so in the future, but Jax's glower warns me not to be a desperate ass.

"I'd like to take responsibility for that." I say this cautiously because I'm not certain he won't haul off and punch me. I'd rather he wait until I have an action plan and *then* he can take a shot at me.

Jax exhales. "She's not a problem, Liam."

"I caused it—I fix it. It was my party. I married her. And people wouldn't have been all over her if I didn't have the kind of money I do. She's way too nice to handle that kind of press. They're calling her the princess of kink."

Thanks to the photos that leaked of Hana and me on the Ferris wheel. My legal team had them taken down, but too many people have seen them and copies keep popping up. Photos of Leda and me keep circulating, too, which only adds fuel to the fire.

"And *Mrs. Kink*," Jax growls. He's clearly been spending time on the internet. It's bad. I have a lawyer working on it, but since most of what's out there is innuendo and out-of-focus pictures, it's an uphill battle.

"Yeah." I scrub a hand over my face. "So that's not good. And it's my fault."

"So it's all about you."

Now it's my turn to give him a look. "There's something about Hana."

I pause, marshaling my arguments. This would be easier in an email I could review and revise. "Marrying her wasn't a mistake," I continue. "I feel things about her. For her. I'd like to have a chance to really be a husband to her."

Admittedly the only husbandly examples I've seen have been more of the what-not-to-do variety, but that's not going to help my case with Jax.

"Just tell her you're sorry and grovel," Jax says finally. "When I say this isn't rocket science, you should know exactly what I mean."

"Apologize?"

"What's she mad about?"

I think about it for a moment. "Top three? I really don't remember our wedding, I didn't act thrilled to be accidentally married, and I bought the mortgage on her farm so now she thinks I legally own her business and that I did it either to fuck with her or to prevent her from messing with me. Also, I used her to feel bad about myself the night of the party and my public visibility is the reason her naked photos got the traffic they did. She's also drawing comparisons between herself and Leda."

"That's six," Jax says, as if the actual number matters. One way to hurt Hana is one too many. "Are you treating her like Leda?"

"Not a chance."

"So you didn't have a controlling interest in her business that could be misconstrued by anyone with internet access?"

I shove a hand through my hair. "It wasn't like that. Leda stole from me. Hell, she stole from everyone. I had a legal obligation to take steps when I found out. Leda is a thief. Hana was vulnerable and I was just trying to make sure she wasn't anymore."

"And yet Hana came to the obvious if mistaken conclusion that you'd disrespected her and screwed around with her career behind her back *and* that you couldn't be bothered to come up with a decent excuse."

"Pretty much." I pull off my suit jacket and drop down onto the grass. From here I can see a square of blue sky framed by the curly gables of a row of Queen Annes. A couple of puffy clouds scoot by and I wonder what Hana is doing. I imagine her swimming in the ocean, maybe in a pink string bikini.

"How do I get her to forget and move on?"

Jax drops down beside me. "You have to show her that she can trust you. It would help if you apologized with actual words, but you're emotionally stunted, so I get that's a challenge for you."

"How do I get her to trust me?"

"You weren't there for her and you kept shit back. You should have been up-front about what you were doing and she should have had veto rights."

"I'm not going to let her tell me what to do or not do."

"You made her feel bad. Now you have to make her feel safe. Stop thinking with your dick for a minute. Also, don't ever make me say those words about my sister again." Jax frowns. "Use your brain. She was feeling vulnerable and she took a chance on you. You took that chance to use her to further your career and buy her farm. You made it seem like she didn't count for much. You have to even things up and make yourself vulnerable to her. It's like basic math."

"I can't have a relationship. You saw my parents. You know what they were like. Do you want a guy like that for your sister?"

Jax shakes his head. "Are you trying to talk me into helping you talk with Hana or out of it?"

Okay. I can figure this out. "Look, this is new for me. I don't know how boyfriends work, so this whole promotion to husband is like going from fry cook to head chef at a Michelin-starred restaurant. I know there's a lot riding on this and I actually don't want to fuck it up."

While I wait for him to process that, I lie back on the grass and stare at the sky. Sometimes it's nice to stop racing to the top. Mostly because I'm already there, but you know, it's good to look around. Stock up on vitamin D. More clouds skate pass. I glance at Jax but he's still looking up contemplatively. Okay. So it's boring as fuck and I need to fix this thing with Hana.

He finally shifts his gaze from the sky to me. "Do you want to be married to her?"

"Are you going to punch me if I'm honest?"

"Probably."

"Long-term I've never seen myself as a married guy. But I thought we were working out and I have… feelings for her."

Jax groans. "If you can't bring yourself to say those two little words—*I'm sorry*—then you show her."

I nod. Okay. Show, not tell. I don't like even thinking about apologizing. It makes me queasy, but I can demonstrate good faith.

"Because you'd better be sorry," Jax adds.

It's way too late for that rule. I think about sex and Hana a thousand times a day. "Give me examples."

Jax stares up at the sky for a long time. "So you can start with presents. Flowers. Thoughtful shit that shows you're thinking about her and that you know something about her other than her panty size. Whatever you do, for fuck's sake, don't make it about sex."

"Buy stuff. Got it."

"But then," he continues, "you have to open up. You have to go all the way. Make yourself vulnerable so that she feels like she's getting to know you and can trust you. It's math, right? You use math all the time. If you want to fly your sorry ass to a planet, you have to figure out how much energy it will take to get to the orbit you need to reach based on the size of your ship. Then you see if your engines can provide that."

"And this math works for you?"

Jax reaches over and punches me lightly in the shoulder. "I'm still single, aren't I? But I know what happens if you don't talk. You're going to fight and there will be misunderstandings. You have to sit down with each other and really listen. And if your spaceship of love burns up on reentry or you crash-land in the ocean, at least you tried."

"I'll have planted my flag," I say mock-solemnly. "Touched down and left my mark. I'll be sure to report back to mission control with each new...development."

Jax growls something I don't ask him to repeat, but I win a reluctant grin from him. Honestly, I'm just glad I don't have sisters to protect from billionaire assholes.

Decision made, I start mapping out the steps in my apology. I've screwed up big-time, so there's no way a simple, two-word *I'm sorry* cuts it. Plus, this is Hana we're talking about. She deserves the biggest, best apology in the world.

CHAPTER NINETEEN

NEW MISSION

Liam

GOING PUBLIC SUCKS. I don't like to talk about myself—
my private life is mine. The usual group of reporters
and photographers follows me to the studio, yelling questions and taking pictures. I've always been
the center of attention for my business successes,
but this is different. They don't care what deals I've
closed or how the software products championed by
my company could change the world for the better.
They just want to hear about how I banged Hana
Valentine and then married her at a sex party. I have
to refrain from punching a particularly obnoxious
reporter when he alleges Hana's been seen with another guy since our breakup.

It's almost a relief to hit hair and makeup, where
the makeup artist makes me look pretty and covers
up the shadows under my eyes. I pace back and forth
in the greenroom until it's my turn to go on set. The

producers make all of the guests walk out through a narrow corridor and then between the rows of guests. I'm supposed to slap hands and make nice, but I feel like the steer in the chute at a rodeo. I stride over to the interviewer, waiting for me in the middle of the studio, ignoring the polite applause.

Barbara, the hostess, spends way too much time explaining to the audience who I am. She seems to think this requires a blow-by-blow description of every dollar I've ever made. More than once, she flashes pictures of a girl I've been seen with on a big screen behind the two of us. This is not efficient, so eventually I lean in and put my hand on her arm.

"Can we just stipulate that I have the reputation of being a dick and that I've earned it?"

"Is that how you would describe your relationship with Leda Swan? The two of you were quite the item for months. And then you broke up and the investment world learned that you'd cut the funding for her company. Two months after that, her company closed its doors. Would you characterize that as a dick move?"

I suck in a breath. "Leda and I did have a personal relationship, but that relationship never entered into the boardroom. It did not affect our business dealings. In fact, Barbara, I'd suggest that it was the other way around: our business relationship made me rethink our personal one. I couldn't condone dating a woman who would steal from her own company. My being a dick was purely professional, not romantic."

Barbara looks out at the audience and then back at me. "So you believe Leda was a thief?"

I keep it simple. "Yes."

"What do you believe she stole?"

My heartbeat quickens. I haven't shared this information with anyone outside the district attorney's office. I'd planned to keep it that way, but not at the cost of losing Hana. "Money. Mine, her investors', anyone who put so much as a dime into her company. I'd initially invested in her company at her request before we started dating, but things started to not add up on the business front. When I did some digging, I found that large amounts of investment funds were unaccounted for. Either Leda was unethical or incompetent."

Barbara raises her eyebrows. "And which did you decide she was?"

"Unethical."

"And why would that be?"

"Because I realized that the portfolio of patents held by Leda's company was worth less than a roll of toilet paper in a Quilted Northern warehouse. She didn't have a working product. She wasn't close, but she told everyone it was fully functional and ready to take to market. The financials I'd seen were deliberately misleading, as were the product demonstrations. Sometimes, companies fail. It can be hard to develop a concept into a finished product and that's not criminal. If you never had a product in the first place, however, that's wrong in my book."

"And you didn't think you should share this information with the other investors so they could try to recoup their money?"

"There was nothing left. All the money vanished. Some of it went for payroll and rent, utilities and office furniture. Most of it, however, simply disappeared from the company bank account."

"So why say nothing?"

I lean forward. This is the tricky part. "I don't like to air my personal business, Barbara. Going public about my belief in Leda's wrongdoing might have been perceived as the vendetta of a disgruntled boyfriend."

Yes. Look at me. I'm such a choirboy.

"So you're saying you chose to do nothing?"

"No, I'm not saying that. There were a lot of rumors, as we both know. People thought—think— that I shut Leda's company down because she broke up with me." I wink at Barbara. "And because I'm a dick."

The audience laughs appreciatively.

"And you didn't care?"

"I don't worry about words. They're just words, or so I thought, and I'd like to be judged on my actions. I worked quietly behind the scenes with the appropriate law enforcement agencies to share what I knew; it's up to them to pursue charges or not. Not knowing about this private decision of mine, the board of Galaxtix let me know that they had their own private concerns, largely about my looking publicly like a first-class dick. They suggested I do something to fix my image problem."

"And how did you do that?"

"Well, I wasn't interested in apologizing to Leda. I made that clear. If you know me, you know that I don't apologize. Instead, I got married."

The people in the audience start whispering.

"I had a chance at a life with a really great person and I used her to clean up my image with the Galaxtix people. She doesn't deserve that. Any guy would be lucky to have her standing by his side, but I acted like I didn't see her. I'm hoping to convince her to give me a second chance, but I don't know what it'll take."

Barbara smells blood. "Why do you want a second chance, Liam?"

I look at the camera. "I love Hana. I want her back. I'd like to be the guy holding her when we're ninety and we're looking back on life. And I definitely want to be the guy living that life with her. For her."

CHAPTER TWENTY

FRANKENWEENIES AND TEQUILA

Hana

I MOPE AROUND Hey Honey Farm, making long, delusional lists of home improvement projects that I leave unstarted in favor of binge-reading Harry Potter. I buy myself an enormous bouquet of purple roses, hoping I'll feel better by the time they wither. One bunch turns into two; by the third, I buy a rosebush in the interests of economy. I lie around on the beach mainlining frozen cocktail pouches. I promise myself that I'll pull it together soon. I knew chasing Liam was a mistake, but I did it anyway, and now I have to sort my shit out. I'd rather not do it with every online gossip site in the country speculating about my motives in marrying Liam at a sex party. Pictures come out, purporting to be "a well-known couple" doing it at that party; the photos are super blurry and I'm not convinced they're actually me and Liam, but it's hard to fight rumor and innuendo.

So I keep my head down, vow to stay off the internet, and hire a perky agriculture major to temporarily cover the farmers' markets for me. There's only so much public humiliation a girl can take.

Liam texts me. Sometimes he asks if we can talk, but he also checks to see if I'm okay and whether there's anything he can do for me. I ignore his texts. I can't bring myself to block his number and sometimes my fingers itch to google him, although I refrain. I'm not ready yet to see him living his best life. At some point, I suppose I need to either find a lawyer or take Jax up on his offer to use his because Liam and I can't go the rest of our lives being half-married. Mentally, I give myself the rest of the month to mope before I get myself sorted out.

Moping mostly involves revisiting the scene of our sex crimes. I drag a backpack of romance novels and frozen cocktail pouches down to the beach for a self-care day and then spend an embarrassing amount of time trying to find the exact spot where we had sex. I cry too much into my faux margaritas, but that's also self-care. Eventually I'll stop feeling these things and it won't hurt so much.

Jax comes with me one weekend. He's been hanging out with me more and I'm grateful. He somehow manages to be both enthusiastic about providing me with emotional support and spectacularly bad at it at the same time. I'm pretty sure he doesn't realize that our trip to the beach is some kind of weird historical sex tour.

I wander up and down the sand, but no particular

spot looks familiar. It's a beach and the tides come and go, so I'm not sure what I expected to find. I kind of wish we'd done something gross and irresponsible like leave the condom behind so that I could find something, even if it's nasty, but no such luck.

"What are you looking for?" Jax asks.

I'm staring at a stretch of sand just above the high-tide mark. In addition to a few broken bits of driftwood, there is a mediumish abalone shell that's survived its journey to the shore mostly intact. Jax nudges it with his foot. He's wearing his motorcycle boots even though it's a million degrees out today because he's a freak who doesn't like to go barefoot.

"Liam and I spent an afternoon here. I'm trying to remember exactly where."

Jax slings an arm around my shoulder. "My offer to kill him stands."

"Thanks." I rest my head against his shoulder before sliding out from underneath his arm. He weighs a ton. "But family doesn't let family commit felonies."

He peers at the sand. "Is this a girl thing?"

"What?"

He gives me a look. "Do you want me to build a shrine here so that you can commemorate the exact spot where Liam boned my baby sister? We could erect a little plaque that says *We did it here* and then other people would know to avoid the used sand and I could buy a flamethrower and sanitize the place."

"Is that supposed to make me feel better?"

I'm pretty sure the only thing that will do that is

time, which sucks. If heartbreak was something you could fix with money, Jax would do it.

He crouches down and starts drawing in the wet sand with his finger. "Did you write your name in the sand? Like with little hearts and the date?"

"No, Jax, we did not. *Liam and Hana forevah* wasn't part of the plan."

"Liam's a dumbass and you deserve better." He rocks back on his heels and eyes his handiwork. He's a terrible artist.

I squint at the doodle. "You're going to have to give me a clue. You haven't improved much since you were five."

He grins up at me. "I was trying to draw Liam's wiener."

Huh. I guess it's possible that his drawing represents two circles and a tiny cocktail wiener of a penis. I'm not sure how this is supposed to make me feel better, but I appreciate the effort.

Three weeks after my sex life becomes a trending topic on the internet, Jax kidnaps me. Since he does this with his motorcycle and he calls ahead to let me know he's coming, he'd make a terrible felon but his thoughtfulness gives me time to hide inside the house and turn my phone off. Ignoring his Neanderthal pounding on my front door turns out to be impossible, though, so eventually we compromise. I open the door and he agrees to give me enough time to swap the yoga pants I've been wearing all week for jeans and boots. Road rash will not improve my life.

I don't ask where we're going until we're out on the main road. Since I'm wrapped around his back, this is not good timing. The helmets and the road noise don't help, either, although he's driving like a granny out of consideration for my wish not to die in a fiery crash. This conversation goes about as well as can be expected.

He bellows a question that sounds like "ax ug ekaxaupp?"

I attempt to translate it, but I've got nothing. "Are you taking me to your evil lair?"

"Pum feekow us pit spaxa dax."

I repeat my original question but eventually give up. It turns out he's decided that what I need is a girls' day, starring himself as a volunteer girl. He pulls off the road when we get to a Zen-like day spa halfway up the California coast.

After he finally convinces the receptionist that we're not a couple (ewww), we have massages and then wear our swimsuits to soak in a hot tub underneath giant redwood trees. There are mani-pedis as well. Jax looks painfully awkward the whole afternoon, but I appreciate the gesture and his hands turn out great.

When we're finally done being massaged and steamed, we sit in the garden with our tiny cups of green tea. I figure he's tried, so I tell him about Liam and how I angry-cry whenever I think about him, which is better than mindlessly crushing on him or wanting to sit outside his house wearing nothing but a trench coat and heels and wait for him to come home.

Jax makes a ferocious face because I've mentioned sex, but apparently being heartbroken is a free pass. "Look. He's an ass. He's said stuff and done stuff that merit an ass-kicking. I'd really like to take care of that for you, but you don't want me to do it. I get how doing it yourself would be empowering and shit, but the problem is, I don't think you want to do it."

"I do, too."

Jax drains his tiny teacup in one swallow. "If you say so."

I stop talking then because I'm afraid I'll cry. Or that Jax will go drag his former best friend over to my farm and make him be nice to me. I'm not sure I'll be able to resist having Liam Masterson gift wrapped and delivered a second time.

When Jax and I pull up in front of the farmhouse, I thank him and say all the right things. I promise, for example, that I've been miraculously cured by our afternoon together and that I'm officially all better and that whatever Liam says or does will have no effect on me because I am total rock where he's concerned.

"We're over," I assure Jax while I try to remember the best way to disembark from the back of a motorcycle. "In fact, we never really even began, right? He doesn't remember most of our wedding and that's kind of hard to get past."

Jax's face twists. I suspect he wants to punch someone really hard. Probably Liam, and I'm not sure how I feel about that.

"Okay," Jax says. He's turned off the bike and kicked the stand down, so I'm not sure he has plans to leave. "But I think you should hear him out."

Since I'm expecting to hear more threats to inflict grievous bodily injury on Liam, it takes me a moment to process. I use the time to slide-hop off the back of the bike.

I'm not sure I can do it. Having my heart broken hurts, and it turns out pain really isn't my thing. Sure, I'll get over him, but it's going to take a lot of time and I'll probably end up adopting too many cats and binge-shopping on Amazon. Then I'll redecorate the house and cut my hair and book an impulsive trip somewhere tropical where there are hot, single guys who I can hook up with for meaningless sex and abandon when it's time for my international flight home.

"You should give him a chance to grovel," Jax says. "I'd enjoy it and you might learn something."

"Should we revisit what he did before this moment of personal transformation? Those things are great on the surface, but there's a *reason* why he felt the need to do them. He married me as some kind of drunken self-punishment. He decided to stay married to me because it facilitated his *business* agenda. He bought my mortgage. Why would you take his side? Do you have masochistic matchmaker tendencies that I'm unaware of?"

Jax growls something I don't catch. That's fine by me. I don't want to talk about Liam. Ever.

Jax stomps up my front steps with all the finesse

of a linebacker, grumbling more stuff about Liam, me and our "stupid fucking stubbornness." When he holds out his hand, at first I think he's asking for my house key in some kind of well-intentioned but misguided belief that poor, heartbroken me isn't capable of inserting a key into her own door lock without having a breakdown.

But that's not it.

There's a white box propped up against my front door, the kind of shiny cardboard that typically holds an expensive gadget. Jax buys a lot of those, so I have experience. Tied to a yellow-and-white polka-dot ribbon is a note. Jax picks the whole thing up as if it might explode and hands it to me. Of course it's from Liam.

"Did you set this up? Is this one of those bro code things?"

Jax shakes his head. "If it works, I'm going to punch him for not delivering it before I had to spend the afternoon at a spa."

I should toss the whole thing in the nearest dumpster, but that seems wasteful. Plus, I'm curious. I start with the note.

Hana,
There are only two things that matter.
I love you.
And I'm sorry.

This is the first time that Liam has ever said he loves me. It's not even the throwaway *Love, Liam* that could be open to interpretation. Instead, he's gone for broke and flat-out said it. I should probably decide how I feel about that, but my stomach cramps and my heart decides now would be a great time to imitate a racing car. Jax pats my shoulder, trying to sneak-read the note.

I solve that problem by tucking the note between my boobs and open the box. Liam's sent me a space-age-looking rose-gold tablet. Jax mutters something about prototypes and nondisclosure agreements while I try to figure out what exactly I'm supposed to do with it. It's pretty obvious I'm not a tech geek, and Liam's a smart guy, so it's probably got an urgent secret message that will self-destruct five minutes after it plays or something.

Eventually I manage to press what must be the on button or maybe the power button because the tablet comes to life in my hands and Liam's face stares out at me from the screen.

He's sitting in the studio of an online news show. He's wearing another one of his ridiculously expensive Italian suits, his knee bouncing up and down as he fields questions about Leda and her company. The interviewer is an attractive brunette wearing a well-cut suit of her own. After covering Liam's general financial hotness, she moves on to his reputation as a revenge-dealing dick. He, in turn, reveals Leda's financial misdealings and corporate misrepresentations. By the time he's done, I'm pretty certain Leda will be arrested for fraud before too long. He's matter-of-fact and doesn't try to make himself look better. He just lays it out.

The felonious tendencies of his ex certainly go a

long way to explain his break-up and his refusal to apologize to her.

I think that's it, but then Liam looks right at the camera and says:

"I hurt someone I love by keeping these secrets. I shouldn't have done that and it's not something I can fix. I'm hoping she'll give me another chance, but as someone wise once told me, hope is not a strategy. So all I have are two little words, and I hope you're listening, Hana: I'm sorry."

The interviewer starts to say something, but Liam holds up his hand. "I want to be very clear about this. I love Hana. I want her back. I'd like to be the guy holding her when we're ninety and we're looking back on life. And I definitely want to be the guy living that life with her. For her."

Liam thanks the interviewer for her time and then he gets up and leaves. All I can think is that I need to know where he is, what he's doing. Or maybe I just need to replay this video a thousand times.

Jax gently slides the tablet out of my hands. His eyes search my face, probably checking to see if I'm going to cry hysterically or turn into a rampaging monster. I don't know what I want to do. A television interview and a few explanations doesn't magically fix everything, even though I appreciate the gesture.

Jax thumps my shoulder. "Do I need to drive you somewhere?"

He clearly doesn't trust me behind the wheel of a motor vehicle—and he seems to be under the mistaken impression that I'll drop everything and rush to be with Liam, wherever he is.

I shush him and then make him show me how to replay the interview that Liam's loaded onto the tablet. I'm not sure which is more shocking—that he's told me he loves me, or that he's apologized using actual words rather than cash. It's a nice moment, even though I'm not sure how much I can trust it.

CHAPTER TWENTY-ONE

FLOWERS WITH ROOTS ARE THE BEST

Hana

THE NEXT MORNING I walk out on my porch to find a lavender rose tree. It's still in its black plastic nursery pot. Someone's tied a bow around the slender trunk and it smells deliciously fruity. In an odd twist, tiny plastic rocket ships dangle from the branches. For no obvious reason, a tiny plastic astronaut is planting a flag in the dirt. I disentangle the card from a mass of half-opened buds:

Have me?

Love, Liam.

Single Hana should toss the whole thing, but the scent is divine, and it's not the poor rose tree's fault the sender is a dick. I compromise and shift it to the middle of my compost heap. It will make the place look pretty.

I don't know what else to think.

Because everything's shit. Or roses.

Have me?
We got married by accident...
We were drunk.
He didn't mean it...
...Did I—was it more than just a crush even then?
More than just sex, just memories, just...
Everything.

Gravel crunches and I look up. I don't know why I'm surprised to see Liam. I'm sure he brought the rose tree himself, and he's made it clear he wants to talk. He's said it to me, to Jax, to most of San Francisco and to anyone on the internet who would listen, although apparently listening isn't something I'm good at. I look around, trying to figure out if I can slip back into the house and get my head on straight.

My denim cutoffs are literally hanging together by strings in some places and the hole in my back pocket flashes my cotton underwear. When I got dressed this morning, I just grabbed the first thing I saw, which means I'm wearing yellow boots with white polka-dots and an ancient Santa Cruz T-shirt. There's dirt on my left knee and probably a dozen other places. I try and fail to remember the last time I showered. My face warms. If we're going to have this conversation, I'd rather do it wearing something new and expensive. I look like the disaster I feel inside.

"Hey," he says, shoving his hands into his pockets. He manages to look both tired and hot at the same time. It should be illegal how good he looks in his jeans, boots and a space center T-shirt.

I stare wildly at him, not sure what to say. Do I

take a chance and throw myself at him—again? Do I wait for him to do something? Say something? Are we taking turns now, and how will I know what to do?

"Hi," I blurt out too late. I guess it's also too late to hide in the house and pretend I'm washing my hair.

Now that I'm looking at him, I can't help but notice the enormous psychedelic bus parked in my driveway. Unless I'm hallucinating, he's swapped the Veyron for some kind of souped-up school bus. Even from here, I can see what looks like an asteroid belt or planets and planetlings cavorting on one side; there's a supersonic rocket painted on the hood.

"Is that a new project?"

Liam's face lights up. "Yeah. It's great, right? You can't miss it. We're going to bring science buses to local schools to teach kids about outer space."

Naturally, since he's an overachiever, he doesn't have one or two buses. He has an entire fleet and the program is launching in twelve states next month. Like a genuine good guy who has a thing for outer space that he wants to share with kids who haven't quite figured out how to dream that big yet. Liam doesn't need my help learning how to be someone's hero: he's got it covered already. Maybe teenage Hana wasn't so crazy after all.

"No more Galaxtix?"

He winces. "Yeah. I don't know what's going to happen there, but this is good, too."

"You're going to crush it."

He just had to decide it was what he wanted.

I stare at the bus and keep talking, babbling words to fill in the silence. My heart's beating so damn hard that he must be able to see it. I don't care about the bus or all the kids he's going to inspire. They'll probably have a class reunion on Mars in thirty years. It'll be—

"Hana?"

Deflect. "Seriously. Did you drive that monstrosity here? Does it even have seat belts?"

Liam gently pries the shovel out of my hand and tosses it to the side. I should protest his manhandling of my garden tools, but he's pulling off my gardening gloves and I can't move. He throws them in the direction of the shovel and then he presses a kiss against each palm. My heart squeezes in my chest, as if he's placed his lips on it and not my hands. Liam has always been able to get under my skin.

He holds my hands and then he looks at me. I remember all the times I was so certain he didn't see me, that he never would or that he'd always see the girl I'd been and not who I am now.

Have I always seen him?

Did I make up so many stories about his heroic Liam awesomeness that I missed this real, amazing, complex man?

"I think I need to say this again," he says. "I love you. I'm sorry."

"Don't just say that." I squeeze my eyes shut so I don't have to look at his face. "I need you to mean it. I can't play games anymore, not with you, Liam. Not about us."

"I'd like to say *I love you* at least twice a day for the rest of our lives." There's a promise in his voice. "I'll probably have to say the other thing, too. I'm sorry I hurt you. I'm sorry I didn't see what we were before I screwed us up. I thought..."

He winces.

"Me, too." I thought a lot of things, some of them true, some of them as far from truth as Mars is from Earth. "I love you. I miss us, I miss you."

I throw myself at him because why ruin a perfectly good track record of chasing this man? He catches me, cupping my butt in his big hands and lifting me up so our mouths are at kissing level. I shove my fingers into his hair because I'm not letting him get even an inch away and then we devour each other.

Our kiss starts out polite, a hi-how-are-you kiss, a welcome-home kiss. His tongue traces the line of my closed lips, as if he's asking for permission. When I open my mouth, he strokes inside. *I know you.* The kiss gets hungrier, more demanding. The sounds that we make are greedy. *I want you. All of you. Can I?* We kiss wilder and rougher, staking our claim on each other. *All mine, all yours. All* ours.

Liam pulls me closer as if maybe he'd like to crawl inside me, too. With a laugh, he dances me around in a circle. This is both dirty and welcome. My shorts are old and his fingers aren't exactly staying in PG territory.

I pull my mouth away from his. "Are you humming?"

He grins at me. "Yes?"

"I have so many questions." Truly. "The *W* kind of questions—the who, what, when, why sort of thing."

"I'm taking you dancing." He says this as if it makes perfect sense.

"We're in my yard."

"Yeah." He makes another sweeping twirl. "I missed you."

He sits us down on the porch and settles me on his lap. "I need to tell you some things."

"Okay." This comes out less badass than I would like because I'm already breathless. Plus, I may not let go of his mouth entirely. I suck on his bottom lip.

"I'm sorry," he says again. I guess he's either practicing or getting it all out of his system at once. "For using our marriage to spackle over my poor personal decisions. For thinking you were just someone convenient. For not making you feel special or like you counted when you're the most important person in my life."

Liam's thorough. I want to go back to the kissing, but he did make me feel like I didn't matter, that he could have been married to any other woman and that I was interchangeable. "I hate that you don't remember most of our wedding night. That you just woke up next to me and felt stuck with me. That you made decisions for us without asking me what I thought, even if they weren't bad decisions."

His hands tighten on my hips. "I hate that, too. I hate even more that I didn't realize what a lucky bastard I was that I got to start straight at 'and they lived happily ever after.' I'd like to start over, if that's what you want. I don't want to not remember the night you promised to love me forever. And I definitely want to be partners. *Full* partners."

I'm not sure what he's getting at. "You want to date?"

"No. I mean, I can if that's what you want. I thought we could redo the memory kinds of moments."

"I have no idea what that means." It takes me longer than it should to make this perfectly valid point because Liam's kissing me again.

"I'd be happy to demonstrate." His voice is rough but happy.

"Is that a euphemism?"

"Not yet. Hold that thought." I'm not certain how I feel about his master plan to restart our relationship, but I definitely know what I'm feeling underneath me and I was sort of expecting we'd have the rest of our conversation naked and in bed. He slides me off his lap, which is unexpected.

He strides over to his ridiculous bus and disappears inside. It would be so much easier to just focus on how cute Liam is with his science program and how his hotness makes me want to jump him right here on my porch. It's just that's not all of Liam. He's smart and sometimes—okay, often—ruthless and once he's got a goal, he's pretty much all-out until he's reached it. He's used to people falling all over him because he has a ton of money and they want a piece of it, so they pretty much roll over and do whatever he suggests because he radiates authority and power.

It's at odds with the guy holding a plastic cake carrier. I attempt to reconcile my bad-boy billionaire with a stress baker or whatever's sent him in the direction of cake.

"Here," he says when he gets close. Automatically, I take the cake carrier he's holding out. He's giving me…cupcakes?

"Thank you?"

The frosting is lavishly uneven, bright green blobs with dabs of pink and blue. There may not be any food coloring left in the entire state of California. It's almost blinding. He's spelled out *I love you* with what looks like marigold petals.

"It's our wedding cake," he tells me. "We didn't get to have one, so I made you one, although I'm definitely not vouching for the quality. You'll have to grade me on effort. Also, I borrowed the flowers from your garden, in the spirit of full disclosure."

"It's perfect."

He holds out his other hand, the one that isn't holding the cupcake carrier. "Will you marry me?"

He's offering me two gold wedding bands, a his and a hers.

A second chance at us.

A chance at having all of him and giving him all of me.

"Yes." I take his hand.

* * * * *

DEVOURED

CATHRYN FOX

MILLS & BOON

This one is for you, Sylvie Howick.

Thank you for all you do for me. You are a gem.

CHAPTER ONE

Peyton

"WHERE THE HECK is he?"

I mumble curses under my breath as I pace around my condo, weaving around packed boxes that are ready to be shipped to Malta first thing tomorrow morning, right before I jump on board my brother's Learjet and get flown to the island myself.

"You talking to me?" my best friend Carly asks.

I spin as she comes into the room with a glass of white wine and unceremoniously flops onto the buttery-yellow sofa. I'm going to miss Carly. I'm going to miss that sofa. Heck, I'm going to miss New York, too, but my dream job of teaching English to young students in Europe calls—and I'm eager to answer.

A bubble of excitement wells up inside me as I envision myself in the modern school located in the quiet community of St. Julian's, standing before a bevy of eager minds ready to learn a new language. Thank God, I studied Italian in college, as well as

Spanish, otherwise this opportunity never would have presented itself.

While I'm thrilled that I'm one of two candidates being considered for the full-time position, leaving my friends, my brother Cason and Londyn, his new wife, and everything else I love won't be easy. Leaving is never easy—that's something I know first-hand. But I'm only a flight away, and I'll have a place to come back to since Carly will be taking over the lease on my downtown condo while I'm in the Mediterranean for the next month, and hopefully longer. But that's going to depend on numerous things...

"No. I'm talking to myself. My 'husband'—" I pause to do air quotes around the word "—is not here yet. He's close to an hour late for our introductory date."

She crinkles her nose. "That's not a great way to start a marriage."

I snort at that. "You're right, it's not." Then again, having my brother choose a pretend husband for me, using the Penn Pals dating app he created when he was an undergraduate at Penn State, is no way to start a marriage, either. Not that we'll end up together in matrimonial bliss. Nope. Not happening. This girl is not setting herself up for that kind of disaster. If there's one thing I learned while being tossed around in the system, it's that I'm not a keeper. If I were, I probably wouldn't have lived in ten different foster homes in the span of five years. I just hope I'm compatible with whoever Cason chooses. We'll be living together in close quarters, and it'd be horrible if we didn't at least *like* each other.

"Is that what you're wearing to dinner?" Carly asks, her blue eyes tracking down my body as she cradles her wineglass like it's a treasured heirloom.

My pulse jumps as I glance at the snug black cocktail dress that's been sitting in the back of my closet for a year. I don't even remember the last time I had a need to wear it, but thought it would be perfect for tonight. "Why, what's wrong with it?"

She grins and twirls a strand of her hair around her finger. "Just that you look hot in that little number, and you don't want this guy to fall in love with you, do you?"

"Please," I say. "Tonight's dinner is so we can get to know each other and talk logistics. This arrangement isn't about love. It's about securing a full-time teaching job for me, and for him, it's about getting a big chunk of money for helping me get it."

I pull the tube of bright red lipstick that Londyn gave me from my purse and swipe the creamy, hydrating wax over my lips.

I turn to face Carly, anxiety welling up inside me when I check the clock for the millionth time. "What if he doesn't show? What if he changed his mind?"

"With the amount of money you're paying him, he'd be crazy not to show, and spending time with you…" She pauses to look me over again. "That's no hardship for any man, my friend." She snaps her fingers. "I also think you should exercise your matrimonial rights and get it, gurl."

I chuckle. "It won't be like that, Carly. We won't be having sex." Like I even know what sex is any-more…or ever. My days have been busy teaching at the local elementary school and I've been falling asleep at night while filling out forms for this new job. Truthfully, the last time I had sex was in col-lege, and that fumbling experience left me cold and underwhelmed. I've pretty much blocked it from my mind and have been flying solo since.

There is, however, one thing—one man—I wish I could exorcise from my brain. But no, the kiss I shared with Roman Bianchi, my brother's best friend, still pings around inside my head like a runaway pinball, and that, my friends, is something I wish I could change. I try. Believe me, I try. But when I'm alone in my bed, my body stubbornly aware of how excruciatingly delicious it was to have his lips pressed against mine, a possessive claiming of my mouth that left me shaken and overly stimulated, I can't help but think back… Then he broke it off abruptly and laughed as he walked away. If his goal was to get me to hate him, he succeeded. He also suc-ceeded in ripping my pride to shreds and reminding me I'm not lovable.

Stupid jerk.

"I need to call Cason," I say. "I pray my brother has a backup plan just in case the guy gets cold feet."

"I love that color lipstick on you, by the way," Carly says. "It goes nice with your auburn hair."

I grin. "Londyn gave it to me the night Cason pro-posed to her. She said it has aphrodisiac powers." A snicker full of disbelief rises up in my throat. "I seriously doubt that."

She glances at me over the top of her wineglass. "Hmm…"

"What?"

"You say you don't believe it, yet here you are applying a generous amount to your lips, anyway." Her grin is slow. "I wonder what Freud would say."

Seriously?

Could I subconsciously be hoping it works? Subconsciously hoping to entice my pretend husband, because I'd like to have one good sexual experience in my life?

Nah.

"You're a psychologist." I recap the lipstick, toss it into my purse and fish out my phone. "You think everything is a Freudian slip."

She reaches for the remote. "Probably because it is."

I laugh at that, and just as I'm about to call my brother, someone raps on the door. My heart jumps into my throat and I spin.

"He's here."

Why the heck am I suddenly so nervous? I give myself a once-over in the mirror and smooth my hand over my long auburn curls. Should I have put my hair up? Maybe spent a little more time styling it? God, what am I doing? This isn't a real date. This is just two people who are going to be spending time together, pretending to be married, getting the first meeting out of the way. During our flight tomorrow, we'll have lots of time to work out the kinks… I mean details. Yeah, details. That's what I mean, and *kink* was not a ridiculous Freudian slip. Not at all.

I don't think.

"Are you going to answer the door?" Carly asks, and I take in her grin. I have no idea why she thinks this is anything more than an arrangement. It's not.

I drop my phone back into my purse, and with a big smile on my face, I swing the door open. But as soon as I see the tall figure invading my front stoop, my jaw falls open, all pretense of happiness dissolving as I set eyes on none other than the big stupid jerk himself.

"What…what are you doing here, Roman?" I ask and try to glance around him, to see if my pretend husband is on his way, but his big, dumb body and impressive height fill my doorway and block everything else out—even the gigantic full moon.

"Well, hello to you, too, Peyton."

I take a fast breath, but my lungs are tight, constricted. "Why are you here?" I ask, and hate that I sound like a damn chipmunk jacked up on Red Bull.

His dark gaze moves over my face and slips lower to take in my dress, and goddammit, my traitorous body warms in all the wrong places. This is the man who kissed me and then laughed in my face. Sure, we were at Sebastian and Rylee's wedding, and the champagne had been flowing, but who does something like that? Who stares at me all night, turning my blood to molten lava, then plants the hottest, sexiest kiss on my lips, and walks away laughing?

A stupid jerk, that's who.

I give him a once-over. It's been a year since I set eyes on him, and I'm not sure how it's possible but this updated version of the man I hate is filling me with unwanted images—of him slipping between my thighs and bringing me to orgasm. My sex clenches, an impatient reminder that I crave being touched—properly, just once—and standing before me is a delicious specimen who undoubtedly knows his way around a woman's body.

You hate him, remember?

I shut down my overstimulated imagination and take in the tightness of his jaw, the rigid set of his muscles when he says, "I'm here to take you on a date and get to know you."

I stand there immobilized, my lungs void of air as his words sink into my rattled brain. "Surely to God you're not—"

"Your pretend husband?" He arches a brow. "Yeah, that's me, and I apologize for being late," he says, not looking one bit sorry at all. In fact, he looks completely pissed off, like he doesn't like this situation any more than I do. "There was an issue."

"An issue!" I say, my voice bordering on hysteria. "I'll say there's an issue."

"Well, this just became interesting," Carly mumbles under her breath as she turns the TV off and slips into the other room.

Interesting?

It's anything but interesting. It's a damn disaster. No way am I flying to Malta with Roman Bianchi and pretending to be married to him. I can't stand the man. In fact, I hate everything about him. Except his face. Yeah, I don't really hate that. And his body. That's pretty banging, too. But his tailor-made suit, yeah, I hate that. I just don't hate the way it highlights his broad shoulders and tight muscles, and reminds me my battery-operated boyfriend hasn't been cutting it for some time now.

Good lord, Peyton. Get it together.

I close my eyes tight, hoping when I open them again he'll be gone, his presence nothing but a figment of my imagination, but *nooooo*, when my lids snap open he's still standing there, his gaze latched on mine. I swear to God, in the nanosecond I had my eyes closed, the man grew taller, broader…hotter.

"I take it your brother never told you he asked me."

My gaze narrows on him. "This can't be happening."

I go for my phone again. "I need to call Cason. There must be a mix-up." I shake my head. "Why would he ask you?"

"Because I'm one of his best friends and he's completely overprotective of you," he says, something warm and personal in his voice as he speaks about my brother. "Trust doesn't come easily to Cason and he knows I'd never mess with his kid sister."

His words are combustible, like a spark to tinder, and it fuels the anger in my blood. "I'm a grown woman. I don't need my brother coddling me, and for God's sake I can mess with whoever I want."

"Are you saying you want to sleep with me, Peyton?"

"No," I say quickly, maybe too quickly, judging by the smirk on his face. "I don't even like you."

"Good, because I don't want to sleep with you, either." He scrubs his face, and I catch the flash of anguish in his eyes before he blinks it away. "In fact, I'm done with women," he mumbles under his breath. "Another reason Cason trusts me with you."

My body stiffens, and for one split second, my heart goes out to him, the hate inside me momentarily evaporating, making room for sorrow to fill the void. I might not like him, but that doesn't mean I don't have compassion or care about his well-being. Two years ago, his fiancée up and left weeks before the wedding. My heart squeezes. I can't imagine how awful, how excruciatingly painful, that was for him.

He kissed you, laughed and walked away, Peyton.

Anger flares bright at that brutal reminder, and I turn my focus to my phone. I'm about to punch in Cason's number when Roman's big hand closes over mine to stop me, his touch sending sparks of sensation through my body.

"He asked me to do this, so I'm doing it." He pauses, and I almost flinch at the seriousness in his face when he adds, "I'm not about to let him down."

No, I'm the only Harrison you don't mind letting down.

"We're doing this, Peyton," he says, his voice firm, businesslike.

I hate the tension in my body, the way it comes alive the second he's in the vicinity. My nipples tighten in betrayal, revealing my arousal, and I pray to God he can't see what he's doing to me.

"No, you obviously don't want to do this," I say through clenched teeth. "I'll get someone else." His thumb brushes the inside of my wrist, a gentle sweep that I'm not sure he's aware he's doing. Heated memories of the hungry kiss we shared come back in a sensual rush. As illicit images dance in my mind's eye, the visual caress teases and torments the needy spot between my legs.

"Whether I want to or not is not the point," he responds bluntly.

"I'll call Cason," I say, and squeeze my thighs together in an effort to subdue the heat in my body, but I'd have more luck stopping a runaway train with my pinkie finger. "We'll find someone else through the app. I'm sure there are plenty of other guys willing to help in exchange for cash."

"Maybe so, but Cason won't allow them." His head dips, and while his breath is soft against my face, it's like a tangible caress to my needy cleft. "You know I'm right. I'm all you got, Peyton, and we're doing this."

Anger and desire war with each other as I stare up at the man I hate. My traitorous body remains hot and achy from the way his hand is still holding mine, but I know there's one thing I'll never have to worry about with Roman Bianchi.

Him falling for me.

"Fine then." I snatch my purse from the hallway table. "Let's go to dinner and work out the kinks."

"Kinks?"

His brow arches and I give a fast shake of my head. "Details. I meant to say details."

Fuck my life.

CHAPTER TWO

Roman

"We could have taken Cason's plane," Peyton says, her lips turned down at the corners, a pouty little frown that shouldn't arouse me, yet somehow does. Christ, how she makes that petulant look sexy is beyond me, and don't even get me started on her yoga pants and T-shirt with *Save the Bees* emblazoned across the front. She always was an activist for any kind of wildlife at risk. "It was all fueled up, ready and waiting for us this morning."

"Now why would I tie up Cason's plane when I have a perfectly good plane of my own?" I ask as she drops into the light tan leather bucket seat beside me and crosses her arms in a defensive move. She's either being very protective of herself, or she's trying to hide the way her lovely, lush nipples are poking against her thin, summery T-shirt, compliments of the cold air flowing in from the overhead vent. Or maybe they're hard for a different reason. I'm not sure, but either way my tongue would love to spend some serious time on her body, trying to find out.

Don't go there, Roman.

Jesus, the last thing I should be thinking about is Peyton's gorgeous curves, or how everything about her kept me wide-awake last night, my cock hard and needy as visions of her in my bed—my mouth and hands on her delicate skin, devouring every delectable inch of her—filled my thoughts.

Simply put, she used to be Cason's kid sister. Until she wasn't. Now, well, now she's all grown up, with big green eyes and that mess of curly red hair that drives me mad. It's all I can do not to grab a fistful, tug it until her mouth is poised open and kiss the living hell out of her.

Shit.

She goes quiet as we settle in, making a show of dragging a magazine from her big bag and dropping it on her lap as the plane makes its way down the runway. Her silence is a welcome reprieve. But I won't think, not even for one minute, that she'll be quiet for the whole flight. Last night over dinner, she raked me over the coals, nonstop. Christ, she grilled me on everything, and by the time I dropped her off at her condo, I sported more char marks than the porterhouse steak I'd ordered.

The hum of the engine at full throttle fills the cabin, and the second the plane levels off I settle back with my tablet, ready to do some reading and a bit of work on the long flight ahead of us. I blink at the stream of letters before me yet can't quite seem to focus. I shift and lift my head when I can feel Peyton's laser-sharp glare burning a hole in my forehead. Jesus, if this plane had an emergency eject seat, and she was near the button, I'd be catapulting through space—violently. Not that I blame her for hating me. It's what I need from her.

"What now?" I ask, and set my tablet on my lap, realizing just how tightly it was clenched in my hand. I stretch out my fingers to circulate my blood and brace myself for impact when Peyton uncurls her fingers from her magazine and sets it aside with a calmness that belies the fire in her eyes.

Never one to disappoint, she glares at me and asks, "Why are you doing this, anyway?" Her gaze narrows, like a bird of prey ready to move in for the kill. A burst of icy air from the overhead vent rustles her long curls and does little to cool the heat building inside me.

I pinch the bridge of my nose, desperate to keep this about business. "Would you like a drink?" I ask, needing one, two or maybe even ten before she begins her interrogation again.

"No, well, yes." She flips her palm over, a gesture I've gotten used to over the years. "But I want answers first." Her tenaciousness is something I've gotten used to as well. I can't say that I dislike her determination and conviction. She has a resolve few do and won't stop until she's satisfied.

Shit, don't think about all the ways you can satisfy her, Roman.

Dammit, I'm thinking about it.

"We've been over this, Peyton. I told you last night, numerous times. I'm helping out a friend. My *best* friend. End of story. I'm not sure what else you think this is."

"I know you and Cason go way back, but this... this is going above and beyond friendship, in my book."

"Not in mine."

"All right then," she says, and I prepare for a change in tactics. "But agreeing to this whole charade after..." She arches a brow without elaborating. Not that she needs to. We both know she's talking about the kiss I never should have initiated—then stalked off like a complete asshole afterward. The heated memory burns brightly in my brain and continues to taunt my dick.

I'll never forget that warm summer night in the Hamptons during a friend's wedding. I could have easily taken her upstairs to my hotel room, where we would have done depraved things to each other, things that my best friend never would have forgiven me for. Thank God someone from the wedding party bumped me from behind before we were spotted making out in the corner like a couple hormonal teens, and my one working brain cell kicked some sense back into my balls seconds before I threw her over my shoulder and carried her out of the ballroom—caveman style.

"I'm helping a friend out," I reiterate for the millionth time.

"I mean, I know you're getting paid. It just seems

a bit much," she adds, and pulls a tube of lipstick from her purse. She smacks her lips together and my gaze drops. How the hell am I going to make it through this plane ride when she does things like that? Her innocent sexuality is going to be the death of me. "The air is dry up here," she explains as she removes the cap and rolls out the lipstick.

"Yeah, dry," I agree. "And it's not about the money," I say. The truth is, I'm not getting paid— I'm a goddamn millionaire and don't need her or her brother's money—but it's best I let her believe I'm getting compensated. She can't wrap her brain around me doing this favor for Cason as it is.

Is this really all about Cason?

Hell yeah, it is. It has to be. I can't be doing this because I want to spend time with her. I'm not a goddamn masochist.

"I expected some unemployed college student desperate for money, not a…a grown man, who's practically Italian royalty at that, with a steady career." Her lips part and thin, as she layers the creamy pigment over her luscious mouth, and I swallow the groan of want threatening to crawl out of my throat. "Can you see why this confuses me, Roman?"

Sweet mother of God. After last night, I was hoping I'd never see that fuck-me-red color on her lips again.

Do not think about her luscious painted lips parting for your cock, dude.

Dammit, I'm thinking about it.

My dick stands up, clamoring for a front-row seat

as that welcome—or rather unwelcome—image plays out in my mind's eye. Yeah, no, it's welcome.

I swallow, and shift to hide my erection. "He's just always been there for me, okay?"

I went to Penn State to get away from my overbearing Italian family. New to America, and a fresh-faced kid on campus, the change of scenery was all a bit intimidating. Cason was there though, my friend, my roommate, the guy who took me under his wing and brought me into his tribe. A guy who'd been kicked around his entire life, he knew firsthand what it was like to be excluded and made sure every damn newbie felt wanted. After college, I chose to live in New York and took the position of head web developer when Cason created Hard Wear—an on-line clothing business that caters to men.

"My family is in Sicily, remember?" I say, playing the ace that had been in my pocket.

"Yeah, I know."

"Malta is just a short ferry ride away, and this is a way for me to go visit them. I haven't been home since—"

My insides go cold as I let my words fall off, but she gets it. I haven't been home since my ex up and left weeks before my wedding. It's been two years, and my sisters still call to check on me—far too much. I tell them I'm fine, and I am, yet they remain intrusive, overbearing, and are always butting into my life—which is why I'm better off in New York where they can't stalk me on a daily basis.

I love them. I truly do, but I'm a grown man who

can make his own decisions. I scoff at that. I'm not even sure getting engaged had been my idea to begin with. One day I'm dating and the next there was talk of a wedding, and I'm pretty sure it was my mother who put Grandmother's ring on my ex's finger—not that it stayed there for any length of time.

"Roman, I'm sorry," she says, her voice thick and sincere. "I don't think I ever told you that." She reaches out and puts her hand on my knee. Her touch sizzles through my body and caresses my cock. I glance down, and suddenly, as if she just realized she was touching me, she snatches her hand back like I might have just given her leprosy. She links her fingers together on her lap.

"Thank you," I say, a canned response even though I do appreciate her words. "It's fine." Her brows lift, her expression dubious, but the truth is, it's not like my ex broke my heart. When she refused to sign the prenup, it confirmed my suspicions. The women in my life want my name and my money; they don't necessarily want me.

"You'll be visiting them?" she asks.

"Yeah," I fib. Hell, I haven't even told them I'm going to Malta. They'd invade our villa within minutes, before we could even unpack. They'd shower Peyton with love, hugs and kisses, and completely smother us both. "But my main reason for this is to help you get the position. I won't let anything interfere with that."

She gives a slow shake of her head. "I'm just not sure you can pull this off," she says, like she's still looking for a way out of this insane arrangement her brother cooked up.

"I can pull it off," I say.

She crinkles up her nose, scrunching the cluster of freckles that have been holding me captive since she grew into a beautiful woman. "You literally just flinched when I touched you."

I give a casual shrug. "You took me by surprise."

"What if I touch you in public? If you react like that people will know we're pretending. We have to present a happy, loving couple." She pushes back into her seat and lets loose a frustrated sigh. Her head falls back, her eyes unfocused on the overhead lighting. "They say the marriage restriction in hiring single female teachers has been lifted, but behind the scenes it's still practiced." The frustration in her voice is palpable and wraps around my chest like a tight belt. "They won't hire an unwed woman, Roman," she adds, her frown deepening.

I lean toward her, my stomach on fire at the unfairness in the world. She wants this job, and goddammit I'll help her burst through that glass ceiling and do whatever it takes for her to get it. No one, and I mean no one, deserves to have their dreams realized more than this woman does.

"That's not fair," I say, my tone just dark enough to have her gaze flying to mine. What, is she surprised that I agree with her?

"You're right. It's not."

"You should get the job on your own merit," I say. "You're smart, one of the smartest women I know.

You're dedicated, and kind, and let me tell you, I've never met any woman wanting to give back to a society that was so cruel to her. If they can't see your value, that's on them." She goes quiet, so quiet worry weaves its way through my body. Shit, maybe I shouldn't have been so blunt when reminding her of her past. "Peyton?"

She blinks, the sound of her swallowing breaking the silence. "Thank you."

I wave my finger back and forth between the two of us. "As for you touching me and me not flinching, I guess we'll have to practice," I say.

"Are you suggesting…" Mimicking my motion, she waves her hand back and forth, her words falling off as her dark lashes fall slowly over alarmed eyes.

"What I'm saying is we'll have to figure out a way not to react when touching each other." Not going to happen. "What did you think I was saying?"

"That." She nods. "That's what I thought you were suggesting. How do we go about that?"

"I'm not sure."

"We'd better figure it out, don't you think? To-morrow we'll be meeting my boss and the other teachers and the person I'm in competition with for the full-time position."

As she rambles, I study her mouth. The woman is sweet and sexy and so goddamn lush, but her never-ending questions and underlying accusations make me want to tie her up and busy her mouth in many other ways. Dirty ways. Delicious ways. Ways that would undoubtedly shock this sweet, young girl and have her pleading for mercy.

Seriously, you wouldn't believe what I'd do, the lengths I'd go to, to see those lush red lips parted, begging me for…anything. It's almost frightening and I have to fight it down with every fiber of my being. I redirect my thoughts to get my damn erection under control. Once my dick is marshalled into submission, I stand and reach over her head.

She flinches and presses herself into the leather seat. "What are you doing?" she asks. But holy Jesus I don't miss the breathlessness in her voice or the way her skin flushed from my closeness. Yeah, okay, it's true, the pull between us is insane, like so far off the charts, it's a nuclear explosion waiting to happen.

But it's not going to happen.

Cason didn't just take me under his wing in college. He's my best friend, the guy who had my back all through college, the guy who took a chance and hired me for a crucial position in his fledgling company and he was there to pick up the pieces when I finally faced the fact that women don't want me for me, they want to marry into my family. Honesty is important and my ex's betrayal gutted me.

Hypocrite much?

Okay, yeah, it's true. I screwed up with Peyton last summer. I can blame it on the romantic atmosphere, the consumption of champagne, and if I try really hard, I can blame it on heartbreak. But the simple truth is this: I wanted Peyton. I wanted her like a drowning man wants a life raft, a thirsty man wants a drink, peanut butter wants jelly.

Yeah. It's bad.

It's really bad.

And now? Well, and now I have to spend the next few weeks in Malta pretending to be her husband, and not exercise any of the rights that go with that.

I adjust the overhead vent. "I'm turning the air off. You're shivering."

"Oh, thanks."

Back in my seat, my gaze seeks out hers and I say, "Seems you need to work on not reacting, too."

"What are you talking about?"

"You damn near jumped out of your shoes when you thought I was about to touch you, Peyton."

Her green eyes are stormy, like the warm Mediterranean Sea stirred up during a squall. "You took me by surprise is all," she says, throwing my words back at me. But we're both smart enough to know what's going on here.

I grin. "Yeah, okay."

"You say that like you don't believe me," she shoots back, and weariness fills my bones. I'm done bickering and answering questions. I reach into my pocket and pull out a small velvet box. Her eyes widen and her hand goes to her chest.

"What…what is that?"

I open the box and present a ring. She gasps, her startled gaze flying to mine. "Roman?"

"This is why I was late last night. I was having issues getting this from my safety deposit box. There was some kind of mix-up."

She shakes her head. "I don't understand."

"What's not to understand? If we're going to pretend we're married, we have to cover all bases. Presenting you with my grandmother's ring is the first base."

Don't think of first base, Roman.

I'm thinking of first base.

My gaze drops, my mind back on her lush breasts. "I don't know what to say."

"Say yes," I respond with a grin, wanting to lighten things up a bit. She frowns, and I don't miss the way she inches back. "What?"

"I don't want to wear your grandmother's ring."

I nod, a measure of disappointment gathering in my gut. For some reason, I thought Peyton might have reacted differently than my ex, that she'd respect and appreciate tradition. "It's a family custom... I just thought." She closes her hand over mine just as I'm about to snap the box shut.

"You don't understand, Roman. It's weird for me to wear the ring you gave your ex. I don't feel right about it."

My throat thickens and I give a humorless laugh. "It wasn't on her finger very long, Peyton. She said it was old and not her style. She wanted something newer, something shinier."

Her eyes widen. "Was she out of her mind?"

I actually think I was the one who was out of his mind for getting swept up in the proposal, for allowing my family to make decisions for me. I'll never allow that to happen again.

I take the ring from the box and hold it out to her. She lets me slip it on her finger, and for the briefest of seconds this feels all too real. I'd be wise to remember it's not, and she's completely off-limits.

"I'm committed to this, Peyton. You *will* be teaching children English," I say. "The full-time position is as good as yours. I promise, and I never break my promises."

"No, you just go around breaking hearts," she mumbles so low under her breath I'm not sure I heard her correctly.

"What?"

She nibbles on her bottom lip and after a few false starts she finally says, "We never did talk about that night, Roman."

My insides go dark as I push back into my seat. "Nothing to talk about. It was a mistake. I had too much to drink," I lie. I don't want to be a prick. I don't want to hurt her—again. But I can't tell her I'd lost all control of myself and was sure if I didn't have a taste of her, right that very second, I'd combust. I don't want to lead her on or let her think there could be more between us. I never want to let Cason down, and I broke the bro code once. I'm not about to lose my control and do it again. Nothing short of a brain tumor stealing my ability to think with clarity could make me kiss her a second time.

"Now what was that you said last night about us working the kinks out?"

Ah, shit, now why the hell did I say that?

"Details," she says quickly. "We need to work out the details."

"Isn't that what I said?" I ask to cover my slip, because no way, no damn way on the face of this earth am I going to think about Peyton and kink in the same sentence ever again.

Goddammit, I'm thinking about it.

"No," she says quietly, breathlessly, heat coloring her cheeks. "It's not what you said."

"It's what I meant to say." I push from my seat. "Now how about that drink?"

Unless, of course, she does want to talk about kink.

CHAPTER THREE

Peyton

I WAKE TO find a set of intense brown eyes watching me carefully. I stiffen and blink, glancing around as memories infiltrate my brain, and that's when I realize I'm on Roman's plane and we've just landed in Malta. Excitement wells up inside me as I reach for my phone and check the time. It's nearing midnight local time, six hours later than New York.

"Did you get any sleep?" I ask Roman as he finger-combs his dark hair, not that any of it is out of place. No, Roman Bianchi is always put together, and as I look at him, I wonder what it would take to rattle the man and shatter his hard-earned control.

"Just a bit." He shoves his tablet into his leather briefcase and smooths his hands over his button-down shirt and dress pants. "It was hard with all your snoring, though."

What the hell? I stare at him. My God, his delivery was so deadpan, I almost think he's telling the truth, either that or the long trip gave him a sense of humor. I open my mouth to come back with some smart-ass comment when the door to the cockpit opens. I turn to find two men stretching their limbs as they step into the cabin.

"Roman," the pilot says, his gaze sliding to me. He gives a curt nod. "I hope you enjoyed the flight."

"It was a great flight, thank you," I say.

Roman steps up to address the two men and I turn my attention to my belongings. I shove my magazine into my bag, and the ring on my left finger sparkles beneath the overhead lighting. I stand up straight, my heart jumping a little bit as I take a moment to admire the gorgeous diamond and gold band.

How could his ex-fiancée not want to wear something so precious? I can't blame Roman for being off women after getting his heart broken. Something twists deep inside me. That had to have been a horrible experience for him and I profoundly hate that he's resigned himself to the idea of spending his life alone. Then again, who am I to judge?

I flinch as Roman slides his big hand around my back, his warm scent filling my senses. Yeah, it's true. I'm really going to have to work on my reactions and figure out a way to *not* like his touch so much.

"All set?" he asks, his voice low and groggy... sleepy and sexy.

"I'm ready." I frown and reach into my purse. "I have the name of a cab company here. I'm supposed to call when we land."

He snatches his briefcase from the floor. "It's been taken care of."

"You arranged a cab?"

With his hand on the small of my back again—jeez, I wish I didn't really like that so much—he guides me to the door. "Something like that."

"Well, you either did or you didn't, Roman."

"You know, it was so peaceful when you were sleeping." I open my mouth, ready to tell him where he can shove his peace, but he smirks and adds, "Until you started snoring, of course."

Hell, who is this man? I'm not sure, but I have to say, I love this unusual playful side of him. Although I'm not about to tell him that.

"I do not snore," I mumble, hiding a smile, the warm night air falling over me as I begin my descent down the metal staircase. Our luggage is delivered to us from the baggage compartment, and Roman picks up both suitcases. I packed pretty light, assuming I'd pick up a few local dresses and accessories. I want to fit into the community as much as I can.

He leads me inside the airport, which is much bigger than I envisioned but fairly quiet this time of night. We move through customs and less than an hour later, we're standing on the sidewalk and I'm searching for our cab when a stretch limo pulls up in front of us.

Roman opens the back door as the driver greets us and sets our luggage in the trunk. "Nice car," I say, as I slide in. "A taxi would have done just fine."

He takes an exaggerated breath and lets it out

slowly as he slides in beside me. "Elias is our driver for the next month," he explains. "Anywhere you need to go, he'll take you."

I blink once, then twice, my sleeping brain taking a minute to understand. "I don't need a driver, Roman," I say, and take in his strong profile as he buckles himself into his seat. The driver, or rather, Elias catches my eye in the rearview mirror and gives me a smile before he pulls onto the road. I lean forward to give him the address to the small villa I rented. Roman touches my arm to stop me.

"What?" I ask.

"He knows where we're going."

"How could he? I never told him. I never even told you."

"He knows where we're going, Peyton."

My gaze goes from Roman, to Elias, back to Roman. "Wait, what's going on?"

He settles in his seat and stretches out his long legs. "I've made other arrangements for us."

"You can't do that."

"It's already done."

I glare at him, but he turns and glances out the window.

"You're a bully, Roman."

"Call me whatever you want." All business, like he's sitting in a boardroom, assigning orders to his staff, he reaches for a water bottle, uncaps it and hands it to me. "Your brother asked me to look out for you, and that's what I plan to do. He told me where you booked, and I didn't like the area, so I found us something more suitable, and it's closer to your work."

I take a long pull from the bottle and hand it back. "I can take care of myself." I lick a bead of water from my bottom lip. "I'm not a child."

He inhales sharply and tears his gaze away from my mouth. "Oh, I know. Believe me, I know." He tips the bottle to his lips and I watch his Adam's apple bob as he finishes it.

"What's that supposed to mean?" I ask.

He shakes his head. "Nothing."

"It's not nothing, Roman. You said it, so it's something."

"Can we just drive to the villa in peace, Peyton? I'm exhausted."

"No, I want to know what you meant, and I don't snore, I—"

"We're on the same page here, Peyton. A team." His gaze drops to mine, focuses on my mouth again, when he asks, "Do you have to question everything I do?"

"When it comes to you, I—"

Before I realize what's happening, he cups my chin, drags me closer, and presses his lips to mine. Sweet baby Jesus. My protest dies a sudden death on my tongue, and as much as I hate this man, I sink into his kiss as it stirs a need inside me. His warm lips move over mine, commanding, possessive, unwavering and…antagonistic. Nevertheless, I moan into his mouth, my hand gripping the front of his dress shirt. He breaks the kiss and I just sit there, perfectly still, my mouth still poised open. He inches back and cold air moves in between us, snapping some sense back into me.

I swipe my mouth with the back of my hand, his alluring taste lingering as I glare at him. "Why did you do that?"

"Did you hate it?" My mind doesn't seem to want to work as his deep voice trickles through me, caressing all the parts he stirred awake with that fierce kiss. "Well, did you?"

He can't for one minute think I hated it. Not after the way I moaned. "Yes," I state flatly, and lift my chin a notch.

"Good, then every time you start yelling at me, or argue or give me a hard time, I'm going to kiss you."

"Like hell you—" He gives me a warning glare and my mouth slams shut. Although, and I hate to admit it, there is a part of me that wants to be defiant, just to push his buttons…just to get him to kiss me again.

Stupid jerk.

"I hate you," I mumble under my breath, sounding like a ridiculous, petulant child.

"Good."

Good?

Really?

He wants me to hate him?

"I wasn't yelling," I mumble. It's true, I wasn't, but I can't deny that I was beginning to annoy myself with all the questions.

We drive in silence, the heated tension between

us enough to fog the window. After a short drive, we pull up in front of a building and I peer out at it. The place is pitch-black, and I can't see much other than it has two stories and a rooftop.

"This is it?" I ask.

"Yes, let's get settled. It's been a long day."

I had very little sleep on the plane, most of it interrupted with unsolicited dreams of the man beside me, but as I take in the place, a new kind of energy sizzles through me. I doubt I'll fall asleep tonight, but that's not unusual. I wrap my arms around my body as I climb from the car, and Elias retrieves our luggage. Roman speaks to him for a moment and we head toward our villa.

"Where exactly are we?" I ask in a low voice, not wanting to wake anyone in the neighborhood.

"We're in Upper Gardens. It's a quiet community in St. Julian's, and very close to all amenities."

"How far are we from the school?"

"Walking distance," he says, his voice low, matching mine. He punches in a code to the door and pushes it open.

The night air is warm, but my body is chilled. It's always chilled, even more so when I'm in new situations or going on little to no sleep. I remember as a child lying wide-awake in bed for hours on end, my body arctic cold as I waited for the knock on the door to come—it always came—telling me it was time to go to a different foster home. I step closer to Roman and try to absorb his body warmth, but the cold remains.

"If the school is walking distance, why do I need a driver at my disposal?" I ask.

He mumbles something about me talking too much under his breath and I'm about to ask even more questions when he flicks on the lights and my words fall off. I glance around the spacious villa, beautifully decorated in black, chrome and white. The kitchen is sleek and modern, the living area lush and inviting. All the clean lines of its open concept give it an airy feel, and I like it. A lot.

I drop my purse and Roman stands at the door as I enter the place, taking it all in. I check the fridge and cupboards to find them fully stocked. After cataloging the main level, I hurry up the stairs to find two gorgeous bedrooms, floor-to-ceiling windows giving a clear view of the water, and a lovely contemporary shared bathroom in between the rooms. The place is absolutely breathtaking—and completely out of my budget.

I hurry back downstairs and find Roman locking up behind us. "Not so fast," I say. "We can't stay."

He turns to face me, and his eyes are half-lidded, tired from the long day. "You don't like it?"

"Of course I like it. What's not to like?"

"Then what's the problem?"

I raise a brow and give him a look that suggests he's dense. "Roman, I'm a teacher. I can't afford this kind of luxury." My brother might be a multimillionaire, but that doesn't mean I don't pay my own way in life. I pride myself on my financial independence. Cason put me through college but I insisted on working part-time to provide for incidentals, even though he didn't want me to.

"It's covered, Peyton," he says flatly.

"Why would you do this?" He hesitates, like he's not sure how to answer. A second later he closes his hand over mine. His touch is so soft, so achingly tender, my stomach takes flight. His eyes narrow.

"You're still cold," he states.

I pull my hand away. "I'm fine." He angles his head like he doesn't believe me, but I don't give him the chance to say anything. "I can't believe you rented this place without even asking me, and had it stocked full of supplies."

"I just wanted you in a safe place, close to your school, and the kitchen is stocked because we need to eat."

"Roman, I—"

He captures my hand and when he pulls me close, my body meshing with his, I can't for the life of me remember what it was I was going to say. His head dips and I hold my breath. Is he going to kiss me again?

Do I want that?

Oh God, I do.

"Before you say another word," he begins, his voice an octave lower, "come with me."

Giving me little choice in the matter, he ushers me up the stairs. We don't stop on the bedroom level. Instead we go up another set of stairs and he pushes open a heavy door. It takes me a second to realize we're now outside.

"Oh my God," I say when I see the breathtaking view from the rooftop. It's even better than from the second-floor bedroom. I turn and take in the long stretch of pool and crisp white outdoor furniture, shadowed beneath a pergola. I breathe in as the warm wind blows by, carrying the fresh scent of flowers with it. "It's gorgeous."

"I thought you might like the view."

"You mean you thought it might shut me up," I say, but I'm losing the will to fight. This is all too much for me, but it was incredibly sweet of him.

"Peyton," he says, and spins me around until I'm facing him, our bodies flush. He rubs his hands up and down my arms to warm me. Awareness flitters through me, and I can't seem to ignore it. "Maybe this isn't about you," he says. "Maybe it's about me. Maybe I just wanted to stay somewhere nice, something that suits my needs and lifestyle more."

He's selling it, but I'm not buying. I don't for one second believe this is about him. He might be a man used to luxuries, but everything in me, every ounce of women's intuition I possess, says he picked this place for *me* because *I'd* like it—and that confuses the hell out of me. One minute he's kissing me and laughing in my face, the next he's flying me here on his Learjet, putting a gorgeous ring on my finger and swearing he'll do whatever it takes to help me get this job.

This isn't about you, Peyton.

It's about my brother and their bond, and I'd be wise to remember that. Air leaves my lungs in a hiss, much like a leaky balloon deflating. What? Did I want this to be about me? No, I don't even like this guy.

"It's not a big deal, okay?" he says, but it's kind of a big deal for me.

"I don't want you to pay my way, Roman." The truth is, while I appreciate him wanting me to live in comfort—because he has some obligation to my brother—I don't want to rely on anyone. Outside of my brother, I can't ever let myself get used to someone else caring for me. Self-preservation has taught me to rely only on my small family of two. I just can't set myself up for that kind of heartache. I don't think I could survive being chewed up and spit out again—especially not by this man.

His head dips and those dark eyes of his narrow on me. His smile is slow and sincere. My stomach tightens as the hardness in his dark eyes melts, reminding me of a steaming mug of hot chocolate on a cold winter's night—the kind of warmth that comes close to thawing the chill in my bones, but never quite succeeds.

"Okay," he says. "You can pay me back."

I nod and my tightly strung muscles relax, slightly. "Good."

"Can we go to bed now?"

CHAPTER FOUR

Roman

PEYTON'S GREEN EYES widen at my slip and I quickly backtrack. "I mean, we should get some sleep. It's been a long day. Tomorrow will be busy for you. You have to meet the children, the teachers and the school's principal, and we need to be ready to make a good impression." *Okay, Roman, you can stop rambling any time now, and while you're at it stop picturing Peyton naked.*

"True," she says, and pushes her hair from her face to expose the pink flush on her cheeks. "Sleep is a good idea. Which room do you want?" she asks as we head inside. She starts down the narrow stairs and I follow behind.

"Why don't you take the master suite," I say, the room I normally take when I come to Malta to unwind. If I told her I owned this place, that my family owns many villas on Malta, it might set off another argument, and I'd have to quiet her with a kiss, which can't happen again. Her brother is my best friend.

That doesn't stop my dick from hardening at the thought of kissing her a second time today. "I'm fine in the smaller room."

She nods and glances at me over her shoulder, her jaw set, a stubbornness about her. "I do plan to pay you back, Roman."

I smile, liking that about her. Not her stubborn streak—that's just plain annoying—but I like that she's a girl who wants to pay her own way through life, even when she doesn't have to. She's always refusing her brother's financial help, and this is my villa—already bought and paid for.

"I know you do," I say quietly.

"I just…it might take a while."

"Or we could find another form of payment," I say, and when she reaches the landing her gaze flies to mine. No doubt she's thinking I'm talking sexual favors here. I'm not. I want her to want me regardless of what I do for her. Wait, no, I don't want her to want me. What am I thinking?

Dammit.

"Such as?"

"You could cook for me." I rub my stomach as I remember Cason's amazing seafood pasta. "If you cook anything like your brother, then that's all the payment I need."

"I'm a good cook," she says, and folds her arms across her body, a small quiver going through her. I make a mental note to adjust the air-conditioning. "I actually enjoy being in the kitchen."

"I hate it."

She glances down and a small smile touches her lips, like she's remembering happier times. "Cason and I did a lot of cooking together." She chuckles lightly. "I used to wear swimming goggles when I cut up onions. That always cracked him up."

I laugh. "Really?"

"Yeah." She rolls her eyes. "I was a weirdo. You don't have to say it."

"Nah, not a weirdo. That's genius-level intellect, my friend."

She chuckles and it curls around me, warms my soul. I like seeing her smile. I'd love to see her do it more often, but the world has not given this sweet girl much to smile about over the years.

She puts her hand on me and gives me a little shove. "You don't have to be a smart-ass."

"I'm serious, and you're the smart-ass, not me." I join her on the landing and throw an arm around her shoulders, nudging her chin with my fist. "No, I'm the one who's older and wiser, so you're going to have to trust me on that."

Her body tightens beneath my arm, and that's when I realize just how close I've pulled her, just how nicely her body fits with mine.

"I… I don't really trust too many people, Roman," she admits, a heaviness overtaking her as her eyes narrow, and I could kick myself. I didn't mean to dredge up demons from her past.

I give her a comforting squeeze before I pull my arm back. "I know. I don't either," I say, not wanting her to feel alone in this. "Not anymore, anyway."

She shakes her head, a bit of the tightness in her muscles gone. "I guess that's one thing we have in common."

"What a pair we make. You'll cook for me, then?"

She waves one hand around the long hallway. "You're here in Malta, away from your work, your friends and your beloved New York, helping me get a job. Cooking is the least I could do, don't you think?"

"It's a nice break from reality for a while and for the record, none of this is a hardship, Peyton." Nope, not a hardship at all. But that's not to say it's not *hard*, and when I say hard, I'm talking about my dick, of course.

She laughs. "Funny, Carly said something like that to me yesterday. She also told me I should be exercising my marital rights, pretend marriage or not." As soon as the words leave her mouth, her eyes widen. "I didn't mean… I wasn't suggesting we should do that." She gives a fast shake of her head. "That was before I even knew it was you, anyway."

"You mean you considered it before you knew it was me."

"No," she blurts out, a little too quickly. With the tip of her finger she pokes my chest and I wish to God she'd stop touching me. "Now that I do know, that's not happening. Ever."

"Yeah, we're not going to do that," I agree. I'm only going to think about doing it, repeatedly, while using my hand.

She exhales, and that's when I realize how weary

she looks. She pushes her hair from her face. "I don't even know why I said it."

"You're tired," I say, giving her an out.

"You're right. So why do you hate cooking?" she asks, redirecting the conversation. "You're Italian. Aren't all Italians supposed to be great cooks? Or is that a cliché?"

I laugh. "I grew up with five older sisters, Peyton. I couldn't get near the kitchen. Not that I wanted to. I was busy with sports anyway."

She nods, and a small, little-girl-lost smile touches her mouth. "That must have been so nice, Roman. I love my brother, dearly, but I always kind of wanted a sister, too. There was this one place…" Her voice falls off and a deep sadness invades her eyes. My gut twists, and it's all I can do not to pull her into my arms. She shakes herself out of her reverie and says, "Anyway, all those sisters. It must have been awesome."

"Are you kidding me?" I ask as she inches toward the bigger bedroom, stopping outside the door. "I had to set my alarm for three in the morning just to get some bathroom time."

She laughs. A sweet melodic sound that strokes my dick. "That does sound horrible," she says.

"Don't even get me started on the makeup and hair products. Everywhere, Peyton. Everywhere. In my cereal, on my soap, on my clothes. Do you have any idea how many girls accused me of cheating on them?"

Her brow arches playfully. "A lot, huh?"

"Well, I wouldn't say a lot." I grin. "A few, maybe."

She lifts herself up to her full height and squares her shoulders. "Well, you'll be happy to know, I'm not high-maintenance. I promise no hair on your soap, in your cereal or on your clothes."

What about in my bed?

Nope. Nope. Don't go there.

Before I can think better of it, I reach out and run a long strand of her silky soft hair through my fingers. My knuckles brush her cheek, and her chest rises with her fast intake of breath. "It's okay, I've gotten used to it over the years." I laugh as I think about that. "I think you'd really like my sisters."

"Really?"

I nod. "Yeah, you're kind of annoying like they are." Her mouth drops open and she whacks my chest. I snatch her hand before she can pull it back. "Kidding," I say, and brush my thumb over her wrist.

She shakes her head. "I do talk a lot sometimes, I know," she says.

"I don't hate it, Peyton." My gaze drops to her mouth. Damn, so sweet and succulent, it's all I can do not to dip my head for another taste while I think about sinking myself inside her. Kissing her in the limo was a bad idea. I have no idea what came over me. Maybe I should get checked for a brain tumor. I swore to God, I was never, ever going to put my mouth on her again. Yeah, I can blame it on her incessant chatter, but I think it had more to do with watching her sleep, hearing her soft breathing sounds and even softer murmurs. The type of noises I'd imagine she'd make between the sheets—while I was on top of her. "Not like you hated that kiss," I taunt.

Her lips pucker, like she'd just eaten something sour. "Yeah, I really hated that."

"Do you hate a lot of things?" I tease. "Besides me, I mean?"

"No, I reserve most of it for you," she jokes in return, a sly little grin on her face.

"I figured." I let my hand fall. "I guess I should let you get to sleep." I'm about to leave when her hand on my arm stops me.

"Roman."

I swallow as the softness in her voice seeps through me and zaps my balls. "Yeah."

"Your sisters." She leans against the wall, like she's not in a hurry to end our banter. "They're all older?"

I pause, and take in her big green eyes. She knows they are. I told her they were. Just a minute ago, and on the plane when we were going over the logistics of our fake marriage. She blinks up at me, and my gut tightens as realization dawns. She wants to talk, wants to hear more about my big family because she never had one of her own.

"Yeah, they're all older," I say quietly. She nods and smiles. "Do you...want a family?" I ask, even though Cason told me his sister was anti-marriage.

Her soft smile falls and she looks at me like I must be an idiot. It's one of the nicer looks she's given me tonight. "Hell no. I never plan on getting married, Roman."

"Another thing we have in common," I tell her.

"I guess so." Her eyes narrow and she looks past my shoulders, like her thoughts are a million miles away. "I learned early on that I'm no Cinderella and Prince Charming doesn't exist," she says, like all life's curveballs haven't bothered her at all. Maybe they haven't—and maybe I was born yesterday. One thing is for certain, she's a fighter, a woman who goes after what she wants. That's damn admirable if you ask me.

"Your sisters," she says, bringing the conversation back to me.

"You'd really like them, Peyton."

"I bet I would."

I wince as I think about that. "Not that you're ever going to meet them."

The light in her eyes fades and her smile tumbles. My heart follows suit. Shit, I keep saying the wrong things tonight.

"No, of course not," she says. "I wasn't suggesting… I didn't think."

"It's just that—"

"No. I don't want to meet them," she says quickly, and I study her face, not sure I believe her. "We're just here pretending. No need for me to meet them and give them the wrong idea."

"Peyton, if they got wind of us—"

"Yeah, right, I get it." She waves her hand. "Anyway, it's late. We better get some sleep." She steps into her bedroom, effectively cutting off my explanation. "Oh, wait, my suitcase."

"I'll grab it," I say, my pulse pounding against my throat as I make my way down the stairs. She might be hell-bent on remaining unattached, but if anyone needs a family it's her. No way can I let my sisters think I'm married, though. I can't even imagine what they'd do. Yeah, maybe I can imagine. All five of them would invade the villa and all their interfering wouldn't be good for Peyton or her job. Christ, we'd probably end up married for real, before either of us realized it, and neither one of us wants that.

I double-check the lock on the door, grab our bags and head back upstairs. I rap quietly on her door, and when I hear the water running in the bathroom that adjoins our rooms, I open her bedroom door and set her bag inside. With sleep pulling at me, I head to the other room and stretch out my tight muscles.

I unbutton my shirt and toss it onto a chair. As I walk to the window to take in the view, I tug my zipper down and kick off my pants. The bed calls to me, but a swim on the rooftop pool might be a great way to stretch my tight muscles. The shower shuts off and a few minutes later, footsteps on the floor reach my ears.

Dressed in my boxers that can easily double as a bathing trunk, I quietly leave the room and pad softly to the rooftop. I walk to the deep end of the pool and dive in; the water is cold and refreshing against my hot skin, but does little to snuff the heat deep inside me. I honestly don't know how I'm going to be around my best friend's kid sister and keep my hands to myself. Shit, I never should have kissed her.

It won't happen again. Cason's trust is too important to me. I spend the next fifteen minutes gliding through the pool, working to exhaust my mind so I'll be able to shut down and get some sleep.

I resurface in the shallow end, wipe my hand over my face and jerk back when I spot a figure standing at the pool's edge. "Shit," I say, my gaze lifting higher to see that it's Peyton.

"Sorry," she says, and even though I don't want to—yeah, okay, maybe I do—I let my gaze roam over her, taking pleasure in the tiny pair of sleep shorts that showcase her long sleek legs, and tank top that does little to hide her lush breasts. If she moved just right, I'd get a lovely view of her nipple. Good God, am I fourteen? My dick is sure acting like it as it twitches and urges me to go for it. I sink lower into the water. She folds her arms over her body and hugs herself, cutting off my exploration.

"I wasn't expecting anyone to be standing there," I say.

"I knocked on your bedroom door and you didn't answer. I heard a noise up here and figured I'd find you."

"You found me."

She scrunches her face up, her body wound tight, and I know her well enough to recognize when she's unsure about something. She has a lot of tells, much like her brother. Unease worms its way through me as she shifts from one foot to the other.

I narrow my gaze. "What's wrong?"

"I just...this is going to sound ridiculous." She

backs up a bit and drops her arms, a cascade of auburn hair falling over her breasts as she glances down.

"Hey, what is it?" I ask, and as my arousal morphs into worry, I step from the pool. Water drips from my body and puddles at my feet as her gaze drops to take in my near nakedness.

"Wow," she says under her breath, and damn, the fact that she likes what she sees isn't helping my hands-off situation at all. Tonight, however, under the covers, it's going to be all hand on dick.

"Peyton," I say, and her head lifts, a dazed look in her eyes. "What's wrong?"

She swallows, briefly closes her eyes, and when she opens them again she stares uncomfortably at the majestic view in the distance. "I just wanted to ask you if it was okay if I left the bathroom light on, and the door leading to my bedroom cracked. It's an adjoining bathroom, so I wanted to make sure you were okay with that." Her look is almost sheepish when she adds, "It's a strange place and all, and if I have to get up in the middle of the night…" Her words fall off and my stomach sinks. This isn't about strange places and needing to go to the bathroom at night. It's about Peyton not liking the dark. Sweet little Peyton who was tossed around in the system, oftentimes getting separated from her brother, is afraid of the dark, and that's so sad. My heart squeezes so tight I could damn near sob. Goddamn I hate how cruel the world was to her. I hate how cruel I was to her, but I need her to hate me.

"I don't mind at all," I say around a lump in my throat.

"Okay, thanks."

She stands there for a moment. "You should put a shirt on. You look cold. Pants, too." I follow her eyes down to see the bulge my boxers are doing a piss-poor job of hiding.

"I'm fine," I say, even though I'm far from it. "You're the one who's always cold."

She glances around and I stare at her ass when she walks up to a cabinet beneath the pergola and opens it. She goes up on her toes, stretching out her long, sexy legs, and visions of me taking her from behind hit like a punch and nearly knock the wind out of me.

"Jackpot," she says, and pulls out a big white towel. "At least wrap yourself in this before you freeze to death."

"I'm not cold," I say again.

Ignoring me, she shakes it out and our hands touch as she tries to throw it over my shoulders. Warmth, need and lust hit at the same time, and a growl crawls out of my throat as I envision my hands on her body, removing those sexy shorts and burying my mouth between her soft thighs.

"Shit," I murmur under my breath, and put the towel around her quivering shoulders instead. I tug her to me, offering the warmth of my body and anything else she might like.

Get it together, dude.

"Roman," she says as she swipes her tongue over her bottom lip. "What…what are you doing?"

My head dips, my lips inches from hers. I want to kiss her. Jesus, there are a lot of things I want to do with her. I breathe her in, let her sweet, flowery aroma feed the hunger building inside me.

"I'm not the one who is cold and wet," she says with a huff.

Oh God, Roman. Don't think about her being wet.

"You need to put the towel around you, not me," she continues.

"Peyton," I growl as she tries to shrug the towel off.

"What?"

"Leave it."

"Leave what?"

"Just…stop, okay," I say, my voice thick with lust.

"Stop what?"

"Stop talking," I say, the push and pull between us arousing me more. "You know what will happen if you don't."

"I am not going to stop—" Her protest dies on her lips and my words slowly register in her brain. Yeah, that's right, Peyton, you either shut up or I'll shut you up.

"Roman," she murmurs, her gaze moving over my face. A beat passes between us, and then a change comes over her. Her body relaxes, her throaty little moan letting me know exactly what she's thinking—what she wants. Oh, hell no! She steps closer, crowding me. "What if I don't want to stop?" she challenges.

Jesus Christ, is she really going there? She knows I can't—won't. I clench down on my jaw, hard enough to break bone, and work to fight the need racing through my blood. I can't let her get the upper hand here. If I do, I just might give her what we both want.

"Aren't you going to answer me?" She presses against me and her breath comes out a little quicker when my hard cock rubs against her stomach.

Summoning every ounce of control I have, I grip her shoulders and move her an inch back, welcoming the rush of cooler air falling over me. Her green eyes darken, turn venomous. She gives a humorless laugh and I put more distance between us before she kicks me in the shins.

"Typical Roman."

I grip my hair and tug. "What the hell is that supposed to mean?"

"Always starting something you can't finish," she shoots back.

"I can finish."

"Doesn't seem to me that you can." She's throwing me a challenge and I'll be damned if I don't want to pick it up.

Back the hell down, dude.

"If you weren't Cason's kid sister—"

"What does that have to do with anything?"

"He's my best friend, which means you're off-limits."

She goes quiet, her gaze latched on mine. "Do you know what I like about you, Roman?"

"What?" I ask.

"Nothing," she says, and a bark of laughter climbs out of my throat as I stand there staring at her back as she heads toward the stairs, an extra little shake in her sweet ass that teases my dick.

"Good," I say.

She glances at me over her shoulders. "You like that, though, don't you?"

"Yeah. I do," I say, my voice a husky murmur.

"You want me to hate you."

"I need you to hate me, Peyton. If you didn't, I'd bend you right over that table and bury myself inside you." She goes still, deathly still. I guess I got her attention now. "Would you hate that?" I ask.

A beat of silence, and then another. "Yes, I'd hate that," she finally says, the big fat lie hovering in the air, taking up space between us.

"Good."

CHAPTER FIVE

Peyton

I'D BEND YOU *right over that table and bury myself inside you.*

Okay, I might hate him—or not—but yeah, I seriously want him to follow through with that threat, which is probably why I spent all of last night tossing and turning between the sheets, imagining that dirty scenario playing out in real time.

No man has ever talked to me like that before. Is it shameful that I liked the deliciously filthy description of what he wanted to do to me, that it fueled all my darkest fantasies? Maybe, but I don't really care about that. Maybe it's the fresh Mediterranean air stirring a desire in me, or maybe I want to explore our kiss, expand upon it. I really don't know, but I'm as surprised as Roman that I suddenly want to get dirty with this man, want to be shameless and wide open to experience what I've never experienced before.

Go for it, Peyton.

At least now I know what's going on with him. There's an insane pull between us but he has some misguided loyalty to my brother where I'm concerned. I'm a grown woman for God's sake, and who I choose to sleep with is my business. It's about to become Roman's business, too. Oh yeah, he's about to learn firsthand that Cason has no say in my sex life.

The sound of Roman moving in the bathroom reaches my ears, and I kick my blankets off, my mind visualizing him stripping down to jump in the shower, his hard body hot and naked beneath the stream of water. Sweet baby Jesus, last night, the sight of him in the boxer shorts—the soft cotton the only thing separating my mouth from his very generous bulge—well…let's just say that eyeful awakened every nerve in my body. I've seen naked before, but not that kind of naked. He was all hard muscles and testosterone—the view completely hypnotizing—and it was a quick reminder that I haven't been touched in a long time, and never by anyone like him.

I slide from my bed, and through the crack in the bathroom door, I catch sight of Roman in the shower, his large body obscured in the steamy glass. What a shame. That thought makes me chuckle. Honest to God, I don't even know who I am with him. I'm not the type of girl to go lusting after a guy; heck, I haven't even wanted a man's hands on me since college—not that any guys were fighting to go out with me, either.

And why have you been flying solo, Peyton?

Oh, maybe because I've been hung up on Roman

for far too long, and it's definitely time to do something about it. I'm not looking for a future, but why shouldn't I exercise my marital rights while we're pretending? What would it hurt? Neither one of us wants anything more. We both know where the other stands, so why not have a bit of fun?

Why not, indeed?

I hang up a few of my dresses and putter around, a plan forming, taking shape in my mind. I bite back a grin as I think about my next move and all the ways I can press his buttons—sexually. Oh, this is going to be fun and the poor guy isn't going to know what hit him.

The water turns off, and his footsteps slap on the tile floor. I hum to draw his attention. His movements still behind me, and I bend to get the last of the things from my bag, purposely aiming my ass toward him. My sleep shorts lift, exposing the swell of my ass, and excitement skitters through me when I hear a low rumble, the deep sound reminding me of a wild animal's hungry growl. I stand and turn, blinking innocently at the man peering at me through the door that has been left ajar. For the first time in my life, I'm suddenly glad I'm afraid of the dark.

"Good morning," I say, trying to sound casual as he stands there, in nothing but a towel knotted around his hips. My nipples swell, and I don't bother to hide them as he grips the doorknob, his eyes dark, fierce like an animal about to take down its prey. "Don't bother closing it," I say. "I'm going to jump in the shower behind you. Do you mind if I soap up with your body wash? I forgot to bring some."

"Peyton," he grumbles, his voice low and dark as his attention strays from my face and falls to my peaked nipples.

I put my hands on the small of my back and push my hips forward, like I'm stretching out my tight muscles. "Yes?"

"About last night. What I said," he begins, sounding rattled, unsure. He grabs a fistful of hair as he waves his other hand between the two of us. "We just can't act on this, okay?"

"This. What do you mean by this?" I ask, feigning innocence as the bathroom door widens to give me a better view of his body. Lord, talk about a big yummy snack. Everything about the man is hard. Every damn inch of him delicious, and there are an awful lot of inches. I resist the urge to throw my hands up and shout out a cheer.

"You know what I'm talking about," he growls through clenched teeth, a good indication that he's wound as tightly as I am. Damned if I don't like that.

Sexual tension arcs between us, sizzles in the air like a live current, as I say, "Just so you know, my sex life is my business, not my brother's. If I wanted to sleep with you, or bend over so you could bury yourself inside me, the choice would be mine to make."

His throat works as he swallows. "Don't you think I have a say in it, too?"

"Yes, of course. I'm just saying. I'm a grown

woman, Roman, or haven't you noticed?" I stretch out a little more and his eyes darken.

"I've noticed."

"What I do with my body is up to me." I sink down onto the edge of my unmade bed, and by small degrees I inch my knees open. A welcome invitation he's fully aware of judging by the clenching of his muscles. "The fact is you want me to hate you, and I do, and that creates a huge problem."

"Yeah, huge," he mumbles, and I resist the urge to see if he's currently sporting anything huge.

"Pretending to like each other, or even touch each other in public, will be a hard task."

"Yeah, hard," he says, and I bite my bottom lip as I fake a repulsed shiver.

"I'm just thinking about the difficulties we're going to face."

"Oh, is *that* what you're thinking about?"

"I can't even imagine how much I'd hate it if you touched me. If you put your hand here," I say, and lightly run my finger up my inner thigh, "it would be horrible. The thoughts of you using your tongue." I crinkle up my face. "That would be worse, I'm sure."

"Peyton," he says, his nostrils flaring, his control fraying around the edges. "Don't."

"Don't what?" I bite back a smile as his rough voice caresses my body, the air in the room vibrating with the tension arcing between us. He stands before me, his chest rising and falling rapidly, as he battles an internal war, one I intend to win. My flesh tightens as I lightly stroke myself, a light feathery caress that stirs the restless desire in me.

"Just don't."

"Don't what?" I ask again. "Don't imagine how awful it would be to have your hands on me, your mouth between my legs, devouring me, you mean?"

"Fuck." His voice is deep, tight, revealing the lust he's trying to keep in check.

"Right, and *fucking*." I roll my eyes as my heartbeat speeds up. "My God, don't even get me started on imagining how much I'd hate that."

He stares at me, his pupils dilating, each breath harsher than the one before. "Peyton," he says again.

"Yes?"

"Maybe…" He begins and stops. He scrubs his chin, agony all over his face.

"Go on…" I encourage, and his gaze drops, watches my fingers dip under the fabric of my shorts. A little whimper catches in my throat as I widen my legs even more to tease him. Tempt him.

As I take in the strength and power of the man before me, a tortured sound rumbles from the depths of his throat and his laser focus centers on the hot spot between my legs. "Maybe you don't have to imagine it?"

Yes!

"Excuse me?" I say as I study the bead of water dripping down his chest, disappearing into his towel. My throat dries. My God, the man is perfect, and judging by the bulge in that towel, he wants me every bit as much as I want him, and I damn well plan to do my best to make it happen.

Like an animal free of its tether—untamed and feral—he shoves my door open. It hits the wall with a thud as he steps into my room, and pleasure gathers in a knot deep between my thighs as his presence overwhelms the space, making me feel small and delicate beneath his glare. But his size doesn't intimidate me. No, it actually empowers me, makes me a little more brazen.

I lift my chin, unafraid. "What exactly are you suggesting?" I ask, my voice laced with need. As he stares at me, another thought hits. What if he starts something, only to laugh and walk away? Do I have it in me to survive his rejection twice?

"Why don't we see just how much you're going to hate me touching you." He cocks his head. "I told you I was committed to this charade, and it's clear we're going to have to know what we're dealing with if we want to pull off a fake marriage."

"An experiment then. Hmm, I think—" My words fall off when he closes the distance between us, pulls me to my feet and grabs a fistful of my hair.

Heat courses through me as he tugs, none too gently. I breathe in his freshly showered skin as his head dips, his lips close to mine. His gaze moves over my face, and his rapid-fire breathing washes over my flesh as his lips twist.

"Do you hate this?" he asks.

"Yes, I hate it," I say, my voice deep and raspy from arousal.

Kiss me, already.

His big hands grip my sides and slide upward, his touch like fire to my skin. He stretches out his thumbs and brushes them over my nipples, effectively shutting down my brain. I moan and his resulting grin arouses me even more.

"Do you hate this, Peyton?" he asks, his voice a bit shaky. Maybe he's not as in control as he seems. Do I, Peyton Harrison, his best friend's kid sister, have the ability to rattle his composure and lance his self-control?

Let's see if I do.

"Yes, I hate it," I say, and arch into him.

"I can tell." His thumbs tease my tight buds, his touch flowing through me, teasing the needy spot between my legs. One hand slides up my leg and he grips my hip, his touch taunting the cleft between my thighs. His fingers bite into my skin, a rough touch that feels far more sensual than a gentle one.

"How about this?" he asks, and plants his mouth on mine. His kiss is hard, deeply brutal and bruising. Everything about it sends a sharp spike of need through me. I moan into his mouth and my hands slip around his big body, taking pleasure in the heat of his skin. His tongue plunders, tasting the depths of my mouth as he rubs himself against my stomach. My God, I love what I do to him.

He tears his mouth from mine and cups my breast. "What about this, Peyton?" he asks as he weighs my aching breast in his hand. "Do you hate this?" My voice disappears on me, so I moan instead. He cups my other breast and kneads me in his palms. "Moan for me. Show me how much you hate it."

My head falls back and I moan louder. It spurs him on. He dips a hand into my shorts, and with the rough pad of his finger, he circles my clit. "I bet you hate this, too." I gasp as he strokes me, his finger slick and wet from my arousal as it thrums against my clit. "What about here, Peyton?" He inches a finger inside me, to the second knuckle, and goes completely still when my sex clenches around him. "I bet you'd hate it more if I tossed you onto that bed and put my cock in here instead of my finger."

"Ohmigod," I cry out, his rough touch and crass words doing the craziest things to me.

"Would you?" he asks, his finger still unmoving inside me, like it's some kind of cruel punishment. I try to buck forward, try to drive him in deeper, damn near ready to lose my mind, but he grips my hips and holds me still, a knowing grin on his face.

"I would totally hate it," I say.

"How much?" he asks.

"I guess I don't really know. I guess you might have to do it before I can put a measurement on it."

"Hell," he growls, his mouth skimming my body as he sinks to his knees. He grips the elastic on my cotton sleep shorts and drags them down, just enough to expose my sex. He inhales me deeply, then exhales and my muscles contract as his hot, shuddering breath strokes my clit. He stares at my sex with heat and hunger, and he wets his lips as he parts me with his finger.

"Jesus Christ, Peyton." Tortured eyes glance up at me. "So damn perfect," he says, and I vibrate beneath his admiration. "This sweet little pussy…" He shakes his head as he strokes along the length of me. I practically orgasm and when he glances up at me again, it's clear he knows how desperate I am for it. "Have you been touched before?"

"Barely."

"Why?" he asks.

Oh, because you're the only man I ever really wanted to touch me. "The truth is, Roman, my one and only time was with a sloppy college boy who didn't know his way around my body." I take in Roman's dark eyes and everything tells me he's a man who knows just how to stroke all the spots that will bring me pleasure. "Guys never really paid attention to me, and that was okay by me because I didn't really want to be touched after that experience," I add honestly. It's true—guys didn't want me and I didn't want to be touched, unless it was by this man. I keep that bit of information to myself.

His eyes lock on mine. "You want me to touch you?"

"Yes."

"To see how much you hate it?"

"Uh-huh."

"I'll touch you, Peyton." His fingers sweep over my damp curls. "I'll touch this sweet little pussy until you're screaming my name in orgasm, but I have a condition."

"What?" I ask as he moves his finger a tiny inch.

I whimper and put my hands on his shoulder as my flesh tightens.

"I don't want you to just tell me how much you hate it. I want you to show me, too."

Fire licks through me. The man wants me to open up for him, bloom under his touch. "I can do that," I say.

"Good girl," he says, and I'm rewarded with the rest of his finger. He slides it all the way into my body, and I whimper.

"One more thing, and we need to make this clear."

"What?" I ask, pretty sure I'd agree to running through fire naked to get him to keep going.

"This is all I can give you."

"Trust me, Roman. I don't want more. No kids or family for me. I am not a girl you have to worry about," I say, eager to settle his worries. I am not going down any road—or aisle—with him, and don't want anything in return.

I try to widen my legs, but my shorts hug them tightly together, and damned if that doesn't come with its own excitement. As lust floods my body, something niggles at me. "I need one thing from you," I whimper.

"Just one." He ever so lightly moves his finger inside me, tease that he is.

"Maybe more," I say, my body on hyperdrive, but we're about to cross a line that neither of us can come back from. Yes, I'm seducing him. In the end, however, I don't want to be with him if it's something he'll never forgive himself for. "Promise me this. No regrets, Roman."

"Peyton." His hot breath washes over my tingling flesh. "I've struggled enough. Keeping my distance from you has been pure torture." My pulse jumps at the admission. An agonized groan catches in his throat. "I can't do it anymore," he says, his control snapping like a tightwire.

"Can't?"

"Don't want to."

"I don't want you to, either," I say, and touch his face. "Okay, no regrets. After I sign the contract, we go back to the way things were. A clean slate, okay?"

"Deal."

"You know, though. You know what I think I'd really hate," I say.

"No, what?"

"I would probably really hate it if you shoved me to my knees and put your cock in my mouth."

"Sweet hell," he grumbles under his breath. "We're going to find out, right after I devour this barely touched pussy of yours and watch you hate every damn second of it."

Yes, please.

He slides his wet tongue over me, and I let loose a loud moan, my fingers digging into his shoulder. "Oh, yeah," I murmur. "I hate that so much."

His chuckle races over my skin, and my entire body quivers. I move my hips to ride his tongue and this time he lets me. His thick, slick finger slides in and out of me, and I shut my eyes as pleasure dances along my nerve endings.

He flattens his tongue and swipes it over my clit, long leisurely strokes, every movement unhurried, like he has all the time in the world to simply give pleasure. I whimper and move and grind against his mouth. I'm shameless, I know. But goddammit, the man has a magical tongue. A second finger joins the first, stretching me in the most glorious ways. I moan in response, showing him just how much I hate it.

He draws my clit into his mouth. "Ooh," I say, a hard tremble working its way through my body. I run my hands through his hair, tug on it as he slides his fingers in and out of me. I lose myself in the sensations, so damn wet and slick as he penetrates me, pounding a little harder, I struggle to hang on, never wanting this moment to end.

With his fingers still inside me, he tugs my shorts down and nudges me backward until I hit the bed. He manipulates my body, moving me around easily until I'm on the mattress, my legs spread wide, my body his for the taking.

"Do you hate this?" he asks, his fingers soaked as he pulls them out.

"God, yes," I cry out.

"Take your top off," he demands in a soft voice. "Let me see your tits."

I quiver at his bluntness and remove my shirt. My pink nipples are hard, and he adjusts his hand to apply his palm to my clit as he lifts his head to take one hard bud into his mouth.

"Roman," I cry out as his fingers resume their pounding and he sucks on me. My muscles clench around his fingers, the glorious things he's doing to me shutting down my brain until all I can do is feel: his fingers pounding, his palm rubbing and his mouth devouring my nipple. I call his name again and judging by the way his muscles clench, it's easy to tell he likes the sound of it on my lips. "I hate this," I say, and he bites down on my nipple, pain and pleasure mingle, bleed into one, and I lift my hips, sensations zeroing in on my sex as my body explodes.

Dizzy, I close my eyes, hyperaware of the way my body is responding. I hold his mouth to my breast, crazed and breathless as I continue to spasm around his fingers, my hot juices slicking down my thighs. Heat spreads through me, my stimulated flesh tingling as I lose myself in the release.

"God, yes," I say, and he goes back between my legs, his tongue a soft caress on my pussy as he laps me up, long, hungry licks that warn he, too, is about to come apart. I put my hands on his shoulders, move my pussy against his face, and once he's had his fill of me, he leans back on his heels. I gasp when I see the unchecked need shimmering in his dark eyes, hot, needy…savage.

Lord have mercy.

Unnerved, my body shakes and I take a wheezing breath. This man is going to wreck me, use me like I'm a sacrificial offering, a pawn in a game I can't win, and leave me strung out like an addict when we're done. More importantly, I'm going to let him.

Without a word he stands and I wet my lips as he unknots his towel, exposing his beautiful body as the cotton sails to the floor. I take in the gorgeous length of him, thick and heavy and throbbing to be touched. Need flutters through me and I almost climax again.

"I wonder how much I'll hate your big cock in my mouth," I say shakily, and sound vibrates in his throat as he briefly closes his eyes, a tremor moving through him.

"On your knees, Peyton."

I drop and put my knees on the towel. I brace my hands on my thighs and open my mouth for him.

"Have you done this before?" he asks.

"Are you asking if I've ever sucked your cock before?" I say.

"Hell, Peyton. Do you always have to be a smart-ass?" I grin. The truth is, there's a storm going on inside me, and I hide behind humor. His face softens. "Peyton, do you want this?"

"I've never sucked your cock before, or any cock," I say. "But I want this."

He tugs my bottom lip between his fingers and slides his thumb into my mouth. "Suck," he says, and I do. His resulting growl is a good indication that he likes what I'm doing. A thrill goes through me. He yanks his thumb from my mouth and wraps his palm around himself.

"Hell," he growls when I moan. "That is so hot," he murmurs, and strokes himself. His cock hovers near my mouth as he fists himself, long hard strokes that show me what he likes. "Spread your legs. I want to see your pussy," he says.

Hands still on my knees, I widen my legs, and he strokes himself from base to tip as his hot gaze caresses every inch of me. "Do you hate what you see?" I tease.

"Yeah, I can't stand it." A couple long strokes over his cock and then, "Open your mouth."

I whimper and do as he says. Putting my hands on his thighs, I wait for him to feed his hard length down my throat.

"You want this in your mouth, Peyton?"

"Yes," I say.

His eyes squeeze shut for a brief second, and it's easy to tell he's fighting for his control. "Are you going to hate it?"

I swallow as his lids flicker open and he stares down at me. "I am," I say.

"What else do you think you'll hate?" he asks, circling and teasing my mouth to open more.

"I'll probably hate spreading my legs wide for you and letting you put this hard cock in my pussy." Lord, I've never said anything quite so dirty before. It almost brings a giggle to my throat.

"Are you going to hate me wrecking you?" he asks, his voice thick, heavy with need.

"Uh-huh," I say as he pulses against my mouth, reducing me to a hot, quivering mess dying to taste him. His hips power forward, his body flexing, and he finally offers me an inch. I moan around his length and he grabs my hair, his fingers bunching in my curls.

"That's it," he groans.

I tighten my lips to suck, sealing them around his bulging veins. While I've never done this before, one thing is for certain, I hate it. Yeah, I hate it so god-damn much I want to take him even deeper. I want him to spurt down my throat. I want to taste every drop of his release, knowing it was me who made him this hard, this aroused.

I grip him in my hand, feasting on him like it's my goddamn job, and his breathing is so ragged and rough, his male scent that much sharper as he fights release.

"Enough," he says, and I whimper when he pulls from my mouth. "Get on that bed and spread your legs. Let's see how much you'll hate it when I'm inside you."

My legs are so rubbery, it's all I can do to stand up, get myself on the bed and spread my legs wide. He growls as he lets his gaze roam the length of me. Then he walks backward and my heart lurches. My God, has he changed his mind? Is he going to leave me like this and walk away laughing?

I go up on my elbows, my skin hot and flushed and achy for his touch. "Roman?" I say.

"Don't move. You stay just like that, Peyton. I'm going to get a condom, then I'm going to fuck the hell out of you once and for all. Will you hate that?"

"Yeah, over the years," I begin, so breathless it's a

bit hard to talk, "when I touched myself, and thought about you inside me, I hated it."

"You've thought about my cock a lot, huh?" he asks as he tugs on it.

"A time or two."

"You rubbed that sweet pussy while you thought about it?"

"Uh-huh."

"Did you come on your finger, Peyton?"

"I did." I slide my hand down my body, rub my breasts and go lower to swipe the soft pad of my finger over my clit. "I would get so wet."

"I like how wet you get."

"That's what you do to me," I admit.

"This is what you do to me," he says, and glances at his cock. "I imagined this so many times in my mind. There are so many ways I want to take you."

"I bet I'll hate them all."

He grins. "Yeah."

"Roman."

"Hmm," he says as I continue to touch myself.

"Condom."

"Right." He moans and I slick my finger over my clit as he disappears. A second later, he's on the bed, ripping into the wrapper and sheathing himself. He falls over me, heavy and strong, and captures my lips. He kisses me hard, claiming my mouth in a frenzied rush. I put my legs around him and lift.

He breaks the kiss and buries his mouth in the hollow of my neck, tasting my skin as he probes my slick opening.

"Please, fuck me," I cry out, and he pistons forward. A gasp catches in my throat as he rams into me, seating himself high and going perfectly still. His cock stretches my body, hits places, deep places I never knew existed. His head lifts and he stares down at me.

"Worst damn thing I ever felt," he says, and begins to move his hips, creating need and friction in my core. I wrap my arms around him to hang on, but it's no use. I'm free-falling without a net and if the landing doesn't kill me, it will ruin me forever. It's frightening. Exhilarating.

"Roman," I say. "I want… I want."

"What do you want?"

"I don't know."

"You want it like this, baby?" he asks, picking up the pace, hard blunt strokes that force the air from my lungs.

"Yes." Thank God he knows what I need even when I don't.

His big hands grip my shoulders, and he presses hot, openmouthed kisses to my neck and chest. His body shifts, the angle forcing him in deeper.

"My God," I cry out as he hits my cervix. He pounds against me, stimulating, rubbing, penetrating so deeply, hitting me at just the right angle, a full-body orgasm rips through me. I open my mouth but no words come when a deep shudder sends waves of pleasure from the top of my head to the tips of my toes.

He goes still inside me and curses under his breath as I shatter around him. "Jesus, Peyton," he says as

I ride the high and bask in each and every glorious pulse. So, this is what sex is like? Damn, I'd have been having it every single day if I knew it was this good. Then again, I'm sure it wouldn't be like this with anyone other than Roman—and the truth of the matter is, what this man does to me, it's a bit frightening.

He moves again, and my body tightens around him. "You got me there," he says, and slides out, only to jerk forward and fill me again. "Right there."

I scratch my nails along his back, scoring his flesh, like I'm marking him as mine, and he pulses inside me. He finds my mouth again for a deep, bruising kiss as he gives in to the pleasure and comes high inside me. His heart pounds against my chest, his body slick, hot and spasming as he collapses on top of me. He kisses my damp flesh again. His rough tongue trailing along my shoulder, as his one hand goes to my face. He cups my cheek and his head lifts, the tenderness in his gaze a complete contrast to our frenzied sex.

"Peyton," he says, and I struggle to get my breath.

"Yeah."

"Fuck."

I laugh at that, loving that I reduced this man to a quivering mess. "Yeah, we just did."

He chuckles against my flesh and shakes his head. "Did you hate it?"

"I've never hated anything more," I say.

"We'll see about that."

CHAPTER SIX

Roman

I CANNOT BELIEVE I just had sex with my best friend's kid sister. Not only that, I owned her, took everything she was giving and gave it back to her just as hard, maybe even harder. The truth is, her sweet, barely touched body came alive under my greedy hands, and I swear to God, knowing I was the one who could do that to her... Let's just say it rocked my world, and I've never come so hard in my entire life. She might have given me everything, and I damn well took it, but it was Peyton who held all the power, in a fundamental way.

I cast her a glance as we walk down the sidewalk, the early-morning sun beating down on us, but the warm rays have nothing to do with the glow on her face. No, I'm the reason her cheeks are flushed with heat. I take in her light blue dress, perfect for the classroom, and smooth my hand over my tie. Peyton's look is more casual than mine, but I'm comfortable in a suit and tie—my usual business attire. I don't need it for my job, but I grew up always having to look my best in public.

As people hurry by, heading to their workplaces, she hums under her breath, and I wish she'd stop. Now every time I hear that sound on her lips, it will take me back to her bedroom. We shouldn't have done that. No, I should have been stronger. An uncomfortable pressure builds in my chest. Christ. If her brother ever found out…

He can't find out.

He won't.

No regrets, Roman.

"Peyton, about Cason, I—"

She puts her hand up to stop me. "First, I know how important he is to you and I'm not going to let anything happen to your relationship. Second, what I do with my body and who I sleep with is not his business," she says, and my shoulders relax.

I'm an honest guy. Shit, I pride myself on it, and I'm a complete and utter asshole for A, sleeping with Peyton, and B, keeping it from Cason. I guess in the end, the fact that neither of us wants more, that we will go back to a clean slate when we're done here, means Cason never really has to know. Never has to know the guy he trusted with his sister, the guy he could always count on, betrayed the hell out of him.

Shit.

"You ready for this?" I ask, and her smile is a bit shaky when she lifts her head to me. A small shiver goes through her despite the warmth in the air.

"Yeah, I think so."

"You're cold."

"Probably just from nerves."

I frown down at her. "You always seem a little bit cold, Peyton."

She shrugs and I put my arm around her and draw her body close.

"Look at that, you didn't even flinch," I tease, wanting to ease her tension. This job is important to her. Being there for young minds, making them all feel important, loved and cherished—all the things she'd never felt, from anyone but Cason, growing up—is her life's goal.

She chuckles. "I guess it's a good thing we had that little experiment, then."

"That's what we're calling it, is it?" My gaze goes to her lush mouth. She opened that mouth for me this morning, the sweet sight more welcoming than a hard rain after a summer's drought. Christ, she took me so deep into her throat. Deeper than I would've ever expected her to take me, and how is it that oral sex with a woman who'd never given it before completely eclipsed every experience from my past? I wanted to come down her throat, fill her mouth with every last drop, but I needed to be inside her. Needed her snug sex muscles to milk my release more than I needed my next breath.

Dark lashes fall slowly over emerald eyes, and her look is demure, coy. "Yes. That's what we're calling it."

Shit, I love this teasing side of her. But two can play that game. "Fine, but I'd prefer if you didn't use the word *little* when you're referring to sex with me."

Her jaw drops open and her gorgeous green eyes go wide. "Did the humorless Roman Bianchi just crack a joke?" She reaches up and puts her hand on my forehead. "Are you sick, running a fever… delirious?"

I shove her hand away. "All right, smart-ass."

She grins at me, but her nervousness about her first day seems to have ebbed, and for that I'm grateful. We cross the street when the light turns and both go silent. After a long while she speaks.

"Roman," she says quietly, so quietly I almost miss it.

"Yes."

She shades the sun from her eyes and glances down the street. I follow the direction and spot the school in the near distance. "Thanks for this," she says.

"My pleasure," I say, and mean every word of it. This girl needs a break, and I'm happy to give it to her. "Like I said, it's a nice reprieve from reality." With my arm still around her, I give a comforting squeeze. "We got this."

"Yeah, I think we do."

"Cason told me a bit about the job. He said you were in competition for the full-time position. How is that all working?" She breaks from my arm and sneezes into the crook of her elbow. I frown when she turns back to me, take in the red in her eyes. "Are you getting sick?" Maybe that's why she always seems to be shivering.

"I think it's actually allergies."

"Allergic to Malta?"

"Probably the different foliage they have here."

"Do you have any meds for that?"

"I'm sure it will pass," she says, and offers me a smile. "Back to your question. The full-time teacher left for maternity and made the decision not to come back. I'm one of two candidates hired for the month of June. I'm not sure who the other person is. We both work in the classroom until the end of the school year, and whoever 'fits' the best will be offered the full-time position in September."

"Why Malta?"

"The opportunity presented itself. I want to offer something to the children, expand their horizons. I feel like I can give back more in a place like this."

"Does it have to be Malta?"

"No, but these jobs aren't easy to come by and I want to be in a community in need, know what I mean?"

"I do."

A woman and her young son, who looks to be about three, stroll down the sidewalk, and I catch the loving way Peyton watches them, her lips curving at the corners. For a girl who doesn't want a family, or kids—doesn't believe in Cinderella or Prince Charming—she sure has a longing smile on her face. Maybe that's why she became a teacher—maybe all the children help fill the hollowed-out holes in her life.

"And you have to be married?"

The small family passes and her chest expands as she takes in a deep breath and lets it out ever so slowly. "Technically the marriage bar has been lifted, but it's practiced behind the scenes here. I don't like to deceive anyone, Roman, but I couldn't take a chance. I'm hoping once they see me in action with the kids, my marital status will no longer matter."

"I get it, but it's all ridiculous. It's the twenty-first century, for Christ's sake."

She shrugs. "I know, but this job means everything to me. Which is why—"

"Which is why I'm your husband." My body stiffens at the words. Wow, why the hell did that come out so easily, sound so right?

"Fake husband," she corrects.

"Isn't that what I said?"

"No."

"I meant to."

"Yeah, I know."

Children file into the school and it brings a smile to her face.

"You really like kids, huh?"

She laughs, but it's forced, and a gust of breeze blows her hair from her shoulders. "When they're someone else's kids, I do."

I nudge her. "I bet you'll love being an aunt."

She goes still, her eyes wide with excitement. "Wait, do you know something about Cason and Londyn that I don't?"

"I hardly think I'd be the first to know. I just mean, I'm sure they'll have kids at some point."

Her big smile wraps around me. "I guess I never thought about being an aunt before." She blinks up at me. "Do any of your sisters have kids?"

"Yeah, and I'm a shitty uncle."

Her face twists, a dubious smile. "I doubt that."

"I try to be a good uncle. I really do. But whenever I visit, it's like the Spanish Inquisition and children are thrust into my arms. I feel like if I touch one, I'll get infected."

Her laugh fills my soul with happiness. "Infected. Like they're a disease?"

"No, maybe the word is addicted, or hooked." I shake my head. "What I'm trying to say—"

"What you're trying to say is having kids is the norm, and people can't understand those like us who are child-free by choice."

"Isn't that what I said?"

She laughs and whacks me. "Oh yeah, that's exactly what you said. But no, I get it, and isn't that just another thing we have in common?"

I give her a teasing wink. "It's safe to say we recently discovered quite a few things we have in common," I say, my cock twitching in remembrance as a sexy pink blush colors her cheeks. Jesus, I want her again. Want to bury my face between her legs and taste her sweetness as I bring her to orgasm. I capture her hand, and without even thinking bring it to my mouth and press a kiss to her fingers. As soon as I do, we find ourselves at the school, the doors swinging open. Peyton turns, and I let our hands drop but continue to hold hers.

"You must be Peyton Harrison," a gentleman in his late fifties, dressed in a light gray suit, says.

Her smile widens and she takes his outstretched hand. "I am, and you must be Mr. Galea."

"Please, call me Andrew."

"It's so great to finally meet you, Andrew." She lets go of my hand and waves it toward me, palm up, as she introduces me to the man I can only assume is the principal. "This is my husband, Roman Bianchi."

Andrew frowns, and I stiffen. I have no idea why I feel like I'm back in grade school getting caught in a lie. Maybe because I *am* in the middle of a whopper of a lie. But it's for a greater purpose in an unfair situation, making it justifiable in my mind. Sleeping with Peyton and lying to Cason about it, however, no greater purpose involved there, and not at all justifiable. Then again, I won't have to lie to his face, because he won't ask if I'm sleeping with his sister. He trusts me like that. Like Cason, I'm a guy who prides himself on the truth, too. But this is my best friend's kid sister, and I'd do anything for him. Okay, who the hell am I kidding? This is Peyton, and I'd do anything for *her*. Even let her seduce me into her bed.

"Roman Bianchi," the man says, and my breath stalls as my name sticks on his tongue, like he's trying to figure out where he'd heard it before. Shit, maybe we should have made up a fake last name. "Do you have a sister named Aurora?"

"Actually, yeah, I do," I say, and reach for Peyton's hand again when her eyes widen.

"My goodness, I had no idea I was in the presence of royalty," he says.

I hold my hands up to stop him. "The Bianchis are an old family, but we have no titles to our name. And please, I like to keep a low profile."

"Yes, I always heard that about you." His gaze goes from me to Peyton, and he must be remembering my failed engagement.

"We've kept things quiet," I say. "You can imagine why."

He nods, his blue eyes thoughtful. "Of course. I must tell you, though, your sister and my old college friend Lorenzo Costa are husband and wife."

Worry cuts like a sharp blade. "You went to college with Lorenzo? What a small world," I say, hoping to make light of it.

"Small indeed," he agrees, and my stomach is so damn tight with worry, I give Peyton's hand another fast squeeze. Shit, this is not good. If word gets out…

"Do you talk with Lorenzo very often?" I ask around the knot in my throat. Christ, I'm here to help Peyton, not screw everything up for her.

"No, it's been a while. I must give him a call soon. Catch up."

"Like I mentioned, I do appreciate my privacy." I roll my eyes playfully. "If you know my sisters, I'd never get a moment's peace if they knew I was here."

He laughs like he does indeed know my family. "They are all lovely women and I'm a younger brother in a big family, too, so I fully understand what it's like to have intrusive sisters." He claps his hands together and turns to Peyton, and I relax a bit hoping we just dodged a bullet. "How about a tour, and then I'll take you in to meet the staff before introducing you to your new students?"

"That sounds lovely," Peyton says, the hitch in her voice noticeable only to me, and only because I know this woman. I give a little nod to let her know I got this, that everything will be okay. Her big eyes scan my face, and she relaxes slightly with my reassurance. Jesus, this girl trusts me, and I better be able to back it up and make sure I don't mess this up.

We walk through the colorful halls and children's laughter reaches our ears. "Richard is already here," he says.

"Richard?" Peyton asks.

He shakes his head. "My apologies. Richard is the other teacher. An American, like you. He, too, is vying for the full-time position. His darling wife is with him. They've been here for over an hour." I glance at my watch. "He's eager to get started, I guess," Andrew adds. "I bet you will all hit it off."

I want to ask why he's holding a ridiculous competition in the first place. Peyton is clearly the best candidate and I don't even have to meet Richard, the eager beaver, to know it.

As if reading my mind, Andrew turns to me. "This is a much-coveted position, and while Richard and Peyton were top candidates, it's important to us to see them in their role."

I wrap my arm around Peyton. "I'm sure you'll be extraordinarily impressed. She impresses me every day."

"How did you two meet?" he asks.

"Roman and my brother are best friends. They met in college, Penn State. Perhaps you know my brother, Cason Harrison. He's the creator of Hard Wear, quality fashion for men, and Soft Wear, quality fashion for women."

Andrew's eyes widen. "I have heard of that app. I believe my wife uses it."

Peyton turns from us, sneezing into her arm again. "Sorry, allergies," she explains as she fishes a tissue from her purse. Andrew gives us the grand tour and we end in the teachers' lounge. He introduces us and everyone greets us with smiles and open arms, until he presents Richard and his wife, Paula, both of whom I instantly dislike. Oh, they're smiling, but I grew up surrounded by fake, and know it when I see it.

"If you'll excuse me for a moment," Andrew says and disappears, leaving us with Richard and his wife.

"I'm looking forward to getting to know you both better," Richard says. "Where are you residing for the month?"

For the month?

Okay, now that shit just pisses me off. He's acting like he's already got the job and Peyton might as well not get too settled.

"Not far," I say, when his gaze lands on me. I work to keep my cool and add, "In this community."

Paula flashes me a saccharine smile. "Looks like we're neighbors. We must socialize." She puts her hand on her husband's chest. "In the evenings of course. Throughout the day, I'll be home tending to the house and supporting my husband." Her eyes turn to me. "And you, Roman? What will you be doing when your wife is at work?"

I move closer to my *wife* and anchor her body to mine. As the protector in me roars to life, I fight the instinct to stand in between her and these assholes. Peyton is tough on the outside and has the ability to handle this guy and his wife. It's what's underneath her bravado that worries me, the flare of some deeper emotion she keeps tucked deep, protected by an impenetrable and unscalable wall.

"I'll be home supporting my wife, too," I say, remaining on my best behavior as my fingers curl.

"Like a house husband?" Paula presses manicured nails to her chest and lets out a mocking laugh, stoking the anger in me. "How adorable."

"So nontraditional," Richard, and when I say Richard, I mean asshole, pipes in.

"You don't want to stay home and have a family, Peyton?" Paula asks.

When Peyton's face pales, a muscle twitches beneath my eye and I open my mouth, not about to let anyone belittle her or question her choices, but she puts her hand on my arm.

"I'm not saying that. I'm saying I'm an independent woman," Peyton says. "My choices are my own, as are yours, and I hope we've come to the point where women have stopped shaming each other for their choices. We can have a family whether we work or stay home. I mean it is the twenty-first century after all."

Atta girl!

I glare at Paula as she lifts her chin. "Yes, of

course," she says. "I guess I'll always be that old-fashioned girl. Not that there is anything wrong with what you're doing," she says, her voice sweet, but the malicious glare tells a different story. "We just prefer to do things differently. That's how it is in the Ozarks, where we come from, our values are much like they are here in Malta. Very different from New York, obviously."

Two elderly ladies step into the lounge and I shake my head as Paula and her husband dismiss us and turn to charm them. I rub the knot from the back of my neck, hardly able to believe people like that still exist in this world. Then again, maybe that's exactly what they're looking for in Malta. Old time-y values. Peyton, however, has more values in her pinkie finger than almost anyone and while there is nothing wrong with staying home, no one and I mean no one should shame a woman for wanting a career. Peyton's choices are hers, and hers alone—and that comes to her sexuality, too. As that epiphany hits me like the slap of a teacher's ruler, it occurs to me she's right about a lot of things she said to me, mainly that she can sleep with whoever she wants to sleep with while she's here—as long as it's me.

Christ.

I love her brother dearly but all of a sudden I can't help but think maybe someone ought to tell him Peyton is a grown woman and her decisions are her own.

Andrew steps back into the lounge and claps his hands.

"Before I introduce you to your students, who are

ready and excited to meet you, I would like to extend an invitation to you all, a get-to-know-one-another dinner at my home tonight."

"We'd love to," Richard says quickly. Peyton, however, casts me a quick glance.

I appreciate the check-in; it's what most married couples would do. Making decisions together is something I watched my folks and my married siblings do over the years. I can't help but wonder if her reaction was because she's playing the part or she doesn't want to ask too much from me. But I'm here for her. This woman is beautiful and selfless, and became a teacher to give back and make sure every child feels cherished. Whatever she needs from me, she gets.

"Sounds great to me," I say, and the smile that splits her lips is enough to destroy any man. My heart tumbles a little in my chest, and I give a big swallow.

You're here to help her, dude, maybe engage in a few marital benefits, and nothing else.

"It's settled then. Let's go say hello to your students."

I put my hands on her shoulders. "Wish me luck," she says.

"You don't need it. You've got this, Peyton." I bend and press my lips to hers. I brush her mouth lightly, and at first the public display of affection startles her. Within seconds, she warms to my touch, to the show I'm putting on—or at least I'm trying to convince myself it's all for show and simply for our small audience. Peyton's mouth lingers beneath mine, like she's in no hurry to pull away, and

I slowly break free and pull myself up to my full height. Paula, clearly one never to be outdone, goes up on her toes and kisses her husband.

I put my mouth close to Peyton's ear and a quiver goes through her. "I'll be at home, waiting for you," I say. She nods, but the surprised yet appreciative look that comes over her face is a fast reminder that outside of her brother, this woman has never been able to count on anyone. I want her to be able to count on me.

Peyton casts a quick glance over her shoulder and I give her a little "you got this" nod as Andrew leads them from the room. It warms my heart and reminds me there really is still a lot of good in this world. Her brother must be so proud of the woman she's become. He just needs to realize she is a woman and not a small, parentless child he has to protect due to a neglectful grandmother, followed by years in the system.

Speaking of siblings.

My phone pings in my pocket and I don't have to check it to know it's my sister, Aurora. I gave them all personalized rings. I toy with the phone and fight down a burst of unease as Peyton and Richard follow the principal out the door. I hope Andrew didn't excuse himself so he could put a call in to his old college buddy—my sister's husband. Shit, if word of this gets out, all Peyton's hard work, hopes and dreams will go down the toilet. I can't let that happen.

I'm about to leave when Paula lifts her head, her eyes narrow. "I can't quite figure it out, but you look so familiar. Have we met before?"

CHAPTER SEVEN

Peyton

I SIT AT the front of the class and my insides are aflutter as all the little ones pack up their belongings and get ready to head home. My day was amazing. Meeting such wonderful children all eager to learn a new language. I'm in a different country yet deep inside, I feel oddly connected to it, like it's where I belong. Strange, I know, considering I've never belonged anywhere before.

Throughout the day I had to dig deep to recall my years of Italian studies. Maybe I should ask Roman to speak to me in his mother tongue to keep me on top of my game. I pack my briefcase and wave to the children as they file from the classroom. I'm about to follow behind but instead roam around the classroom, a small smile on my face as I take in the artwork we did today.

"All set?" a voice asks from behind and I turn, startled. My wide eyes narrow, and my heart misses a small beat when I find my "husband" standing there, looking so casual and relaxed, so sweet and sexy at the same time, I can't help but second-guess what I'm getting myself into with him.

"You startled me."

I quiver under his steely gaze and the air around us vibrates when he says, "Payback for sneaking up on me last night in the pool."

"First, I wasn't sneaking up on you," I say as his eyes visually caress me. "And second, I had no idea you were the vengeful type."

"I can be vengeful," he says, and saunters toward me, his hands shoved into the pockets of his khaki pants. His clothes are casual this afternoon, but no less devastating. Breathless—it's the only way to describe what his presence does to me.

I inhale shallowly as my body buzzes to life. "That polo looks amazing on you," I say. Heat floods my body as my gaze falls to take in the way *he* makes the shirt look good, not the other way around. I can only assume he wore a suit this morning to help make a good impression, and I truly appreciate his attention to detail—inside the bedroom and out.

He steps up to me, slides one hand around my body and with no finesse pulls me to him. Our bodies collide, and as he inhales, filling his lungs with my scent, I shiver under his touch. "Is that right?" he asks, splaying the hand on my back, his fingers lightly brushing the swell of my backside. Ripples of sensual pleasure move through me, and my little fluttering breath gives away my arousal. His grin is knowing when he says, "You know what I think would look even better on me?"

His sexy smile rattles me even more. "What?" I ask; the brown in his eyes deepens, a telltale sign of the lust building inside him. "Me?"

He laughs. "You took the word right out of my mouth," he answers, his voice raspy and fractured. Once again I can't help but think he's not as in control as he seems. I'm not sure why but it secretly thrills me when this man becomes unhinged.

I brush my thumb over his bottom lip and press my breasts into his chest. "Well, now that this mouth of yours is empty maybe we can fill it with something else."

His cock instantly hardens against my leg, and he gives an almost resigned shake of his head. "I can't believe you said that."

"You mean you can't believe *I* said it before *you* said it." I laugh and poke his chest. "You were thinking it. Don't even try to deny it."

"Not trying," he says with a cocky grin. The more time we spend together, the more playful he becomes. Before this trip, he kept that side of himself locked up tight. I guess humiliation in the past—he was dumped just before his wedding—forced him to keep his guard in place, and perhaps he doesn't feel the need to protect himself with me after we both made it clear where we stood. I get that he's still worried about his friendship with Cason, but I'm not a girl to kiss and tell. Heck, up until this morning, and the time he ravished my mouth at the wedding, I wasn't even a girl who kissed, period. Damned if I haven't been missing out, though. Then again, it's not like I'd want another man's lips on mine. No, and right there, that fact alone, could very well lead to a problem.

No regrets, Peyton.

I push that thought from my mind as he glances over his shoulder. His grin is mischievous, playful when he turns back to me, his eyes zeroing in on my mouth. His hips move, pressing against me, conveying all his needs. Desire twists inside me as I ache to lose myself in him a second time.

"Want to shut the door?" he asks, his voice a rough whisper that glides over my flesh and hints at things to come. Intimate things. Dirty things. I'd be lying if I said I wasn't excited by the prospect.

"No," I blurt out, and he cocks his head, his brow raised, his tanned skin glistening in the rays of sun streaming in through the big windows. I lean into him, soak in his warmth. The scent of his skin, clean soap infused with testosterone, swirls around me. "Well, yeah, of course I want you to shut the door." That brings a smile to his face. "But I'm not about to jeopardize this job."

His demeanor changes and he steps back, putting a measure of distance between us, and I instantly miss the connection. "Right. Sorry about that." He taps his head and winks at me. "Loss of blood there for a second."

"Don't be sorry." I sidle back up to him, put my hands on his chest, loving his strong heartbeat beneath my palm. "I kind of like that I can do this to you."

"Ah, something you *like*," he says, a slow nod of his head. "That's different."

I run my finger along his cheek, the bristles on his late-afternoon shadow rough against my flesh. How would it feel between my legs? "Let's hurry home. I'll show you what else I like doing to you."

He frowns. "Don't we have to go to Andrew's for dinner?"

I glance at the clock. "If we hurry, we—"

He snatches my hand and ushers me out the classroom door before I can even finish my sentence. Hand in hand, like two lovestruck teenagers, we laugh and hurry outside the school. I sneeze again when we pass by the same purple flowers.

He casts me a quick glance, and beneath the lust I spot genuine concern. "Allergies?" I nod, and he slows his steps when I become a bit breathless. "Tell me about your day," he says, his brow furrowed, real interest on his face. "Did you enjoy it as much as you thought you would?"

"It was so much fun. The kids are all wonderful." He grins at me and I talk endlessly, as I sometimes do, as we continue to make our way back home. We reach the villa and I'm winded from my incessant chatter. "I'm sorry," I say.

"For what?" Roman pushes the door open and gestures for me to enter.

"I talked nonstop and never even asked how your day was." I frown and his mouth drops to my lips, stoking my need for him as I push past him. "That was thoughtless of me."

"There's nothing thoughtless about you, Peyton." His voice is almost tortured as he says that, like it's something he can't quite comprehend, like it scares him a bit. Inside he shuts the door and pushes me against it. "And if you really want to know about my day, let's just say we're about to get to the highlight reel."

"Does the highlight reel have anything to do with me?" I slide my arms around his neck and take pleasure in his strength and sureness. The man is a powerhouse, and while I feel small in his arms, I also feel cherished.

"It has everything to do with you. Don't you realize you're the star of the show?" He runs his thumb over my bottom lip, and warm sensations grip me. "This mouth. I've been thinking about it all day." His nostrils flare and my nipples tighten with arousal. "I'm going to destroy it." I suck in a breath, his filthy words derailing my ability to think. He inches closer, his lips a breath away from mine, and I'm about to open for him, welcome his ravishing tongue inside, when my nose tingles.

"What…what if I'm getting a cold?"

His eyes are glazed, completely enraptured with my mouth, a hungry wolf about to feast on a lamb, when he says, "I thought you said it was just allergies."

"Can we take a chance?" I rake my hand through his hair and make a mess of it. The mussed-up look works for him. Then again, any look works for him. "I don't want you to get sick." Why the hell am I trying to talk him out of this when I want him to strip me bare and make a complete and utter mess of me?

He laughs, but it's more like a tortured growl and my body burns in response. "You think a cold is going to keep me from claiming this sweet mouth?" Oh God, I shouldn't like how he wants to claim me. I shouldn't like it at all. But I do.

He presses his body against mine, and his cock is so hard, I'm pretty sure the entire marine corps couldn't stop him from touching me. "I don't want to get you sick."

Just shut up already, Peyton.

"Yeah, I know. You're sweet like that." His demeanor changes, and in the blink of an eye the wild animal vanishes, the hunger receding, giving way to a soft smile as he pulls me from the door. "Come on," he says, the tenderness in his tone like a gentle caress over my skin, and I work to ignore the strange possessive tug on my emotions.

This is just sex, Peyton.

"Where?"

He leads me into the kitchen, and on the counter I see every kind of allergy medication known to mankind. "What did you do?"

He gives a casual shrug, like it's nothing, but it's not nothing to me. "I didn't know what kind you took."

I pick up box after box after box. "You have enough here to obliterate allergies from mankind."

"Just need to obliterate them from you," he says.

My heart thumps, my insides going to mush.

It's just sex, Peyton.

Why then, when he does stuff like this, does it feel like so much more?

"Roman," I say. I'm so touched by his thoughtfulness, it's hard to push the words out.

"I told you I was committed, Peyton. You're going to get this job and you're not going to be taken out by allergies."

I fight a stupid tear and my chaotic emotions scramble in all directions, every sentiment I've locked up over the years trying to crawl over the jagged-edged wall I erected early on in life. But there are too many moving parts, racing at a speed I'm not accustomed to, scattering before I can lasso them back in. I swallow, a silly attempt to rein them all in, but I can't let him see how much his random act of kindness has touched me or have him thinking I'm going to fall for him because of one thoughtful gesture.

Oh, but it's been more than one, Peyton.

"It's just…"

He puts his hand around my neck and spreads his fingers, lust once again returning to his eyes. "Maybe I had ulterior motives," he says, bringing this back to what's really between us—sex—and I'm grateful for that. No need to mistake the physical for the emotional. A person can attend to your basic needs—shelter, food, water…allergy medication—but that doesn't mean they care deeply about you. A lesson learned at a young age taught me that, and I'm not about to forget it now. I can't.

"Ulterior motives, huh?" I pop a pill from a bubble pack as he pours me a glass of water.

"Maybe I need you healthy so we can experiment more, see what else you hate—or what you like." I grin. This morning I put all my best efforts forth to seduce this man, but now that we've broken the seal—or rather removed our clothes and gone at each other like wild animals during mating season—this man is all in. He hands me the glass and I take the pill. I swipe my tongue over my lip, and much as I expected, a small moan escapes his throat.

"What was that you said about filling your empty mouth?" I ask, and arch a brow.

His grin is crooked. "I believe that is what *you* said."

I feign innocence and back up toward the stairs. "Me? I can't believe you would accuse me of saying something like that, Roman."

"Where do you think you're going?" he growls when I reach the stairs.

"I don't think I should be around anyone who would accuse me of saying something so...dirty."

"Get back here, Peyton."

I rush up the steps and his footsteps pound on the kitchen floor.

I glance over my shoulder. "Not until you tell the truth."

"Peyton," he says, his warning voice churning with passion.

"Admit it was you who said it."

"Calling me a liar, are you?" he grumbles, his deep, thick voice curling through me and teasing the needy little cleft aching for his attention.

"If the name fits."

As his long legs carry him up the stairs fast, and

he begins to close the gap, I bypass the bedrooms and go straight for the rooftop. He's hot on my heels and I can't stop laughing when I reach the top step, kicking my shoes off and tearing at my dress the whole way. I'm in nothing but my bra and panties when I reach the pool, and without bothering to remove them I dive in.

I swim to the shallow end, and when I surface, Roman is right there, his clothes soaked, and a bubble of joy wells up inside me. I can't remember the last time I had fun like this, or laughed this hard. Honestly, for the first time, I feel like the weight of the world isn't on my shoulders and I can just be… me. I'm guessing it's because we both know where the other stands.

Where exactly is it you stand, Peyton?

I shut down that inner voice—I cannot fall for him—as his arms slide around my waist. In a move that is less than gentle, he anchors me to his solid body, and I register every delicious detail of his hardness.

"Want to know what fits?" he asks, the lust in his eyes heating the surrounding water and pushing the chill from my bones until I'm almost warm.

"What?" I ask, breathless. He puts one hand between my legs and pushes my panties to the side. A thick finger presses inside me, and my breath hitches. God, that feels good.

"My cock, right here. That's what fits." His mouth finds mine for a mind-numbing kiss and I quake as he begins to finger me. His thumb slides up, stroking my cleft, increasing the sensations, and I quiver at the sweet agony.

He tears his mouth from mine and puts it to my ear. "Want to know something else?"

"Yeah."

"I don't take too kindly to being called a liar." His hands slide down my back and he splays his fingers over my ass. He kneads my flesh, his hands full of ownership as he tugs, to widen my cheeks, and a cold rush of water stimulates all my sensitive nerve endings.

"Say it again, and I'll own this ass," he growls.

"Oh God, yes," I cry out without thinking, and his soft chuckle curls around me.

"Oh, you *like* that, do you?"

"I…don't know," I say. "My guess is I'd hate it."

His growl of laughter vibrates in the air, ripples through the water, and I move my hips, try to work his finger around inside me.

"Yeah, I can tell how much you'd hate it." He slowly pushes his finger in deeper. "Maybe I'll have to find another way to punish you." He bites his bottom lip, his shoulder muscles flexing beneath my fingers, and my sex clenches, desperate for him to take the ache away. "Maybe I'll put you on the side of the pool, spread you wide, shove my fingers inside you and give you a good hard licking."

I close my eyes as the sensations and image pull me under, and I don't dare say a word for fear he'll change his mind. As I revel in all the things he's threatening to do to me, a strong palm cups my face.

"Look at me, Peyton," he says, and my lids lift. The intensity in his eyes is as frightening as it is exciting. His hand leaves my cheek, a slow exploration downward, his fingers sliding between my breasts, his hot gaze following behind. A second later my bra is gone, and his look is ravenous as he lifts me, taking one nipple between his teeth. His lips close over my bud, hungry, demanding, and I arch into him, loving this feral side that takes without asking. I've never wanted to open myself, give myself up like this before. But it's a game we're playing and I can't forget it.

The water moves around me, and that's when I realize he's walking me to the edge, his deep growl rumbling through my body. He settles my bottom on the stone decking. Strong fingers grip my thighs and spread my legs. Need zings through my body and my throat instantly dries.

His mouth finds mine for a ravenous kiss and my entire body heats, a small moan catching in my throat. He pushes himself against my leg, and with my panties pushed to the side, he works magic with his fingers and I grow impossibly slicker. I thrust my pelvis, demanding more.

"Have you thought about me today? Thought about all the things I was going to do to you?"

"Uh-huh," I say as he pushes a finger into me, and pulls it out, his concentration deep, like he's working out some mathematical computation.

"Yes. Have you been thinking of me?" I ask in return. He slides his finger into his mouth, and for whatever reason watching him lick my slick arousal from his finger is like a goddamn aphrodisiac. Pressure builds inside me, and I tremble and pant.

"Roman," I murmur, my gaze focused on his mouth.

He pulls his finger from his mouth and pins me with a glare, his hard body holding me in place, trapping me beneath him. "What, you want a taste?" He leans into me, his soft lips on mine, but his tongue, oh there's nothing soft about that as it roughly invades my mouth, wars with my own tongue, like a king about to conquer an army and claim the bounty. I'm the bounty.

His mouth slides from mine, stopping to tease my nipple between his teeth in his quest for the treasure between my legs. I've never felt like it was a prized possession, something to be worshipped, until this morning. He growls around a hard nub, tugs at it, and pain and pleasure tangle for dominance.

I lean back on my arms, brace myself as he feasts on me. My nipple pops from his mouth, and he licks a path downward until he finds what he's looking for. His growl of pleasure wraps around me, and my skin tightens as the late-day sun shines on my body, sizzling the water on my exposed flesh, but I can't think about that. No, I can't think about anything other than his tongue and the lashes he's giving my clit, a brutal punishment so intense it ignites every nerve ending and pulls a cry from my throat.

"My God, Roman," I say, impatience in my voice

as I lift, bucking against his face as his tongue swirls through my slick heat doing delicious things to me.

He growls and holds my hips, better positioning me as he feasts, his mouth ravishing my pussy, hungry little laps that drive me insane. His fingers tease, delve deep, slick in and out of my channel, but then he changes tactics and scrapes his teeth over my engorged cleft. Small tremors grip me as he spears deeper inside me, pounds into my flesh, hot, dirty plunges that possess my body, and tease the building pressure.

I sit up and grip his hair to hold on. My senses explode, my body jerking in reaction to the intense pleasure. The man is wrecking me, and my struggle to hang on splinters, breaking me in two. Air leaves my lungs, and my words are nothing but a pleading whimper when I say, "I'm going to come." Oh God, am I ever going to come. So hard, I'm going to shatter in the most profound ways, ways there are no coming back from.

I throw my head back and my muscles convulse around him, shock waves rocketing through me as he nudges me over the edge until I'm flying. Flying and falling, living and dying all wrapped into one as the man frees my body in a way no one ever has before, in a way I've never been able to achieve solo.

I'm panting by the time he stops, but dark eyes meet mine, and giving me no reprieve, he tears my panties from my hips and pulls me back into the water. With my legs around him he backs up until he's sitting on the steps, water lapping at his ankles.

He tugs his pants down, just enough to free his cock, and pulls me toward him. "Ride my cock, Peyton," he demands. I widen my legs to straddle him and he growls as I reposition.

His crown presses against my opening, and delirious with need, he grips me and tugs me firmly down. I gasp as he fills me, and lean forward and lay my forehead on his shoulder, trying to catch my breath.

"I want you to ride me," he growls into my ear. "I want to watch myself slide in and out of you."

I savor the dirty, delicious way he wants me, the way he couldn't even get his pants off before he had me on top of him.

"Look at what you're doing to me," he demands, his eyes dark and feral as I tear my gaze away and look between our bodies. I lift, and his erection is wet and slick as he slides out of me.

"So hot," I say, my muscles rippling.

"Jesus, I feel you." His body tenses as my thigh muscles burn. He grips my hips and manipulates my body to take the strain from my legs. He's so damn strong he lifts me easily and pulls down until his steely length fills every inch of me. "Do you hate how hard you make me?" he hisses through clenched teeth.

"I hate it," I cry out. "I hate your cock. Hate the way you fill me up. Hate when I shatter around you."

"Keep riding me, Peyton." My nails dig into his shoulder, but he doesn't so much as wince. "I want you to make me come."

Oh God, it's crazy how much I love it when he

talks dirty. I let him move me, twist me to the way he needs me, and he lifts his hips, powering into me. My body flushes hot, and I reach between us to stroke my clit.

"Yeah, just like that." His nostrils flare, his lips part, and he thickens even more inside me. I'm so damn wet, his rapid thrusting picking up the pace until the friction is unbearable, control a thing of the past.

I briefly close my eyes, fearing I'm losing my damn grip on reality as this man drives into me, his fingers biting into my hips. Tomorrow I'll have little bruises and the thought thrills me. He jerks me up, then pulls me down again, so goddamn hard, he hits my cervix, and draws another full-body release out of me.

"Roman," I cry out, and practically collapse on top of him. My body shakes, a hard quiver, so power-ful and intense, it leaves me trembling, on the brink of tears. Soothing hands drift up from my hips to wrap around me.

"I got you," he says, and my heart squeezes at the tenderness in his voice. I move my body as he cradles me, rotate my hips around his thick cock, wanting more, wanting everything as a new, almost frightening kind of hunger takes hold. "Take what you need, Peyton," he says, like he can see into my soul, understand I'm still that small frightened girl who asked for nothing. My throat squeezes tight, my hair falling forward as I lean into him. "Take every-thing you need," he says, his voice rusty and harsh, thick with an emotion I can't identify.

I rock against him, knowing I'll never truly have

what I need, not from him or any other man. My breasts rub against his face, and I lift, only to slowly sink back down. His hands move to my face and he cups my cheeks, bringing my mouth to his. He groans into my mouth, and I swallow his moans as he lets go, giving in to the need gripping his body. I struggle to breathe with each hard pulse inside me.

"I feel you," I murmur, the pleasure so intense as his release sears my insides and stimulates all my nerve endings, and I come again. "Oh my God, Roman," I breathe into his mouth.

"I know, Peyton, I know," he moans, and peppers kisses to my nose and cheeks and chin. "Jesus, I know," he says. I inch back to take in the darkness in his eyes, the need he's desperately trying to hide. Or maybe I'm imagining it. I've wanted for so long to be wanted and needed, maybe my mind is playing tricks on me and the sex is messing with my perception of reality. He cups the back of my head and brings my face to his shoulder. His hand strokes down my hair, his touch so soft and gentle, my stupid heart misses a beat. Once again, I let my mind wander, live in a fairy-tale world where Roman and I could be more. Is that what I want? I bask in it for a second, until his worried voice breaks the spell.

"Shit, we just made a big mistake."

CHAPTER EIGHT

Roman

I LIFT HER from my lap, and we both collapse on the warm decking. The warm late-day sun disappears behind a heavy cloud, darkening the rooftop—not to mention my mood. Talk about a colossal mistake. What the hell is wrong with me? What was I thinking? Oh, maybe I *wasn't* thinking—not with the head on my shoulders—because I simply couldn't get inside this sweet girl fast enough, but goddammit she deserves better from me.

"Roman?" Peyton's eyes are wide when they search mine, seeking answers, and the fear I see there is like a punch to the gut. Christ, I'm not even sure she's breathing.

"I didn't—" I begin, but stop when the worry in her eyes deepens, triggering a pang of unease deep inside me. I push the hair from her face. Shit, what is going through her mind? "I didn't use a condom," I tell her. "I completely forgot, and I'm so damn sorry."

She nods and the breath she'd been holding leaves

her lungs in a whoosh. "Is that all?" she finally says, and I put my hand on her shoulder, her muscles relaxing under my touch. *Is that all?* That's her reaction? What the hell? I thought she'd be as upset as I am, but she seems to be okay with it. What am I missing here, or more importantly, what the hell did she think I was going to say? What could be worse than not using a condom, especially when we have no future?

I brush my thumb over her skin. "What did you think I meant?"

"Nothing," she says quickly, and averts her gaze, but I'm not having any of that. I want openness and honesty between us. I cup her chin and bring her focus back to me. That's when I see it, right there in the depths of her eyes. This sweet vulnerable girl puts a big smile on for the world but underneath it all, she's still lost, still vulnerable, still thinks she's unlikable...unlovable.

"Did you think I meant me sleeping with you again was a mistake?" I ask, wrapping the question in a soft voice.

"I guess, maybe."

"Because of my relationship with Cason?" Yeah, he'd give me a beating if he ever found out—hate me for the rest of my life, likely—but she said she'd keep our secret and I trust her.

"Well...no. This isn't about Cason."

"Then what?"

She shakes my hand from her chin and turns from me, her long auburn curls falling over her chest. "Can we not talk about this?"

I take a curl between my fingers, rub softly. "I want to talk about it, Peyton. We're friends." Honestly if anyone can use a true friend, someone she can trust implicitly, it's Peyton. "More than friends right now, actually," I tease, hoping it brings a smile to her face.

"Look," she says, her dark tone cutting into my thoughts. "It's no big deal. I just thought you changed your mind about all this."

"Because I no longer wanted you?"

Shit, right there. Right there, all over her face, lies my answer.

She tries for a casual shrug, but fails miserably. "I just thought you'd changed your mind."

My God, her screwed-up childhood really did a number on her. I probably didn't help when I kissed her and walked away, leaving her to believe she wasn't likable. I just hadn't wanted to betray her brother.

Doesn't matter, I never should have started something I couldn't finish. Not with Peyton. If I could kick my own ass I would. What I can do now, however, is show her she's everything any man would want, and more. I roll toward her, my body pressing against her leg.

"I like being with you, Peyton." I brush my hand over her cheek. "I like *you*."

She grins and glances down past my waist. "I can tell."

I chuckle at that. Sure, I'm physically attracted to her, but I like her. She's a kind, caring and giving woman. I haven't come across many of those in my life, besides my family. I thought my ex was all those things, but look how that turned out. I hope someday Peyton finds a guy who can give her the family she says she doesn't want, because I get the sense that she's just too frightened to put herself out there, afraid that she's not enough, afraid of getting close, of getting hurt…again.

"You know, for years I kept you at a distance, but you were right when you said it's your body, yours to do with as you wish, and who you sleep with is none of Cason's business." The truth is Cason is completely overprotective of her. I can understand that, though. It was just the two of them against the world. Everything about Peyton, from her big green eyes to the way she tries to hide her vulnerabilities, brings out the protector in me, too. I'd like to put her in a bubble and keep her sheltered from a world that has been cruel to her. Of course, she'd introduce her foot to my nuts if I tried. She's a grown woman and mistakes or not, her decisions regarding her life and her body are hers.

"Coming around to my way of thinking, are you?"

"When you're right, you're right," I say, and trail my finger down her arm. "But we should have used a condom." My gaze narrows in on her. "I'm clean, but neither one of us wants a family, right?" I say, my gaze roaming her face. Will she agree with me, or finally admit that she wants more from life? I used to want a family. I used to want a lot of things, but

I gave up the idea when I realized women value my status over me.

"That's right, we don't, and it's okay. I'm on the Pill. It regulates my cycle."

A ridiculous laugh bubbles up inside me and spills from my mouth.

Peyton's brows arch. "What, does it make you uncomfortable to talk about a woman's menstruation cycle?"

"Hell no, it's just…" I shake my head. "This… us… I never in a million years pictured this…" I wave my hand back and forth between our bodies. "Correction, I've pictured this, a thousand different ways, but I never thought we'd be having sex, on a rooftop no less, forgetting condoms and talking about your cycle." I flop onto my back, a grin tugging at my mouth. I like the openness and honesty between us. A little too much, actually.

Careful, Roman.

"You didn't stand a chance, Roman," she says, a playful tone in her voice.

"Oh?" I angle my head to see her green eyes glistening with mischief.

She blows on her knuckles and brushes them over her chest. "I go after what I want, and I wanted you."

Liking that far too much, I roll on top of her and she squeals when I grab her hands and put them over her head. "You're a tease, you know that." I brush my lips over hers as I begin to harden again.

"You say that like it's a bad thing," she says, and

lifts her hips to grind against my swelling member. My God, I can't get enough of this woman.

"I think we have another problem." I press my lips to hers when she arches a questioning brow. "I want to fuck you again."

Her eyes dim with desire. "Pretty sure that's not a problem."

"It is when we have to be at your boss's house."

Her lids fly open. "Ohmigod, you're right. We need to get moving."

I roll off her, stand and pull her to her feet. Our bodies mesh, and she smiles up at me. "Thanks for saying that about my body being mine. I'm glad you see it that way and can finally understand why I get so frustrated with Cason."

"Doesn't mean he's not going to kill me, though."

She frowns and glances at my chest, her finger rolling around my nipple. "Yeah, I know he will. Are you regretting this, Roman? Are you sorry I seduced you?"

"Hell no," I blurt out, and it brings a smile to her face. "I was fighting a losing battle with you, and I want to be honest. I tried to tell myself that coming here with you was all for Cason. That was a lie."

"It was?" she asks, a small hitch in her voice.

"I wanted to be around you. I didn't plan for anything to happen between us, but I just wanted to be around you." A garbled laugh catches in my throat. "I must be some kind of masochist, huh?" She smiles and I put my hands on her shoulders to display just how serious I am when I glance down at her and continue with, "I also really wanted to help you, Peyton. What you want, well, if it's important to you, then it's important to me, too." She's important to me. She always has been.

Sometimes I think I didn't stop the engagement, went through with the wedding prep, because this girl could never be mine, and it was a way to make that clear—to myself. Even though the engagement failed, Peyton and I still can't have a real relationship. We want different things and her brother would disown both of us. She needs her brother more than life itself. I need him, too. The most important thing, though, is for nothing to ruin what they have. I'd never forgive myself if I came between brother and sister.

I swallow. Hard. "I don't want any kind of trouble with Cason, Peyton."

She goes up on her toes and gives me a soft kiss. "You won't. He never needs to know about this. It's not his business, anyway."

"Yeah, I know," I say, but that doesn't help with the guilt spreading through me. I give her a nudge, setting her in motion toward the stairs. As I gather our clothes, I realize there's something she needs to know. "You said you were only with one guy in college, but it's not because guys weren't attracted to you."

"What makes you say that?"

"Well, one, you're the most beautiful woman I've ever set eyes on, and two, your brother was well-known on campus. The guys all sort of knew not to mess with you."

Stark naked, her hand goes to her hip and her mouth drops open. Could she be any more adorable? "You have got to be kidding me."

"Nope, sorry." I give her a sheepish look. "Your brother would have killed anyone who got too close."

Her green eyes flare with anger. "I'm going to kill him."

I drag her to me. "Hey, you can't tell him I told you."

"How can I keep that in?"

"Please."

"Fine, Roman. I'll keep the secret." She rolls her eyes at me and I smile. I like having secrets with Peyton. "Let's go get ready."

Forty-five minutes later, Elias is dropping us off at Andrew's house. "See, we needed a car after all," I tell her.

"You don't always have to be right about everything, you know," she says, and playfully elbows me in the gut. We walk up the cobblestoned walkway, and she wraps her arms around herself and shivers as the night air falls over us. I put my arm around her to warm her and as we approach the door, it swings wide open and a very attractive lady with short dark hair and dark eyes greets us.

"You must be Peyton and Roman. Right on time." Her smile is warm and inviting as she takes our hands and gives a welcoming squeeze. "I'm Sofia, Andrew's wife. We're so glad you could join us tonight. Richard and Paula are already here." Her lips thin and her light laugh wraps around me. "I didn't have time to do my hair," she says, and even though she's still smiling, I sense the tension beneath. "Please excuse the mess of it."

"Your hair looks fine," Peyton says, and points to her own. "Look what the humidity is doing to mine."

Sofia laughs, steps back and waves her arms. "Come in, please."

She leads us through her gorgeous home and Peyton glances at the pictures on the wall. "Are these your children?" she asks.

A look of longing comes over Sofia's face. "Yes, twins. They're both studying in England."

"How nice."

"Not for me," she says with a laugh, and Peyton grins.

Understanding and warmth dance in Peyton's eyes. "You miss them."

"I do, terribly," she says, and gives Peyton a wink. "Someday you'll understand that."

"Yes, I suppose so," Peyton says, playing the part of my wife as the two share a bonding moment. Laughter comes from the deck.

"Sounds like the party has started without us," Sofia says, her voice a bit tight, and Peyton casts me a quick glance, her eyes telegraphing a secret message. I nod slightly. Yeah, I get it. Sofia doesn't appear to be a fan of her early-bird guests.

We step out onto the back deck, and I glance out at the Mediterranean Sea, which is right on their doorstep. "Nice place you have here," I say.

Sofia smiles at me. "Thank you. Let me fix you a

drink." She angles her head. "Let me guess, a scotch drinker."

I chuckle. "How did you know?"

"A woman knows these things," she says. "Peyton, how about you?"

"Wine girl."

"Ah, I knew there was a reason I liked you," Sofia jokes, and Andrew stands to greet us.

"Great to see you both again," he says, and gestures to the empty chairs around the table. We greet Richard and Paula, who are both sipping on some kind of cocktail, and Sofia comes back with our drinks and sits at the other end of the table, opposite her husband. She turns to glance at Peyton.

"How was your first day?" Sofia asks, and before Peyton can say a word, Paula jumps in to explain how much her husband loved meeting the children, and how they all loved him in return. I resist the urge to roll my eyes. We all listen quietly, politely of course, since most of us around the table have manners. I reach out and put my hand on Peyton's leg to give it a squeeze. The look on her face suggests she wants to give a hard eye roll, and I grin back.

When Paula finally stops talking, Sofia turns to Peyton. "How about you, Peyton?"

"It was enjoyable. I really liked—"

Paula gasps and we all go quiet. "You're Roman Bianchi," she blurts out.

"That's right," I say, and roll the ice around in my glass.

Paula taps her husband's arm repeatedly. "Richard, Richard, this is Roman Bianchi. Remember we read about him in the paper. He's from a family of Italian elites. His ex-fiancée left him before their grand wedding. There was a whole spread done on him."

I shift, uncomfortable as she rudely narrates the horrible articles splashed in the trash magazines.

"I remember," Richard says, and I don't like the gleam in his eyes as his gaze goes from me to Peyton, back to me. "You went into hiding for a while."

"I wasn't hiding." Both Andrew and Sofia go quiet, clearly uncomfortable by the direction Richard is taking this conversation. "I was in New York working."

"New York's most eligible bachelor." He laughs lightly, but it belies the vindictive look in his eyes. "I believe I recall you saying something about being a bachelor for life?"

I put my arm around Peyton and her body is stiff. I laugh and take a drink of my scotch, playing it off. "You can't tell me you believe everything you read in the paper, now can you, Richard?"

"No," he says, and pushes back in his chair to mimic my relaxed posture. "You're right about that." He focuses in on Peyton's ring. "Tell me, how long have you two been married?"

"Six months," we both say quickly, maybe too quickly.

"Newlyweds," Sofia says. "How romantic."

"A big wedding, with all your family?" Richard asks.

"No, we wanted a private wedding. I love my family, but they can be overbearing at times, so we just sneaked off. I'm sure they'll want to throw us a party when we go to Sicily to see them."

"I'm looking forward to meeting them all," Peyton says.

Richard's mouth drops open. "You've never met them then?"

"It all happened rather fast," I explain. "They'll meet her soon enough and fall for her as hard as I have."

"Malta is such a great place to spend your first year together," Sofia says, and waves her hand toward the sea. "I grew up here of course, but Andrew is from Italy, and we honeymooned right here on this island. It's where we're happiest." She points to a strip of beach in the distance. "We actually exchanged vows right there, all our family and friends in attendance."

"Perfect place," Peyton says, a longing in her eyes that she can't hide from me. She doesn't want a family my ass, and as far as big weddings, there was a point in this girl's life where she wanted to be Cinderella. I'm sure of it.

"Where did you get married?" Sofia asks.

Peyton coils her hair around one finger. "Oh, we just had a civil ceremony in Manhattan."

Sofia's eyes go wide. "Oh, my, I can't believe Roman's family let him get away with that."

I grin; obviously her husband told her who I was and the two know my history and that of my overbearing family.

"This is such a great island to raise a family," Paula says, and puts her hand over her stomach, giving her husband a small grin like they might have a secret.

Sofia beams. "Great indeed. My kids had a wonderful childhood here with the beach so close."

Paula gazes at her husband. "We would love to raise our family here, too," she says. "Of course, we're very traditional, and I'll be staying home to raise them, just like my mother did. That's how children end up with good old-fashioned values." She picks up her glass and eyes Peyton over the rim. "Did your mom stay home, Peyton?"

Holy shit. Is this woman for real?

"Actually, I lost my parents when I was young," Peyton says.

"Oh, so sorry to hear that, dear," Sofia says, and I shift uncomfortably. Something tells me Paula has done her homework on the competition and is using Peyton's childhood to her advantage. Every protective instinct I possess kicks into high gear.

"Do you plan to have children, Peyton?" Paula asks.

"Of course, someday," she says, a small waver in her voice that I don't miss.

I take her hand and bring it to my mouth and give it a kiss. "We plan to have plenty of children," I say.

"Will you continue to work?" Paula waves her hand. "I mean, if maternity leave is in your future, what would happen to the students?"

"I'm sure I can figure out a way to help pick up the slack," I blurt out without thinking.

Paula laughs. "You mean you'll help out in the classroom? What qualifications do you have?"

"I might not have a degree in education, but I speak numerous languages." What am I saying? I know nothing about teaching children, but if it means helping Peyton, I'd probably stand on my head and spit nickels for their entertainment.

"How unorthodox," Paula says.

"Andrew," I say, shifting the direction of the conversation. "Do the children have computer access?"

He steeples his fingers and lets his index fingers bounce off his lips. "We have a small lab, not enough for every student of course. They all must take turns."

"I'd be happy to volunteer my time and teach basic coding skills."

Andrew's eyes widen. "We could never ask that much of you."

"You're not asking. I'm volunteering, and I'd love to help."

A wide smile splits Andrew's lips as Peyton looks at me, her mouth agape. "That's a generous offer, Roman, and I'd love to discuss this in depth with you. Right now, I must get the barbecue going."

"I'll get the salads from the kitchen," Sofia says, and takes a look at our glasses. "And it looks like we could all use a refill on our drinks."

Richard jumps up. "I'd be happy to help with the barbecue. I'm sort of known for my barbecue skills back home."

I scoff silently. I'm sure he's known for a lot of things back home.

"I'll help you in the kitchen," Paula announces, and stands.

"No, please sit and enjoy your drink," Sofia says, a little too quickly.

Refusing to take no for an answer, Paula smooths her hand over her skirt and follows Sofia inside.

The women disappear inside, and as Richard brags about his skills, I lean into Peyton. "What the hell?"

"Wow…just wow."

"You don't like them either, huh?"

She frowns. "Do you think she's right? Do you think my values are going to stand in the way of me getting this job?"

"Your values are just fine, and your heart is in the right place, but we're going to have to be very careful. If we're not…"

I let my words fall off. Shit, maybe I wasn't the right guy for this job. I thought I could blend in when in fact, I could be the one to ruin her dream job. But the thought of any other guy pretending with her, touching her, kissing her, exercising marital rights with her…well, that just doesn't sit well with me. Not anymore, anyway.

I am so screwed.

CHAPTER NINE

Peyton

"You don't have to walk me to work every morning, you know," I say, secretly liking his strong, solid presence beside me, not to mention the way he holds my hand, swinging it a little as we stroll. For the last week, he's insisted on walking me to work, and I always put up a fight, simply because I like pressing his buttons.

He groans and pinches the bridge of his nose. "Haven't we been over this?"

"Yes, but—"

"Jesus, girl, are you forgetting what happens when you argue with me?"

"Maybe I want you to kiss me." I lift my chin an inch. "Right here in the street."

"Fine." He grabs me by the waist and tugs me to him. His warm lips find mine, and I sink into the sensations as he ravishes my mouth. His growls reverberate through me, and I wrap my arms around him, loving how I can rattle him like this. He breaks free, leaving me breathless. "Just for the record, you don't have to give me a hard time every time you want a kiss."

"A hard time, huh?" I tease, and press against him.

"Cut it out. I do not need the mother of all boners right now. Not when you have to get to school, and I can't push you to your knees and enjoy this sweet mouth of yours."

Heat races through me and he gives a playful grin, knowing how much I like it when he talks dirty. "Was that payback for rubbing up against you?" He looks away and whistles innocently. It brings a laugh to my lips. "You're going to pay for that."

"Can't wait." He gives my ass a smack. "Now come on before you're late. We don't want to give Paula and Richard any more ammunition."

My shoes tap on the sidewalk as we head toward the school. "He's actually been pretty nice this week."

His hand tightens around mine. "You've heard the saying, keep your enemies close, right?"

"Yeah."

"Don't trust him, Peyton."

"I won't." We both go quiet for a second, lost in our own thoughts. I break it by asking, "When do you think you're going to visit with your family?"

He frowns. "Soon. I've been busy with some work for Hard Wear and haven't really had a chance."

"You did tell me that was one of the reasons you wanted to come here with me, yet you don't seem to be in any hurry to visit them."

"I know. It's true. I just…don't want them to know what's going on here, with you and me."

I crinkle my nose, a part of me wondering if they really would like me, or would they think I'm not good enough for their brother. Could that be why Roman really doesn't want them to know? On some level does he think the unwanted girl with no parents wouldn't fit in with his family?

"I hate for you to be so close and not see them, though," I say.

"It's fine, Peyton. When this is all over, and you're the new full-time teacher—and we're officially over—I'll visit them. They never have to know about any of this."

"I've always wanted to visit Italy," I say, putting a little cheer in my voice to hide the unease welling up inside me as I think about him leaving here, disappearing from my life—like so many others have before. "Not that I'm saying I want to go with you or anything," I quickly clarify.

He studies my face, opens his mouth and closes it a couple times. Finally, he says, "Are you going to pretend we broke up after you sign the contract, or pretend I was needed back in New York and carry on with the charade that we're married? We never really talked about that."

Even though I get the sense that's not what he really wanted to ask, I say, "If you have no intentions of ever getting married, I guess continuing to pretend is an option, isn't it?"

"I might not want to get married, Peyton, but I'm still a guy," he teases with a wink.

Yeah, I get it. Pretending we're still married means he can't be seen out with other women. Okay, so why does the idea of him being with another woman bother me so much? Then again, do I really have to ask myself that question? "How about we cross that bridge when we get to it," I say as I try to wipe the visual of him in bed with another woman from my mind. "Right now, let's just focus on me being the best candidate."

We stop in front of the school and he turns to me. "Tonight, let's get out. Go sightseeing, go to a restaurant. I'll make us a reservation for somewhere nice."

"That sounds like fun." I go up on my toes to kiss him. "Just so you know, you don't have to walk me home from work today. I'm a big girl. I can find my own way."

"Okay, I'll probably be too busy today, anyway."

Disappointment settles in my stomach. Damn, I was only kidding. I was hoping he was going to fight me on the matter. I smile to cover the ridiculous turmoil careering through me, settling around the vicinity of my heart.

The first bell inside the school rings and I reach for the door. "See you later."

I hurry inside and head to the staff room to grab a coffee before the second bell rings. I make it quickly and reach my classroom as the children start filing in. On my desk there's a little pink box.

I open it to find a gorgeous cupcake with pink

icing inside. I glance at the note, with my name on it. Paula made me a cupcake? I might not believe in Cinderella, but Snow White and the poison apple, that's a different story. Just then Richard pokes his head into the door, a big smile on his face.

"I see you found your surprise."

"How lovely of Paula," I say.

Anita, the math teacher in the class across the hall, peeks in. "I'm saving mine for break, although I was tempted to call it breakfast dessert and dive in."

Richard laughs at her and I mentally kick myself for believing the worst of Paula. She's obviously just trying to win the staff over with sweets.

"Saving it, huh?" Richard says with a laugh. "Then how did you get that blue icing on your nose?"

We all laugh and Anita, good sport that she is, quickly wipes it away. "Well, I didn't eat the whole thing," she says, a sheepish look on her face. "I only had a nibble, and it was delicious." She glances at my box. "What color icing did you get."

"Pink," I say.

"She made a different color for everyone. Based on your auras," Richard says.

I don't really believe in such things, but I do appreciate the effort. "Tell Paula thanks," I say when the second bell rings and they head to their respective classrooms. As I watch them go, Roman's words of warning jingle in the back of my brain.

All the lovely little children sit at their desks, their hair combed neatly, their faces scrubbed and shiny.

"Okay, class," I say, and pull a package of cards

from my bag. "We are going to learn animal names in English." I hold the picture up of a llama making a funny face, and the kids chuckle.

Before I know it, the bell signaling the end of the day rings, and the kids pack up their desks. My heart is so full as I watch them file from the classroom, and without even thinking I press my hand to my stomach. Not because I'm wondering what it would be like to have a child of my own, but because it's suddenly very grumbly.

I take a sip from my water bottle and put it back into my bag. My stomach growls a bit louder and I swallow uneasily.

"Hey."

My heart leaps at the sound of Roman's voice in my doorway. "What are you doing here? I thought you had work to do."

He jerks his thumb over his shoulder and he has a teasing grin on his face when he says, "If you don't want me—"

"I want you," I say.

He steps up to me and pulls me to his body and I slide my arms around his neck. "Yeah, I can tell," he says playfully.

"How about we go home and I get you naked."

My body warms at the idea as I say, "What time is our dinner reservation?"

He puts his mouth close to my ear. "The only thing I'm hungry for is you."

A thrill goes through me. "What a coincidence,

because the only thing I want to put in my mouth is you."

His breathing changes. "Jesus, girl. Keep that up and I'll bend you over this desk." He inches back and his brow furrows.

"What?" I ask.

"Are you okay? You actually look a bit pale." He touches my forehead. "No fever, but you're kind of cold and clammy."

"I'm always cold," I say, brushing it off, but he's right, I'm not actually feeling great.

"Not like this, Peyton."

"My stomach is a little funny, actually," I say. "It just started. Maybe I'm coming down with something."

"Let's get you home."

Home.

I like the idea of Roman, me and…home. I've always lived in houses, never homes, and I'd be wise not to think this time is any different. When he leaves, I leave the villa. I'll have to find something permanent for myself, something I can afford.

He leads me outside, and I wince as the sun shines down on me, the contents in my stomach churning. Roman keeps casting me quick glances, like he's worried I'm going to go down for the count. I'm a little worried about that, too.

I pick up the pace and he hurries along with me. By the time we reach the villa, I'm in a full-blown sweat and whatever is in my stomach wants out.

"Roman," I say, and grab his sleeve. "I'm not feeling good."

He scoops me up and hurries upstairs to the bathroom. "Are you going to vomit?"

"No." Oh God, this is so embarrassing. "Please leave."

"Peyton, I don't want to leave you." He stands over me as I grip my stomach. "I think you need my help."

"Roman, please, you need to leave right now," I blurt out, never more embarrassed in my life. "Trust me on this."

He hesitates, but the pleading look in my eyes must have convinced him. He steps into the smaller bedroom and closes the door behind him.

"Go downstairs," I yell, mortified. "I need to die in peace."

"Call out if you need me," he says as I hurry out of my clothes and drop down onto the commode, my entire life flashing before my eyes. "This cannot be happening," I cry as pain rips across my abdomen.

Sounds of Roman moving about in the kitchen, and possibly cooking something, reach my ears, although the thoughts of food turn my stomach even more.

After a long while, I wash up and Roman raps on the door. "You okay in there?"

"I'm going to our bed to die," I say.

"Can I come help?"

"Yeah," I say. I swallow against a dry throat as my weak legs carry me to the bed Roman and I have been sharing for the past week.

I collapse onto the mattress, and Roman enters from the hall. The concern in his eyes wraps around me like a blanket. He sits down next to me and pulls the cover over my now-freezing body.

"Do you think it's the flu?"

"I don't know. I have severe pains in my stomach."

"Maybe it was something you ate."

I run through everything I put in my stomach. "We had the same big breakfast, and you're not sick."

"What about lunch?"

"I was so full from breakfast, I skipped lunch."

"Same." He presses his hand to my forehead. "Do you think you can drink something?"

"Yeah, I'm really thirsty."

"I'll be right back." I close my eyes, and a minute later Roman is back with a tall glass of ice water.

"Can you sit up a bit?" He helps me up and I sip the water, praying to God it doesn't go through me and thinking it will, judging by the way my stomach is protesting.

"It came on so fast," I say.

He helps me lie back down and lightly brushes my hair from my face. "Are you tired?"

"A little bit."

"Do you want me to leave you to sleep?"

Before I realize what I'm doing, I reach out and take his hand. "Do you think you could stay for a minute?"

"Of course."

"Tell me about your day," I say, as if we're an old

married couple sharing stories like it's the most natural thing in the world for us to be doing.

"I did some work and talked to Cason. He called to see how things were going."

"I've been meaning to call him." I swallow as another wave of pain rips across my abdomen.

"I told him things were going good."

I groan. "They were. Right up until today. I mean they still are but…ugh, whatever this is, it's not good."

Concerned eyes rake over my face. "Do you want me to call a doctor?"

"I haven't had a chance to find one here yet."

"I could take you to Emergency, or I could call my sister Maria," he says. "Her husband is an emergency room doctor. He might be able to diagnose you over the phone."

"Then they'd know you were here."

"I think your health is more important than that, Peyton." He lightly brushes his hand over my forehead, and it feels good. "I can deal with their interfering if it means helping you."

"Keep doing that," I say as his hand soothes me. "The warmth of your hand feels good." He disappears for a second, coming back with a damp cloth. He lightly presses it to my flesh and it instantly makes me feel better. "That's good." I sigh. "Don't call anyone, though. I think it's just something I ate."

"I'm not sure, Peyton. We ate the same things and I'm fine."

"I'm sure it's just a bug. Promise me you won't

call." I don't want to bring the wrath of his family down on him, and he's spilled enough lies for me already. I'm not about to put him in a position where he has to lie to his family, too.

He dabs my head a few more times, sets the cloth down and fixes the blanket around me when an almost violent cold shiver moves through me. "Okay, if that's what you want." I don't miss the reluctance in his voice, but I don't think I need to go so far as to seek medical help.

"Roman."

"Yeah."

"Thanks for helping me," I say. Honestly, I'm so not used to counting on anyone, and he has gone above and beyond in so many ways. He's so kind, and so giving, and honestly that's just going to mess me up more when we go back to a clean slate. "I wish it wasn't you, though. I wish it wasn't you here with me," I murmur.

His shoulders tighten, and the wounded look on his face hurts my heart. "Why would you say that? I thought we'd become friends."

I pick up a pillow and put it over my face. "It's not that. We are friends, it's just… It's so embarrassing for you to see me like this," I say, my voice muffled. He takes the pillow away and sets it beside me, and the understanding and compassion in his eyes eases the mortification inside me.

"Don't be," he says softly. "I had older sisters, remember? They embarrassed me all the time. Someday I'll tell you about all the terrible things they did to their baby brother."

"Tell me now," I say, wanting him to stay longer. I like his calm, steady presence. I like…him.

His mouth twists like he's in pain, and I shouldn't laugh but he looks so adorable right now. "Fine, remember I told you how much they liked to be in the kitchen."

"I do," I say, and snuggle closer to him, to bask in his strength and intimate familiarity. My lids fall shut, and I relax to the sound of his deep voice.

He laughs and the rumble soothes me. "This is really horrible but when I was around five, my sister Lucy, who is a year older than me, had this Easy-Bake Oven. She made a chocolate brownie but didn't have any icing sugar. She made up this weird concoction of yogurt and regular sugar, and I think she put some mud in there for color." I open one eye and chuckle when he scrunches up his nose. "Of course, she talked me into trying it first. It was pretty bad."

"Oh, how horrible." I take in the small smile touching the corner of his mouth. "You're smiling."

He scrubs his face. "Yeah. I guess I miss Lucy. We were the closest. We did everything together."

"Like Cason and I did."

"If I ever had kids, I'd want a dozen so they could all have one another. I complain, but goddammit, Peyton. They do mean the world to me."

As he shares something very touching, very private with me, my heart thumps a bit faster. "I thought you didn't want children."

"I don't." He blinks a couple times, like he's trying to get his head on straight. "Isn't that what I said?"

"It's something you said before. Not what you just said."

"Oh, it's what I meant to say." He picks the cloth back up and dabs my forehead. "Just for the record, Peyton, you'd be an amazing mother."

"What makes you say that?"

"The kindness and compassion you have for kids."

"When have you ever seen me with kids? Hey," I say when a guilty look crosses his face. "What did you do?"

He gives a slow shake of his head. "Even sick, you're questioning me."

"When you look like the damn cat who swallowed the canary, yeah I'm going to question you."

"I was out for a stroll today, just to get some fresh air. I saw you in the schoolyard with the kids."

"You're a creeper, Roman," I murmur, and snuggle in tighter.

"I just wanted to make sure everything was going okay and you were happy."

I chuckle. "Still a creeper." My stomach squeezes, but this time it's from happiness. I like the thought of him checking up on me, just to make sure I'm okay and happy. "You're sweet," I say without thinking.

"Keep that to yourself. I have a reputation to uphold." He laughs softly. "Close your eyes and sleep."

I do as he says. A second later his warm lips are on my forehead and a soft sigh escapes my throat.

Don't fall for him, Peyton.

If I put that on repeat in my brain, will it sink in?

As his warmth and closeness cocoon me, his steady, even breathing sounds soothe me. I'm seconds from drifting off when a horrible thought occurs to me. My lids fling open.

"I did eat something different."

CHAPTER TEN

Roman

"Yes, Lucy, I'm fine. Working away as usual." I pinch the bridge of my nose as my lovely sister grills me about my love life, or lack thereof, on the other end of the phone.

"Why do you sound like you're close? Typically your calls from New York don't come in this clearly," she asks.

"I'm just…outside," I say, not a lie. Peyton had been up half the night with stomach cramps and slept through her alarm this morning. I shut it off. She's in no shape to go in to work, and when my phone rang, I ran to the rooftop to answer it, not wanting to wake her.

"You sound tired."

"I am tired." I spent the better part of the night worrying about Peyton and debating on calling a doctor, not to mention refreshing her water to keep her hydrated after every trip to the bathroom. There wasn't much time for sleep. I yawn, and something niggles in the back of my brain. I reach for it, and when I'm finally able to grasp it, I blurt out, "Wait, why wouldn't you expect me to sound tired? You're calling in the middle of the night." At least in New York it's the middle of the night. A long pause takes up space between us, like she's trying to figure out a way to tell me, and worry zings through me. "Lucy, is something wrong?"

"It's Mamma. She worries about you being all alone. She's not getting any younger, Roman. You need to find yourself a wife and settle down." I open my mouth, ready to blurt out that I did, just to ease my mother's worries. I stop myself before I do. While that might make my mother happy, it would bring a whole lot of trouble to this situation Peyton and I are in.

"Can you please tell her she has nothing to worry about? I'm happy, and life is good." I smile. Despite Peyton not feeling well, this last week has been good—probably the best week I've had in a long time, or ever. Yeah, being with Peyton has been fun, and I can't remember the last time I had fun or felt this alive. But in a few short weeks, after she signs the contract and I say I have to head back to New York for work, we erase this time from our memories and go back to a clean slate.

Why the hell does that idea bother me so much?

"That's why you called? To tell me our mother has been worried?" I glance at the gorgeous sea cliffs in the distance; a colorful blue bird chirps as it takes flight. "You're not telling me anything I don't know, so why the call in the middle of the night, Luce…"

"What was that?" Lucy asks.

"What was what?"

"If it's the middle of the night there, why do I hear a bird chirping?"

Shit.

"Sound machine," I say quickly. "Helps me sleep." Wow, aren't the lies just rolling off my tongue lately.

"I though you said you were outside?"

Crap.

"I'm back inside now."

"Sounded like a blue rock thrush."

"How would I know what it is? You're the bird-watcher, not me."

"It's the national bird of Malta. Don't you remember when we were kids, we used to chase them when we vacationed on the beach?"

"Vaguely," I say, my stomach twisting. "What I remember most is you making me eat mud. I'm going back to sleep."

Her chuckle fills the space between us. "No, wait. I called because I couldn't wait to tell you something."

I lean against the glass rail and let the sun warm my face. "What's up?"

"You're going to be an uncle again."

My heart squeezes tight. My God, the baby Bianchi sister is going to have a baby. How is that possible? "I'm so happy for you, Luce…" I can just picture the big smile on my sister's face. She was the youngest girl, and I came after her. The two of us were closer than any of us and Jesus, I really miss her. My heart thumps a little harder.

"I wanted to tell you before the others, that's why I called in the middle of the night. Sorry if I woke you."

My throat tightens. "Don't be sorry," I say, and cradle my phone. "I'm glad I was your first call."

"Roman."

"Yeah?"

"Miss you, bro." My heart squeezes tight. "Can you come home soon?"

"Yeah, I'll see you soon, Luce…" I think about next weekend. Maybe I can sneak off to Italy for a quick visit with my family.

"Love you," she says.

I spin when I hear movement behind me, and turn to find a pale Peyton watching me, her big green eyes wide and glassy. How much did she hear? Will she be upset that I'm planning a trip sooner rather than later, and leaving her behind, after admitting how much she'd love to visit Italy? She's been left behind enough, and yesterday I got the sense she'd like to go, but under the circumstances what choice do I have?

"I have to go. I'll see what I can do about visiting," I say, my voice thick with emotion. "Talk to you later, and love back." I end the call and shove my phone into my pocket. I examine Peyton's pale face. Honest to God, if that cupcake Richard gave her was tainted, he's going to have some explaining to do—to my fist.

"Hey," I say, and sink down in front of her. I press my hand to her forehead. "How are you feeling?"

"I spent time on a farm one summer," she begins. "My foster family had an orchard." I eye her. Jesus, is she delirious? I wait for her to continue, to see where she's going with this. She swallows and practically peels her dry tongue from the roof of her mouth.

"Okay," I say. "And…"

"They had this tractor." She lifts her arms and widens them, sounding a bit loopy and tired. "It was huge. It tilled the ground or something." She uses her fingers and opens and closes them like she's plowing the soil. "Anyway, I feel like that tractor ran me over, then backed up to finish the job."

I can't help but laugh at her description and it brings a small smile to her face. "I'm so sorry, Peyton."

"Not your fault." She takes a breath of fresh morning air and groans. "I need to get ready for school." She stands on wobbly legs. I jump up and catch her, scooping her into my arms.

"The only place you're going is back to bed."

She tries to wiggle from my arms. "No, I have to get to work."

"I already called Andrew. I'm going to be in the computer lab with the kids today."

Her mouth drops open. "Roman, I can't ask that of you."

"You're not. I'm happy to shape young minds, and maybe I'll have a hand in producing the next Bill Gates or Steve Jobs."

"Andrew agreed?"

I set her into the chair under the pergola and drop down in front of her. "He's pretty excited about it, actually."

She frowns. "Ohmigod, now I'm going to be in competition with you, too."

"Hardly. If you want to know the truth—" I stop to feign a shiver "—I'm scared shitless."

A little chuckle rumbles in her throat. "Why?"

"Kids, they kind of scare me. They can be evil little beings, you know. One time when I was in high school, my young nephew thought it would be funny to put blue dye on my toothbrush. It was my senior year and I was going on a date with this girl I was crazy about. Let's just say it was my one and only date with her."

"Why did he do that?"

I shrug. "I actually think my sisters put him up to it."

"Are you kidding me?"

"They passed it off as an April Fool's joke but deep down I think they were trying to sabotage my date."

She frowns and puts her hand on my cheek. She doesn't feel as clammy as she did last night. "That wasn't very nice," she says, siding with me, and I like that. Couples need to stick together, no matter what. Not that we're a real couple, but Peyton would undoubtedly be a ride-or-die kind of girl when it came to relationships. If she were open to one, that is.

"Sisters." I push her curls from her face. She's a hot mess and never looked cuter.

"They must have had a reason." She eyes me, curiosity all over her flushed face. "What did you do to them?"

"Me!" I exclaim, indignation in my tone as my head rears back in shock. "I'll have you know I was a saint, Peyton. A damn saint."

She laughs at that and the sweet sound goes through me.

"A *damn* saint? Yeah, and I'm Mother Teresa." Long lashes blink over tired green eyes. "Seriously, why did they do it?"

"I think it was because they didn't like the girl I was going out with. They all thought she wasn't good enough for me."

"Wow, tough crowd."

"Right—now do you see what I mean about butting into my life?"

"Yeah, I guess, and I bet they'd hit it off with Cason. He's always up in my business."

"You really do know how it feels."

"Something else we have in common," she says, and glances down, her brow furrowed. Her head lifts and her eyes are brimming with questions when she looks back up at me.

"What?"

"Did they like your ex-fiancée?"

"Yeah, they did. I think at that point in my life they were anxious for me to settle down and have a family. They either missed the signs or she fooled everyone."

"Fooled everyone?"

"Never mind. It's not important."

I'm about to stand when her hand on mine stops me. "Roman, if it's important to you, it's important to me." She pastes on a smile. "I am your wife."

I am your wife.

Shit. Shit. Shit.

I really shouldn't like the sound of that so much.

"She didn't want me for me, Peyton," I say, and go quiet as her eyes narrow, her brain absorbing that information. "She wanted my name and all that came with it."

"I didn't know. I'm sorry."

"I'm not," I say without thinking. The truth of the matter is, I was sorry to find out my worth to women, but deep down, I think I might have felt a measure of relief when she called off the wedding.

And why is that, Roman?

Oh, because she wasn't Peyton.

Well, shit.

She goes thoughtful for a moment. "Do you… think they'd like me?"

"Yeah, of course." I lightly nudge her on the chin. "I told you that already."

"Yeah, I know, but I'm probably not the kind of girl they'd like to see you with."

I stare at her long and hard. "Why would you say that?"

She rolls her eyes. "Come on, Roman. I hardly come from the right background."

"Why would you think that matters?"

"Are you seriously asking me that?"

"You think pedigree matters to my family?"

"Oh, it matters, Roman. When you're on my side of the tracks, it matters. I'm judged all the time. You have no idea what that's like."

Her words pierce my skin and I stand abruptly. "Is that what you think?" Jesus Christ, I'm judged all the time, too. I'm judged because I was born with a silver spoon, she's judged because she wasn't.

"No, I don't mean that." She squeezes her eyes shut, hurts from her childhood written all over her face. "Things aren't coming out right." Her glassy eyes meet mine. "If that came out as an insult, I didn't mean it. I think you're a really great guy."

"You won't for long." She gasps when I pick her up and carry her back to bed. "You're staying here for the rest of the day."

She wiggles and tries to protest as I cover her. "I don't feel right about this, Roman."

"Stop," I say, and pin her down. Her breath catches and I grin. "Oh, do you hate me restraining you right now?"

"Yes, you're such a bully."

I laugh at that. "Yeah, I am, aren't I?" I brush her hair from her forehead, everything in me softening. "I want to take care of you, okay?"

"Roman—"

A growl rumbles in my throat. "It's okay, Peyton.

It's okay to let someone else help." I dip my head and cup her face. "I'm not going to hurt you. I promise. Can you trust me on that?"

She swallows and water fills her eyes as she glances away. My heart nearly shatters. This sweet girl hasn't been able to count on anyone but her brother, for fear of being cast away like she was nothing more than yesterday's newspaper.

Goddammit, I want to be the person she can count on.

"Yes," she says.

"Good. I'm going to the school today. End of discussion."

"Bully," she murmurs under her breath.

"What's that?" I ask, a warning in my tone.

"Nothing." She pulls the blanket over her head and whispers, "Bully." Her chuckle wraps around me and I shake my head. This girl is killing me.

"You're going to pay for that."

"I know," she mumbles, more chuckles.

"Get some rest, Peyton."

I'm about to leave the room when she flings the covers off. "Roman."

I hover in the doorway. "Yeah?"

"Who are you going to see soon?" She flips her hands over, palms up. "It's not my business and you can tell me that. It's just when I walked onto the rooftop, I overheard you." Her eyes blink rapidly, and one thing I've come to learn about her is when she's upset about something, she rambles on. Another thing we have in common. "If you have someone here you want to see, some girlfriend or something—"

"It was Lucy," I say.

The apprehension on her face morphs into a smile. "Oh, your sister." Relief visible, she adds, "Easy-Bake Oven."

I laugh at that. "Yeah, she's the one, and I think I'm going to call her that from now on." I step back into the room. "She's pregnant. She wanted me to be the first to know."

Peyton closes one hand over her heart. "That is so nice."

"She wants to see me."

She smiles up at me, a longing on her face. "You should go see her."

"Yeah, I think I will." Before I can stop myself, I blurt out. "Will you come?"

What the ever-loving hell am I doing?

"I…" She grips her blankets, squeezes them in her hand. Her expression is troubled when she says, "I don't think that's a good idea."

Her words hit like a punch to the gut. Not good, Roman. Not good at all. Nothing good can come from introducing her to the family. I'd have to lie and tell them we were married, or let them in on the charade—they wouldn't be happy about that, and the fewer people who know, the better. Despite all that, I still want my family to meet her, and that's all kinds of messed up.

"Maybe I won't go."

"It's okay if you do," she says, smiling up at me, but the sadness on her face tears at my heart.

"I'll think about it." I'm about to step away but turn back and say, "Jealousy looks good on you, by the way."

Her eyes widen and her mouth falls open. "Excuse me?"

"When you thought I was talking to a girlfriend or something…"

"I was not jealous. I was curious. I'm very curious by nature, in case you didn't know." She folds her arms and lifts her chin an inch. "I was being nice, Roman."

"I like when you're nice," I say, and let my gaze drop to her mouth. The energy in the room changes, vibrates with the heat between us. "For the record I like when you're *not* nice, too." That remark gets me a pillow across the face.

I laugh and walk back to her. "That's quite a throw you have there. Little League?"

"The end of the school year fair is coming up. There'll be a dunk tank. I signed you up for it." She lifts her arms and flexes. "I've been warming up my pitching arm."

My God, she is so adorable. "Do you hate me, Peyton?"

"Yes," she says with a grin.

"Let's just hope all the evil little humans in the classroom don't feel the same way, otherwise they'll eat me alive."

She grabs my arm. "Roman."

"Yeah."

"They're going to love you."

"Right, what's not to love?" I joke. She rolls her eyes hard enough to give me a headache and I chuckle, despite the windstorm sweeping through my gut. The one person I want to love me doesn't. We're playing a game, having sex and having fun, but when push comes to shove, she's built a wall around her heart—something else we have in common—and her brother would disown us both if he ever found out. How could we ever be together after this?

More importantly, how could we ever be apart?

CHAPTER ELEVEN

Peyton

THE WARM SUN seeps in through the crack in the curtains and falls over my body, stirring me awake. My lids open and it takes me a second to remember where I am. My entire body tingles, my stomach full of butterflies, as I remember my morning conversation with Roman and that adorable smirk that crossed his face before he left me to sleep. When he teased me, saying he likes me nice and *not* so nice, his expression was filled with pure adoration and playfulness. Honestly, I love the way he looks at me. Roman Bianchi is so sweet, funny and playful—completely sensitive to my needs—how is a girl not supposed to fall for him?

Oh boy.

I can't go there. No way, no how can I go and fall for a guy who is completely off relationships. I'm off them, too, but that still doesn't change the fact that I'm crazy about Roman, always have been, and nothing good can come from that.

I push my blankets off and pad to the bathroom. I reach for the light, only to realize it's on. It's been on since Roman put me to bed last night, leaving the light on and the door cracked. My heart thumps a little harder in my chest and my throat is a gritty mess when I swallow.

God, where is my self-preservation when I need it most?

I step into the bathroom and gasp at my reflection in the mirror. Holy, I'm surprised the man didn't run back to New York. I cringe at the dark smudges under my eyes, and at the mess of hair on my head that would make Carrot Top look like a fashion model. I hurry into a warm shower and wash the remnants of the flu, or whatever this bug was, away. I can't for one second think Richard or his wife would stoop so low to put something in a cupcake to knock me on my ass—or rather the commode. We're adults, not devious children, right? I've dealt with enough of them in my childhood, and thought adulthood would be different. Maybe I'm wrong. Roman seems to think so.

Once clean, I dress and head downstairs to find a loaf of bread and a mug with a tea bag in it on the countertop. I pick up the note he left, and my throat tightens as I read his perfect penmanship.

Try to eat something and text if you need me. See you soon. I'll make us dinner, but it might not be edible!

A strange ache, deep in my chest, right around the vicinity of my heart, tugs at me. I drop down into the kitchen chair, note clutched between my fingers. I read it again and again, yet no matter how hard I try, I can't stop that wall around my heart from fracturing. My phone pings and I jump. I fish it from the bottom of my purse, and a stupid smile tugs up the corners of my mouth as I read the message.

Hope you're feeling better. I'm still alive. The evil little humans haven't taken me out yet.

I hold the phone close and laugh, a new kind of lightness in me as I text back.

Feeling much better. I'm up to making dinner no problem. Whatever I had has passed.

I stare at the phone and three dots appear, only to disappear. I guess he changed his mind on whatever it was he was going to say. I shoot a text off to Cason to let him know things are going well and set my phone down. My stomach growls and I make some toast and tea, appreciating Roman leaving this all out for me. After I eat, I glance around, suddenly bored with myself. I'm usually on the go, having a million things to do, and I actually have no idea how to relax.

Well, I have some idea…

But Roman is at work, so I'm left to my own devices. Maybe I'll head to the school and creep on him the way he creeped on me. I scoop up my purse and head out into the sunshine. Face tipped to the sun, I stand on the porch for a second. I truly love it here in Malta, and I haven't even really explored it yet. Something about the place gives me a sense of peace, of home. Would it be the same if I weren't here with Roman?

I'm too afraid to answer that.

I walk along the sidewalk leading to the school and pass joggers, and mothers pushing their children in strollers, and elderly people out for a walk. I'm not sure I ever remember my heart being so full.

As I approach the school, laughter reaches my ears, and I check my phone to see it's afternoon break at the playground. I walk around the school, spot Roman and cover my mouth to stifle a chuckle. The kids are pulling him in all directions. I lean against the brick building, a huge smile on my face as I watch him join them in a game of basketball, where evidently, it's him against the entire classroom.

"Hey, not fair," he calls out, when one of the kids distracts him so the other can get the ball. They all laugh, obviously loving how they're able to get the better of him. I stand there a few more minutes, and my smile falls as a flash of sadness envelops me. The man has been hurt in the past, has sworn off marriage and children. It's a shame, really. He's having the time of his life with them right now and it's clear he'd be a remarkable father. Dammit, I hate that past hurts have forced him to guard his emotions. Maybe it's time he let go of the past and move on to the future. My throat tightens. Yeah, I'm one to talk.

I fold my arms and hug myself as a cool chill moves through me. The sun is shining on my body, but the cold is always there, right below the surface. I'm about to push off the wall when I catch a shadow on the ground. I turn to find Richard coming toward me. I stand up a bit straighter.

"Late start to your day, isn't it?" he calls out, his loud voice grabbing my attention. He checks his watch and closes the distance between us.

"I was ill."

He raises his eyebrow and looks me over, like he's judging me. "You seem fine now." He finishes his perusal and I square my shoulders.

"I am now, but I was ill all night." I narrow my eyes as I remember Roman asking if Richard could be behind my illness. "I think it might have been something I ate. Maybe the cupcake."

Richard's head rears back, and he glares at me. "Are you suggesting my wife did something to your cupcake?"

"I'm not—" I say.

"I can't believe you would accuse her of something so vile... How dare you..."

"I never accused her of anything," I say, as my stomach clenches. Yeah, I'm beginning to believe more and more that Paula did something underhanded to keep me from the classroom, and with the way he's defending her, he's completely unaware.

I stare up at him. Even though I saw the worst side of many people growing up and trust no one, I still can't quite wrap my brain around the idea that Paula would go to such lengths to knock out the competition. Unease grips my throat. What else would she do to ensure he won the full-time position?

He rocks on his feet for a few seconds, and while I turn to take in Roman's solid presence on the playground, I can feel Richard's eyes drilling into me. "Where exactly did you say you and Roman were married?" he asks. My gaze flies back to his. His tone might be deceptively innocent, but every intuition I possess tells me there is nothing innocent about the abrupt change in conversation. This man is on a fishing expedition, although from the smug look on his face, he might have already reeled in a big one.

I tamp down the anxiety threatening to rise. "Oh, it was just a small ceremony at city hall in Manhattan," I say, and try not to shift or look uncomfortable as the lie spills from my mouth. "Why do you ask?" I take a deep breath, not sure I want to hear the answer.

He goes quiet, leaving my mind to call on every worst case scenario, and after a long pause he says, "I was just wondering, because Paula said there are no records that you two were married in NY State."

"Why on earth would she look that up?" I ask, almost afraid of the answer. "Is she that bored at home?"

He purses his lips and my gaze goes to Roman, who is now standing perfectly still, watching the two of us. Richard looks back to me. "Why don't you answer the question?"

"You didn't ask one, and I'm sure it's just a filing mistake. I'll look into it." The school bell rings. "If you'll excuse me," I say, ending our discussion as I walk away. I head toward Roman, who is standing still on the basketball court, his eyes dark and deep, locked on mine as I saunter toward him.

I keep my steps even and measured, resisting the urge to run, not only to put distance between Richard and me, but because of the need to be close to Roman, to revel in the way his strength always wraps around me. I step up to him, and as he lightly runs his fingers down my arm, he dips his head, positioning his mouth inches from mine. Being close like this, his strong hands on my body, has a way of soothing my worries—making me think things will be all right. But not everything will turn out all right, and I can't think about the loss that's going to slice through me when this man goes back to New York.

"What are you doing here?" he asks, his voice low and steeped in concern.

"I feel 100 percent better." I crinkle my nose. "And I was bored." Okay, maybe *bored* isn't the right term. Maybe *lonely* is a better way to put it. Without his big presence in the villa, it was just a big open space. Stark. Empty. Lonesome. That's insane, considering I love alone time.

He frowns and rubs his hands up and down my arms to chase away the goose bumps. "Did you think I couldn't handle this?"

"Well, you did say you were terrified," I say with a laugh. "But I can see you have everything under control."

"The kids are great."

"Honestly, I just needed a breath of fresh air."
Needed to see you. "The kids seemed so happy to
have you here."

"Not true. They were all asking for you."

My heart flips and my gaze rakes over his irre-
sistible face. My God, what have I gotten myself into
here? "Really?"

"Really." Concerned eyes move over my face.
"You do look a lot better."

I laugh at that. "After last night. My God, I
couldn't have looked worse today had I tried."

"Not true. You were adorable."

"You, my friend," I say, and poke his chest, "have
become an awesome liar."

He frowns at that. "I don't lie, Peyton. Well, except for this pretend marriage, but we're fighting an
unfair system and had no choice." He looks past my
shoulders. "What did asshole want?"

Unwanted thoughts of Richard push back the
warmth in Roman's touch, leaving room for dread to
invade and spread through my blood. A hard quiver
goes through me. "He asked about our wedding, and
where we got married. Paula's been doing some digging. I think they know something, Roman."

"They don't know anything." He clenches his jaw
and his muscles ripple. "They're just trying to rattle you."

"I never let on, but I think he succeeded." I shake
my head, guilt eating at me. "This was a bad idea. I
shouldn't have dragged you into this mess."

"It's fine." He shakes his head, takes a deep breath

and lets it out fast. "Maybe we should just get married for real," he blurts out.

My entire body goes stiff. Holy, that flu must have affected my hearing, because no way did he just say we should get married for real. "What did you just say?"

"Maybe we should have a ceremony here, something small. We could play it off that we decided to renew our vows on the beach."

"Are you serious?" Maybe I'm still in bed, lost in fever and having a bad dream.

But the thoughts of being with Roman, coming home to him every night, the two of us sharing hopes, goals, the good and bad, is not a bad dream at all. It's a fairy tale and I don't believe in them. I need to keep myself grounded in reality. It's the only way I won't get hurt.

"You still there?" he asks, his gaze roaming my face. "You went somewhere else for a second." He frowns. "I'm not so sure you're over this flu just yet."

"I am. I'm fine. You just took me by surprise."

"I can tell." He laughs, pulls me to him and after all the kids file back inside, he presses a kiss to my forehead. "You can stop looking at me like I just grew another head, Peyton."

"I'm not going to ask you to go through with a ceremony, Roman. You've done enough already, and I know how you feel about marriage."

"You're one to talk," he says, his voice low and intimate. His eyes narrow, like he's waiting for a counterargument. But I have none.

"When you're right, you're right. Not denying that I'm a bachelorette for life, but you've already gone above and beyond for me." I glance over my shoulder. "I'd better get inside. The second bell just sounded. I can take over now."

"Nice way to change the subject," he says with a snicker. "We'll talk about it tonight, then." He inches back. "And *I'm* finishing the day off with the kids. You go home and rest."

"Home is boring."

Without you.

"Go for a swim, and if you really are feeling better, why don't you do a search on restaurants, and we'll go out to eat tonight and do some sightseeing."

"I'd love that."

He kisses my forehead, takes a fast glance around and gives my backside a little whack. "Go."

I yelp. "Are you sure?"

"Positive. I'm actually having fun teaching these kids how to code. They really seem to enjoy it."

"Okay, if you're sure. I'll head back and find a nice place to eat tonight."

We walk back to the school, our bodies close, our knuckles brushing, and it's insane how much I miss his touch, his closeness, when he disappears inside. My phone pings and I welcome the distraction.

I smile when I see the call is coming from Carly. I quickly slide my finger across the screen. "Hey, Carly, I've been meaning to call you."

"Uh-huh. You get married and forget all about

your best friend," she teases, her voice light and full of laughter.

"Very funny. I've been crazy busy."

"Doing what? Playing house with New York High Society's Most Eligible Italian? The man is unbelievably hot. The pictures in the paper don't do him justice."

"I don't think of him that way." Her laugh of disbelief nearly deafens me. "Okay fine, he's hot."

"Oh my God," she says.

"What?" I ask.

"You slept with him."

I glance over my shoulder. I'm not sure why. Maybe I expect Richard to be leaning in to hear the call. I lower my voice and say, "So what if I did?"

"Peyton," she screeches. "That is awesome."

"Yeah, it kind of was, or is…because we're still doing it."

"Tell me everything."

I laugh. "Let's just say, it's possible he's ruined me for every other man."

"Is he, you know?"

I frown and saunter down the sidewalk, sneezing as I pass the foliage I seem to be allergic to. "No, I don't know."

"Is he big?" she blurts out, and I cover my mouth.

"I'm not telling you that."

"Like hell you're not, and actually you don't have to. I already know he is. I can tell by your voice."

"Going all Freud on me again, are you? How are things back there?"

"Same," she says. "But I want to hear about you."

"Things are going really good." A mortified sound crawls out of my throat. "You're not going to believe this, though…" I begin and for the next ten minutes, as I make my way back to the villa, I fill her in on where I'm living, how Roman took care of me last night and jumped in to help out with the students.

"Wow, what a guy. He almost sounds too good to be true."

"I know, right? But he's my brother's best friend and said he'd do whatever it took to help me get this job." She goes quiet, too quiet, and my stomach squeezes as I press in the code to open the front door. "What?" I ask.

"You like him."

"Yeah, he's okay," I say as need wells up inside me. Honest to God, I do like him, a lot. I always have. But I swore long ago I'd never give anyone the power to hurt me. Is that what I'm doing here? Have I given Roman the power to hurt me?

My entire body tenses, and the toast I washed down with tea threatens to make a second appearance.

"How does he feel about you, Peyton?" she asks, her voice changing as she goes into professional mode.

"I'm not a patient, Carly. Please don't analyze this. We're just two consenting adults, having a little fun while we pretend to be married."

"I just don't want to see you hurt."

I step inside the villa, and the cool air-conditioning

falls over me, although I'm not sure that's the reason I'm shivering. "I'm a big girl. I know what I'm doing."

I don't.

Not even a little bit.

"Okay, my morning break is over. I have a patient waiting. Call me soon."

"Will do."

I end the call and fight off the unease circling my stomach. I grab my laptop and do a search on restaurants. I find one not too far, make a reservation and head upstairs to get ready. I want to look nice for Roman tonight. I find my prettiest dress, spend a long time on my hair and makeup, and when I finally emerge from the room, Roman is coming in through the front door.

I hurry down the stairs and his gaze lifts to take me in. The heat in his eyes is like a visual caress over the tingling spot between my legs. My God, the man is addictive.

He drops his briefcase and stalks toward me. "You look beautiful." He slides his arm around me, and like a damn caveman drags me to him.

"Have I ever told you how much I like when you touch me like this, all rough and hungry and impatient?"

His lips quirk. "You didn't need to. But we have a problem."

I stiffen. "Does it have something to do with Richard?"

"No," he says, and I relax into his touch. "It has

something to do with me wanting you naked so I can put my dick in you."

I laugh.

"Not a laughing matter, Peyton," he growls, and rubs his growing erection against my stomach.

"No, not a laughing matter at all," I say, my voice husky as his lips find mine. "And I suppose we have a few minutes," I say, stepping back. He reaches for me, but I dodge him.

"What are you doing?"

"I was thinking. We do have about a half hour before our reservation, and if you're fast—"

"I can be fast," he says, and I bite my lip to stop my chuckle as my entire body heats up.

I move to the back of the sofa. "I guess if we need to do this quickly, it's a good thing I don't have any panties on to get in my way."

Raw need shimmers around him like an aura. "You're kidding me."

"Would I kid about something like that?" I lean over the sofa and lift my dress, exposing my body to him.

"Shit, Peyton. I'll take over your job every day if it means I get to come home to this."

I laugh. "Roman?"

I glance at him over my shoulder and my body quakes as he licks his lips, his eyes zeroing in on my sex as I spread my legs. "Yeah?"

"I believe you said something about bending me over a table and burying yourself inside me." The sound of his zipper releasing curls around me. "This isn't a table but…" I swallow as his crown breaches my wet sex, and my fingers curl into the fabric of the sofa as he powers into me. "Oh my God."

He pumps and grips my hips for leverage, burying himself to the hilt. I love the way he loves my body, the impatience in his touch like he can't get enough of me, like he can't get deep enough. I know the feeling.

"Jesus, girl, why are you so hot and wet?"

"Maybe because I was thinking about you thrusting into me like this all day."

He pants and grunts, his hot breath on my flesh as he slams into me. "Were you home touching yourself, wishing it was my cock inside you?"

"I wanted to, but I wanted to save my orgasm for you."

"You want to come, Peyton. You want to come for me?"

"Uh-huh," is all I can manage to say as he rides me, fast and hard, blunt strokes meant to get the job done. There's no choreographed moves with this man, no time for the finesse this afternoon. No, he's here on a mission, his sole focus on getting us both off. Damned if I don't like that.

I'm so slick and aroused, he slides in and out of me smoothly, the skin-on-skin friction creating an even deeper intimacy between us. After the night we forgot to use a condom, there was no sense going back.

"Yes," he groans, his body all muscle and power as he takes me hard and fast. He slides a hand around me and touches me where I need it most. I jerk against his probing fingers, and a groan tumbles from my throat. "You like that, babe? You like when I take you from behind like this?"

"Yessss," I hiss.

"Tonight, when we go out, you're going to sit there all sweet and prim but we'll both know you'll still be feeling me inside you."

"Roman," I cry out, and he leans in and digs his teeth into my neck. The second he does, I feel myself lose all control, chanting his name over and over as I come.

"Oh shit," he moans against my flesh, and his hands go back to my hips. With each hard thrust we work toward his orgasm now, and I move with him, my sex muscles clenching and unclenching around his hardness. His breath catches, his fingers bruise my hips, and I let loose a cry as he fills me with his hot release. He pulses inside me, his muscles hard against my soft flesh as he rides out the bliss. As I revel in the pleasure coursing through me, he falls over my back.

"Peyton, Jesus," he says as he pants against my flesh. "I loved coming home to this," he adds, and nibbles my ear.

"I loved it, too," I say, my heart hitching, warning me to be careful here, not to let this man into sealed-off places, even though it's too late for that. I'm in big trouble here.

CHAPTER TWELVE

Roman

I GLANCE AROUND the cozy Italian restaurant in the middle of downtown St. Julian's. "You picked my favorite restaurant, you know."

Peyton lifts her head from the menu and her smile slays me. "Really?"

"It's almost like you know me."

She cocks her head. "I know some things."

I lean toward her and lightly rub my fingers over her wrist. "I know things, too."

Her smile is warm and her eyes are steeped in desire when she asks, "Did you spend a lot of time in Malta?"

"When we were kids, we vacationed here. My family owns property."

Her jaw drops open. "The villa. It's yours, isn't it?"

"Yeah."

"Why didn't you tell me?" she asks.

I let loose an exasperated sigh. "You really have to ask that?"

"Yes."

"You would have argued with me." I stretch my legs out beneath the table. "You always argue with me."

"No, I don't."

"Yeah, you do."

She lifts her chin. "I don't argue about everything."

Grinning, I lean back into my chair.

"What?"

"You're arguing about not arguing with me."

She laughs. "Okay, I'll give you that. Seriously, I didn't know you spent time here, or owned property, and I appreciate you letting me use your villa, but I still plan to pay you for helping me out."

I arch a brow at her. "You think I'm going to let you do that?"

She glares at me, those lush lips pinched into a fine line. "Roman…"

"It's not been a hardship, Peyton."

Her demeanor changes, softens. "Yeah, it's kind of been fun." She sets her left hand on the table and eyes the ring on her finger, and I don't miss that look of longing in her eyes.

The hostess leads two people to a table behind us, and I go quiet until they're seated. I lean toward Peyton, my words for her ears only. "Any more thoughts about what I suggested earlier?"

Her shoulders tighten. "You mean getting married?"

"I just don't think we should risk anyone finding out."

Is that why you're asking, Roman?

Is that the only reason you're pushing for this?

She frowns. "I know what you're saying. We've come this far, and Richard's wife is obviously the kind of woman to play dirty, to make sure her husband succeeds."

The server comes back to take our orders, and as I glance over the menu, I notice Peyton keeps looking beyond me, like she sees someone she knows. I casually look over my shoulder after handing the menu back.

"What's going on back there?" I ask.

"I'm not sure. Two girls over there keep looking at me and whispering back and forth."

"You know them?"

"No, maybe they know you."

I touch her hand. "Maybe, but I'm here with you tonight, and you're the only one I want to talk to."

I pull my hands back when the server comes with our bottle of wine. He pours some into my glass, I taste it and nod. Once he's gone, I say, "I'm glad you're feeling better. I was pretty worried about you."

Her smile is sweet, grateful. "Thanks for taking care of me all night. I'm just glad whatever it was passed."

"I had a talk with Richard."

She toys with the stem on her wineglass. "He told me you did."

"I don't trust that guy. I still think he was behind whatever made you ill."

She sets her napkin on the table. "I'm going to make a quick trip to the ladies' room. I'll be right back."

"I'll be right here."

I pull my phone from my pocket and check messages as I wait for her to return. There are a few from my sisters, and one from my team at Hard Wear. I read it quickly, but it's something I can deal with later. I put my phone away and pour another splash of wine into our glasses as the server returns with bread. The warm scent fills my senses. I look toward the hall leading to the washrooms. What is taking Peyton so long? A knot coils in my stomach. Jesus, I hope she's not sick again. I'm about to stand, go to her, when she comes from the hall, her face a little pale.

What the hell?

She hurries to her chair. "Are you okay?"

"Yeah, that girl who was staring followed me to the bathroom. She asked who I was to you. I told her you were my husband, and she said you were old friends."

I turn and see the woman coming from the bathroom, headed our way. Holy shit. Here comes trouble.

Anna's eyes go wide, and she holds her arms out to me, a big surprised smile on her face. I stand and bring her in for a hug.

"Anna, it's so nice to see you. It's been a long time."

"Too long, clearly," she says, her gaze going from me to Peyton, back to me again. "I saw you two earlier, and let me say, it comes as quite a surprise to find out you're married. Lucy never said a word to me about it."

My throat tightens. "It was a fast ceremony, and we've been keeping things quiet."

Her dark eyes narrow in on me, and my stomach twists. "Are you saying your family doesn't know?"

I smooth my hand over my tie. "We prefer to keep it that way, for now."

She laughs, but it holds no humor. "Oh, Roman, what kind of mess have you gotten yourself into?"

"No mess at all." I force a laugh. "You know my family. They wouldn't give the newlyweds a minute to themselves. We'll tell them when we're ready."

"Yes, I suppose you will," she says, and casts Peyton a glance. "It was lovely meeting you, Peyton. Let's see if you can keep his interest. He tires of relationships very easily. Prepare yourself." Before Peyton can respond, Anna flips her long black hair over her shoulder and saunters away.

I sit back down and blow out a breath. "Shit."

"This isn't good, is it?"

"No."

"What happened between you two?"

"We dated but we were teenagers. She's a friend of Lucy's and has chased me forever. I was never really that interested, but Lucy wanted me to take her out, so I did. It was brief, and I broke it off before she could think we were going somewhere with it. I'm pretty sure she was more interested in my family name than me."

"I think she hates you." She gives a low, slow whistle. "If looks could kill."

"I know." I rub the knot in the back of my neck, tension tightening my muscles. "Trouble is coming, Peyton."

"Trouble?"

"Trouble in the name of Aurora, Lucy, Maria, Emma and Bianca."

She leans toward me, clutching her napkin. "You think she's going to tell your sisters?"

"Is she on her phone?"

She looks over my shoulder and grimaces. "Yeah, looks like she's texting." I shake my head, my appetite gone as Peyton wrings her cloth napkin. "Want to get out of here?" Peyton asks.

"Only if you do."

"Why don't we get our food to go and eat at the park. Somewhere private?"

"Okay." I call the server over and tell him our change of plans. Ten minutes later we're walking the downtown streets and heading to the park for a picnic. My phone has been going off in my pocket for the last five minutes, but I just ignore it. I can't answer them until I figure out what it is I'm going to say. We grab a seat at a picnic table, and I hand Peyton her take-out container with her penne chicken.

I settle in beside her and I dig into my ravioli as she stabs a piece of pasta.

With her fork halfway to her mouth, Peyton says, "You're going to have to answer them, Roman."

"I know, but I'm going to need a full stomach for the wrath that is about to come down on me." She nods and my mind races as we eat in silence for a few more minutes. The sun dips lower in the sky, and the streetlights begin to flicker on.

"This food is delicious," Peyton says, breaking the quiet.

"I know, right? That's why it's my favorite."

She lifts her head when a family of four saunters by. A smile touches her mouth. "Your family has other properties here in Malta?"

I nod. "I have some really fond memories from my childhood here."

Her smile widens and she sets her fork down and pushes her container away. "That's so nice."

"Come on, let's walk." I gather up our trash and dump it into a nearby garbage can.

We head down the street, busy with tourists, and pass by all the lovely outdoor cafés. We stop by an alleyway and I gesture with a nod. "This is my old stomping grounds. Right there, that's where I lost my virginity," I tell her with a smirk.

Her brow arches. "Really?"

"Yup."

"Romantic."

I laugh at that. "I was seventeen."

Her arm slides through mine as we walk, and I'm

not even sure she realized she did it. Being together like this is just so natural for both of us. "Young."

I give her a wink and hold her tighter. "She was eighteen."

"Ooh, a cougar," she teases, and I laugh, leading her to the walkway along the bay. We stop and stare out at all the boats bobbing in the water. She inhales, breathing in the salty air, and lets it out slowly. "I love it here."

"I do, too," I say, and give her a little bump with my body.

"What made you stay in the States when you could have this every day?" she asks, and waves her arms around.

"I needed to be away from my family for a while." She looks down at her feet and my gut squeezes. Christ, this woman would do anything for a family and I spent years running away from mine. "Sometimes it's nice to go where you can be under the radar, you know," I add. "Somewhere where your every move isn't scrutinized."

She nods. "I can understand that."

"Yeah?"

"I'm under the radar. People don't really notice me." I go completely still as she continues to walk. The second she realizes I'm not beside her she turns. "What?"

I shake my head, taking pleasure in her thick, auburn hair, the warmth and honesty in her green eyes, and the way that sexy dress hugs all her curves.

"You have no idea how beautiful you are, do you?"

She shrugs at the comment. "You don't have to say that."

"When you walk into a room, all heads turn, Peyton. You don't even know."

She looks away to gaze out over the water. A visible shiver moves through her, and I close the distance. I shrug out of my jacket and drape it over her. "I spent so many years trying to be invisible, Roman."

My throat practically closes over as pain grips my heart. I put my arms around her and pull her in. I press a kiss to the top of her head. "I know."

"If I didn't cause any trouble, if they rarely saw me…" She goes quiet for a long time, and I just hold her quivering body to mine, tucking her safely beneath my arms so no one else can hurt her. "I…" Her voice hitches, and she adds, "I guess I figured if I was small and invisible, they wouldn't be so quick to get rid of me."

Jesus, I hate that her childhood was so damn brutal and her scars are still so raw. "No one is going to hurt you anymore, Peyton. I won't let them."

She puts her hand on my chest, and her eyes are watery when she lifts her gaze to mine. "My very own knight in shining armor," she says.

I chuckle. "I thought you didn't believe in fairy tales."

"I don't," she says so quietly, so softly I almost missed it. I hug her tighter when a hard quiver racks her body.

"We should get you home. You're freezing."

I make a move to go but she stops me. "We should end this, Roman. I don't want your sisters angry or hurt, and you've…you've helped enough."

"No," I say so forcefully, her eyes widen. "I'm seeing this through to the end. I told you that right from the beginning and I'm a man of my word."

Really, Roman. Is that the only reason you can't walk away from this?

"But your sisters—"

"I'll deal with them." I put my arm around her and we hurry back to the villa. Once inside I carry her shivering body up the stairs to the shower. "We need to warm you up." I peel the zipper down on her dress, and there is something so completely open and honest about this sweet, vulnerable woman as she stands there stark naked, gazing up at me, I could fucking sob. The world might not have wanted her, but I sure as hell do.

I'm in love with her. So lost in her, I'll never find my way out. Not that I want to. I might have been engaged, but this is the only woman who's ever truly mattered to my heart. I strip down and help her into the shower, ignoring my pinging phone for the time being. Right now, Peyton needs my attention.

I turn the water to hot and pull her under the rain showerhead.

"Mmm, that is nice," she says.

"Getting warm."

She laughs. "I don't think I've ever been warm in my life."

"Come here." I pull her back to my chest and soap

up my hands. I run the suds over her body, cupping her breasts as I clean her. She rests her head against my shoulder, and a warm, contented sigh escapes her mouth. I spin her and rinse her clean. Once done, I turn the water off and towel-dry us both before I wrap her in a clean one, and knot another one around my waist.

She yelps when I scoop her up and carry her to the bed, setting her down gently and crawling in beside her. She snuggles into me, her skin warm and fragrant. I lightly touch her arm, trail my hand lower. Her sexy moan wraps around me, and I part her legs to caress her sex.

"Sore?" I cringe. "I sort of went a little caveman on you earlier."

Her soft chuckle strokes my balls. "I loved it."

"I loved it, too."

I love you.

She widens her legs even more and the welcoming way this woman invites me into her body, giving herself to me entirely, is one hell of a mind fuck. I put my finger inside her and her eyes roll back.

"Hate that?"

"Hate it sooo much, Roman."

"Yeah, I can tell."

I move my finger in and out of her until she's dripping and so close to release, but I pull back, needing to be inside her when she comes. I roll on top of her and her smile is soft, her mood far more mellow tonight, despite the storm we're going to face tomorrow. But we'll cross that bridge when we come to it. Tonight, all I want to do is make love to this woman.

I piston forward and slide my cock into her. She wraps her legs around me and hugs so tight, I nearly come. "Jesus," I murmur, and push her hair from her face. "Do you have any idea what you do to me?"

"I have a little idea."

"Didn't we agree that you weren't to use the word *little* when we're talking about sex," I say, and a laugh bubbles out of her. I laugh with her, and it changes to a moan when she brings my mouth to hers for a deep kiss. She breaks it and cups my face.

"There's nothing little about you, Roman."

"That's better," I say, and move in and out of her.

"You have a very big…heart."

"Hey," I say, and she chuckles.

She wraps her arms and legs around me and pulls me closer, until every inch of flesh is meshed together. This. Right here. This is what I want. Peyton in my bed, and in my life. Tonight. Tomorrow.

Forever.

Her eyes are at half-mast as she gazes up at me, and I lose myself in her just a little more. Impossible, I know, but I have never in my life loved a woman the way I love her. I'm 100 percent positive the wrath of five will be at my door tomorrow, demanding answers. As I think about that, with Peyton coming underneath me, the answer to our dilemma comes to me in a flash.

Peyton doesn't want to get married. She's a sworn bachelorette. But what if we did go through with it,

if I lived here with her, stayed in Malta, maybe she
would warm to the idea of a real husband. As far as
her brother is concerned, I'll have to deal with that
when the situation arises. All I know is I'm crazy
about this woman, who came from nothing and wants
to give everything. She's nothing like my ex. She's
never said or done anything to lead me to believe
she's the type of girl who'd marry for title or position. I could never be with her if she was. I hug her
tight, knowing what I need to do next. I just hope
she doesn't get frightened and run the other way.

CHAPTER THIRTEEN

Peyton

VOICES—LOUD VOICES—pull me awake and I roll over to find the other side of the bed empty. I jackknife up and the blankets fall to expose my naked body. I scramble to pull them back up before someone comes busting in, and try to figure out what is being said, but everyone seems to be talking at once, and in Italian. My tired brain can't seem to keep up.

I quietly slip from the bed and pull on a T-shirt and pair of yoga pants. I make a quick trip to the bathroom to fix myself up the best I can, although there is nothing I can do to wipe the contented smile off my face. Yeah, one look at me, and whoever is downstairs is going to know I was up all night making love with Roman.

Making love.

While I love it fast and hard, his touch was a bit different last night. Tender, gentle, so profound it seeped under my skin and wrapped around my heart. Yeah, I know. Not good for a girl who's a sworn bachelorette. But I feel myself falling, despite everything.

I open my bedroom door, and as my fuzzy brain clears, I gasp and wrap my arms around myself, knowing exactly what's going on. My God, I can't go down there. How can I face his family, let lies spill from my lips? I'm about to slam my door shut, crawl under the covers and stay there until everyone leaves, but footsteps pound on the stairs.

Roman's dark eyes meet mine, but he doesn't seem upset at all. Maybe I'm mistaken. Maybe his family hasn't invaded, demanding answers.

"My family is here," he says, and leans against the doorjamb.

My heart sinks. "Are you okay?" I ask.

"They want to meet my bride."

My stomach tightens. "Roman, you shouldn't… we can't pull this off with your family."

"Just for a little while. We have to let them think we're married. The fewer people who know the truth, the better." He exhales loudly. "Believe me, none of them can keep a secret and we wouldn't want them accidently spilling the truth here."

"I guess you're right, but how are they going to feel when we have to end this?"

He goes thoughtful and puts one hand on my cheek. "How about we cross that bridge when we come to it?"

"I hope we don't have to jump off the bridge."

He laughs, a big, deep laugh that eases the tension inside me and brings a smile to my face. "I don't think it will come to that." He bends and gives me a soft kiss. "Come on, they're dying to meet you."

A jolt of unease freezes my legs. "I don't know." What if they don't like me? What if they try to break us up like they did when they put blue dye on his toothbrush?

It's not a real relationship anyway, Peyton.

"It's going to be fine," Roman says, reading the worry on my face. "They're going to love you and vice versa. I promise."

"Am I dressed okay, maybe I should—" His lips close over mine, swallowing the last of my worries. He inches back, takes my hand and leads me down the stairs. As we walk, the scent of waffles reaches my nose.

"Are they cooking?" I whisper.

"Of course. They said I was looking too thin and need more meat on my bones." He puts his mouth close to my ear. "The only thing I need on my bone is you."

I chuckle at that. For a guy who was worried sick about his family, and lives in a whole other country to keep them from meddling, he sure doesn't seem upset with them being here now. He actually seems… happy. But I'm out of my element here, and so not the type of girl they'd want to see their baby brother with. Roman says otherwise, but unlike them, I have no real heritage, no family outside of my brother. I've accepted my lot in life. My past made me the strong woman I am today, but I'm smart enough to know how things work in the real world.

I reach the bottom step and all eyes turn to me—all eyes that resemble Roman's. It's not hard to tell they're all family. "Oh God," I whisper under my breath, completely overwhelmed, but Roman puts a strong, supportive arm around me and pulls me to his side.

"Everyone, this is Peyton. Peyton, this is my family."

I give an awkward little wave. "Hi."

A beat of silence and then one sister spreads her arms. *"Bella!"*

She comes toward me and Roman says, "I should have warned you. They're all huggers."

Before I realize what's happening, I'm being passed around, each squeeze tighter than the last. The women touch my hair and face, and their praise wraps around me.

"Mia sorella," Lucy says when she gets a hold of me, and my heart pinches tight. I can't believe these women are so accepting, calling me their sister. I seek Roman out in the flurry, and he's leaning against the kitchen island, a huge smile on his face.

One of the sisters, I think it's Aurora, speaks quickly in Italian. I struggle to grasp what she's saying.

"English," Roman says, and she turns back to me.

She fists her hands. "I ought to give it to Roman for keeping you from us, *bella*."

"I told you. We wanted time alone before we let you know," he explains. "We were going to tell you soon, isn't that right, Peyton?"

"Yes, that's right," I say, pushing the lie past a tight throat. Pretending to be married for a job at a school that practices unfair hiring rules is one thing, but straight-up lying to the people he's closest to doesn't sit well with me. Not even a little bit.

"I think the waffles are burning," Roman says.

Aurora leaves my side, and that's when I spot an elderly woman on the sofa, her purse clutched in her lap, a small smile on her face.

"You must be Roman's mother," I say, and move toward her.

She nods and pats the sofa. I sit beside her and she cups my face. She kisses both my cheeks and takes my hand in hers to examine the ring.

"It fits you perfectly," she says, and I'm not sure she's talking about the size of it.

"Thank you, Mrs. Bianchi."

"Phooey," she says with a wave of her hand, and everyone laughs. "You, my sweet *bella*, can call me Mamma."

I take a fast breath as tears pound behind my eyes and threaten to spill. This sweet woman wants to be my mamma. I nod, my throat so tight I can barely swallow. "Okay, Mamma," I say and Roman must pick up on the hitch in my voice because a second after those words leave my mouth he's there, right there, pulling me into his arms.

"You have an amazing family," I say as I turn to him.

"Yeah, I know."

"But we have a problem," he says quietly as dishes clang in the kitchen.

I blink up at him, but don't see worry in his eyes. "What problem?"

"Remember I told you they were interfering?"

I nod.

"We want a real wedding," his mother says, and pushes to her feet. She holds one finger up. "Only then will I forgive Roman for getting married behind my back."

I blink rapidly. "A real wedding? What do you mean?" I glance around, and realize four out of the five sisters are on their phones; the fifth is in the kitchen dishing up waffles. One sister is talking about flowers, one about a dress. My God, are they making wedding arrangements for us? "What's going on?"

"They want to see us exchange vows. It won't be a big ceremony. Just a small one with family."

"Roman…" I'm about to say no, he's done enough, but there's a part of me that just can't. I actually want this. I want this to be real with Roman, and…maybe, just maybe he wants it, too.

He puts his mouth to my ear, his warm breath sending shivers along my spine. "It will solve our problem with Richard, Peyton."

Or maybe not.

"Please say yes, Peyton," Lucy asks, and pulls me in for another hug. I take a breath, completely overwhelmed with all this.

Say no, Peyton.

No matter how much I might want this, I can't go through with it. I have to say no. I have to.

"What do you think?" Roman asks.

"Roman, do you—"

"I do," he says, and for a brief second it catches me off guard, like I might have actually just proposed to him and he might have just agreed. My stomach rolls, wanting so much for this to be real.

"Do you?" he asks, and the room goes silent—a huge task for this group, I'm sure.

I take in all the hopeful, expectant looks. I can't bear to disappoint them, even though going through with a ceremony, only to nullify the marriage later, will undoubtedly leave me scarred and emotionally wrecked. "I do," I say, and the girls all start clapping and jumping up and down and talking a mile a minute in Italian.

Okay, I need a minute alone here to get my head and my heart straightened out. But no, that's not about to happen. The next thing I know I'm being led to the rooftop, with *Mamma* beside me as all the sisters bring up plates of food.

They set plates at the table, and the first thing I do is go for a coffee. Hard to believe I agreed to marry Roman, and he agreed to marry me, all before my first cup. I can only hope it's strong. I catch the way Roman keeps watch over me as his sisters fuss and talk details.

"Yeah, sure," I say when Emma suggests we exchange nuptials on the beach near the family villa. Questions about flowers, dresses and food get thrown at me, and my gaze seeks out Roman's. He opens his mouth, no doubt to tell them to back off a bit, but I hold my hand up to stop him. His presence is solid, and I really like having him in my corner, but I've got this.

I've never had a big family, and I've never had sisters. This might not be real, and everyone is going to be devastated when Roman and I end this, but right now—even though my family comes from nothing, and they might disown me when they find out—I just want to bask in the love and warmth and exuberant energy they're displaying. Can it really hurt for me to enjoy these ladies while I can and pretend that I'm family, too?

Yeah, I'm pretty sure it can, but I'm in too deep to pull the plug now.

"For flowers, I don't want any of those local purple ones, they make me sneeze." Roman relaxes and pushes back in his seat.

"No purple flowers," Emma says, and we all laugh and dig in to our waffles.

"What about your family?" Maria asks. "Will they want to come for the nuptials?"

My heart jumps into my throat. What do I say, I'm a nobody with only one brother? I open my mouth and close it again, not sure what to tell them, when Roman pipes in.

"This one will be for my side of the family," Roman says, and while I'm glad he jumped in to help, I also can't resist thinking he might not want them to know who I really am. He's a great guy, but he had a very different upbringing than me, and there are certain expectations placed on him, certain things he must live up to—marrying beneath his status is probably something that would be discouraged. Then again, I could just be projecting my fears. Maybe the only one worried about it is me. But to answer her question, no, my family won't be coming. No need for Cason to be made aware of our wedding, when it's not a real one.

I barely take my last bite when Lucy snatches up my plate. "Okay, let's go," she says, her dark eyes brimming with excitement.

I take in her little baby bump and my heart misses a beat. It would be so much fun to be a part of this family, watch that baby grow and be there to spoil it. "Go where?"

"We have one week to pull off a wedding," she says.

"One week?" I blink numerous times and take in the bobbing heads. "Why one week?"

"We have duties to get back to," Aurora says.

"Wait, where are your children and husbands?" I was so caught up in the excitement, I never stopped to consider they had lives to return to, children needing their mothers, husbands needing their wives.

"Our babies are with our husbands and nannies," Maria says. "They'll come next Saturday for the wedding."

My gaze moves around the table and I plant one hand on my hip. "Why do I get the feeling this wedding was in progress before any of you arrived?"

Bianca gives me a sheepish look. So far she's been the quietest in the bunch. "Probably because the second Anna reached out to Lucy, we were packing and making arrangements."

"I didn't stand a chance, did I?" I ask, and Roman mumbles something like, *I told you so* under his breath and all I can do is laugh.

"Okay, let's go," Lucy says.

The next thing I know I'm in the shops, and we're picking out flowers and cake and food. With little time to find the perfect dress, I'll have to pick one from the rack, but I don't mind. I don't want to spend a lot, although so far I haven't spent anything. These women insist on purchasing everything, but I don't want them to waste a lot of money on me. They just wave me off every time I try to protest.

They march me into a bridal shop and even without an appointment we're made a priority. I suppose that's how it is when you come from money.

The sisters all take a seat on the sofa and pull me down with them. The clerk, Lucille, a gorgeous middle-aged woman with long dark hair and big brown eyes, asks me to describe my favorite dress, and I basically sit there with my mouth hanging open. How on earth would I know? I wasn't like other little girls, dreaming of their Prince Charming. No, I was sticking close to the walls trying to be invisible. There was no time for fairy tales in that cruel world I grew up in.

"I…don't know."

She takes my hands and pulls me to my feet.

"Let's have a look at your body shape." I stand there like a mannequin on display as she spins me around and everyone excitedly gives their opinion on what would look best on me.

"I don't need anything fancy," I say. "Just simple."

The clerk taps her chin, her brown eyes narrowing as she goes quiet, thoughtful. "I think I have the perfect dress," she announces, and the women all clap their hands, excitement on their faces, and I can't quite help but get swept up in it.

"Okay," I say, and let her lead me to a change room. I step inside and strip to my underwear and she comes in with a gorgeous white gown.

"I think this ball gown will be perfect for you."

My heart races a little faster in my chest as she removes it from the hanger and helps me into it. The second I see the dress on me, the silhouette perfect for my shape, I swallow hard and fight the barrage of emotions pushing tears into my eyes.

"I knew it," Lucille says, and clips it in a few places. "We have to do a few alterations, and we'll put you at the top of the list of course."

My throat squeezes tight, my legs a little wobbly. "That's so kind."

"Anything for the Bianchis." She stands back. "What do you think?"

"I love it," I whisper, my heart aching in my tight chest. "But I can't go with the first dress, can I? I mean, I've watched the shows and it takes girls forever to pick their dress, right?"

A wide smile splits her lips. "When it's the right one you know."

My pulse leaps. She's right. When it's the right one, you know. A surge of love wells up inside me. At the wedding last summer when Roman kissed me, it sealed the deal. For years I thought he was the right guy, but that kiss was electric, setting off a storm inside me that would forever ruin me for other men. Maybe deep down, he feels it, too, but is too afraid. A little bubble of hope wells up inside me. Is it possible that he wants this, too, and is using Richard as an excuse? I spin around and there is nothing I can do to wipe the ridiculous smile from my face. I've always tamped down hope, too afraid of disappointment—too used to disappointment—but this just all feels so right.

"Should we go show the others?" she asks.

I nod, my hair bouncing around my shoulders as we step out and she puts me on an elevated pedestal. I glance in the mirror, and I really do feel like Cinderella. Is it possible that fairy tales really do come true?

"Okay, turn around, dear," Lucille says.

I spin and everyone smiles with lots of oohs and ahhs. The way they're all looking at me makes me feel like I'm someone very special, even though I spent my whole life telling myself I wasn't.

"It's perfect," Mamma says. "She'll take it."

I laugh at that and Lucille looks at me. "Do you say yes to the dress?"

I take in all the expectant eyes and put my hands to my chest. "I say yes to the dress."

* * *

I glance around my empty classroom. Honestly, I can't believe the week I've had, or that it's Friday afternoon already—my wedding is less than twenty-four hours away. For the last week, when I went off to teach, Roman's family would forge forward to put the perfect wedding together for me.

I push to my feet, ready to head home to my new…family. I smile and resist the urge to pinch myself. Honest to God, I'm just afraid to let myself get too excited.

"Oh, I didn't see you there," I say, finding Richard in my doorway.

He puts his hands in his pockets. "The big day is tomorrow, huh?"

"Yes, we're renewing our vows for his family," I say, disliking the smirk on his face.

He gives a humorless laugh. "Renewing? You say that like you guys are already married."

"Yes, well, if you'll excuse me." He steps farther inside, blocking my escape. I try to go around him.

"You're lying," he says. "You were never married. This is all a farce, some sort of fake arrangement you have with Roman. Go ahead, admit it." He scoffs. "Not that any of it matters now, not with you both sealing the deal for real tomorrow."

I lift my chin an inch. "I don't owe you any explanation, Richard."

"No, but you owe me one," Andrew says, entering the room from the hall. Richard's smirk widens, as he turns and slinks out, leaving me alone with Andrew.

"Peyton?" Andrew says, his brow furrowed. "Is it true? You and Roman were never married?"

My stomach clenches so hard I'm sure I'm going to throw up. "It's…um…the marriage bar…" Good God, no matter how I put it, it's never going to look good for me.

"We don't have a marriage bar." He angles his head, his eyes narrowed, studying my face. "Not anymore."

"I realize that, but from my research, and those I've talked to, I heard it was still practiced." As more words stream out, I attempt to turn the oncoming tide with, "I just thought it would be okay. No big deal. Harmless lie."

"I see." He adjusts the collar on his shirt and stands a little straighter, exuding his authority. "You lied, then?"

"I don't really think—"

"Presenting yourself as married when you're not is a lie, Peyton," he says, his voice taking on a hard edge that shoots daggers of worry through my body.

"I just thought…" I take a breath and change tactics. I can't lose this job. I just can't. This has been my dream for so long and I've connected with the children. "I'm good at my job, Andrew. You can see that. Marriage was an obstacle and that was my only way to get around it, so I could show you how good I am at my job. I wanted you to judge me based on my merits, not my marital status."

"Being single is something I would have accepted. Lying, however… I'm afraid you don't have the morals for this job, Peyton." As he frowns and shakes his head, my heart goes into my throat. "If you'll please take all your things with you when you leave."

My knees nearly collapse as the room closes in on me. I grip my desk and I take a few quick breaths as air squeezes from my lungs. Is this really happening? I open my mouth to plead but he shakes his head to stop me.

"That will be all," he states, and disappears out the door.

"Ohmigod," I say, and fall back into my chair.

I just lost my job.

I sit there for a long time, trying to wrap my brain around this turn of events, until the hum of the lawn mower outside my window sets me into motion. I have to tell Roman and once I do, there will be no need for us to go through with the wedding.

With my life crumbling around me, I force one foot in front of the other and somehow make my way back to the villa. "Roman," I call out, my voice as shaky as my hands as I drop my purse. I race through the villa and go to the rooftop, but he's nowhere to be found. I run back downstairs to grab my phone from my purse, but papers on the kitchen island catch my attention. Maybe he left a note.

I run to the island and pick up the papers, and as soon as I realize what I'm holding I sink into the closest chair.

A prenup.

A level of separation between those who have and those who don't.

A piece of paper that reminds me who Roman is, and who I'm not.

Tears press against my eyes and bile punches in my throat. An almost hysterical laugh explodes from my mouth. I drop the papers onto the floor like they're disease-ridden and slowly back away. Yeah, I should have seen this coming. People like Roman and his family need to protect themselves from someone like me—a girl from the wrong side of the tracks who will never be good enough, never really be accepted or loved for who I am.

I never, ever should have let myself believe in fairy tales.

CHAPTER FOURTEEN

Roman

"Okay, I have to run. Peyton should be back at the villa by now," I say, and my sisters all take turns giving me a hug. I absolutely love the way they took Peyton under their wings, readily accepting her and showing her love and affection, just like I knew they would.

Before I leave the family villa, I take a look at the beach below, the perfect spot for us to exchange vows tomorrow. A seed of hope wells up inside me. It's all kind of surreal, really. I'm not sure I can quite wrap my brain around the fact that I'm marrying my best friend's sister. After my gold-digging ex walked out, refusing to sign the prenup as is tradition in our family, I closed my heart off. But things are different with Peyton. She's sweet and beautiful, open and honest, and yeah her brother is going to tear me a new one, but once he sees how serious I am about her, how much I love her—that this wasn't just about sex—I think we'll be able to bring him around to our side. It's better to ask for forgiveness than permission, right? Besides, he wants his sister happy, and I damn well plan to spend the rest of my life making her exactly that.

I step outside and hop in the car waiting for me. "How are you doing today, Elias?"

"Very well, Roman, and you seem quite happy yourself."

I smile. "Tomorrow is a big day for me," I say.

"To the villa?"

"Yes, thanks."

As we drive through the streets, my heart beats a little faster, I'm so anxious to get home and pull Peyton into my arms. Being away from her for any length of time practically kills me, and that just makes me laugh. I pull out my phone to see if she messaged me, and disappointment wells up inside me.

Man, I've got it bad.

I stare out the window and take in the scenery. I might have to travel to the States every now and then, but most of my work can be done here and meetings can be held online. If Peyton wants to stay in the villa we can do that, or if she wants to buy a new place, I'm open to that, too. Whatever she wants, she gets.

Elias stops the limo in front of my villa, and I thank him and rush up the steps. I punch in the code and step inside.

"Peyton," I call out. "You home?" I note that her purse isn't by the front door, but she could very well have taken it to our bedroom. I take the steps two at a time and find the bedroom empty. I go all the way to the rooftop, but she's nowhere to be found. Perhaps she hasn't returned from school yet. I shoot her off a text and when she doesn't answer, I head back outside and walk to her school. I try the front doors and find them locked. Strange.

I walk around the school, only to find it's closed for the weekend. I check my phone again, worry gnawing at my gut. Is it possible that she went to the family villa, expecting I'd still be there? I shoot a text off to Lucy.

Hey, Lucy, is Peyton with you guys?

No, why, what's up?

Oh, nothing, she's probably just doing a bit of last-minute shopping.

You sure everything is okay?

Perfectly fine.

I shove my phone back into my pocket, but something isn't right. I feel it deep in my gut. I hurry back to the villa and make my way through the place again, but Peyton is still missing. I step into the bedroom. Something is off. I walk around the bed and to the closet. I open it and my heart sinks into my stomach.

"What the hell?"

I hurry to the other bedroom, check the closet there, but her things are nowhere to be found. In the bathroom I find her cosmetics and toothbrush gone.

Peyton packed up her belongings and left? I take a breath to calm myself, working to figure out why she would have done this, and I almost laugh when it occurs to me she's probably staying at a hotel tonight. Tradition dictates the bride and groom don't see each other before the wedding. Still, why wouldn't she have mentioned it? Perhaps she left a note and I haven't seen it yet.

I head to the kitchen to check, and my foot kicks up papers. I snatch them up and realize it's the prenup I left on the counter this morning, every intention of discussing it with Peyton tonight. Why the hell is it on the floor? I falter backward a bit, my mind racing and slowing on the most logical explanation here.

Peyton found these papers and bailed.

I sink into the chair, unable to believe this. I pull my phone out again and send another text. When it goes unanswered, I dial her number, but it goes straight to voice mail. Has she blocked me? Worry sets in, and I pick up my phone and check flights out of Malta. There isn't one until tomorrow, so it's not like she's taken off today, unless she chartered a private flight.

Fuck me.

I drive my fingers through my hair and pace and continue to wait for her response. When my phone finally rings, my heart leaps—except it's my sister. "Hey," I say, sounding completely irritated.

"Ah, are you okay?" Lucy asks.

"I don't think so."

She lowers her voice. "What's up, Roman?"

"I think she's gone, Luce. I think she saw the prenup and changed her mind." I glance around the empty villa. It's stark and hollow without her in it.

"That doesn't sound like Peyton."

"I didn't think so, either, but her things are gone, and she's not answering my messages."

"Maybe she's staying somewhere else tonight."

"I thought that at first, but *all* her things are gone."

"That doesn't make sense." She goes quiet for a moment. "Could something have happened at school?"

I tug on my hair as it gets harder and harder to breathe. "I don't know." I swallow but there's nothing I can do to hide the panic in my voice.

"You know the principal, right? Why don't you give him a call?"

"Okay, good idea. Thanks, Luce."

"Let me know, okay?"

"Don't say anything to the others, please."

"You know I've got your back, Roman. I wouldn't have made you eat mud if I didn't love you."

That pulls a chuckle from me. "Later, Easy-Bake. Love back."

I find Andrew's number and call his place, but no one picks up. Determined to get to the bottom of matters and hoping I'm making a huge deal out of nothing, I call for Elias and get him to drive me to Andrew's home. I'm out of the car before it even comes to a complete stop, and I dash up the stairs. I pound on the door, and Andrew opens it, a frown on his face.

"If you're here to try to get Peyton's job back for her, you're wasting your time."

My heart stalls and I grab a hold of the rail, squeezing until my knuckles turn white. "What are you talking about?"

His eyes narrow on me, assessing my face. "She didn't tell you?"

"No, I can't find her."

He nods, like he understands that. "Now that she's out of a job, she's probably going back to the States."

"Why is she out of a job?" Jesus, what the hell happened today? "She's the best person for it, Andrew."

"Is she now?" He taps his finger on his chin and worry explodes inside me. "Do good people lie about being married, Roman?"

I suck in a fast breath. "Oh, shit."

"Yes, exactly."

"You know we're getting married tomorrow."

"It was never about the marriage, it was about the lying."

"Come on, Andrew, you have to give her another chance," I plead. "A marriage bar is ridiculous. You must know that."

"I'm sorry, Roman. The contract has already been signed by Richard."

My throat squeezes tight. "You're making a big mistake."

"If you'll excuse me, I'm in the middle of something."

He closes the door and I stand there staring at it for far too long. How the hell did he find out? It had to have been Richard, and while I'd like to track him down and introduce my fist to his face, right now it's Peyton I'm worried about. She needs me. Phone in hand I head back to the limo and shoot a text to Peyton, telling her I know about the job and we need to talk.

Three dots pop on the screen and I stop breathing, waiting for her words to come in, but when they do, my jaw drops.

Peyton: Thank you for your support. You're off the hook. Marriage is no longer needed.

"What the hell?" I say as my life crashes down around me. She's letting me off the hook? Doesn't she know how I feel? A groan catches in my throat. How could she know? I was too afraid to tell her, too afraid she'd bolt.

Goddammit, even though I never expressed what she meant to me, she had to know, right? Or have I been reading what's between us all wrong? I sit in the back of the limo and pull the prenup from my back pocket. My mind searches for answers. Was I only a means to an end with her? Now that she no longer needs me for the job, is she done with me, or did this prenup have something to do with her running away? My ex left because I asked her to sign one and she refused, and that lesson taught me she wanted what I had, that she never wanted me for me. Is the same thing going on with Peyton? Does she want my name and what's in my bank? I shake my head slowly, refusing to believe that for one single second. But while my heart says one thing, my brain reminds me of past hurts.

No, she's not like that.

I sit in stunned silence as Elias drives me back to my villa. I give him a generous tip and head inside. With a headache brewing I go upstairs and into the bathroom. I toss back a couple pills and plunk down onto the bed. I turn my head sideways, and that's when I see my grandmother's wedding ring, sitting beside the lamp.

I jackknife up and reach for my phone. Goddammit, I can't let this happen. I just can't. I walked away from her once and it nearly destroyed me. I know there is more between us; I felt it in her touches and kisses, felt it when we made love last night. So why did she run away? Is she afraid I'm going to hurt her?

There's only one person who can help me figure out what's going on, and it's time I come clean. I pull up my contacts and press Call. The phone rings, and I take a deep breath when Cason answers.

CHAPTER FIFTEEN

Peyton

"COME ON, WE'RE going out," Carly says.

I sink deeper into the comfy sofa and plant my feet on the coffee table. "Nope, I'm not going anywhere."

"Yes, you are."

I pick up the remote and flick through the stations. I haven't left my condo in two weeks, not since I lost my job—and the man I love—and hopped on a plane to come home. Someone raps on my door, and I sit up a little straighter, my heart missing a beat. I honestly have no idea why I would think it's Roman. We had fun, played house for a while, but now it's over. I'm sure he's glad he's off the hook for marriage.

God, I miss him.

But I had to leave. I couldn't go through with a sham of a marriage—one I wanted to be real—after seeing that prenup. Does he really think I'm like his ex, that I wanted to get my hands on his money? I swipe at a stupid tear that threatens to fall—I've cried enough. Why should I shed tears for a man who doesn't know me or trust me at all?

Oh, because no matter what, you still love him.

Carly pulls the door open and my sister-in-law Londyn takes one look at me and shakes her head.

"Go away," I say, and take a sip of wine.

"She's worse than I thought," Londyn says.

"Yeah, she's been in those pajamas so long, the second she takes them off they're going to run to the washing machine themselves."

"I'm right here," I blurt out. "I can hear you."

"Come on, we have a long day ahead of us," Londyn says.

I stroke my wineglass and twirl the red wine inside. "What are you talking about?"

Londyn stands over me. "You know you look a little bit like the Joker right now."

I arch a brow at her. "I remember when you used to be nice."

"You have red wine all over the corners of your mouth and on your pajamas."

"Wine is my precious," I say, lifting my nose an inch.

"Get up," she demands in that no-nonsense voice of hers.

I snort. "I remember when I used to like you."

"You still like me, now get up. Cason is getting his plane ready."

"For what?"

She gives an exasperated sigh. "Did you forget?"

"Apparently."

"We're going to Belize, for Gemma's bachelorette party." She plants one hand on her hip, clearly frustrated with me. I don't blame her, all this self-pity and arguing is getting on my nerves, too. If Roman were here, would he kiss me to stop me from arguing?

Stop thinking about him!

I crinkle my nose. "Isn't that like a month away?"

"You've been moping so long you don't even know what day of the week it is anymore." Londyn hastily takes my wine from me and pulls me to my feet.

"I don't want to go." I stand there like a petulant child and dig my feet in. "I don't even like her fiancé."

Londyn waves a warning finger at me. "Who she marries is not your call."

"Well, if it was, I think she should be marrying Josh Walker."

Londyn smiles. "Yeah, she used to use his services at Penn Pals. I remember. I thought those two would end up together."

That's when an idea hits. I think it's brilliant, of course, or it could just be the wine. "Maybe we should kidnap the bride."

"We are not kidnapping anyone. Gemma is a good friend," she says, her voice softer. "We all need to support her. Now come on."

I pout. "You don't play fair."

There's someone else I know who doesn't play fair, either.

God, will I ever get him out of my head?

"Gemma is counting on you," Londyn says.

Okay, okay, I know she's right. Gemma and I met at Penn State and I have been looking forward to her bachelorette. It came much faster than I thought, but then again, I have lost all track of time.

"Will there be wine?" I ask.

"Yes," both Carly and Londyn say at the same time.

"You don't have to yell." I saunter to the bathroom, take one look at myself in the mirror and cringe. I rub the corners of my mouth. Londyn was right. I am channeling the Joker. Carly and Londyn are whispering something in the other room, but the shower drowns out their voices when I turn it on. I scrub off with hot, soapy water and head to my room to pack a bag, only to find it's already packed for me.

"Who did this?"

"I did," Carly says, her arms crossed as she leans against the door.

"How did you know what I wanted to pack?" I'm about to open the duffel bag but she stops me.

"Don't."

I frown and narrow my eyes. "Why are you acting so weird?"

"I'm not acting weird," she says lightly as she brushes me off with a wave. "You just had too much wine."

I nod. "That's fair."

"Everything you need is in that bag. Trust me."

Trust me. Isn't that what Roman asked me to do once. Where was his trust in me?

I eye her. "If you're sure…"

"I'm sure."

Londyn stands by the open door. "Come on, we need to go now."

One hour later, I'm on my brother's plane, ready for the long four-hour flight to Belize. I yawn, and my muscles relax. It's been a long time since I've slept well. Whenever I close my eyes, visions of Roman dance in my mind. I swallow hard. Is he relieved I never went through with the marriage?

He said he'd do anything to help me get the job, but agreeing to marriage, or rather being the one to suggest it, seemed a little over-the-top. That alone, not even taking into account all the other things he did for me, is why I thought he might want more. Why I thought that this was not about my job, and more about the two of us and how great we were together? I guess I was wrong.

Were you, Peyton?

I recline my comfy seat, let my lids fall shut, and the next thing I know, Cason is shaking me awake.

"What?" I say groggily, and blink my eyes into focus. Both Carly and Londyn are gathering their things.

"We're here."

"That was fast."

Cason's eyes narrow on me and he pats my hand gently. "Everything is going to be okay, Peyton."

"What are you talking about?" I ask, knowing, deep in my heart, that nothing is ever going to be okay again. I've lost everything. Cason doesn't know the whole truth, though. I kept my promise and never said a thing about my relationship with Roman. He only knows I didn't get the position.

"You trust me, right?" he asks.

"Of course I do."

"Then you know everything I do is with your best interest in mind, right?"

"Cason, what are you talking about?" I shake my head to clear the rest of the sleep away. "You're freaking me out a little here."

"Promise me you won't be mad," he says, a softness in his voice, making it the tone he used with me when I was a frightened child.

Everything inside me stiffens. "About what?"

He casts Londyn a quick look and she nods. "We didn't really go to Belize."

I jump up and look out the window. "Where the hell are we?"

"Come on, I'll show you."

I quickly gather up my things and exit the plane. Once we're on the ground, I look at the airport, but still can't figure out where we are. It's not until we land in customs that I realize I'm in Italy.

Italy!

Where Roman's family lives.

Oh, hell no!

"I'm getting back on the plane," I blurt out.

Cason takes my hand and tugs. "You said you trusted me."

"Cason, why are we here?" I don't want to see Roman. We're done. But I can't tell him that because he never knew what we were doing behind closed doors.

"There is something I want to show you, then we can turn around and head right back to the States."

My stomach cramps. "I don't get it. What about the bachelorette party?"

He gives me an exasperated sigh. "Do you have to question everything?"

"Yes."

"Fine. I'll explain everything shortly. Right now, I need you to trust me."

With my stomach in tight knots, we go through customs and outside there is a limo waiting for us. We all pile in and I put my travel bag by my feet. I have no idea what my brother is up to. All I know is that I do trust him and if he wants to show me something, I'm not going to say no. If it has something to do with Roman—and how could it not—I'm going to kill him.

As we drive, a cold chill moves through me despite the warm temperatures outside, and I dig into my carry-on duffel bag to see if Carly packed me a sweater.

"What the heck?" I ask, when I pull pair after pair of sexy underwear from the bag. "You didn't pack me any clothes."

She looks away, avoiding my gaze, and once again I can't help but think she's acting strange. "I didn't think you were going to need them," she says.

"Why on earth wouldn't I need clothes for a bachelorette party?" I snort. "Then again, I guess we're not really going to Gemma's party. I still don't understand all the underwear, though."

"To answer your earlier question, Peyton," Cason says, "Londyn and Carly are here because we *are* going to a wedding. Just not Gemma's."

"Then I do need clothes." Maybe I'd better lay off the wine, because nothing is making sense. The car comes to a stop and we all climb out. I glance around at the big open field, which goes on as far as the eye can see. "Where are we? Whose wedding?"

I take a step forward and go completely still when I spot Roman cresting a hill, walking toward me. But he's not alone—behind him I spot his entire family.

My legs go weak and Cason puts his arm around me. "Cason…"

"You two need to talk."

I glare at him. "You were behind this?"

"Yes," he says, a calmness in his voice that does little to soothe me.

"Why?"

"All I ever wanted in my entire life was to make sure you were safe and loved, Peyton. But you're grown up now, and it's time to stand on your own two feet and make your own decisions. A conversation I shared with someone very wise opened my eyes to that."

I gasp. "Really?"

"Roman and I talked, for hours. Now it's your turn to talk to him. What happens next is up to you. He's a good man, Peyton. In fact, he's the best, and if there was ever a man I wanted in your life, it's him. I know you'll make the right choice."

"You don't understand."

"I think you're the one who doesn't understand."

He gives me a little nudge until my legs are moving and the next thing I know, Roman and I are standing alone in a wide expanse of field, our family and friends in the distance.

"What's going on, Roman?"

"I'm sorry about tricking you into coming."

I cross my arms. "Say whatever it is you have to say."

"We have a problem."

I try to keep my breathing steady, but his proximity is seriously messing with my body and brain. "What kind of problem?"

"You see, I hurt you, Peyton, after I swore I never would. But you have to know I didn't do it on purpose. I'd never do it on purpose." I blink up at him, and he continues with, "I love you, Peyton. I've always loved you. I never thought you could be mine, but now, well, I'm going to do everything in my power to make that happen."

My throat dries. "You…love me?"

He laughs and shakes his head. "Is that what I said?"

I stiffen. Oh God, did he not mean it? "Yes, that's what you just said."

His smile falls, his face completely sober, when he says, "Then that's what I meant." He takes my hand and when I see love and desire reflecting in his eyes, happiness wells up inside me.

Roman loves me!

Wait, why is he suddenly frowning?

"I'm sorry you lost your job."

Hurt tightens my heart, and I blink back the tears pounding behind my eyes. Richard's wife might have been out to get me fired unbeknownst to him, but at least he was good with the kids, and they loved him in return. Their well-being is important to me. "Thank you."

"Teaching kids English in another country is still your dream job, right?"

"It is. But I don't see that happening now."

"Look around." I glance around at the wide-open space and catch my brother's eye. He looks on with worry, and my heart thumps. He's done right by me my whole life, and I love him for it, but I'm a grown-up now who can stand on her own feet, make her own decisions. "This is where your new school is going to be built."

I falter a little, my pulse leaping in my neck. "What?"

"I bought this land, and it took weeks to get all the permits I needed. I would have come for you sooner, but I wanted to make sure everything was in place."

I raise my shaky hands to his face. "Roman, I can't believe you did this." Then again, maybe I can. He's been nothing but good to me, going above and beyond to help me out…because he *loves* me.

Roman loves me.

"I don't know what to say," I push out, my voice as shaky as my body.

"Say yes." He drops to his knees, pulls a box from his back pocket and opens it. Tears flood my eyes and spill when I see his grandmother's ring. "I love you, Peyton, with all my heart. I want you in my bed and in my life, I want you for the good times and the bad. I want to go on this journey called life with you by my side. I want to be equal partners, and I don't care about the prenup."

My head spins, my heart so full it's ready to burst, but with everything he's saying to me, everything coming at me so fast, my mind focuses on the last words out of his mouth. "Why don't you care about the prenup?"

"Because I know you're nothing like my ex, that you're the most giving person I know and you don't care about my name or money. You care about the person behind all those things—you care about me. The prenup is simply a tradition, something that has been in my family for generations. I never even really thought about how it would make you feel. I'm an idiot like that sometimes."

"You're not an idiot, Roman, and I didn't know it was tradition," I say, my heart pounding so hard, I'm a little light-headed. "When I saw it, I thought…"

"I know what you thought, and I'm sorry. I never meant to do anything that made you feel like that lost girl from your childhood. The one who was afraid she wasn't enough and would never be enough. I never meant for you to think I wanted you to sign the prenup because I didn't trust you. I do trust you, Peyton. You're everything to me and to my family. You're kind, sweet, giving and so goddamn lovable that when I found the villa empty—" he shakes his head, agony all over his face "—it broke my damn heart. At first, I couldn't understand it. I thought you were done with me, thought you were discarding me because you didn't need me to be your husband anymore. I jumped to conclusions because of past hurts, but then I recognized that's not something you would ever do. I called Cason and realized the prenup brought back past hurts for you, too."

"It did, and I'm sorry, too, Roman. You've been nothing but sweet and helpful, and you showed me I have value, made me feel important."

He once confessed that helping me was more about me and less about my brother. Everything in his touch and actions told me he cared. After reading the prenup, I didn't want to believe him anymore, and I expected him to hurt me like everyone else. Self-preservation and a childhood in the system does that to a person. But there was a part of me that always believed him...believed in him. I was just so afraid. But I don't have to be afraid anymore.

"The prenup... I don't know, it just reminded me that I should never let myself believe in fairy tales, because..."

"Because there's still a part of you that believes you're not enough. But you have to let that go. You're everything. You're more than everything." He takes a deep breath and lets it out slowly. "The truth is,

Peyton, you *can* take care of yourself, I know that, but all I want to do is protect you and give you the world." His throat makes a noise and he puts a hand on my face. "I don't want to live without you. Correction, I *can't* live without you."

"You can't?"

"No." Eyes full of love and sorrow study my face. My heart races and happy tears full of joy spill down my cheeks. "Can you let me do that?"

"All I ever wanted from you was your love, Roman. Those other things aren't important to me."

He smiles. "Is that your way of saying you love me?"

"Of course I love you," I blurt out. "I've always loved you. For as long as I can remember I loved you."

"Then say yes."

"No," I say, and he falls back onto his heels.

Fear and sadness invade his dark eyes. "No?"

"No, if it's tradition, then I want to sign the prenup. I didn't know that before. I thought it was about me, but it's not, it's about your family and tradition and I want to respect that."

He smiles, stands and pulls me to him. "Right there, Peyton. That's why I *don't* want you to sign it."

I take a big breath, about to answer him, then glance up to see our families. "Wait," I say. "Why is everyone here?"

"Because if you say yes, I want to get married this very second. All the arrangements have been made."

"Oh."

He chuckles. "Yeah, oh, and I'm not the only one out here holding my breath here, Peyton. My sisters can't wait until they can call you sister, Mamma can't wait to call you her new daughter, and I can't wait to call you my wife."

I put one hand on my hips and shake my head. "You just took it upon yourself to make arrangements without consulting me?"

"I just thought—"

I throw my hands out, palms up, and those watching must think we're fighting. "And never considered if I wanted it to be on a beach or a church, or a… I don't know, somewhere else," I say, totally pressing his buttons and wanting to frustrate him.

"This is where your school is going to be built, I thought you'd like—"

"What about where I want to live?"

"If you liked Malta, I thought you'd like—"

"You thought I'd like all of this, did you? Maybe I don't like any of this, Roman. Maybe I *hate* it."

I grin up at him and that's when he clues in to what I'm doing.

His smile is slow, sexy. "Do I have to kiss you to stop you from arguing with me?"

"Yes, Roman."

He pauses, his lips inches from mine, hope invading his eyes. "Wait, what are you saying yes to?"

"I'm saying yes to being your wife, to living here, to building a school here, a future here, and celebrating a wedding today with our families."

He runs his thumb over my cheek and I melt

into him. "Are you going to hate all those things, Peyton?"

My heart beats so fast, I'm sure I might faint, but if I do, this man will be there to take care of me, and more importantly I'm going to let him. "I'm going to hate every single one," I say.

"Good."

Cheers erupt behind us as he picks me up, puts his lips on mine and as his love and warmth wrap around my body and heart, he spins me, pushing the last chills from my body. I kiss him back, deeply, passionately, my flesh absorbing all his heat and love, and for the first time in my life something miraculous happens to my body.

It warms.

*****

COMING SOON!

We really hope you enjoyed reading this book.
If you're looking for more romance, be sure to
head to the shops when new books are
available on

Thursday 18th
February

LET'S TALK
Romance

For exclusive extracts, competitions
and special offers, find us online:

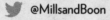 facebook.com/millsandboon

 @MillsandBoon

@MillsandBoonUK

Get in touch on 01413 063232

For all the latest titles coming soon, visit
millsandboon.co.uk/nextmonth

MILLS & BOON

THE HEART OF ROMANCE

A ROMANCE FOR EVERY KIND OF READER

MODERN

Prepare to be swept off your feet by sophisticated, sexy and seductive heroes, in some of the world's most glamourous and romantic locations, where power and passion collide.
8 stories per month.

HISTORICAL

Escape with historical heroes from time gone by. Whether your passion is for wicked Regency Rakes, muscled Vikings or rugge Highlanders, awaken the romance of the past.
6 stories per month.

MEDICAL

Set your pulse racing with dedicated, delectable doctors in the high-pressure world of medicine, where emotions run high and passion, comfort and love are the best medicine.
6 stories per month.

True Love

Celebrate true love with tender stories of heartfelt romance, fr the rush of falling in love to the joy a new baby can bring, and a focus on the emotional heart of a relationship.
8 stories per month.

Desire

Indulge in secrets and scandal, intense drama and plenty of siz hot action with powerful and passionate heroes who have it all: wealth, status, good looks…everything but the right woman.
6 stories per month.

HEROES

Experience all the excitement of a gripping thriller, with an int romance at its heart. Resourceful, true-to-life women and stron fearless men face danger and desire - a killer combination!
8 stories per month.

DARE

Sensual love stories featuring smart, sassy heroines you'd want a best friend, and compelling intense heroes who are worthy of t
4 stories per month.

To see which titles are coming soon, please visit

millsandboon.co.uk/nextmonth